Stradi's Violin
Book I

Blenda Bligh

Blenda Bligh

PublishAmerica
Baltimore

© 2007 by Blenda Bligh.
All rights reserved. No part of this book may be reproduced, stored in a retrieval system or transmitted in any form or by any means without the prior written permission of the publishers, except by a reviewer who may quote brief passages in a review to be printed in a newspaper, magazine or journal.

First printing

All characters in this book are fictitious, and any resemblance to real persons, living or dead, is coincidental.

ISBN: 1-4241-9460-1
PUBLISHED BY PUBLISHAMERICA, LLLP
www.publishamerica.com
Baltimore

Printed in the United States of America

In loving memory:
Lee Roy Strickland
Ruby Marthena Trammell
Ann Roscow Bligh

Special Dedication:

*Pauline Trammell Strickland, my mother,
for her encouragement and inspiration.*

Acknowledgements

Alan David Bligh, my wonderful husband for his love and support, and our children, Quin, Luisa, Alanna and Joel, and our granddaughter, Kinzie; thank you for being my greatest fans and having faith in me!

Prelude

The catastrophe that occurred would paralyze America for more than a decade. Optimism faded quickly with the economic collapse that caused the loss of hopes, dreams, homes, and jobs. Families were torn apart as the struggle for survival became paramount in an unbelievable era known as the Great Depression.

Chapter 1

The gusty Texas wind was blowing against the slight frame of Ellen Gibson as she trudged through the dingy, dust-laden streets of south Austin. The shabby clothes she wore could not distract from her beauty. Wisps of curly blonde hair framed her elfin face, and her startling blue eyes were framed by dark, thickly curling lashes. Her full lips were usually curved in a becoming smile, but right now she was biting her lips in her effort to struggle against the fierce wind as she desperately fought to get home before dark. Home was across the tracks in what was crudely referred to as Shanty Town. As she struggled to keep her balance, her thoughts were on her missing husband that had left her with two small children and another one on the way.

Dan was handsome and dark haired with laughing green eyes. He was always teasing her and playing games with the children. At least, that's the way he had been, until the Depression had stolen his vitality and broken his spirit. The factory where he worked had closed without warning. As days of job hunting went by without success, Dan had sunk deeper into despair. That's when Ellen discovered another side to her husband—a dark side. He would sit brooding then suddenly would grab his coat and rush out of the shack as though the walls had suddenly closed in upon him. He never told her where he was going, and anxiously she and the children would wait for him to return. As he became more and more withdrawn, and despair crushed his spirit, he would suddenly lash out in frustration saying hurtful things that she hoped he didn't mean. Knowing her slight frame intimately, he soon discovered that she was with child. In anger he riled at her for placing this additional burden on them. Seeing the sadness in her face and tears gathering in her beautiful blue eyes had been the final straw. He grabbed his coat and rushed out as he had so many times before, only this time he didn't come back.

At first, Ellen had been almost insane with worry, but when the authorities assured her that her husband's disappearance was not uncommon for the times, she was heartbroken. Dan's abandonment was so sudden, that she was convinced he would come to his senses and realize how much they needed each other. She was certain that, in time, he would come back.

The only job she was able to find was in a department store, where she worked long hours as a sales girl for five dollars a week. It wasn't nearly enough, and the children were always hungry. Ellen could endure the poverty, but her heart ached when the children were forced to go without. Seeing the expectant look on their faces, as they depended on her for all their needs, was a large burden for such slender shoulders. Ellen wondered how long she would be able to look after herself and the children.

The streets narrowed and darkness was falling as Ellen rounded the last corner. Straight ahead, she saw the shack that sheltered them, but it was to the shack further down the street that she hurried. The door was slightly open, and a young boy poked his head out. As soon as he saw her, he began to jump up and down and yell, "Mama's home! Mama's home!" The welcoming enthusiasm brought a smile to her face and lifted her spirits.

Pushing the door wider, she stepped inside, and immediately was surrounded by two lively youngsters, each vying for her attention. She stooped and kissed the upturned faces and then turned to the old woman sitting quietly in the rocking chair.

"Aunt Kate, how are you?"

She was not really Ellen's aunt, but she was "Aunt Kate" to everyone who knew her. Her face was somber, and she was looking at her with sad, weary eyes, causing an uneasiness to sweep over Ellen.

"What's wrong?" she asked calmly while her insides were a bundle of raw nerves.

"Sit down, child," Aunt Kate stated in her quiet, gentle voice, "I have some bad news."

Ellen's heart sank as she wondered what was to befall her next.

"You remember my son? Well, he found work in Charleston, and he's coming to get me next week. Says I'll be better off with him."

Feeling the impact of those words, she slumped in the chair and bowed her head. The old woman reached out an unsteady hand and gently touched her head.

"Child, I don't know what else I can do. I can barely get by as it is."

She struggled to control the tears that sprang to her eyes. The children had grown quiet, and Ellen knew they were watching her. Sitting up straight and managing a tiny smile, she looked at the kind old woman.

"I'm glad that your son found work, and that he's coming to get you. These are hard times and you need each other."

Ellen heard her voice break as she said this, because she was thinking how much she had come to depend on this woman. The old woman read her mind.

"Ellen, I know that you need me to look after the children for you, and I hate leaving you like this. Maybe you and the children could come with us to Charleston?"

Even as she said it, she knew in her heart that it would not be possible. Her son was fortunate to have found work, and the two of them would barely be able to survive on his earnings. A feeling of helplessness swept over her, making her vulnerable. She was angry at this terrible depression that had hit the country, and left so many jobless, homeless and hungry. Mostly, she was angry with Dan Gibson for going off God knows where and leaving behind his young wife and children.

"Aunt Kate, we couldn't possibly go with you. We have to be here when Dan returns." Ellen hurried on, sensing that she was about to be interrupted, "He is coming back, I know it!"

The last was said with such desperation, that the woman's heart ached for Ellen.

"He's looking for work and when he finds it, he'll come back for us." She was unaware of the frantic note that had crept into her voice.

The children could sense her fear and anxiety. They stood in front of her, clamoring for attention. Jim tried to pull his mother to her feet.

"Come on, let's go home, Mama."

Slowly, she stood with Lilly in her arms. Then she bent and kissed Aunt Kate gently on the cheek.

The old woman's voice was filled with grief. "What's gonna happen to you and the children?" The tears that she had tried to withhold were making their way down the crevices of the age-lined cheeks.

"Now, Aunt Kate, don't you worry about us," she admonished sternly. "We're going to be just fine."

"I wish there were something I could do!" Sadly she bowed her head.

Gently, Ellen reached for her hand as she spoke. "You can remember us, and say a prayer for us each night."

Aunt Kate could tell that despite her young friend's brave front, she was scared. Without her to look after the children, they would be alone all day while Ellen worked.

"I'll see you tomorrow," she smiled, as she ushered the children out the door.

They hurried down the street to the dark, one-room shack that looked as forlorn as Ellen felt. Still, it was a roof over their heads, though lacking in even the barest of necessities. Since there was no electricity, she quickly lit the kerosene lamps.

"Mama, I'm hungry," Jim whined.

"I'm hungry too," Lilly chimed in.

He was already looking in the cupboard for something to eat.

"Okay, you kids get cleaned up while Mama fixes supper and, Jim, you're in charge. See that you both wash up."

"Yes, Mama," Jim replied, as he moved the stool up to the washbasin for them to stand on.

Ellen sincerely hoped that she would be able to keep up a cheery front for the children. All the time she was laughing and talking to them, her mind was racing ahead wrestling with all the problems she would be facing with no apparent solution.

She had one small potato left in the cupboard, with which she made watered down potato soup. *Payday is tomorrow*, she thought, *and I can buy some more food.* Feeding the children was about all she could manage, and there was nothing left for clothes or shoes. The rent would be due soon and that was six dollars a month.

The children interrupted her thoughts as they began to get ready for bed.

"Don't forget your prayers before going to bed," she reminded them.

"Okay, Mama, it's my turn to pray," said Jim. They knelt by the bed as Jim prayed, "Dear God, please give Mama money so she can buy food. Help us to be good, and God bless Mama, Daddy, Aunt Kate, Lilly, and me. Oh, and please bring my daddy home soon. Thank you, sir. Amen."

"Amen," echoed Lilly as they scrambled into bed. Lilly slept with Ellen, and Jim slept in a make-shift bed in the corner. "Mama, aren't you coming to bed?" she asked.

"In a little while," her mother responded. "Go to sleep, now."

Silence settled over the house, except for the creaks and groans caused by the howling wind. Ellen sat at the kitchen table with her head in her hands. She had been trying to formulate a plan of some kind, but the task seemed hopeless. Her thoughts chased each other round and round until she felt her head spinning with the effort.

Mostly, she worried about the baby she was carrying. No one knew, not even Aunt Kate. She couldn't see any reason to tell the old woman. It would only make her feel worse than she already did about leaving them. No, the baby would be her secret. Anyway, she was hardly showing, and her hand-me-down clothes were amply covering her slight frame so that her secret was safe.

Ellen sighed. "Six months, six *long* months, since I've seen or heard from Dan." She ran her hands through her hair feeling weary yet restless.

She got up and walked over to pull the covers back on Jim. Tenderness for her son made her forget her problems for a moment. *He is such a good boy*, she thought. Six years old, and, yet, he seemed so much older. The worst part was in knowing he belonged in school, but how could she let him go? More than ever, she needed him to look after four-year-old Lilly. He seemed to understand, and she was teaching him how to read from the Bible. Ellen bent down, and kissed the button nose that had a faint sprinkling of freckles. He had sandy hair and big brown eyes that melted even the hardest of hearts.

Walking to the bed, she looked down at her sleeping daughter. *Little angel, what kind of life can I provide for you?* Inwardly she agonized, as she took in the tiny replica of herself, with blonde hair and blue eyes.

Ellen's hands moved over the gentle swell of her stomach. *What will this child be like?* Thoughts came flooding through her mind and worry lines wrinkled her brow, as she asked herself how she could possibly raise another child in these appalling conditions? The fact was she would be unable to work after the baby came, so how would they live?

Pacing back and forth, she fought hard against the despair that threatened to overwhelm her. Dan would come back, and everything would be okay. He probably thought it was better to go away for a while and find work, but he would come back for them. He had to!

Ellen stopped pacing as weariness took its toll. She slipped off her clothes and slid into bed next to Lilly. The little girl snuggled closer to the warm body. Ellen stared into the darkness, willing her mind to rest, but knowing that sleep would not come easily. A single tear slipped from beneath her lash and rolled down onto the pillow.

Today was a slow day at the store and customers were scarce. Maize was chattering incessantly, and it was giving Ellen a headache. Maize was Ellen's co-worker, a vivacious brunette who was the epitome of a chatterbox. The only time she was quiet was when Mr. Boswell made an appearance from the back room where he did all his paperwork. Mr. Boswell was the owner, and he liked to come out front whenever any of his regular customers were in the store. He always said that they felt more important if he spoke to them. Ellen's thoughts were interrupted by the tinkle of the bell above the door. Amanda McGowan swept through the door.

In was not in Amanda's nature to show kindness or generosity. However, if it was to her advantage, and helped her attain something she desired, she could be charming. If someone displeased her, retribution was sure and swift. She never suffered fools gladly, and all who knew her could attest to her quick temper.

Some said that a bout with the measles at the age of eleven, which left her totally deaf, was the reason for her unpredictable nature. She never allowed anyone in the same room to turn their back on her, or to speak unless they were looking directly at her. Expertly reading lips, she seldom missed a word that was spoken. Her voice was perfection, trained in well-modulated tones, precise and clear.

Wealth and education lent her an air of sophistication and self-confidence. Being a woman of tall stature gave her a regal bearing, which was further emphasized by the long, chestnut hair worn in braids and wound about her head like a coronet.

Her mere presence intimidated, but it was her eyes that people dreaded most. It is said that eyes are the windows of the soul, but Amanda's eyes were a flat brown. There was no sparkle, and it was whispered by some, "No soul."

"Boswell, come here!" The voice was one that Mr. Boswell recognized immediately, and he wasted no time in presenting himself.

"Dear Amanda, how lovely to see you," Boswell crooned, as he took Amanda's hand.

Ellen and Maize watched with interest. For a moment, Ellen thought he was going to kiss the perfectly manicured hand. Pulling herself up to her full height, Amanda stated in no uncertain terms, that she was not his "dear" anything. She thrust a large, round hatbox into his arms.

"I am returning this thing you refer to as a hat, and I want my account credited immediately!"

The hat had been in her possession for over four months and she had worn it many times. Mr. Boswell was no fool, but Amanda's cold eyes stared into his in a silent battle of wills, daring him to argue.

Dropping his eyes, he slowly walked over to the desk and wrote out a credit receipt. He hated the triumphant smirk on her face, but what he hated most was the condescending tone she now used to speak to him.

"Dear, Boswell, *always* a pleasure doing business with you." Turning, she haughtily walked out the door, never once looking in the direction of the open-mouthed Ellen or Maize.

Without a word, their employer stalked back to his office and slammed the door. For the reminder of the day, Maize talked about the rude and uppity Mrs. McGowan.

Chapter 2

Jake McGowan was born with the proverbial silver spoon in his mouth. He came from a family of old money and publishers. His great-grandfather *was The Lone Star Chronicle's* first proprietor and editor.
Over the years the newspaper had grown and flourished to become a top contender in the publishing industry. There was a fine board of editors and publishers who ran the paper without a hitch. Even though Jake was the heir and proprietor of *The Lone Star Chronicle*, he respected and generally accepted all of the board's decisions governing the running of the newspaper empire.
Jake had started at the bottom just as his father before him. He had learned it all from the bottom up, and now he wasn't much more than a figure-head. A man with too much money and too much time on his hands, he had turned to drinking and the occasional other woman. He was over six feet tall, a striking man with graying black hair that was as thick as when he was twenty. In his late thirties, he was in the prime of life, and yet, he felt that his life was over. He had felt that way for a long time, and the only time he didn't feel anything was when he used alcohol to numb his senses. For Jake, life had become a vicious circle.
He had married Amanda when she was eighteen, and he had just turned twenty-five. They had met at one of those political shindigs in New York City where he was covering a story. Amanda was no shy,

shrinking violet, and even at her young age she had a commanding presence. She was talking animatedly to a group of her peers about women's suffrage and had attracted quite an audience. Center stage was Amanda's favorite spot.

Jake soon learned that most people shied away from Amanda, not because she was deaf, but because she was intimidating in a way that they didn't understand. It was her way of looking at a person, which caused even the most confident and poised to become uneasy and awkward in her presence. Education had given Amanda the confidence to rise above her handicap. Having a physical disability actually made her stronger and gave her a kind of power over other people that she thoroughly enjoyed.

Jake wasn't put off by her condescending attitude toward those whose intellect did not match her own, or by her handicap. She inspired mixed emotions in him. Paradoxically he was fascinated and repelled. However, the fascination won and he conned one of her adoring followers into an introduction. Amanda was never one to miss an opportunity, and she saw one in Jake. She discovered that he was wealthy and his family welded a lot of power back in Austin, Texas.

Her own mother and father had died in a train wreck a few years ago and the only family she had left was an older sister who had put her through school. Recently, she received word that she would have to fend for herself soon, because the money had run out. Her sister begged her to come to Virginia and live with her. To Amanda, death would have been preferred, because living in some backwater town in Virginia was not what she had in mind. Jake McGowan, and his wealth provided the perfect opportunity for the life she craved. Ambition was Amanda's middle name, and she was determined that nothing would stop her from getting what she wanted.

She teased and tormented Jake by going out with him one day, and refusing to see him the next. If he balked at her inconsistencies, she became a charming lady or a sultry siren. She beguiled and beckoned and withheld, until Jake gave in. He was unaware that she was reeling him in hook, line, and sinker.

Falling in love with Amanda was a fatal mistake. His poor judgment allowed her to have the upper hand. Soon, she made all the decisions and Jake, like a lovesick puppy, followed. Constantly, she pushed and prodded to make sure that he cultivated the right people, the movers, the shakers, and all the ones worth knowing.

Jake didn't even remember proposing, but before long, he found himself embroiled in plans for a high-society wedding. The wedding held all the glitter and pomp associated with Amanda's high idea of what her station in life should be

It was what came afterwards that Jake blotted from his memory. The honeymoon at Niagara Falls was a nightmare. He tried to be gentle, but Amanda riled and fought against the alien invasion of her person. She called him names that he didn't think a lady should know. Playing the martyr was second nature to Amanda, but Jake felt like the lowest sort of scum. His guilt cut the honeymoon short, much to Amanda's delight, and they left for home earlier than planned. Home was the mansion on the hill overlooking Austin.

The days and years that followed were like a blur to Jake. Mostly, an alcoholic haze, brought about by the booze that he drowned himself in. As he thought about the wasted days and years, and about what his life had become, he knew it was time for him to do something about it.

Soon, he promised himself, *Soon, I'll do what I should have done years ago. I'll ask, no, I'll demand a divorce!* The force of his thoughts bolstered his courage, and he strode down the street, determined to confront his wife. His steps faltered, then slowed as he passed the bar on the corner. *No, don't stop*, he argued, *you must talk to Amanda.* In his mind's eye, he could see her looking at him with those cold, hateful eyes. His spirit plummeted and he could feel his courage ebbing away. He turned toward the bar. *One drink*, he thought, *one little drink.*

It was a blustery day, and the wind whipped around the beat up old ford. Aunt Kate's son was stowing the last of the bags in the trunk of the car when the wind sent his hat sailing off down the street.

"I'll get it!" yelled Jim. Halfway down the street, he triumphantly rescued the abused hat. He came running back just as Aunt Kate and Ellen came out of the shack with the last of the boxes.

"Well, I guess that's everything," Aunt Kate said as she gave the boxes to her son.

Lyle took the hat from Jim, and thanked him for rescuing it, while he awkwardly shuffled his feet as he impatiently waited for the goodbyes to be said. He knew that his mom hated leaving Ellen and the kids. He felt awful about it, too, but there was nothing he could do.

Jim threw his arms around Aunt Kate, "Don't leave," he pleaded. Lilly not wanting to be left out, wiggled her way between Jim and Aunt Kate, "Don't leave, don't leave!"

The old lady smiled down at both of the children, her arms going around them.

"Now, you kids be brave and take care of your mama."

"Jim," she turned to the boy, putting her hand on his head.

"Yes, ma'am?" Jim looked at her expectantly.

"You're the man of the house so you be sure and take care of your mama and Lilly. Don't let nothin' bad happen to them, you heah?"

Puffing out his small chest, he appeared to stand three feet taller. "I promise to take care of them, Aunt Kate!" he solemnly vowed, the seriousness of his face making her smile.

"Good," she patted him on the head as she turned to the Ellen. "Well, lets not drag this out. I'm too old for this kind of unpleasantness."

Lyle was holding the door open for her. She turned to get into the car, then stopped, and looked back at her surrogate family. They were looking at her so forlornly. Aunt Kate could feel the tears threatening at the back of her eyes. As they each realized the moment of parting was upon them, they rushed forward in one last bone-shattering hug. Lyle couldn't stand it any longer.

"Come on, Mama, we've got to get going. There's a long drive ahead." She stumbled to the car with eyes swimming in tears.

Hesitantly, Lyle turned to Ellen, and the children, he was crushing his hat in his hands, and turning it round and round as he spoke, "I wanna thank ya' for bein' so kind to my mama," and without allowing Ellen time to respond, he hurriedly climbed into the car.

Slowly, they pulled away from the curb, and started down the street with Aunt Kate looking back. Jim and Lilly were jumping up and down, waving to her. The last thing she saw, before the car turned the corner, was Ellen's lonely, forlorn figure waving goodbye.

"Now, you kids stay inside and don't you dare open the door for anyone!" Ellen admonished her children before leaving for work the next morning, "Jim, you're in charge. You watch out for Lilly and keep her safe until I get home."

"Yes, Mama," he solemnly swore as he stood shivering before the kerosene stove. Ellen was worried. She knew that her children were too young to be left alone, but she didn't know what else to do. She had to work so they would have a place to live, and food to eat.

Lilly interrupted her thoughts by pulling on her skirt, "Mama, I can help Jim." Ellen smiled, and ran her fingers through Lilly's tousled blonde curls as she knelt before her, and searched the little girl's face.

"Yes, dear, you're mama's big girl, and you and Jim must look after each other."

Ellen felt a lump rise in her throat as she looked at Lilly. Reaching out she stood and lifted the little girl up in her arms. Lilly responded by wrapping her tiny arms around Ellen's neck as though she were afraid to let go of her. Kissing the button nose, she bent to put her down, but Lilly tightened her hold and clung to Ellen's neck. Gently, she broke the hold.

"Lilly, I have to leave now, but I'll be back soon. You be a good girl and mind your brother."

Quickly, Ellen left, because she could sense that Lilly was about to protest.

Two fat tears rolled down the cherub face, and Jim put his arms around his little sister.

"It's okay, Lilly, Mama will be home soon." Pushing at her brother to break his hold, she ran to the window, and strained up on her tiptoes to peer out the dirty glass pane. At that moment, Ellen looked back and saw the tiny head above the window- pane, and the pink bow lips forming the word "Mama." Ellen turned away, and steeled herself not to think about the sad, little face in the window. With heavy heart, she continued the long walk to work.

The days passed quickly, but leaving the children did not get any easier for her or for them. When she was at home the children followed her around, scarcely letting her out of their sight. Even though Jim and Lilly knew that she had to go to work, they seemed to resent it. Ellen knew that they were thinking about their father, afraid that she would leave them as he had. To reassure them, she would rush home from work as quickly as she could. Nothing seemed to help, and Ellen could sense their unhappiness.

Lilly begin waking up and crying during the night, and Ellen had to hold her and talk to her until she drifted off to sleep again. For the hundredth time, she wished that Aunt Kate were still across the street.

Ellen's unhappy thoughts were interrupted, by the tinkling of the bell as the formidable Amanda McGowan swept through the door. As usual, the woman did not look Ellen's way. She sat a large bag down in front of the counter, and headed for some brightly colored scarves displayed in the front window.

Ellen hoped that Maize would come out of the back storeroom where she was unpacking some boxes, or that Mr. Boswell's office door would open. As she stood there unsure of what to do, Amanda turned her frosty stare in her direction.

"Girl, do you work here, or, are you the store dummy?"

"Yes, Madam. I... I mean I work here," Ellen stammered.

Amanda's eyes moved distastefully over Ellen's shabby, but clean clothes. She felt herself shrinking before those measuring eyes that clearly found her lacking.

"Don't just stand there gawking! I require your assistance now!"

Ellen felt her face flushing at the unkind rebuke, as she jerkily moved around the counter toward Amanda. Her foot stumbled over the bag that was left standing in front of the counter, forcefully knocking it over. The splintering sound of shattering glass broke the silence in the store. Ellen stood paralyzed, staring in horror at the bag lying on its side. Seeing her stricken, dismayed face, Amanda guessed at the reason, and hurried around the counter, stopping when she saw the bag. Stooping to open it, she inspected the contents. Amanda made a noise in her throat that sounded like a snarl. Ellen stood rooted to the spot as she stood up and began swearing and shrieking obscenities at her.

Maize and Mr. Boswell both came rushing out at the same time. The startled look on their faces would have been comical had there been something to laugh about. Before Mr. Boswell could recover, Amanda began to berate him, "Boswell, what kind of idiots do you employ? This, this person," she sputtered as she pointed at Ellen, "has broken a very valuable vase, an antique to be exact. It cannot be replaced as it is one of a kind, unlike your employee, who is all too common!" Hardly drawing a breath, her ranting continued, "I demand that you fire her immediately!"

There was complete silence as heads turned towards Mr. Boswell. Nervously, he wrung his hands as he tried to placate the irate woman.

"Now, Amanda," he uttered in his most pacifying voice, "I'm sure it was an accident and Ellen didn't do anything intentionally. Let's just try to be calm and work this out."

Amanda drew herself up to her full height and glared at Mr. Boswell. "Don't you dare patronize me; you incompetent fool! That vase was worth far more than this, this *hovel* you call a department store!" Not allowing Mr. Boswell the opportunity to interrupt, Amanda continued her tirade, "If you don't dismiss this person," she waved her hand in Ellen's direction, without bothering to look at her, "I shall call your most, shall we say, affluent customers, and I can guarantee," she punctuated her words by jabbing her finger into his chest, "your store will not be on the list of places to shop. Let's see," she mused, putting her finger to the side of her chin, "there's Mrs. Danfield, Mrs. Worthington, Mrs. Levy, Mrs. Carlton,." peering at him from beneath her lashes to see what affect her words were having, she paused, "shall I go on, Boswell?"

His face was pale and he was breathing heavily. "No, that will not be necessary, Amanda." He had taken out his handkerchief and was wiping his perspiring forehead as he spoke, "I am well aware of the influence you carry in this town."

"Then you do see things my way?" Amanda sneered.

"Please listen to me," he pleaded, "Ellen has two small children to support. Her husband left...."

"Stop!" she demanded, "I'm not interested in any hard-luck stories! Are you going to fire her or not?"

The unyielding look on Amanda's face let Boswell know that he was defeated. How he hated having to give in to the Amandas of this world, but he had to face facts. The Depression had made everyone crazy. He had obligations, mouths to feed, and bills to pay. Slowly, and regretfully, he turned toward Ellen, but his eyes couldn't meet hers.

"Ellen, I'm afraid I have to..." before he could finish Ellen made a sound that caused Mr. Boswell to look at her. She had stuffed her fist hard against her mouth to hold back the great gulping sobs that were shaking her body. Ellen didn't wait for her employer to finish the sentence, before running blindly out the door and down the street.

There was silence except for the tinkling of the bell above the door that she had left open.

Mr. Boswell turned to Amanda, and she could see the hatred burning in his eyes. It amused her to know that she had power over him and that he wouldn't stand up to her even for one of his poor, unfortunate employees.

"I trust things were handled to your satisfaction, Amanda!" he said in a stilted voice, and he could feel the rage boiling beneath those words as he forced himself to exercise control.

"Oh, yes, dear Boswell," Amanda deliberately gushed.

Temptation was strong to put his fingers around the pearl-draped neck and choke the life out of the creature before him. Without another word, he turned and stalked to his office and slammed the door. It vibrated from the force of his anger.

Amanda's cruel laughter could be heard through the door as Boswell laid his head on his desk in utter despair for what he had done.

Maize stood silent, still in shock at the drama she had just witnessed. Before she could recover, Amanda had swept out the door and into the chauffeur driven car.

Chapter 3

As she settled herself in the back of the car, her eyes closed in complete relaxation. She was very pleased with herself. *What a delightful ending to an otherwise boring day*, she thought. A tiny smile curved her mouth as she thought about what had transpired.

Welding her power over people was what Amanda loved most. It was her orgasm, and she reveled in the chaotic aftermath. She was thinking about how Ellen had looked when she realized that Boswell was not going to stand up for her.

Laughing to herself, she thought about Boswell trying to placate her so that he could keep his precious employee. The old fool had even tried to make her feel sorry for his little waif by mentioning something about children. Children, she never liked to think about children. It always brought back the past. Yet, her thoughts betrayed her, bringing unpleasant memories back to haunt her.

She was twenty-one, and her marriage to Jake McGowan had been anything but pleasant. She didn't love him and had never loved him. Jake was just a means to an end. She loved the social position, and the power his position provided her. His so-called lovemaking was distasteful to her, and after their honeymoon fiasco, she had moved into her own bedroom. When Jake confronted her and complained about their separate living arrangements, she informed him that he would have to accept that the intimacy of their marriage was over.

Generously, she had given him permission to seek out other women for his physical needs as long as he was discreet.

Jake had been furious. He slammed out of the house and that's when his drinking problems had started. Amanda knew that Jake was weak where she was concerned, and the drinking made him weaker. She also knew that it made him more dependent on her, and that he would never have the nerve to divorce her. Oh, yes, she reasoned, she knew how to control Jake.

At least, that's what she had thought, until that one night when Jake had come home drunk. Amanda had been reading in bed for some time when suddenly the door banged open, and Jake stood in the doorway. She had riled at him for barging into her room, and demanded that he leave at once. He laughed as he weaved his way toward her.

Never dreaming that she would be in any danger, she had remained in bed. When he bent close to her, the smell of cheap perfume and booze sickened her. She raised her arm to push him away and he grabbed her, pinning her to the bed. She fought like a mad woman, but Jake had won.

Afterwards, she lay stunned, her pride shattered. She couldn't believe it; her husband had actually raped her. Blind with rage she looked at him as he slept, oblivious to the storm going on inside her...and she hated him. "You will pay for this," she vowed, "you will pay for the rest of your miserable life!"

As it turned out, Amanda was the one to pay. About a month later, she discovered that she was pregnant. She hated Jake so much that the thought of giving him a child was something that she would not contemplate. From her days in academia, she had learned from her peers that there was more than one use for a coat hanger. Crudely, without thought of danger to herself, she used the only method she knew to be rid of the unwanted burden. Rage, coupled with the desire to expunge Jake from her body forever, made her careless.

Unfortunately, she took sick with a fever soon after the self-inflicted abortion. Fear took its toll on Amanda's guilt-ridden mind. She was sure God was going to kill her for what she had done. Perhaps, God had a more subtle punishment for Amanda. The infection caused by the coat hanger abortion left her sterile. For years, she had avoided the subject of children, because it made her remember her guilt and the deception that kept Jake tied to her.

Riling at Jake, she had informed him that it was his fault, and that he was to blame for her "miscarriage." Tearfully, she had heaped more guilt on him by telling him that she would not be able to have another child. Jake had been crushed, but, thankfully, his guilt had made him give up on a normal marriage relationship. Distastefully, she pushed aside the thoughts that pricked her conscience on how she had deceived him.

Ten years is a long time. Amanda was now thirty-one, but the guilt continued to haunt her. She came to regard it as a stigma or a blot on her otherwise perfect life. The high society of Austin still would not totally accept her into their tight knit circle. It had even been hinted that her childless condition was one of the reasons she had been denied her coveted pinnacle in their society. The snooty, hoity-toity women had all but rubbed her nose in the fact that she was childless. Sneers and snide remarks about Jake's extramarital activities had stung the haughty Amanda as well.

Almost every night, the same dream plagued her. Dreams about children of various sizes and ages. Included in the dreams was the circle of women from whom she so desperately wanted approval. Always, they were pointing their finger at her, accusing her, taunting her, and never giving her any peace. Imperiously, they informed her that a perfect child would take away the stigma of her handicap. Was this dream some sort of revelation, showing her what to do to gain their approval?

A plan began to take form in Amanda's troubled mind. *A child, yes, that's the answer,* she thought, *I'll get a child, and then they will have to accept me. They'll see that I'm normal and perfectly capable of raising a child.* A satisfied smile curved Amanda's lips, and just as suddenly, the smile vanished. A problem that hadn't occurred to her until now, where would she find a suitable child? *Well, let's see,* she mused, *what about the woman that Boswell had fired? I believe he mentioned that she had children. Her financial condition wouldn't be too good without a job. I'll make Boswell tell me all about her. Surely,* she thought, *a child should be as easy to purchase as an antique vase.* She laughed at her own little joke.

Bread lines formed all across the land. The poor depended on the charity of others and their city or local government. President Hoover did not believe it to be the job of the United States government to provide relief. The city of Austin had set up a "bread line" to provide food for its citizens that had no means of support, and had lost their jobs.

It had been six weeks since Ellen had lost her job. A hard six weeks when Ellen had been so depressed that even the children couldn't cheer her up. She had walked the streets looking for work, but it was the same story everywhere. "Sorry, we're not hiring right now," were words that Ellen had come to dread. Finally, she decided to register for local relief. She was given an identification card.

The bread line was longer than ever and Ellen was tired and she was hungry. The children were hungry. The small amount of food given to them was more often than not of poor quality. Sometimes the bread line had only one type of food to offer. Once they had to live on potatoes for a week. Ellen sighed as she looked at the long line. Her feet hurt from standing so long.

Bitterness claimed her thoughts as she remembered what had transpired six weeks ago. *I can't believe Mr. Boswell fired me because that woman asked him to!* she fumed to herself. *Amanda McGowan must be the most heartless person in the world to have thrown such a fit over something that was an accident!* She had willed in her mind for Mr. Boswell to stand up to Amanda, and it had seemed as though he would until Amanda had threatened him with financial ruin. Tears were gathering again in Ellen's eyes. No one had stood up for her. *Life is so unfair. What have I done to deserve this kind of treatment?* she wondered in self-pity.

"Next!" the voice boomed, jolting her out of her thoughts. At last, she had made it to the front of the line.

Chapter 4

Ellen trudged home with her sack of food finding each step more and more difficult. She was weary, bone weary from standing in line most of the day. Ellen looked older than her twenty-four years. Stress and desperation were adding lines to her face, and lack of spirit made her shoulders droop.

Her pregnancy was near the end, and she was showing. The children were beginning to ask questions, especially Jim. So, she told them that they would soon have a little brother or sister. They danced around her and patted her stomach like it was all some wonderful game. She felt guilty every time she thought about the little addition to their impoverished lifestyle.

As she rounded the corner to where the shack stood, she noticed a car parked in front that somehow looked familiar. Panic gripped her. Had something happened to the children? Ellen quickened her pace. She reached the door, and with fumbling fingers managed to pull the door open. Ellen gasped, shock and amazement held her immobile. It was incredulous that this woman would be bold enough to come to her house!

"Don't just stand there, come on in, dear," Amanda gushed. She was sitting in a chair holding Lilly in her lap. Ellen forced her frozen lips to move, "What are you doing here?" she demanded in a strangled voice. The children were staring at their mother and the woman that had come to visit them. Lilly wiggled down from Amanda's lap, and ran to Ellen.

"Mama, don't you like the nice lady?" Jim broke in before Amanda could respond, "Mama, look at all the food," he yelled, "I bet we have enough for a year!"

Lilly was dancing around the table, picking up various delicacies for Ellen to see.

Her face was pale, and her hands were trembling as she turned to look at her tormenter. "What's the meaning of this, Mrs. McGowan?" Ellen's voice shook as she spoke.

"Why, dear Ellen, I thought it was obvious. I heard about your plight, and felt it my Christian duty to try and help you."

Her voice erupted in indignation at Amanda's blatant hypocrisy, "You, you..." Ellen stammered, "get out of my house!"

She had raised her arm and was pointing at the door as she yelled, and the action had pulled the material of her tattered dress across her protruding stomach. Amanda's eyes widened slightly, and then narrowed as she took in Ellen's unmistakable condition.

The children watched in confusion not understanding their mother's attitude toward the kind lady that had brought them all this wonderful food.

"Mama..."

"Be quiet, Jim!" Ellen warned. Jim hung his head and sulked at the rebuke.

"I'm only trying to help you, Ellen," Amanda stated in her most condescending voice. "However," and she injected just the right amount of hurt in her voice for the children's benefit, "if you don't want my help, I'll take the food and leave now."

At those words, the children set up such a ruckus Ellen thought she'd never be able to quiet them. While she was trying to smooth things over with the children, Amanda watched, and smiled in her self-satisfied way at the chaos she had caused.

Slowly, she walked to the table and began to gather up the food. Being a convincing actress whenever the need arose, she put on her saddest face for the children to see. Watching the delightful treats disappear before their eyes did not bring Lilly and Jim comfort. They pulled away from Ellen, and begin to cry in unison.

Helplessly, Ellen looked at Amanda. She was wearing the same satisfied smirk on her face as when she had gotten her way with Mr. Boswell.

"What do you want from me, Mrs. McGowan?" Ellen asked in a tired, defeated voice.

"I only want to help you and your children," she reiterated as though she were talking to a less than bright child, "and do call me, Amanda. Even though you were in the wrong at the store, perhaps Boswell was too harsh on you." Her words caused Ellen to flinch as she remembered the pain of her boss' betrayal, but the hypocrisy of this horrible woman was even worse.

"You will allow me help, won't you?" she sensed Ellen was about to speak, so she continued, "for the children's sake and," momentarily she paused, "for the sake of the child you're carrying?" Something in Amanda's eyes made Ellen suddenly feel the need to protect her unborn child. Defensively, she placed her arms across her stomach. The gesture did not go unnoticed.

The children's recent bout with tears had left their little faces puffy and swollen, and they were looking at Ellen, expectantly. Her head had drooped in defeat. "Thank you for the food," she mumbled ungraciously.

"What was that, I didn't quiet catch what you said?" Amanda was determined that Ellen would concede the victory to her before she left this hovel.

Ellen's head snapped back, and for an instant some of the spirit and pride that was once so much a part of her, shone through her eyes. "I said, "thank you for the food, now would you please leave!"

"Of course… but," at that one little word Ellen looked at Amanda warily, "You can be sure that you will see me again," her cold, hateful eyes held Ellen's, "and that my dear, Ellen, is a promise!" With those words her flat brown eyes traveled to Ellen's stomach, sending a chill down her spine.

Chapter 5

A crowd of men and women, shouting that they were hungry and jobless, raided a grocery store near the City Hall today.

Jake threw down the paper in disgust. It was happening more and more all over the country. Something had to be done, and soon, too. Jake pulled out his suitcase and began to pack. The riot had occurred in Dallas, and several men had been arrested. Jake wanted to do a story, and interview the men involved. The government was claiming that such riots were organized rather than spontaneous. Jake had reporters that he could send, but he liked to cover this type of story himself. Anyway, his mother lived in Dallas, and he always stayed with her. It was a good excuse to visit her. Amanda never went with him, and his mother never came to visit for obvious reasons. She and Amanda had never gotten along.

Amanda, Jake sighed as he thought of her. He still hadn't gotten up the courage to ask for a divorce. She was up to something, Jake sensed it, but he didn't know what, and Amanda never talked to him unless she needed him for something. Oh, well, he'd find out what it was when he got back from Dallas, he mused. Then, by heaven, he'd tell the witch that he was leaving her!

Amanda watched from the upstairs window as Jake left the house. It pleased her to see the luggage being stowed in the trunk of the car. *Good,* she thought, *he'll be gone for a while.* She turned from the window dismissing Jake from her mind as she thought about the "plan" she was working on involving Ellen and her children. Actually her plan included only one child, and that child was not yet born. Amanda had determined that the child would be hers from the moment she realized Ellen's condition. "My very own child," she mused, aloud. "You'll be the toast of Austin and everyone will know that you belong to Amanda McGowan!"

The flat-brown eyes actually gleamed and sparkled for the first time in many years. Ellen's child was to be Amanda's salvation. It would also be the key to her rapidly deteriorating respectability, and to keeping Jake chained to her side. She laughed out loud at the thought. How Jake would hate her for this final triumph!

"Miss Cummings, Miss Cummings," Amanda yelled for the elderly housekeeper. The woman appeared almost immediately in the doorway. Her iron-gray hair was pulled back severely, and twisted into a knot on top of her head. The thin body was encased in a plain black dress. A stiffly starched white apron was her only adornment. She crossed her hands over her abdomen as she looked at Amanda.

"Yes, Madam, you called for me?"

"Well, is the room ready?" Amanda inquired rather impatiently. Without replying, Miss Cummings gestured for Amanda to follow her to the room in question. She pushed the door wide then stepped aside so that her employer could see.

It was the room next to Amanda's, and over the past few weeks the room had been transformed into a child's nursery. There was a white crib with a large rocking chair nearby. Stuffed animals peeked out of a large corner shelf. There was a white trunk at the foot of the crib filled with blankets, bunting suits, pillows, and everything necessary for the newborn that would live there. A large white wardrobe was at one end of the room. The padded bench beneath the bay windows looked as though it were made for a young person to someday sit, and dream, and wonder about the mysteries of life. A gentle breeze was stirring the lovely lace curtains. Amanda's satisfied gaze took in everything, and seeing the contented look on her face, Miss Cummings allowed herself to relax.

Alice Cummings had come to work for the McGowan family when Jake was a boy of ten. They were good to her and she enjoyed working for them. She could have gone to Dallas with the elder Mrs.

McGowan, but had decided to stay with Jake and Amanda. After all, Jake needed her. She knew that his life had taken an unhappy turn, and that Amanda was the source. It took all of her will-power, but she could not allow her dislike of Amanda to show. The woman would get rid of her in a heartbeat if she suspected anything less than complete loyalty. So, she did her job, and kept her mouth shut.

Chapter 6

The rent on the shack was nearly three weeks overdue. Ellen was frantic that she and the children would be thrown out on the streets with no place to go. Last week, the surly owner of the shack had threatened that they would have to pay the rent or get out. She knew that any day he would be back to make good on the threat. The children were silent as they watched their mother pace back and forth. Ellen's head ached from the effort of trying to figure out what to do. She was tired, lonely, and desperate. Her unborn child was due any moment, and she wondered for the hundredth time what she would do when the moment actually came. She wore the haunted look of a person who has finally come face to face with reality. The reality that Dan was never coming back, and that she and the children were virtually destitute.

Her thoughts were interrupted by a knock at the door. Ellen stood motionless as the sharp knock was repeated. The children raced to open the door, but Ellen called out to them, "Jim, Lilly, wait! Let Mama answer the door." They moved aside as she slowly lifted the latch to admit the man who would throw them into the street without a backward glance.

Ellen was surprised, and a little wary that the man at the door was not their landlord. He was wearing a chauffeur's uniform. He removed his hat and tucked it under his arm as he spoke to her,

"Madam, will you and the children please accompany me to the car? Mrs. McGowan would like a word with you." He turned to walk back to the car expecting Ellen and the children to follow. When he reached the car, he looked back surprised to see that they were watching from the doorway.

"Madam," he began somewhat impatiently. Just then the car door opened and Amanda beckoned the chauffeur to help her from the car. She walked up the path to the shack her eyes never leaving Ellen's wane face. Amanda could see defeat in the eyes of the woman before her. Knowing that Ellen was about to be a victim of her circumstances brought no remorse. All that mattered was that she was about to achieve her goal, and she wore the smile of triumph.

Jim had already squeezed past Ellen's slight form to be near the nice lady that had brought such wonderful food. Only Lilly hung back, clinging to her mother's skirts. It was as though the child sensed some unknown, impending doom was about to enfold them all, and change their lives forever. Ellen absently caressed Lilly's head as she stared at Amanda.

From the looks of things, there was no time to waste, so Amanda came right to the point.

"Ellen, I have a proposition to offer you. I'd like you, and the children to accompany me back to my home where we may talk in private, and the children can have something to eat." She looked at Lilly and Jim as she said this knowing that she would have their full support.

"Oh, Mama, can we?" Jim and Lilly cried in unison. Earlier misgivings forgotten, Lilly joined her bother as they jumped up and down in excitement.

"Stop it! Jim, Lilly, come here immediately!"

The two children were beyond listening to their mother. They were running around the car, and the chauffeur was opening the door for them to get in.

Ellen swayed. Her head was spinning, and she couldn't think clearly. When she looked at Amanda her eyes mirrored her confusion. To Amanda, she was simply a helpless, pathetic creature that had finally realized that there was no escape. As she swayed again, Amanda signaled to her chauffeur. Ellen's slight form was picked up and placed in the car.

Her eyes remained closed, her mind in chaos, as she tried to focus on what was happening to her. Why was Amanda doing this? What purpose could she possibly have? The questions floating in and out of her mind were making her dizzy. She gave up trying to think.

At that moment, another concern captured Ellen's attention, and she moaned as the unmistakable pains of labor bore down on her. The pain was unbearable, and Ellen's eyes were wide and frightened as she clutched her abdomen. Lilly and Jim huddled in the corner of the car, shaken and frightened as they witnessed their mother's pain. The next wave of pain brought oblivion, and Ellen slumped, unconscious.

Amanda instructed the chauffeur to drive faster, and soon she was relieved to see the car approaching the front of the house. Her concern was not for Ellen, but for the unborn child.

The crunch of gravel and the cessation of motion made Ellen open her eyes. She stared at the large house that appeared to cast a shadow of despair over her confused mind, and then cried out as another wave of pain tore through her body.

The children were becoming distraught as they witnessed their mother's labor. Amanda ordered the chauffeur to carry Ellen upstairs, while she had Miss Cummings phone her personal physician. Then she ordered her to take the children to the kitchen and distract them with food. Crying, they pulled away from the housekeeper. Both children demanded to see their mother. They could hear cries coming from upstairs. Something was not right. The tall lady with the "crown" was beckoning to them.

"Come here at once!" Amanda's demeanor brooked no argument. The "nice lady" was gone. "Now, you will stop all this sniveling, and go with Miss Cummings!" The housekeeper could see the indecision in their eyes as they looked at her.

Poor little mites, she thought. *They deserve to be treated better.* The loud snapping of fingers brought Miss Cummings out of her reverie. She encountered Amanda's glaring eyes.

"Miss Cummings, have you suddenly gone senile? I've asked you to take the children to the dining room for something to eat." A hint of red crept into the housekeeper's face at being so harshly reprimanded.

"I'm sorry, Mrs. McGowan, I'll see to them at once," she was gesturing for the children to follow her as she spoke. Reaching down, she lifted a reluctant Lilly into her arms. Lilly's bow mouth was beginning to quiver. "It's okay, dear," the housekeeper soothed, "I'll take good care of you." As she turned to leave, Amanda stopped her,

"Make sure they are kept away from their mother until this is all over and settled." she motioned toward the upstairs room as she spoke while her eyes bored into Miss Cummings.

"Yes, Madam." The message in Amanda's eyes had been read and surrendered to. The elderly housekeeper hurried the children down the hallway to the kitchen.

There was a scream, and the chauffeur appeared in the doorway, disheveled and pale. Amanda read the panic in his face as clearly as she read his lips. "Madam, please, I can't hold her down much longer, and she's in such pain!"

"Oh, all right, I'm coming!" Amanda answered impatiently as she placed her foot on the first rung of the stair. Before continuing up the stairs she saw the front door open. Doctor Hemsley had knocked several times, but he knew Amanda was deaf, and he let himself in. Amanda went quickly to his side, and grasped his sleeve pulling him towards the stairs.

"Amanda, what is go...?" A piercing scream interrupted the doctor, and he ran up the stairs two at a time, with Amanda close behind. He pushed the dazed chauffeur out of the way as he paused in the doorway of the bedroom. The young woman on the bed was writhing in pain, and the bed was soaked. The doctor began to bark out orders as he rolled up his sleeves. Amanda was beside herself, but the doctor was firm in refusing to allow her into the room. She paced the hallway outside the bedroom, wringing her hands and waiting for the doctor to emerge with news.

The labor was long and arduous, and there were moments when the doctor worried whether the fail, young woman would make it. Ellen had bitten her lips so hard they bled. Finally, just before dawn, Ellen's suffering came to an end. She was delivered of a small, but healthy girl. Dr. Hemsley examined the child thoroughly as he cleaned her up, and satisfied that she was indeed healthy, he wrapped her in a warm blanket. Ellen was anxiously watching his every move. Her arms stretched out in a silent gesture towards the child. He smiled reassuringly before placing the tiny infant in her extended arms.

"You, young woman," the doctor gently scolded her, "are going to have to rest, and get plenty to eat in order to gain back your strength." Ellen was weakly smiling, but her eyes were on the little girl as the doctor continued, "Tell your husband that he must take good care of you, and see that you take it easy for awhile." He was aware that the smile had left her face, and he cursed himself for being a fool. He should have known that if the woman's husband were anywhere around, he would have been here by now. Tears were running down Ellen's face, and she blindly put the baby back in the doctor's arms, and lay facing the wall.

"Young woman," the doctor admonished in his sternest voice, "turn around and look at me." There was no response other than the muffled sobbing.

"You must get hold of yourself for the child's sake. Are you listening to me?" he asked in exasperation.

"Please, I am trying to help you!" seeing only Ellen's back, and shaking shoulders as sobs tore through her body, the doctor turned away in defeat.

He carried the infant out of the bedroom wondering what he should do. Amanda met him at the top of the stairs. She almost tore the child out of his arms in her haste.

"The child! Let me see the child!" she devoured the tiny form with her greedy eyes and hands as she checked the now crying infant for any existing flaw or mark.

"Why, she's perfect!" Amanda exclaimed to the bewildered doctor.

"Mrs. McGowan, I don't understand," the doctor began, but Amanda was impatient to be rid of him now that she had what she wanted.

"I think you should be on your way, doctor, as I am sure someone else must be in need of your services."

The puzzled doctor shrugged his shoulders and turned away. To some degree, he felt a sense of relief knowing that he would not need to worry about Ellen. After all, he reasoned, Amanda seemed to be in control of the situation. The baby had stopped crying, and Amanda was clutching the infant to her as though she would never let her go.

The doctor gathered his belongings in silence, and as he turned to leave, he hesitated. Impatiently, Amanda watched him hovering near the door.

"Mrs. McGowan, the doctor started, "that young, woman needs help and"...

"Dr. Hemsley!" Amanda interrupted, addressing him in her most imperious tones, "I am well aware of what is needed. Do not concern yourself further in this matter. Good evening," she dismissed coldly.

The doctor realized he was helpless in the face of Amanda's determination, and nodding in her direction, he quickly left the house.

Looking down at the sleeping infant, her lips curled into a satisfied smile.

"You are mine, all mine!" she whispered to the tiny doll, as she carried her to the nursery.

Miss Cummings quietly closed the bedroom door, and breathed a sigh of relief. At last, the children were asleep. It had taken a long time for that to happen, and they had submitted only after severe exhaustion had taken over their minds and bodies. They were worried about their mother, and the housekeeper felt pity for them as she recalled the dried tear stains on their tired little faces.

She tiptoed down the hall toward Amanda's room, deciding that she would try to talk to her. *After all,* she thought, *the woman must have some compassion.*

Passing the room that had been made into a nursery, she heard what sounded like someone in deep conversation. It was Amanda's voice. She pressed her ear against the door, straining to hear.

"My darling little girl. You shall be the toast of the town. Heads will turn whenever you walk down the street, and people will say, there goes Jenny McGowan, Amanda's daughter!"

Cautiously, she opened the door. Amanda was sitting in the rocking chair staring at the baby, oblivious to anything else. Only when the housekeeper stood directly in front of the rocking chair where she sat holding the infant, did Amanda look up.

"Miss Cummings, I'm giving you the honor of being the first to meet my daughter...Jenny," she said her name almost as though she were breathing a prayer, and as she said it she turned down the blanket so the housekeeper could have her first glimpse of the infant.

The dark, softly curling hair was much more than the peach fuzz that usually adorned the head of a newborn. She was tiny, probably no more than five pounds. Long, dark lashes fanned the rose petal cheeks.

For a moment Miss Cummings was speechless. She didn't ever recall seeing a baby quite so beautiful. Usually they looked like wrinkled monkeys, but not this one. She glanced again at Amanda, and was startled by her demeanor. It was plain to see that the tiny infant enthralled the woman that held her so possessively.

All the same, she thought, *Amanda McGowan could not possibly think that she could just take this child as though it were her own!*

As she started to remind her of this, she noticed her employer's attention had once again been captured totally by the child. Hesitantly, she touched Amanda's sleeve to get her attention.

Reluctantly, she turned her attention from the child to Miss Cummings. The housekeeper was startled as she looked into Amanda's eyes. The eyes that looked back at her were glowing as though life had been breathed into the soul of Amanda McGowan.

Haltingly, the housekeeper told her mistress that the baby needed to be returned to her mother, but before she could continue, Amanda startled her by standing up and thrusting her face close to hers.

"Now, you listen to me, Miss Cummings! This is what I have waited and planned for, so don't tell me what I can or cannot do!" Amanda's face had turned an ugly shade of purple, and her breathing was labored by her impassioned words, "from this day forward you will think of this child as mine and only mine! Is that clear?"

The housekeeper's voice seemed to be caught somewhere in her throat and she mutely nodded as Amanda continued her tirade.

"You will put Ellen and her other children completely out of your mind...they don't exist." The words were hissed through her teeth.

"I will take care of everything, and you will follow my instructions to the letter!" At the look on the housekeeper's face, Amanda snarled a warning, "I can make sure that you do, Miss Cummings."

A look of disbelief crossed her face as she waited for her employer to finish.

Amanda relaxed and swayed back and forth to soothe the awakening Jenny. She was not through with her distraught housekeeper, and smiling to herself she decided to drive the knife home.

"You see, my dear, there seems to be a depression going on, and there's not much work in this country, for say, a poor homeless, might I add, aging housekeeper!"

Miss Cummings tried to regain a small amount of her fast fading dignity.

"Mrs. McGowan, I'll have you to know that the lady who lives a short distance from here, Mrs. Jennings, told me the other day that she would just love to steal me away from you!"

Amanda threw back her head and laughed cruelly.

"Would she indeed, Miss Cummings? And how would she feel about hiring someone who was sent to jail for stealing!" Amanda laughed again at the housekeeper's horrified expression.

"Mrs. McGowan how can you say something like that when you know it isn't true!" she pleaded indignantly.

"You and I may know it, but what about the rest of the world?" Amanda sneered, "I can ruin you. I can make sure that no one in their right mind would ever hire you or even have you in their home."

The woman shuttered at the cruel words, and seemed to shrink before Amanda's haughty stare.

"Have I made myself understood?"

"Yes, Mrs. McGowan, I understand very well."

"Good! It will not be necessary to speak of this again." With those words, Amanda turned away, dismissing the distraught housekeeper.

Jenny began to stir again, and this time she awoke making little mewing, suckling noises, as though she were seeking substance.

The housekeeper fled the nursery. She had no doubt that Amanda would make good on her threats if she dared to disobey her. Jake would not be able to help her. He, too, was a coward in Amanda's presence.

In the hallway, she heard a weak cry from the bedroom by the stairs. She knew it was Ellen's room, and she didn't want to go there. The pitiful cry came again,

"Please, is someone there?" Uncertainly, the housekeeper stood listening. The decision was taken away from her as Amanda came out of the nursery.

"Miss Cummings, I need you to go to the kitchen and take charge of Jenny's formula. It is time for her feeding." The housekeeper turned to do her bidding, but was halted by her employer. "In the future you are to stay away from Ellen. Is that clear?"

Slowly she nodded her head while Amanda's cold eyes bored into her.

"Good, be on your way then!" She could feel the impact of those eyes following her all the way down the stairs.

Now, Amanda focused her attention on the bedroom where Ellen was weakly struggling to get up.

Chapter 7

Jake was struggling into his jacket, as the doctor came up to give him a hand.

"Okay, doc, you've poked and prodded on me long enough, what's the verdict?" Jake was laughing as he said this, but he noticed that the doctor didn't share his humor.

"Jake, I need to get the rest of the charts from my nurse, so go ahead and have a seat in my office. I'll be along in a moment."

"Okay, but it had better be good news if you want me to pay the bill!" He slapped him on the back with a chuckle, but, again, he noticed there was no responding banter from the doctor as turned and left the room. Sighing, the doctor took a deep breath. With every fiber of his being, he dreaded what he must tell Jake.

Doctor Aaron Greeley was a prominent physician in Dallas. He had been Jake's friend and doctor for a number of years. When Jake had first came to him, he complained of being tired a lot, and dutifully, he had checked him over without finding anything of major importance. Over the years, whenever Jake was in Dallas, he came to see him, and usually with the same complaint, about always being tired. He had fixed him up with vitamins and other medications, but still nothing helped.

Then recently more serious symptoms had made themselves known; High blood pressure, pain in the center of the chest, sometimes pain down the left arm, and sometimes in the neck. All classic symptoms, the doctor swore softly as he opened the door to his office where Jake was waiting for him. Sitting behind his desk, he spread the charts out before him, playing for time. He looked up and caught Jake watching him out of the corner of his eye.

Appearing relaxed, he was smoking a cigar. Suddenly, he stood up and stubbed out the cigar in the ashtray. Jamming his hands in his pockets, his eyes met the doctor's.

"Let's not waste each other's time, doc. What's the verdict?"

Nervously, Aaron cleared his throat, "Jake why don't you sit down"...he was interrupted as Jake swore violently. Quickly he strode to the desk and supporting himself with his arms, he leaned across to the doctor.

"Damn it man, tell me now, what's wrong with me!"

Doctor Greeley stood up in alarm.

"Jake, just take it easy, it's your heart!" oh, hell, he hadn't meant to tell him like this. Jake looked stunned, and his face was ashen as he sank down into the chair.

"Jake, you have a heart condition known as angina. The pain you're feeling is because the arteries can't supply enough oxygen to your heart." Jake slowly raised his head, and looked at the doctor.

"What you're telling me is that I'm going to die, isn't that right?"

Frustration colored Aaron Greeley's voice as he tried to explain, "No, not necessarily," he hurried on before Jake could speak, "I've known people to live years with this condition."

Gruffly, Jake's voice interrupted him, "how much time do I have?"

He stared into Jake's eyes as he spoke, "I honestly don't know. If you will take it easy, and rest or lie down every time this pain comes, it will do a lot for your chances. Also, I want you to take nitroglycerin to relieve the symptoms."

Jake was shaking his head and backing away.

Dr. Greeley hurriedly wrote out a prescription. Walking up to Jake, he stuffed it in his coat pocket. Then he put his hand on his friend's shoulder.

"Please, Jake, take this to the emporium down the street, and get the medicine!"

The pleading look, the concern in his friend's eyes, and voice was more than Jake could stand.

"Hey, don't take it so hard and don't look so sad! I know someone who wouldn't be sad at all if I left this earth sooner than planned!"

The doctor looked at him in surprise. The Jake that he knew was very well thought of and liked by everyone. Out of curiosity he had to ask.

"Who would that be?"

Jake laughed as he walked out the door, then he turned and winked, "My loving wife, Amanda, who else!"

Amanda swept into the bedroom just as a pale and trembling Ellen stood to her feet.

"Where is my baby?" she asked weakly. Then she swayed unsteadily as the room began to spin.

"For heaven's sake, woman, lie down before you fall!" Amanda barked.

Ellen sank back onto the bed. A chair was dragged up to the bed, and Amanda sat down. She stared at her so long that Ellen begin to feel uncomfortable, suddenly fear made her rear up, and grab hold of Amanda's arm.

"What has happened to my baby, tell me damn you!" she cried. Amanda removed Ellen's hand from her arm as though disposing of something distasteful.

"Calm yourself, nothing has happened to the child...yet," she added for good measure. At the startled look on Ellen's face, Amanda continued, "You are very weak after having the child, plus you have two other children who will need your attention. Adding to that you have no place to live, a little matter of being behind on the rent, I believe," she paused here to make sure Ellen was still paying attention, "Also, your husband deserted you, poor dear."

Ellen was not fooled by Amanda's false sympathy. Suddenly Ellen leaned over, and stared into Amanda's face.

"Why are you saying all of this to me? Just cut to the chase, Amanda, and tell me what it is you want!"

With those words, Ellen's last bit of strength left her, and she allowed herself to fall back on the bed. She lay staring at the ceiling as she waited for Amanda to speak.

"All right, since plain speaking is what you prefer, here's the situation as I see it. You have no means of support, and you have three children."

As Amanda's voice of doom droned on, Ellen was racking her brain trying to figure out what to do. She and her husband had no family left, well, maybe some distant relatives, but no one that would care what happened to them or their children. She came back to earth with a jolt when she heard Amanda mention Social Service Exchange.

"What... what did you say?" Once again Ellen sat up and stared at Amanda.

"I said that an investigator from the Social Service Exchange would be checking into your situation." Amanda stated blandly.

Ellen had paled considerably.

"No, no, not even you would be that cruel!" she cried in alarm.

"Calm yourself!" Amanda snapped, "There is a way out of this."

Ellen's heart was beating rapidly as she waited for the axe to fall.

Amanda begin, "here is what I propose. You can leave it to me to see about a place for you to live, and a job," she was watching Ellen as she spoke, but there was no response, "You would not have to worry about *anything*," she paused, but Ellen's continued silence irritated her.

"What I'm saying is you and your children will have a chance to live decently," triumphantly, she paused certain that she had made her point, but Ellen was looking at her as though she thought she had lost her mind.

"Why would you do this for me? What's in it for you, Amanda?"

"My dear, I'm simply trying to help you." The blatant lie was more than Ellen could stand.

"Stop lying, Amanda, and tell me what you want!" Suddenly, the gloves were off, Amanda's look was menacing as she stood to her feet.

"I want the baby!"

All the blood had drained out of Ellen's face and for a moment, fear held her immobile. Struggling she got out of bed, and stood on wobbling legs that threatened to buckle at any moment.

"Never! Never will I let you take my child! We'll starve first!" she yelled into Amanda's face.

Quickly, she was shoved into the chair, and as she struggled to rise, Amanda gripped her arms, and restrained her with her superior strength.

"Now you listen to me!" she sputtered through her mounting rage, "if you persist in being stubborn, you'll lose *all* of your children. Do you understand?"

She shook her for emphasis. Ellen's strength left her as the shaking continued, and her head rolled from side to side like a limp, rag doll. She whimpered, then begin to weep in earnest, as great wracking sobs shook her frail body.

Amanda moved out of Ellen's way so she could crawl back into bed. Turning her face to the wall, she continued sobbing as though her heart would break. There was no compassion as she looked at Ellen. She wasn't overly concerned with the situation, just impatient. Ellen would come around; after all, she had no choice.

Jake's eyes were closed as he sat in his mother's favorite armchair facing the window. Unknowingly, his mother had walked quietly into the room, and stood watching him.

He looks so tired, she thought. She knew he had gone to see Aaron Greeley for a check-up, and she hoped everything was okay. Sometimes Jake was not very talkative, and she didn't want to intrude. *However*, she sighed to herself, *I should have said or done something years ago when he married that harpy from hell*!

Rose blushed at her own thoughts. It wasn't like her to speak or think unkindly of anyone, but she loved her son. She knew that Jake had not been happy for years. Rose knew his faults as well. Drinking was one of them, but heaven knows, he didn't start drinking until after his marriage. She sighed once again, silently she thought, but some small sound must have alerted Jake to her presence. He opened his eyes and looked at her from across the room.

"Son, I'm sorry I disturbed you," she apologized as she hesitantly came closer, "I only wanted to check on you, and see that you're okay."

"I wasn't asleep, please come, and join me." He watched as she made her way over to the settee.

Rose McGowan was still a lovely woman…inside and out. Her silver hair was worn in a French twist made secure with the pretty ivory combs that she favored. Her complexion was the ageless peaches, and cream variety that has been the envy of women for centuries. No one would ever guess that she was fifty-four. She was of medium height, thin, and very graceful.

Jake looked at her with admiration and pride as she seated herself across from him. She sensed that he wanted to talk to her so she folded her hands sedately in her lap and waited. Suddenly, Jake reached over and took one of her small hands into his large one.

"Mother," he said, looking into her eyes, "if something were to happen to me, you'd be okay wouldn't you?"

Alarm bells sounded, but outwardly she remained calm. Her hand trembled slightly as she reached up and touched his cheek. "Of course, I would be all right! Son, please tell me what is wrong."

Jake laughed half-heartedly, "Mother, nothing is wrong. I just wanted to know that if something did happen, you'd be okay." Rose said nothing, but her sixth sense told her that something was not right. Her mind was clamoring for something to say, and she said the first thing that popped into her head.

"Jake, how is Amanda? You haven't mentioned her since you've been here."

He rose and walked over to the liquor cabinet and poured himself a generous amount of scotch. He didn't bother to offer his mother any, because he knew she never drank. He turned and raised his drink in salute, then downed the fiery liquid in one gulp.

"Let's see, you asked me a question about my dear wife, didn't you? Well, Mother, she's the same witch that she has always been!"

Bitterness edged his voice, and it broke Rose's heart as she took in her son's defeated, worn demeanor. She stood, and walked over to him. Hesitantly, she put her frail arms around him. He looked at her, and the pain in his eyes was almost more than she could bear.

"Jake, Son, if she causes you this much misery, why don't you leave her?" earnestly her eyes sought his, "You could do it, Jake, you don't need her; you never did." Disengaging himself from her, he turned away.

"Mother, I'm a gutless coward and I've lived this way so long, I don't know if I can change, or even if I want to bother."

The self-loathing in his voice was the last straw. Rose drew herself up to her full five feet, five inch, height.

"Now, you listen to me, Jake McGowan!" this was said as she shook her finger under his nose, "You can do anything you set your mind to. I won't have you berating yourself this way!"

Jake chuckled in spite of himself. "Now, I know why Dad used to call you his "little spit-fire"!"

"Jake McGowan, don't you go changin' the subject!" The twinkle in her blue eyes told him that she wasn't really angry. Glad to be away from the subject of Amanda, Jake picked his mother up and twirled her around the room.

They were both laughing so hard that, at first, Rose didn't notice that Jake had stopped. She was still laughing when he slowly lowered her feet to the floor, but when she looked up at him the laughter died in her throat. Jake's face was grayish. She reached out to steady him as he fell heavily into the armchair clutching at his chest.

"Mother, he moaned...in my jacket...pills...hurry!" Rose needed no second bidding, terror lent wings to her feet as she ran to find the jacket.

Ellen's sobbing finally ceased. She felt limp and lifeless. A cloud of despair and darkness had descended on her, and if she hadn't been raised to be God-fearing, she would have ended her misery. The thought to do so crossed her mind more than once during the last couple of hours. Her children's faces swam before her and she knew she must stay alive for them. Her mind went over and over her tormentor's words. She knew that Amanda McGowan would see that her children were taken from her unless she complied with her wishes.

How can I give up one of my own flesh and blood? What if Dan comes back? Won't he hate me for not taking care of our child? Relentlessly, her thoughts pursued her. Tossing and turning, she tried to escape. Soft moans could be heard as she buried her face in the pillow trying to hide from her dilemma.

"Mommy!" Ellen's eyes flew to the doorway just as Jim and Lilly came bounding toward her. She struggled up, but felt herself being smothered by two small bodies trying to climb on her and kiss her all at once. She smiled and gathered each close to her, one under each arm.

A shadow fell across the bed and she looked up into the watchful eyes of Amanda McGowan.

Resentfully, Ellen spoke to her, "What do you want? Can't I have even a moment alone with *my* children?"

Amanda was not put off by Ellen's attitude. "Of course, you may. And you know the terms, don't you, Ellen? You can have your children with you all the time, a place to live, food, clothes, a job, shall I go on?" Amanda asked.

Sarcastically, Ellen snapped, "I wish you would go on...on out of our lives!"

Amanda pretended hurt. "Why, Ellen, you don't mean that! Whatever would you do without me to look after you?"

The children were silently listening to the dialogue between their mother and the "mean" lady. Their opinion of Amanda since the night before had drastically changed. They cringed, and moved out of her way every time she came near them. Somehow they sensed that this woman had hurt their mother, and they were convinced that she would hurt them also.

There was the matter of the baby, too. Jim and Lilly had both wanted to see their new sister, but were told that they couldn't see her. Puzzled by this, they wanted to talk to their mother.

As though Amanda could read their minds, her attention focused on the children.

"It is past your bedtime. I suggest you tell your mother good night and go to your room at once!" Amanda's voice and manner brooked no argument.

However, being in Ellen's presence gave Lilly and Jim courage to refuse. Jim stood up slowly by the side of the bed.

"We need to talk to our mother."

Lilly put her tiny arms around Ellen's neck and clung, but her eyes never left Amanda.

"You had better tell your children to do as I say! We have unfinished business to discuss." Her eyes held Ellen's for a moment, before Ellen sighed and looked away.

"Jim, Lilly," she drew them to her once more, "I promise we will spend some time together tomorrow." This she said defiantly for Amanda's benefit.

They started to protest, but something in their mother's eyes stopped them. Ellen embraced and kissed them, and they reluctantly left the room without looking at Amanda.

"Very wise of you!" her tormentor snapped. Once again she pulled the chair to the bed and sat down.

"I have secured a position for you as a live-in companion, and housekeeper to a widow woman. She is financially secure, and lives in a large house. You and your two children will be given the entire upper floor for living quarters. Food will be provided as part of your generous salary."

Suddenly, Ellen extended her hand toward Amanda as though imploring her to listen,

"How do you expect me to give up my child? Can't you see it would destroy me! Please, if you have even one ounce of decency in you, don't do this!" Even before she finished speaking, Ellen could tell her words meant nothing.

Amanda was shaking her head. "You have the chance to have a good life, and to provide for your children. If you really loved them, you would jump at this chance to give them the security they need."

As Amanda continued berating Ellen with her words, she defiantly clamped her hands over her ears to stop the sound of her tormentor's voice. Angrily, Amanda jerked Ellen's hands away.

"You had better listen and listen good!" she snarled, "One call to the Social Service Exchange, and an investigator will come, and take your children away! They will be placed in orphanages, do you understand that! I have tried to reason with you, but no more!"

Standing over Ellen, she ranted and threatened until Ellen thought she would go mad if the woman didn't stop.

Realizing that her tantrum was not getting the desired results, Amanda fought for control, and once again resumed her seat by the bed. Taking a deep breath, she spoke softly yet firmly,

"What's it to be, Ellen, shall I call the Social Service Exchange?"

Wearily, she looked at Amanda, defeat evident in her eyes. "Will I ever be allowed to see my child?"

"My dear, Ellen, do you take me for some kind of monster? Of course, you'll be able to see her anytime you want."

Ellen couldn't believe her ears. Could it be possible that Amanda had a heart after all?

"You mean I will really be able to see her anytime I want?"

"Isn't that what I just said?" Amanda replied impatiently.

Reaching inside the bodice of her dress, Amanda extracted a piece of paper. She saw Ellen's look of curiosity.

"I took the liberty of having my lawyer draw up a document giving me charge of the infant," Amanda stated matter-of-factly, "I need your signature," as she spoke she sensed Ellen's withdrawal. "Don't be foolish, Ellen. Think of your other two children, and what this opportunity will mean to them. They'll be able to live decently, go to school. Think, Ellen!" Amanda hissed, "This is your chance to give your children the life they need and deserve, or," she sneered, "would you rather they grow up in an orphanage and remember that their own mother put them there!"

Ellen was shaking uncontrollably as Amanda's words pierced her heart. In triumph, Amanda held out a pen. Ellen's shaking hand took the pen, and through the blur of her unshed tears, she signed her name on the paper.

The gleam in Amanda's eyes grew brighter as she grabbed the pen and paper from Ellen's trembling fingers. "You did the right thing and in time you'll realize it," Amanda gushed.

"In a couple of days, you and your two children will start a brand-new life." With those parting words she left, leaving Ellen to deal with the anguish of her decision.

Rose McGowan was wringing her hands and pacing the floor. She was as frightened as she ever had been for Jake. Aaron Greeley had rushed right over and he was with him now.

My God, she thought, *nitroglycerin!*

She never dreamed that her son had a heart problem. How long had this been going on, she wondered. She stopped pacing when she heard the bedroom door open and close.

Grimly, the doctor walked over to Rose. He could tell she was in a state of great agitation. She started to speak, but he interrupted her by taking hold of her arm and seeing that she was seated first. Then, he sat down across from her.

"Rose, I'm sorry you had to find out this way. Jake should have told you when he came home."

"Told me what, doctor?" she asked, "I know it has something to do with his heart, because of the nitroglycerin." The doctor was nodding his head.

"Yes, he has a condition known as angina." He could tell by her expression that she didn't understand. "Mrs. McGowan, quite simply, he doesn't get enough blood to his heart. This can cause pain, when this happens, he must rest and take the medicine."

Fearfully Rose asked, "Will he be all right then?"

He hesitated a moment before answering her, "Yes, I think so, if he follows my directions," at the look of alarm in her eyes, he rushed on, "lots of people live many years with this problem."

Rose was trying to gather her scattered wits. "Doctor, what can I do to help him?" His heart went out to her as he saw the concern and the tears forming in her eyes.

"My dear," he reached over and took her hand, "you can be there for him, but Jake will have to be responsible for how he conducts his lifestyle and his business. I think he truly understands now what needs to be done."

He gently raised her chin so he could look into her eyes. They were shining with tears.

"Now, Rose, you must be strong. If he sees you distressed, then he will be distressed, and that will never do."

Jake lay on the bed staring at the ceiling, and wondered how his life had come to this. He knew that he had lived on an emotional roller coaster for years, and now he might be running out of time. He had told his mother that he was a coward, and that's what he believed himself to be. Now, he wondered if it was too late to try and change.

All these years he had blamed himself for everything that had gone wrong in his marriage. Starting with the honeymoon. Then there was that night. The night he had come home drunk, determined to take what was rightfully his. He thought if he forced her, she might eventually yield to him. It hadn't worked. For days he'd faced dead, stone cold silence.

Finally retribution had come. Amanda had gotten very sick with a raging fever that had lasted days. He was sick with guilt, and grief when the doctor told him that Amanda had suffered a miscarriage, but that wasn't the worst part. It had left her sterile. The loathing in her eyes whenever she looked at him had caused him to look elsewhere for comfort. The drinking had gotten worse.

Guilt weighed heavily on his shoulders, and Amanda made sure it stayed there. Feeling that he was entirely to blame, he allowed her complete control of their lives. Whatever she wanted, she got and he never demanded anything from her. Drinking had made it all bearable and had given him false courage. Now, that, too, had failed.

It's time to stop, to put the past where it belongs, to finally face my mistakes. "Amanda," he whispered; then his thoughts became jumbled, and he slept.

The sun was streaming brightly through the curtains when Jake finally stirred the next morning. His eyes opened slowly, and his mind cleared as he looked around the room. His eyes rested on the slight figure in the chair beside the bed.

"Mother," he said gently, as her eyes fluttered open and she looked at him.

"Oh, Jake, son, I was so frightened for you." She had risen from the chair, and leaned over to plant a kiss on his forehead. "You gave me quite a scare," she gently scolded.

"Yes, I know, Mother, and I'm very sorry. I should have told you about it yesterday, but I thought I could spare you. Anyway, I don't want you to worry. Remember, I'm a big boy and I can take care of myself." He smiled to take away the sting his words might cause. She smiled knowingly.

"I promise not to play the doting mother, if you will promise me something." Silently, he nodded his head in response. "I want you to promise me that you will slow down and rest whenever you feel the need. Jake," she pleaded, "please, will you take care of yourself? Aaron believes that if you will do as he says, you will be fine."

Jake placed his large hand over her small frail one. "Mother, I solemnly swear to you that I will do my best to stay alive."

"Good," she smiled, "that's all I wanted to hear."

Hesitating, she stood beside his bed, and Jake could tell there was something else on her mind.

"Jake, son, stay here with me," she rushed on afraid he would speak. "The newspaper practically runs itself. You could still run it from here. I would be here for you and I could help you. It would be great having you here. I'll cook all your favorite foods. You can rest."

Jake was waiting for her to run out of steam, before he spoke. Deep down, Jake knew that his mother was worried about the damning affect of Amanda's presence in his life.

"Mother, I have to go back to Austin. Don't worry," he smiled up at her, then his voice and his eyes hardened as he continued, "there's about to be some major changes in my life. Changes I should have made a long time ago, and it's taken a crisis to give me the courage. So, even though I appreciate the offer, Mother, I will rest a couple of days, and then I must go back."

Rose understood his need, and she smiled at him to let him know, but her heart was heavy. Before leaving the room to prepare breakfast, she remembered something.

"Jake, don't you think you should call Miss Cummings so she can tell Amanda that you've been delayed?"

Jake looked at her blankly, "Why?" he asked.

Rose was reminded of when he was a little boy and would ask her a million questions a day. No matter what explanation she gave him, with the guile of youth, he would always demand to know "why."

"Yes," she thought, "why, indeed!"

Chapter 8

The constant clickedy-clack of the train had lulled the two children to sleep. The scenery whizzed past the window so fast it was almost a blur. Ellen leaned her weary head against the back of the seat. Her red-rimmed eyes were puffy and swollen from crying.

Amanda had really won this time. Never in a million years had Ellen guessed that Amanda was sending her and the children away from Austin. She naively thought that they would be living down the street or across town, but never fifty miles away! Up until the time they pulled into the train station, Ellen had innocently believed Amanda. By then it was too late, and all of her pleading and crying had fallen on deaf ears figuratively, and literally. She glanced down at the faces of her sleeping children, and once again, the tears welled up.

The lie, the terrible lie she had told them. Amanda had convinced her that it was the only way to keep them from asking questions. Since they had never seen the baby, Amanda insisted they should be told that the baby was dead. That she was in heaven. They had cried when Ellen told them, but Amanda was right about one thing, after that, they hadn't mentioned her again. They had attributed their mother's sorrow to the death of their little sister.

Amanda had breathed a sigh of relief when the train pulled away from the station. She was elated. She was rid of Ellen and her two children. Jenny was all hers! Foolish Ellen had signed the papers of adoption that gave her sole parental rights where Jenny was concerned. Amanda smiled to herself as she thought of how naive Ellen was to think that she would ever allow her access to the child.

Hurrying back to the house, she thought of one last problem that she must deal with before Jake came home. She had asked Miss Cummings to call Jake's mother, and find out when Jake was due. Then she made the housekeeper face her as she spoke into the phone, so she could be sure of what was being said. She didn't want Jake to know about Jenny until he got home.

The housekeeper sat and rocked baby Jenny, but her mind was on the telephone conversation she had with Jake's mother. Rose McGowan had called right after Amanda had left for the train station. Rose explained about Jake's heart condition, and pleaded with her to take care of him. She had asked her not to let on to Jake that she knew. Rose also said that Jake was adamant about not telling Amanda.

After listening to Rose, and hearing the concern for Jake in her voice, Miss Cummings couldn't tell her about Amanda's latest scheme. She sighed as she thought about this, but what good would it do anyway? She decided that she could be of more help if she kept an eye on Jake, and Jenny, too. She smiled down at the sleeping infant.

Well, she thought, *maybe things will work out after all. This could be Jake's salvation as well as Amanda's. Maybe, Jenny would give Jake a reason to change things, and take care of himself!*

Amanda rushed upstairs as soon as she arrived.

"Miss Cummings, Miss Cummings!" she shouted. Stiffly, the housekeeper got up from the chair with the sleeping infant, just as Amanda reached the door. Amanda watched as she put the child in the crib, and tiptoeing toward her, she motioned her outside the room. Once they were out of the nursery, Amanda wasted no time.

"Whatever I decide to tell Jake about Jenny, you will back me up one hundred percent. Is that clear?"

Amanda expected an argument, and she was ready for it. This would be her opportunity to get rid of the housekeeper, and hire someone who knew nothing about the situation. Her face mirrored her surprise when the woman simply nodded her agreement. Quickly, recovering her composure, she stared at the housekeeper.

"How do I know I can trust you?" Amanda demanded. Indignation at having her character questioned caused the housekeeper to square her shoulders, and hold her head high.

"Mrs. McGowan, I've been a loyal servant of this household for over forty years. I would never say or do anything to hurt a member of this family no matter how much I disagreed with them. I will always remain trustworthy and loyal."

The words were spoken with a hint of pride, and she looked straight into Amanda's eyes as she spoke.

Amanda read her lips, and the truth in her eyes.

"All right, I believe you."

Miss Cummings visibly relaxed.

"But, if I ever have cause to distrust you, I'll get rid of you like that!" she snapped her fingers inches from the housekeeper's nose. Satisfied that everything had been dealt with, she retired to her room.

"Oh, yeah," Miss Cummings snorted as she watched Amanda's retreating back, "I'd never leave Jenny and Jake to the likes of you!"

Several hours later, the housekeeper heard the unmistakable sound of tires crunching on gravel, and the slam of a car door. She made her way down the stairs.

Amanda was doing needlepoint in the parlor, and caught the flash of movement as the housekeeper hurried past the door.

"Miss Cummings!" Amanda shouted as she tossed her needlepoint aside, and went to see where the woman was going. She paused with her hand on the doorknob, and turned to face Amanda.

"Master Jake has arrived," she stated. Amanda brushed her aside.

"You go about your business. I will see to Jake."

She flung the door wide and ran down the steps. Jake had closed the trunk, and bent to retrieve his suitcases as Amanda ran up to him. He looked up in surprise to see a disheveled, and flushed Amanda.

Out of breath from the unaccustomed exercise, Amanda reached over and gave Jake a peck on the cheek. A stunned Jake could only stare at the wild creature before him. He shook his head wanting to shake off any lingering attraction for the woman who had been slowly destroying him.

"What's the meaning of this Amanda? What's going on?" Grimly, he searched her face for answers.

"Why, Jake, I just wanted to welcome you home. I've missed you. You have been gone longer than usual. Your mother is well, I trust?" The latter was said with a touch of irony that did not escape Jake's notice.

"Stop the melodrama, Amanda. You could care less about me or my mother!"

"Why, Jake, how crude! How can you speak such nonsense? You know that it is not tr—"

"Shut up! Just shut up!" Jake exploded. "Unless you have something earth-shattering to tell me, I would prefer that you didn't speak!"

His unyielding features warned her to tread carefully. Unaccustomed to Jake's new manner, Amanda decided to change her tactics.

"Oh, don't be so grumpy!" she spoke airily, "I was just trying to make this a special home-coming for you, because I have some wonderful news."

She paused to see if her words were having any affect on Jake. He was eyeing her suspiciously, wondering what she was up to.

"Look, Jake, let's for a moment, lay aside our differences. This is important, and I think after I tell you what's happened, you'll appreciate why I'm acting this way."

"Oh, I can tell you're acting, Amanda, but I don't know if I'll appreciate it!" Jake responded sarcastically.

Amanda feigned hurt, and with a loud sob, turned and hurried up the steps. Jake shook his head, picked up the suitcases, and grimly followed her into the house.

Miss Cummings, who immediately wrestled the suitcases away from him, met him at the door.

"Master Jake, you shouldn't be carrying something this heavy!" Jake's eyes narrowed on the housekeeper.

"Why not, Miss Cummings?" His look dared her to reveal what she knew. Instinctively, she knew that she must not say anything about his condition.

"Well, I just meant that you shouldn't have to worry yourself about such things." Dryly, Jake responded,

"It's okay, Miss Cummings, I don't think carrying my own bags will endanger me in any way."

A loud sniff turned both their attention to Amanda who was standing in the doorway of the parlor with her handkerchief dabbing away at tears.

Jake turned his back on her to remove his coat, and hat. Amanda caught the housekeeper's attention, and her softly spoken words belied the message that her eyes were sending to the housekeeper.

"Miss Cummings, that will be all for now. I need to talk to my husband in private. There's a "little matter" that you need to attend to upstairs." Her eyes spoke volumes, and the housekeeper did not fail to interpret the meaning.

She also sensed that Amanda was angry with her for talking to Jake without her being able to "see" what was being said. Hurriedly, Miss Cummings left, knowing there would be retribution for her indiscretion.

Slowly, Jake followed Amanda into the parlor, knowing the time for a confrontation had finally come. He wasn't sure how he would handle it, but he had the courage now. That much he knew. He walked over to the fireplace, and rested his arm on the mantle as he absently scraped his boot on the iron grate.

Amanda was tossing her needlepoint into the sewing basket to hurriedly make room for Jake on the couch. He turned to look at her, and she patted the seat beside her. Ignoring the offer, he continued to look at her, but made no move.

'What is different about her?' Jake wondered.

He studied the pale marble skin and the classic features of her face. Her long hair was braided and twisted around her head in the coronet she favored. Jake could count on one hand the scant number of times that he had seen her hair loose. The length of it was something he remembered well. It was long enough for her to sit on. Jake's eyes traveled over her face once more.

Yes, she's still a handsome woman, he thought. Bitterly, he turned away. *God knows, where her heart should be, there's a lump of ice the size of Texas!*

Amanda impatiently cleared her throat, causing him to turn his attention back to her. She gave him what she hoped was a smile, and invited him to sit down.

Jake was truly puzzled. *What in heaven's name was wrong with her?* he wondered.

"Jake, sit down!" At the imperious tone, he stiffened. Quickly, she added, "please."

Jake rejected the seat next to Amanda. He chose the wing-backed chair across from her. It irked her to see him being so independent. Slyly, she thought of something.

"Jake would you like something to drink?" She started to rise, but Jake lifted his arm to wave her down.

He knew what she was thinking - get him drunk and he wouldn't be able to resist whatever scheme she had cooked up! *Damn you, Amanda!* he thought, *Not this time!*

Seeing that her attempts to soften him up had failed, she decided to take the plunge.

"All right, Jake," she began. "Will you promise to just listen to me and not interrupt until I've finished?"

Seconds ticked by and tension filled the room as she waited for his answer.

"I'll listen to you, Amanda, on the same conditions. When you've finished, I have something to say to you. Is it a deal?"

Uneasily, Amanda replied, "Yes, yes, of course."

She was gambling that her news would cancel whatever it was that had Jake so worked up. Deep down she knew.

The fool! she thought, as rage boiled within her. *A trip to Dallas to see his "mama," and he mysteriously has the courage to confront me! The witch! Rose McGowan is behind this surge of independence! Well, we'll just see who comes out the winner won't we?* she seethed.

"Amanda, I'm waiting!" Jake's impatient voice brought her back to earth. She was careful to bank the rage she felt from her eyes as she looked at Jake.

Hesitantly, she began her story.

Jake knew that his mouth must have been hanging open. For the past 20 minutes, Amanda had been telling him the most incredible story.

"So you see, Jake, I just couldn't turn the poor thing away."

He held up his hand to stop her, because it was time to ask a few questions.

"Are you telling me that this homeless woman came to our house in the middle of the night, give birth to a child, and then disappeared?"

"Well, as incredible as it may sound that is the story in a nutshell." At Jake's blatant look of disbelief, Amanda spoke defensively.

"Just ask Mrs. Cummings, if you don't believe me!"

"Sarah!" Jake bellowed, as he strode into the hallway.

In a few moments, the housekeeper appeared at the top of the stairs, and she was holding a tiny bundle.

Jake strode up the stairs two at a time, his eyes never leaving the bundle in her arms. Slowly, the housekeeper peeled the blankets back so Jake could see.

The tiny perfection before him delivered a sharp blow somewhere to his mid-section. His breath seemed to catch in his throat, but not from his heart condition.

She was beautiful. Her eyes opened, and Jake could have sworn that she was looking straight at him as if to ask, "Who are you?"

Suddenly it struck him; he had never been this close to a baby before. He was in awe of the tiny creature and could only stare at her in amazement.

It took him several seconds to realize that Amanda was tugging at his sleeve, and pleading with him to let her keep the baby. He cleared his throat trying to regain his composure. Then choked out a curt reply as he pried Amanda's fingers from his sleeve,

"I'm going downstairs to give some thought to all this, and I don't wish to be disturbed for any reason - is that clear?"

Before she could voice the protest, that he could see coming, he strode down the stairs.

Walking past the liquor cabinet, he grabbed a bottle of scotch, and slammed out the back door. He strode up the hill to the tall, slender Juniper tree, and flung himself on the wooden bench beneath its leaves. The Juniper permeated the air with the aroma of cedar.

This was his special place, and it had been ever since he was a child. When things got tough or he felt confused, he always came here. The Juniper tree grew close to the edge of a cliff and high up here, away from all the problems, he felt at peace. His father and mother had known of his special place.

The bench where he was sitting had been made, and placed beneath the large tree, by his father. Whenever he and his father had a disagreement, he would tell him to go to the Juniper tree and think things out.

STRADI'S VIOLIN

His breathing was labored, and reaching inside his shirt pocket, he took out a couple of nitroglycerin pills. Slipping them under his tongue, he chased the medicine down with a swig from the bottle of scotch, and waited for them to take effect.

Just when he thought he could take charge of his life and make a change - wham! Everything was turned upside down.

A baby, who would have thought a baby would come into my life at this stage. Amanda and I have been at each other's throat for years. How can we possibly consider raising a child?

He ran his hands through the still thick hair at his temples, then he leaned back against the trunk of the tree and propped his feet on the bench. Slowly, the tension began to drain out of him as he felt his body relax. Thank goodness the pills had worked their magic, and his heartbeat had slowed to a steady rhythm.

He thought about what Amanda had told him - if she could be believed. *Well,* Jake reasoned, *it could be possible. The depression was making people crazy, and the woman was alone with two other children to consider.*

Jake thought about the baby, and with those thoughts came the fantasy born from years of longing. His mind drew him a picture of a loving wife, a child, and a real home. Visions of what it could be like danced before his tired eyes.

Suddenly, Jake stood, and walked over to the edge of the cliff. Far below, he could make out the twinkling lights of the city and he wondered if he could make those dreams a reality.

Amanda had been pacing the parlor floor for almost an hour. What was keeping Jake?

Why is he keeping me waiting? she fumed, *He has to let me keep the baby. I won't give her up! She's mine!*

The realization that she was getting too worked up made her stop and contemplate.

I've got to calm down or Jake will never agree to our keeping the child, she admonished herself.

Determinedly, Amanda stopped pacing and seated herself on the couch. She tried to still her fidgeting hands by placing them demurely in her lap. Her heart was racing and her mouth felt dry. Her eyes kept darting to the door, willing Jake to appear.

What if Jake decides to play the Good Samaritan, and look for the mother!

The agitating thoughts brought her to her feet, and she began to pace once more.

I won't let him take her away from me. I worked too hard to get her. I've planned a wonderful life for myself, and Jenny. We will rise to the top of Austin society together, and no one will stop us!

Her eyes darted to the door, and this time her heart almost missed a beat - Jake was standing there watching her. The hurricane lamp cast a shadow over his features, hiding his expression. Unable to stand the suspense, she got up. Stiffly, she walked toward him. She stopped in front of him, and looked deeply into his eyes. What she read made her knees go weak. Jake had accepted the child!

Suddenly, he gripped her by the shoulders, and drew her closer until her face was inches from his own. His eyes pierced hers.

"Now you read my lips and get the message straight. Do you understand?"

He shook her slightly for emphasis. Amanda nodded her head and waited.

"If we are going to raise this child as our own, we are going to start behaving as a family, and that means no more separate bedrooms."

He glared at Amanda as he said this, expecting her to protest. However, much to Jake's amazement, Amanda meekly nodded her agreement. Already, she had determined that Jenny's life must be perfect. She wanted nothing to interfere with the little girl's upbringing. The sacrifice of being a wife to Jake wouldn't matter. Nothing was as important as this chance. She would be able to hold her head up. Those hoity-toity women with their perfect children, and husbands would no longer be able to look down on Amanda McGowan! Oh, yes, for this, she was willing to agree to anything Jake wanted. Let him think he was in control, and making the decisions. What did it matter after all? In the end it would be her triumph.

Jake was frowning down at her, wondering why she was so docile.

Maybe, Jenny's already changing our lives, he thought. Almost instantly, he pushed the thought aside. Amanda could never change that quickly. Once again he gripped her shoulders, making sure he had her full attention.

"One other thing, Amanda. If I should ever find out that you've lied to me about this whole business...you'll pay and you'll pay dearly!"

Amanda felt a chill run down her spine. The way Jake was looking at her made her afraid for a moment. Then she shrugged the feeling away, and looked innocently up at Jake.

"Why, Jake, I would never lie about something this important! We must start trusting each other...for the child's sake," she added hurriedly as she noticed his expression. Slowly Jake released her, shaking his head.

"I don't know if this will work, but I'm willing to try."

"That's all I ask, Jake." Amanda said, smiling up at him.

Jake stared at her for a moment. How long had it been since he'd seen her smile? She touched his arm as she spoke.

"Jake, I must see to Jenny now, if you would like, you may come up to the nursery while I feed her." Secretly, she hoped that he wouldn't want to. In fact, she was hoping that Jake's interest would be obligatory, and that he would soon go his way as before. She considered Jenny to be her property and hers alone. It was unfortunate that Jake was needed to make up the nice little "family" package. Amanda couldn't understand why society put such emphasis on a "father" figure.

Thoughts of her own father ran through her mind. He was a prominent lawyer, a striking figure that she had looked up to. Her mother was a cold, distant woman who never showed emotion or affection. She and her sister had been provided for, but never had they been made to feel part of a family. Her parents viewed their offspring as an obligation or responsibility that society had forced on them.

Naively, she believed that her parents actually cared for her. It was only after she accidentally witnessed a conversation between her mother and father that she knew they would never love her.

She had been a child of eleven when the aftermath of the red measles left her totally deaf. Her father was telling her mother that she was a freak, a *deaf* freak and that they would probably have to take care of her for the rest of their lives. Her mother simply nodded her head in agreement, and stated that she couldn't bear all the pitying looks from their friends.

Amanda didn't wait to observe more of their conversation. She hid in her room and cried until there were no tears left. Then she had calmly dried her eyes and vowed that no one would ever make her cry again.

From then on she was driven to show everyone, most of all her father, that she could be successful and independent. It was a pity her parents weren't alive to see her now.

She was half way up the stairs, when she realized that Jake was striding along beside her. Her eyes widened and she looked at him inquiringly. Jake stood back holding the door to the nursery open.

"Well, what are you waiting for, let's go in, shall we?"

Amanda swept past him before he could see the spark of venom in her eyes. Hurriedly, the housekeeper arose to place the baby into Amanda's outstretched arms.

Jake quietly watched as Amanda took over Jenny's feeding. It was obvious that this tiny creature had completely captivated his wife. His eyes filled with tenderness as he looked at the child. *Well, she isn't the only one captivated,* he mused. Suddenly, his eyes hardened as he thought about the child's mother. *How, could a woman, no matter what the circumstances, give up her flesh and blood to a complete stranger, and then walk away? She must have a heart of stone.* His thoughts were dark as he heaped condemnation on the unknown woman.

Chapter 9

Rivulets of water were running down the windowpane, but the woman staring out was oblivious to the rain.

Jim stood quietly watching his mother, and wondered what she was thinking as she stared out the window. He was supposed to take care of his mom and sister, but he felt so helpless. His mother hadn't smiled since they came here. It must have something to do with his little sister who died, but he was afraid to ask. Jim stood there a little longer, hoping she would notice him.

Suddenly, she spoke, causing him to jump. "Go to bed now, and be sure to check on Lilly." Still she had not turned to look at him.

"Mother, I..." before he could continue, Ellen interrupted.

"Go! Now!" she heard Jim's heart felt sigh, as he turned away.

Peering through the open doorway, she saw her son's too thin body as he walked down the hall with shoulders hunched. She almost cried out for him to come back, but she stopped herself before she could utter the words. She fell across the bed, her soul in agony. Frantically, she clutched the covers to her and moaned aloud, "What have I done, oh, what have I done?"

Jim opened the door to Lilly's bedroom. The light from the hallway spilled into the room, and he could see that she was asleep. Slowly, he tiptoed over and pulled the covers back over the tiny sleeping form. He knew that she would probably kick them off again, but at least he felt like he was doing something. Satisfied that Lilly was okay, Jim softly closed the door.

He went into the room next to Lilly's - his room. It was kind of neat that a house could have so many rooms that you could have your own place to sleep. Nora Thacker must be a very rich lady. Jim hastily removed his clothes and jumped into bed. Then he remembered his prayers, so he got up and knelt beside the bed.

"Dear God," he prayed, "please take care of my mother. You see, Sir, she's had a very hard time since my Dad went away, and my little sister went to heaven. I'm just a kid so I don't know what to do. If you know where my Dad is, please send him home. Amen."

He climbed back into bed, and lay listening to the rain pounding on the roof. The sound soon lulled him into a deep and dreamless sleep

Downstairs in the parlor, Nora Thacker was hashing over some business with her foreman, Isaac Rheinhart. Isaac had been with her for twelve years, and together they had built up one of the finest, working ranches in this part of Texas.

Luckily for Nora, her late husband had made his money from oil wells. They had come here from Oklahoma where her husband had a partnership in several major wells. It was with this money that she was able to continue the ranch. With the depression on, feeding the cattle would have caused her to go broke otherwise.

The ranch was the only thing that had any meaning for Nora. It had been that way ever since her six-year-old daughter had died almost seventeen years ago. A tough woman, with the spirit of a pioneer, she wasn't broken by her daughter's death as her husband had been. Soon after, he had committed suicide, and she had found him hanging from the rafters in the barn.

People tended to leave Nora to herself. It wasn't right for a woman to be so self-sufficient, especially after all that had happened. But people couldn't see inside, they didn't know about the scars on her soul. The physical evidence of her sufferings could be seen too, if anyone had noticed. She looked every bit of her forty-six years and then some. Makeup was something she never wore. On her brown, weather-roughed skin, it would have been ludicrous. Her mousy, brown hair with streaks of gray was cut short and close to her head. Work shirts, and pants were all she ever wore.

STRADI'S VIOLIN

Being inside the house was like prison to Nora. She had to be outdoors. It made her feel alive. Probably, this is why she welcomed Ellen and her two children. Her housekeeper of many years had died several months ago, and Nora had been forced to stay inside more. Now, she could go back to the life she craved, and Ellen and the children could take care of the house.

At first, she had refused to even consider letting them live here, but then the more she thought about it, the more it had seemed the perfect solution. She was a little surprised that her eccentric behavior, and reputation had reached as far as Austin, but then she had also heard of Amanda McGowan and the McGowan newspaper empire. She wondered why Amanda was so interested in helping a poor, vagrant woman and her two small children. From what she had heard about the uppity Mrs. McGowan, the woman had no interest in anyone, but herself.

For the McGowan's, life settled into a comfortable pattern. Not perfect, but in a lot of ways satisfying. Amanda kept Jake at arms length, only showing interest whenever other people observed.

Jake did not trust her, and knew that Amanda's tolerance hinged on Jenny's need for a "family" atmosphere. Still he was not overly concerned, because Jenny was now the focus of his entire world. Everything he planned or thought was based on Jenny's needs for now, and in the future. Jake smiled as he remembered how his mother had reacted when she was first introduced to the tiny bit of fluff. "Why, Jake, she's the most perfect little being in the whole world," she exclaimed to him, as she had lovingly held the small bundle, and cooed to her like any dotting grandmother. Jake's demeanor turned hard, as he remembered the fight he'd had with Amanda, regarding his mother's visit. She had riled and ranted about the elder Mrs. McGowan, but Jake had been adamant.

Rose came only at her son's insistence, because she knew that her presence would not be welcome. Also, after the initial astonishment that Jake and Amanda had adopted a child, she wanted to see Jenny. Secretly, she was very pleased for Jake's sake, because she could see the positive effect the child was having on her son. Amanda had been cold and distant, and Jake had not allowed her to dominate Jenny while his mother was there. This was also a pleasing sign to Rose. At last, Jake was standing up to Amanda! She left after only a few days, but Jake had promised to bring Jenny to Dallas soon.

Amanda had seethed and fumed, but Jake had ignored her.

"Just wait!" Amanda hissed under her breath, "Someday you and that uppity mother of yours will pay for this!" Jenny was hers and no one would be allowed to come between them. Now, with that woman out of the house, she and Jenny could resume their daily walks in the park. She smiled to herself as she anticipated how people would stop and stare into the carriage to see her beautiful baby.

It was true that Austin society had been astounded at the change in Amanda McGowan. They talked among themselves about how the cold, heartless Amanda had been transformed by the "miracle" child. It was also noted that Jake no longer frequented the local bars, and visits to a certain "other" woman had ceased. Despite their somewhat jaded view of Jake and Amanda, one thing was abundantly clear. Jenny was highly esteemed by the entire populace of Austin.

Isaac pulled his hat down further to shade his eyes from the blazing noonday sun. He was busy tinkering with the Ford that Nora seldom used. Personally, he'd rather have used a couple of horses and a wagon, but that would take too long for the much-needed trip to Austin for supplies.

Isaac was a large man, his skin a dark mahogany from the long hours in the Texas sun. The startling thing about this dark man was his blue eyes and blond hair. His ancestors had come from Germany and settled down in Fredericksburg, Texas, to raise cattle.

Wanderlust had claimed Isaac when he was a very young lad, and he had roamed over a large portion of the United States. The lands that his father had parceled out to each of his sons were now gone. Isaac's share had been sold long ago to finance his travels. The Depression had claimed the others.

He was nearing forty, and this was the only place he could call home. In his travels, he had worked a lot of ranches, especially in Montana, and he knew that he was a good foreman. He had learned early to be very careful with his money, and he had quite a stash saved. Not in the bank, thank goodness, or it would all be gone. It was tucked away in an old saddlebag that he stowed underneath his bed.

Soon there would be enough to buy that parcel of land that he wanted so badly in Montana. The man he had worked for had agreed to sell it to him, and he had already made a down payment. In fact, the man had allowed him to build a shack on it. It was Isaac's secret dream, not even Nora knew.

As he turned from the car and wiped his hands on the oil rag, he noticed the kid watching him from the doorway of the house. *Kid's too skinny*, he thought.

Jim stepped back into the shadow of the doorway as the big man looked at him.

Isaac shook his head a little as he stepped onto the running board and swung his big frame into the ford. He looked back at the doorway, the kid was watching him again, his eyes big as saucers as they looked at the old car. Isaac started the engine, the boy jumped. Quickly, Isaac cut the engine then he slowly got up and motioned for him to come out.

Jim hesitated for only a second, before he was out the door and standing beside the Ford. Isaac had to smile at the look of awe on the boy's face as his eyes lovingly caressed the Ford.

"Is this your car, Mister?" Jim asked, not taking his eyes off the car.

"No, it belongs to Mrs. Thacker, but she lets me drive it for her. I have to go to Austin for supplies, and I could use some help loading and unloading the car." *Kids too skinny to be of much help*, he thought. Then he surprised himself by asking,

"Would you like to go along?"

Jim's eyes lit up, and he let out a big yell before bounding toward the house. Laughter made crease lines on Isaac's weathered face, as he watched the excited boy run into the house.

Suddenly, he was back.

"Wait right there, Mister! I need to ask my mother if it's okay." He started off again, but turned back.

"What's your name, I can't keep calling you 'Mister,' and anyway my mama will ask." Before Isaac could answer, he solemnly stuck out his hand.

"Well, I guess you need to know mine, too. It's Jim," he said. A much larger hand enveloped his.

"Name's Isaac—glad to meet you, Jim. What say, we both go find your Mom, and I introduce myself to her?" At Jim's enthusiastic nod, the big man and the small boy headed toward the house.

Ellen watched them approach, noticing how animated Jim seemed and the excitement in his laughter. It had been far too long since she had heard him laugh. Ellen wondered who the large man was - she vaguely remembered seeing him around, and supposed that he worked for Nora, too. They both stopped as they noticed Ellen watching them.

"Howdy, Ma'am. Name's Isaac Rheinhart. I'm Nora's foreman." He stuck out his large callused hand for Ellen to shake. She hesitated momentarily before placing her small hand in his, and introducing herself. "I'm Ellen Gibson." A large hand enveloped hers and she felt its strength all the way to her fingertips.

Jim couldn't contain his excitement any longer. "Mama, Isaac, I mean Mr. Rheinhart, has to go into town for some supplies, and he said I could come too - can I, Mom, please?"

He had hardly stopped to breath as he spoke, and now he felt the air trapped in his chest, in anticipation of what his mother would say. He was looking up at her with large pleading eyes.

Ellen withdrew her hand and shifted her attention from the searching eyes of Isaac Rheinhart to look down at her boy. Instantly, Ellen sensed the need in her small son. It had been a long time since he had the companionship of a man.

Isaac laid his hand on Jim's shoulder as he spoke. "Mrs. Gibson, I promise that I will take good care of the boy. No need for you to worry." Once again he had captured her attention. She drew herself up and looked him squarely in the eye.

"For your sake, Mr. Rheinhart, you'd better and I hold you to that promise!"

Jim let out a whoop of joy as he caught hold of Isaac's hand and tried to pull him in the direction of the Ford. Reluctantly, Isaac tore his gaze from Ellen's, and allowed Jim to lead him away.

Ellen watched them go. Part of her was glad that Jim had found someone, and part was sad that it wasn't his father.

The car sputtered and coughed, Isaac glanced once more at Ellen before easing out the clutch and allowing the car to spring to life. They both waved as the car lurched into action and she couldn't keep from laughing. They were quite a sight - the giant and the small boy in the beat up old Ford.

In the weeks and months that followed, Isaac tried desperately to get to know the elusive Ellen. She avoided him at every turn, and when he did manage to corner her, she had little to say. Jim, on the other hand had plenty to say, and most of the time he followed Isaac around talking incessantly. Isaac didn't mind, because he had become quite fond of the boy.

Lilly had taken up with Nora. Even Nora didn't understand the bond that had sprung up between them. She attributed it mostly to the fact that Lilly reminded her of the daughter she had lost.

Maybe, she mused to herself, *I'm just a lonely, old woman.* Frown lines made deep furrows in her brow as she thought about Ellen. *What on earth is wrong with the woman?* It was as if she carried some awful burden or secret.

The roar of the Ford's engine and the honking horn brought Nora's attention to Isaac and the boy as the car pulled up in front of the house. The car had barely stopped before the boy was out and racing toward the house waving a letter.

"Mama!" Jim was yelling at the top of his voice as he rushed past a bewildered Nora into the house letting the door slam behind him.

"Lands sake! What's got into that boy?" Nora turned towards Isaac, but he wasn't listening.

He mounted the steps, keeping his eyes on the door where Jim had disappeared. "Isaac?" Nora questioned as she pulled on his sleeve.

"Not now!" he growled to Nora as he, too, disappeared into the house. Not knowing what else to do she followed. Jim's excited voice could be heard down the hall.

"Mama," he stood breathlessly in front of her waving the letter.

"We got a letter - I'll bet it's from Dad!"

Her eyes lifted to the man standing behind her son. He answered her unspoken question. The voice that came out was gruffer than he intended.

"It came general delivery."

Lilly, hearing all the commotion had come into the room also. Jim was excitedly telling her about the letter. Ellen's hand shook as she reached for the envelope. It looked very official. The name on the outside return address was North Woods Logging Company in Flambeau, Wisconsin. Slowly she tore open the envelope aware that her audience was becoming more impatient by the second. The letter was brief.

It regretfully informed her that her husband Daniel Gibson had been killed in a logging accident. The company, on company owned land, had buried him. Also the letter informed her, Dan had authorized the company to hold on to his wages, allowing only the cost of food and lodging to be deducted. It also stated that Mr. Gibson had requested the company send the money owed him to his wife and children if anything should happen. With trembling hands, Ellen unfolded the enclosed note stating that the amount of $289.77 would be wired to her shortly. Her hands clenched, and a deep moan escaped her lips. Isaac rushed to catch her as she fell. He carried her upstairs to her bedroom and gently laid her on the bed. Nora hurried to find some smelling salts.

An alarmed Jim and Lilly stood beside their Mother's bed not understanding what had happened. Isaac picked up the letter that Ellen had been reading. Quickly his eyes scanned the contents. Silently, he folded it and laid it on the bedside table.

Ellen was coming to with the help of Nora's smelling salts. Lilly was crying, and Jim was trying to be brave, but Isaac could sense the boy was at the breaking point. Quietly, he motioned for them to follow him.

"Come, kinders, we will talk and you can tell me about your father." He coaxed them out of the room, but as he was closing the door he heard Ellen cry out.

"Dan! Oh, Dan!"

He stiffened, and his hands clenched at his sides. The agony in her voice was more than he could bear.

Chapter 10

"Shoeshine! Shoeshine!" Young Jim called out into the crisp fall air. The year was 1930, and he was twelve years old. He had finally convinced his mother to let him work as a shoeshine boy on Saturdays in Austin. Well, actually, it was Isaac who convinced her, and promised that he would personally take Jim to town, and bring him home by the end of day.

Jim had learned to snap his shoeshine rag and put a shine on shoes that you could see yourself in. He took pride in his shoe shining expertise. A nickel was charged, and he hoped for a nickel tip. Usually, he made anywhere from $1.25 to $1.50.

His favorite customer was Mr. Jake McGowan. He always praised Jim's effort and never gave him less than twenty-five cents! For that reason Jim tried to get into town early so he could get the best spot, which was close to the *Lone Star Chronicle*.

Mr. McGowan had even told him that if he kept up the hard work, in a few years he might give him a job at the newspaper. He had even allowed him to come inside once and Jim had never forgotten the exciting sounds and smells.

Right now, he had a customer and was busily shining shoes, so he didn't know that the subject of his thoughts was observing him from a block away.

Jake pulled the collar to the overcoat up to keep off the sting of the October wind. He wondered how young Jim stood the cold wind that could cut right through your clothes. The boy was wearing patched knickers and a long sleeve sweater that had seen better days. His blonde hair was blowing across his eyes as he feverishly shined the shoes. Jake didn't know why, but the kid's enthusiasm and gumption had touched something inside him. Whether they needed it or not, he always let the boy shine his shoes. Today was no exception.

"Be Still!" The commanding voice of her mother caused her to stop squirming-for the moment. Amanda was trying to arrange six-year-old Jenny's hair to look like the little girl in Harper's Gazette.

"Miss Cummings!" The shrill voice reached the ears of the housekeeper as she came up the stairs.

"That woman will drive us all insane with her obsessions!" The housekeeper fumed, it was no wonder Jake had left the house early this morning. The need to get away from Amanda's constant nagging had plagued them all. Poor Jenny, the only time she got to be a regular little girl was when Mr. Jake took her to visit her grandmother in Dallas.

For the past two years Jenny had been made to take piano lessons. When Jake suggested that perhaps she was too young, it had caused such a tirade and temper tantrum from Amanda that Jake had dropped it. Still, the housekeeper wondered if she should have told Jake what went on when he wasn't there. The little girl was forced to practice no less than three hours a day. Amanda would place her hands on the piano as Jenny practiced to ensure that she was indeed playing.

At first, Jenny had rebelled, but gradually her spirit had been broken, and Amanda had won. If she cried, she was punished, but not so that Jake would find out. Amanda was too clever for that. To control the little girl, she would withhold a favorite toy or doll or some other treat that Jenny enjoyed. Soon the child learned that if she just endured the practice, she would be free of Amanda for the rest of the day.

The only time Amanda showed interest in Jenny was during piano practice, and on occasion, in front of a friend or someone she wanted to impress with Jenny's beauty or talent.

Everyone agreed that Miss Jenny was going to be a stunning woman one day. Porcelain skin and dark curly hair were enough to

STRADI'S VIOLIN

turn heads, but it was her eyes that captivated. They were emerald green with a fire that danced in them, and beckoned all who looked into them to come closer.

Today, Amanda needed to impress someone with Jenny's talent. As soon as the housekeeper came into view, she demanded to know if the Maestro had arrived.

"No, Madam, but I'll let you know as soon as he does," Miss Cummings assured her. "Oh, someone's at the front door now." She started down the stairs when Amanda's voice stopped her.

"Wait, I will let him in. You bring Jenny downstairs in a few moments," she said, as she rushed past the housekeeper to welcome her distinguished visitor.

Franz Leoni of Austria was visiting the U.S., and had promised an old acquaintance, Professor Goltz, that he would stop in Austin. Professor Goltz was the symphony conductor, and was ecstatic at having his life-long friend and mentor visit. Franz Leoni was a renowned maestro of Viennese music culture. He composed and directed, but most of all, he played the violin with an expertise that was envied by many.

The night before, the audience at the symphony was treated to his special talent. The standing ovation he received was not unexpected. In fact, in Vienna, they would have considered it quite uncivilized had he not been given one.

Amanda never let her deafness interfere in mixing with Austin's finest, even if it meant attending the symphony. To her, being seen was far more important than being able to hear the music. Anyway, she had always insisted that she could 'feel' the music.

Professor Goltz had planned a reception afterwards, and a few of the city's elite were invited. Among them were Jake and Amanda. She wasted no time in bulldozing the professor into an introduction with the famous Maestro. Jake was not impressed, and his indifference infuriated his wife. Nevertheless, before the end of the evening, Amanda had connived to have Franz Leoni agree to visit her home.

The man who entered the house was wiry and thin with snow-white hair. His eyebrows were thick and almost met in the center. The dark, piercing eyes beneath would suddenly light up whenever he was amused or excited. As he stood listening to Amanda fawn over him, he wondered for the hundredth time what had possessed him to come here.

"Please won't you be seated, Maestro?" Amanda gestured toward the wingback chair in the parlor.

"Thank you, but please call me Franz." He was getting tired of her 'maestro'.

The woman had said it so much last night that it was beginning to grate on his nerves.

"I will call you Franz, only if you will call me Amanda," she said as she peered at him coyly through her lashes.

He cleared his throat; this was most uncomfortable. Not knowing what to say, he was content to allow Amanda to carry the conversation. As she continued her small talk, Franz gazed around the room, and there it was! Now he knew his purpose for being here. A piano! *This was going to be a sticky situation*, he reasoned. The confounded woman probably wanted to play for him, and then expect him to fall at her feet and proclaim what a talented woman she was or some other absurdity.

"And here she is!" Amanda was saying, "This is Jenny."

The Maestro came back to earth with a thud. He had been so engrossed in trying to figure out what Amanda's plans were that he hadn't noticed the little girl come in. Jenny's dark curls and green eyes were a contrast against the emerald green dress. "How do you do, sir?" she inquired as she placed her tiny hand in his. He looked into the dark, green eyes and felt his heart melt.

"Who is this little, lovely?" he asked looking up at Amanda.

"That's what I've been telling you, Franz. She's my daughter, Jenny, and she plays the piano."

Ah, he thought. *Now, I know why I'm here.*

"Jenny," her mother was saying, "go to the piano and play for Mr. Leoni."

As he watched the little girl obey, he fervently hoped that she was talented. He could tell by the mother's reactions that it would be hell on earth for the child if she failed.

Hesitantly at first, then at her mother's stern look, Jenny begin to play her favorite piece, a waltz by Chopin. It was obvious to the

STRADI'S VIOLIN

Maestro that Jenny spent many hours practicing, but her music lacked spirit. She was rehearsing a piece of music and that was the substance of it. Amanda held her breath as Jenny played, darting looks at Franz.

What is he thinking? she wondered. Nervously, she twisted the handkerchief she was holding until it resembled the knot in her stomach.

Jenny's music teacher had promised that Jenny was good, in fact, quite good. When the piece ended, the little girl came and sat down by Mr. Leoni.

The man still hadn't said anything. *What in heaven's name was wrong with him?* Amanda fumed to herself.

He patted Jenny's hand, "That was delightful, dear."

"Delightful!" Amanda sputtered, "What does delightful mean? Is she talented? I've been told with the proper music lessons, she can become quite an accomplished pianist!"

Unfortunately for Franz Leoni, Amanda was getting quite worked up. She was now standing and glaring down him with hands on her hips. While the nervous Franz was trying unsuccessfully to placate her, Jenny was busy opening the curious box that the Maestro carried with him. She had noticed it when he had placed it at his side earlier. Inside was a wooden instrument with strings, and there was a stick with a string attached. *What is this strange instrument?* the intrigued child wondered. Slowly she picked it up. Yes, she had seen one before. Her mother had taken her to a recital, and a man had made the most beautiful sounds with it. Vaguely, in the background, she could hear her mother and Mr. Leoni arguing, but her fascination with the instrument soon made her forget all about them. Carefully, she placed it under her chin. Instinctively, as though she were born to play this particular instrument, her fingers molded themselves to the strings, and she picked up the bow.

Through the heated argument that filled the parlor and beyond, there came the melodious strains of someone playing a violin. No, not just playing, but someone whose heart and soul were one with the instrument. At first, Franz thought his ears were playing tricks on him. He motioned Amanda to silence, and as he turned and looked at Jenny, his face registered disbelief then astonishment. The little girl stopped playing, and shyly laid the violin back in its case.

"Child!" Franz cried as he knelt in front of her and took hold of her hands. Jenny watched as the Maestro keep turning her hands over and looking at them as though they were something extraordinary. He knew that few people had ever been born with this kind of talent.

Amanda was puzzled, what had Jenny done to the Maestro's violin?

"Mr. Leoni, what has she done?" Before he could answer she had grabbed hold of Jenny's arm. "You naughty girl! Have you broken the Mr. Leoni's violin? Go to your room! You will be punished for this!" Amanda was shaking the child and yelling, when Franz stood up between them.

"Cease your shouting, woman! The child has not harmed the instrument. Jenny was rubbing her arm, and crying when the housekeeper came running in to see what was causing all the commotion. She quickly gathered the crying child into her arms.

"There, baby," she cooed softly, "its all right, Sarah will take care of you."

Franz Leoni was shaking his head, "I wouldn't have believed it if I hadn't heard it with my own ears." He spoke so that Amanda could 'see' what he was saying,

"Madam, it is very unfortunate that you cannot hear what my ears have just heard. Your daughter was playing the violin the way I would give my soul to play. I have had many years of lessons and experience, but I knew I was not one of the "blessed ones."

Curiously, Miss Cummings looked at the Maestro. "What do you mean, sir?"

"Simply this," he stated as he walked toward Jenny, "this child has a God given gift. A rare gift that only a few mortals are privileged to posses." He paused, and stood in front of her, looking deeply into her eyes, "Come," he said softly.

Jenny went into his outstretched arms. He carried her gently to the sofa.

"Now, child, I want you to play the violin for me." Jenny's eyes darted to Amanda for guidance.

Amanda was stunned; she never dreamed that Jenny would be able to play the violin.

Whoever heard of being able to play an instrument without lessons and

hours of practice? she thought. They were all looking at her expectantly. Slowly, she nodded her head in Jenny's direction.

The little girl wasted no time in picking up the wonderful instrument. The moment it was in her hands, her audience ceased to exist. It was just Jenny and the violin. As she played, her soul took wings and danced with the music that filled the room. Amanda sat in a corner, watching. She noticed that both Mr. Leoni and Miss Cummings had tears running down their face. Jenny was in another world. For the second time in her life, since she lost her hearing at the age of eleven Amanda felt that she had lost something dear and precious. She sucked in her breath and refused to give way to tears of self-pity that threatened to disgrace her.

"Read all about it!" The newspaper boy stood on the corner hawking newspapers to passersby. There were some noteworthy headlines, but there was one article of special interest to Jake McGowan. Jake hurried next door to the *Lone Star Chronicle,* where his own copy of today's paper would be waiting on his desk. There was the usual hub-hub, and greetings were thrown his way by employees, but Jake hardly noticed as he made his way to his private office. As soon as coat and hat were dispensed with, he sat down and began shuffling through the paper.

"Ah, there it is!"

"Child Prodigy Miss Jenny McGowan to Study Music in Vienna."

As he read the article, his mind wandered back over the events of the past several months.

He had been astounded at what had transpired the afternoon that Franz Leoni had paid his wife a visit. They all had! No one could have foreseen that Jenny had this incredible talent. It was amazing. All she had to do was hear a piece of music, and then she would pick up the violin and play the same piece to perfection.

Franz Leoni had been beside himself. Proclaiming over and over that Jenny had the "gift." He insisted that she come to Vienna and study with the masters. He had even stayed for dinner and continued talking, but Jake had refused to listen. However, the Maestro would not give up, and he had summoned Jenny to play for her father.

Once Jenny began to play the violin, her talent staggered Jake. He was as moved by it as Franz and Sarah. To deny or hide such a gift would surely be a sin. Franz Leoni had pleaded with him far into the night, and finally it was agreed that Jenny would study music in Vienna. Amanda would accompany her, and Jake would join them at a later time.

Amid protests, the Maestro had given his beloved violin to Jenny before he left. He insisted since she was the one who had truly brought the wooden instrument to life, it belonged with her. Later, when Jake had gone upstairs, he decided to look in on Jenny. She was fast asleep, the violin next to her.

In the months that followed, Jenny had become somewhat of a sensation. It seemed overnight she was performing at recitals, even at the symphony. People were delighted and amazed by the child prodigy. As Jake pondered all this, his thoughts turned to Amanda.

The woman was an enigma. Before all this happened, it had seemed that this was what Amanda wanted more than anything in the world. People saying, "There's Jenny, Amanda McGowan's daughter!" Strangely enough, she hadn't had much to say.

Jenny was in her room crying her heart out. Once again, her precious violin had been taken away from her. The little girl couldn't understand why her mother was so unkind. The violin had become a bone of contention between them. In truth, Amanda was insanely jealous of an inanimate object that had totally captivated her daughter. Lately, she used any excuse to punish Jenny by taking away her violin. She still insisted that Jenny practice the piano three hours everyday, knowing how much she hated the piano. If it had been the violin, she would not have protested at all. Indeed, she loved to play, because she could escape into a world where Amanda could not come.

Amanda swept into Jenny's room. Startled, Jenny looked up, tears still evident by the puffiness around her eyes. "You will not be allowed to stay up here and sulk! You will come down and practice the piano!" At the look on Jenny's face, she paused. "If you don't, the violin will remain put away for one week!"

The tortured look on her daughter's face, pleased Amanda. For some time now, it had seemed like Jenny had been escaping her influence, and becoming far too independent.

"Mother," Jenny sniffed, "I'm ready to play the piano." Amanda laughed, knowingly.

"I thought you might be. I knew you couldn't be without your precious violin for long!"

She smiled as a subdued Jenny preceded her from the room. Once again, Amanda was in control.

Chapter 11

Ellen giggled like a schoolgirl as she backed the Ford over the unfortunate flowerpot.

"Woman!" Isaac growled, "You'll be the death of me yet!"

He pretended to be stern, but secretly he was happy to hear her laugh. He recalled the times following the news of Dan's death, when she had gone about the house pale and quiet. Nora had said to leave her alone and it would pass, but he and Jim had been determined to coax her out of the sorrow that covered her like a shroud. Even though they were successful to a degree, they both sensed that something else weighed heavily on her mind. Isaac silently vowed that one day he would make her tell him what caused her such deep despair.

He was teaching Ellen to drive. Initially, she hadn't wanted to learn, but Isaac had insisted. Since he was going to Montana for a while, he thought that Ellen should be able to get to town if she needed to. Nora couldn't drive the Ford, and flatly refused to learn.

Isaac was going to Montana to claim the land that had been promised to him. He figured while he was there, he'd do some work on the shack. Eventually, he planned on moving to Montana. If he could get the shack fixed up, and expanded into a more home-like atmosphere, well, maybe Ellen...he shook his head to clear his thoughts. That line of thinking was off limits. It had taken a long time to gain Ellen's trust. Sometimes, he felt like his relationship with her was moving in slow motion. He forever had to "put the brakes on." Speaking of putting the brakes on!

"Stop, Ellen, use the brakes!" He yelled at her louder than he intended, but she was headed for the bullpen. She managed to stop the Ford in time, but the engine stalled out. Laughing so hard she could barely speak, she turned to Isaac.

"I guess the driving lessons are over for the day. Her blue eyes twinkled up at him, and he was mesmerized. Isaac's head dipped toward her, but suddenly she began coughing. He frowned; she had been doing a lot of that lately.

"Ellen," he got out his handkerchief, and handed it to her, "are you okay?" She nodded her head, and put the handkerchief to her mouth as another coughing spell erupted.

Isaac swung her down out of the Ford, and she headed for the house. His eyes followed her; he was worried about those coughing spells, and the fact that she weighed next to nothing.

After she was inside, the coughing spasms continued for a moment. When she took the handkerchief away from her mouth, she noticed two bright red spots of blood. Ellen stared at them for a moment before walking to the sink, and washing the stains out of the handkerchief.

The blustery wind swirled around the small group gathered at the train station. They had all managed to squeeze into the Ford to drive Isaac to the station, so he could catch the 4:00 train to Montana. It was not a very talkative group that waited for the train.

Each was absorbed with unhappy thoughts about Isaac's leaving, especially Jim. He had grown so attached to the big man that it was hard to imagine him not being around for three weeks.

Nora was giving her foreman some last minute advice about watching out for con men that might try and talk him out of his land or money. The whistle sounded as the train rounded the bend at Little Junction. They knew it would arrive in a matter of minutes. Isaac's big hand grasped Ellen's small one. He looked deep into her eyes,

"You'll be okay, won't you?" She nodded, afraid to speak, because of the lump that had suddenly formed in her throat.

"Think you'll be able to handle the Ford?" It took some effort, but she smiled up at him.

"I had the best driver for a teacher, didn't I?" Sensing he needed something more from her, she stood on tiptoe and gently kissed his cheek.

"Don't worry, Isaac, we'll all be fine. You take care of yourself, and come back soon," she added in a whisper.

He felt as though his heart would burst, and he wanted badly to grab her, and never let go. They had an interested audience, though. Nora was watching them speculatively. Lilly and Jim exchanged glances, and the approving gleam in their eyes was hard to overlook. Isaac was sure that he was happier than he'd ever been in his whole life. With all his heart, he wished he were returning from this trip instead of leaving.

The train was now in the station, and people were boarding. Promising to return soon, Isaac admonished Jim to be good, and to keep an eye on things. Running to climb aboard the train, he suddenly stopped and ran back to where they were waiting. Nora was about to ask him if he had forgotten something, but he wasn't looking at anyone but Ellen. Roughly, he pulled her into his arms, and before she could protest, he was kissing her. Then he was gone, his tall frame disappearing into the crowd. She stood rooted to the spot, waiting for the ground to stop spinning.

Finally, a bemused Ellen was led away by a smiling Nora. Jim and Lilly giggled at their mother's drunken expression. All but Ellen climbed into the car. She was watching the train as it disappeared down the track. Nora winked at the children.

"You better hope your mother comes back to earth soon, or we may not get home in one piece."

The ship bound for Europe was pulling away from the New York harbor. Streamers, balloons, and confetti lent a party-like atmosphere to the bon voyage farewell. Jenny was standing between her mother and Miss Cummings. She strained on tiptoe to catch a last glimpse of her father before the big ship left the harbor.

Jake, too, was pushing through the crowd milling around the pier, trying to keep Jenny in sight as long as possible. He felt guilty, because Jenny had pleaded for him to go with them.

Silently, he cursed the heart ailment that often times kept him from doing the things he really wanted to. His mother and Sarah Cummings were the only ones who knew about his illness, and he meant to keep it that way. Lately, he had not been feeling well, and he knew it would be pushing it to travel all the way to Europe. *Maybe*, he thought for the hundredth time, *I should not have allowed her to go to Vienna.* Actually, Jenny didn't seem to keen on going, but Amanda had pushed for all it was worth and, of course, so had Franz Leoni. What he couldn't understand was why Amanda had insisted on Sarah Cummings going with them. She was the housekeeper, not a companion. Jake shook his head; he would never understand the woman. Most of the time she complained about the housekeeper, and threatened to get rid of her. Then, out of the blue, she had declared that Miss Cummings would be going with them. Jake offered to hire a companion or nanny for Jenny, but Amanda had resisted the idea so strongly that he had dropped it. Anyway, he had no objection to Sarah's going with them, because Jenny loved her, and Jake knew the faithful housekeeper would take good care of his daughter.

Amanda smiled in her self-satisfied way. Free at last! She was going to Europe, something she had dreamed of doing for a long time. Now, she was actually going, no thanks to Jenny. She turned her disapproving stare on the pinched, wane face of her daughter. *She almost spoiled it for me!* Amanda fumed to herself. Why a young girl would not want to go to Europe and study music, she could not understand. Jenny had moped around with her sad eyes, and a long face, and Jake had come very close to calling the whole trip off. It had taken a lot of finesse on her part to convince her husband that he must not allow anything to stand in the way of this opportunity. After all she reasoned to Jake, Jenny was too young to know what was best for her, and it was their parental duty to guide her so that she would have every advantage in life. Her ploy had worked, and Jake had reluctantly given his approval.

Miss Cummings' thoughts were anything but calm as she watched the fading lights of New York Harbor, and they headed out to sea. She was under no delusions as to why she was making this trip. It wasn't for the phony reasons Amanda had given Jake, either. She was sure that she knew why Amanda had insisted that she come. The woman was afraid that if she left her alone with Jake, she might be tempted to tell him what went on in the house when he wasn't around.

I'm not a troublemaker, she insisted to herself, *but I do know this - Amanda is never at peace with herself. She constantly struggles in an emotional conflict that will no doubt end in her own self-destruction along with those closest to her.* Troubled thoughts caused her eyes to travel to the small child by her side. Six years ago, she kept quiet about the circumstances of Jenny's birth, not because she was afraid, as Amanda thought, but because she truly believed Amanda could change. For Jake's, and Jenny's sake, she had wanted to believe it. Jake's illness also had kept her from saying anything. Her eyes once more focused on the child. What would become of her if anything happened to Jake? It was unbearable to think about it. Since Jenny's fame, Amanda had become obsessive with controlling the little girl's life. Never allowing her to just be a child. Jenny seldom played with other children, and her mother saw to it that she never had any free time on her hands. No time for dreaming or playing with toys. Miss Cummings sighed, and looked down at the sad-eyed little girl, clutching the violin case. It was going to be a rough crossing.

The sun beat down relentlessly on the lone cowboy as he guided the horse down the ravine. Pausing for a moment, he removed his hat, and wiped his arm across his forehead where the perspiration was making little tracks down his face. He turned his brown face toward the sun, and saw an eagle swoop in the distance. He watched for a moment smiling, before he replaced the hat. Isaac felt a sense of peace. It was like coming home.

The long train ride had been boring, and before it had arrived in Wolf Point, Montana, he had been "chompin' at the bits." Impatient for the dream to come true, he hadn't hung around the station any longer than necessary. Someone had pointed out a stable close by where he could find a good horse that didn't cost too much. In this beautiful, rugged land, it was the only way to travel.

As the horse picked its way carefully over the rocky terrain, Isaac was thinking about asking Walter Hutchins about buying a few head of cattle to get him started. He stopped again, and drew in a long breath of fresh air. As his eyes turned toward the west, majestic purple mountains meet his gaze. They never failed to inspire in him a sense of awe. His eyes swept over the valley below. In the distance, northeastward was the Hutchins' ranch. Impatiently, he urged his horse to go faster as they headed in that direction. This was it, he would pay Walter Hutchins the balance due on the land, and it was his!

STRADI'S VIOLIN

The barking dog had caused Walter Hutchins to come outside on the veranda. He shielded his eyes from the bright afternoon sun. As the speck in the distance came closer, he could tell it was a man on a horse. Finally, the rider arrived, and as he restrained the excited dog, Isaac dismounted.

Walter still couldn't tell who the man was, until Isaac tipped the hat back, and smiled into the face of the astonished rancher.

"Why, Isaac Rheinhart, as I live and breath, what on earth are you doin' in this part of the world?"

Isaac's long arm, and strong hand reached out to meet the short, stocky one in a bone-crushing handshake.

"Come on up here on the veranda, and tell me how Texas is surviving the Depression."

Isaac followed the still talking Walter onto the veranda. As he eased into the chair, the rancher laughed knowingly.

"Looks like you're gettin' soft, boy! Don't they have horses in Texas?"

Isaac laughed good-naturedly.

"You surely don't call these mangy, flea-bitten animals horses. Why, in Texas we've got jack rabbits that are bigger and better lookin'!"

His exaggeration caused them to laugh, as they both relived the past, about how the rancher had teased the young, skinny Texan about his bragging.

Isaac was impatient to tell him why he was here, but as the conversation turned serious, he could tell that Walter needed to talk about the woes the Depression had brought in the last few years.

"You know, last winter was the worst this ranch has ever seen. Cattle were starvin'. We didn't have any grain for 'em."

He peered at Isaac from beneath his thick heavy brows, with a look of pleading.

Pleading for what? Isaac was puzzled as he looked into the face of his former boss.

The years had added deeper furrows in his weathered skin and the thick, black mustache was now snow-white. An unthinkable premonition began to take hold of Isaac. The now guarded look on Walter's face, and the eyes that seem to dart nervously without making contact with his, caused him to suddenly stand up. The rancher stood, too, with hands jammed in his pockets. The time for plain speaking had come.

"Walter, you must know why I'm here. I've been sending you what I could for years, and now I've come with the final payment on the land you promised me."

He bent to extract the money from his boot. A hand reached out to restrain him. He slowly rose as he stared into the ashen face of his former boss. With head down, not daring to look at Isaac, he told him that the land had been sold to pay for feed, and worse, yet, he couldn't give him back all the money he had paid over the years. The Depression was blamed for the misfortunes that had caused him to have to sell the land to someone else, after all, the cattle were dying and he needed the money right then, or else he would lose the ranch. He also reminded Isaac that they only had a verbal agreement. No papers had ever been signed or any formal contract written. However, he assured him, he had fully intended to honor their bargain, until the Depression came along and changed everything. Over and over he said how sorry he was, but he couldn't even offer him another parcel of land, because the ranch was in hock to the bank.

If the Depression didn't end soon, there'd be nothin' left. The only sound Isaac heard, through the flow of words tumbling out of Walter's mouth, was the death knoll of a dream.

Chapter 12

Tuberculosis! The word rang in Ellen's ear like a death sentence. She sat immobile as she relived the visit to the doctor. X-rays, along with other samples had confirmed what the physician had suspected. Her lungs had been long infected; one of the symptoms was the irritating cough that had produced the bloodstain on Isaac's handkerchief. Her weakness, and loss of weight was another sign.

The doctor was insistent that she be put in a sanitarium where she would be given every treatment available. When Ellen had protested that she didn't have the money, he explained that the sanitarium was state funded, and her expenses would be minimal. Even though the kind doctor had tried to reassure her that everything possible would be done, Ellen was afraid it wouldn't be enough.

The sounds of the city brought her back to earth. She had been sitting in the Ford for over an hour.

"Where in tarnation have you been?" A worried Nora confronted Ellen the moment she walked in, "We've been holdin' supper for you, but it's probably not fit to eat by now."

Wearily, Ellen removed her hat and coat and hung them on the peg by the door. She stood with her back to Nora not offering any comment.

Worry lines creased Nora's brow as she took in Ellen's fragile appearance. When she turned, there was a look of infinite sadness about her.

Nora's questioning look made her want to turn and run.

"What is it, child?" Nora's usually gruff voice was soft and gentle.

"Oh, Nora!" Ellen sobbed as she ran into the enfolding arms of the only person she could turn to. "Why, why!" her small fist beat against the tough ranch lady's shoulder, as she fought against the sentence that had been handed her. For the first time in her life, Nora was frightened. Something was terribly wrong.

Nora woke at the first light of dawn. As she dressed, her thoughts were anything but pleasant. Nearly four weeks had gone by since Ellen had told her about the illness. It was still hard for Nora to even think or speak the word Tuberculosis.

At first, she had raved and ranted that Ellen must have gotten it all wrong, and that she couldn't possibly have that awful disease. Nora had insisted on going back to the doctor with Ellen, determined to settle this once and for all. The doctor had calmly stated all the facts, and gone over the test results. She couldn't ignore the facts. Also, the coughing spells were coming more frequently and getting more violent.

Nora, with the doctor's help, settled Ellen into a state sanitarium near Dallas, Texas. She had been there almost two weeks. Nora sighed as she remembered how difficult it had been telling the children. Lilly had cried, and Jim put on his bravest front. He had asked questions, and even though it meant that Ellen would have to leave for a while, he had insisted that she start treatment as soon as possible.

"Damn you, Isaac!" Nora cursed her absent foreman as she jammed her hat down on her head to emphasis her frustration at the man. Why, hadn't they heard from him? He was supposed to be gone three weeks, but it had been a lot longer since they last saw him. Ellen was worried, because she was sure something bad had happened to him. Nora reckoned that it must seem to Ellen and the children like Dan leaving them all over again. *It wasn't good for Ellen to worry!* Nora fumed to herself. She needed to concentrate on getting better. Jim and Lilly, the poor kids, had stopped asking when Isaac was coming home. In fact, they had stopped mentioning him all together.

Two months later, Isaac returned to find everything in chaos. He had stayed away far longer than intended, but he'd needed some time to lick his wounds. After Walter had dropped his bombshell about the land, he'd left the ranch in shock. Then for many days, he had ridden the horse over a good portion of Montana. Camping, hunting and fishing served as a balm to soothe his mind and ease the pain of Walter's duplicity. Now, he'd come back to face something far worse than what had happened in Montana.

Nora hadn't bothered to soften the blow about Ellen's condition. Her frustration at his prolonged absence caused her to berate him for his inconsiderate behavior. He didn't try to defend his actions, or tell her why he had stayed away so long. Ellen's situation was intolerable to him. The combined feelings of guilt and grief were almost more than he could stand. She was fighting for her life in some state sanitarium, and he hadn't been there for her when she had needed him the most.

The children! He had let them down so badly. They had treated him politely, but distant. It would take some time to regain their trust and confidence.

Uppermost in his thoughts was to visit Ellen, but Nora and the doctor had vetoed the idea. Ellen was to be completely isolated, and that meant "no visitors," to speed up the effects of her treatment. So Isaac had to content himself with writing letters to her.

Knowing that worry would not help Ellen's condition, he decided to make her think that he had been delayed working on the shack. He wrote to her about how many improvements he'd made on it. A room had been added and a window put in the kitchen. He slyly insinuated, "All it needed now was a woman's touch."

He composed long letters describing the rugged land of Montana, and the purple mountains of which he was so fond. Most of all, he told her about the love he felt for her, and the life he hoped they would share someday.

Jenny's small but sturdy legs had carried her over most of the grounds of Franz Leonie's vast estate. She loved the garden most of all. The summer evenings were filled with the sweet smell of begonias and honeysuckle. Shadows cast by the fading sun made excellent hiding places. Here was Jenny's land of make-believe. Hiding in the shadows, she pretended to be invisible. No one could see her or find her if she didn't want them to.

Once her mother had come looking for her, but Jenny had remained immobile in a dark corner of the garden, and Amanda had passed by without seeing her. Jenny had been delighted. It gave her a sense of freedom that she had never before experienced. Her mother was always criticizing her for some indiscretion, but now she could escape by being "invisible."

How she missed her father and her grandmother! Grandma Rose was always hugging and kissing her, and telling her what a pretty girl she was. Her father talked to her, and made her laugh. The sadness in her eyes deepened as she thought about her mother. Amanda never held her or kissed her or said nice things to her. It seemed the harder she tried the less she pleased her mother.

Her music had suffered, too. Much to Franz Leonie's consternation, she sometimes refused to play the violin. She could feel her mother's eyes watching her, registering their displeasure, so she would refuse to play, thinking it was what Amanda wanted. One of Amanda's lectures, more of a verbal berating, would follow causing Jenny to withdraw completely. No amount of coaxing by Franz Leonie could bring the little girl out of her shell. He would sigh in defeat and settle back in his favorite chair while Amanda and his neighbor, Hans Gunthur, would engage in lively conversation. His irritation would mount as he listened to their inane banter. Since he had introduced the two, they had been inseparable and the woman totally ignored her daughter or else she berated her until the child would try to make herself as inconspicuous as possible. He wondered why Jake McGowan had married such a sallow, self-centered creature. As for Hans Gunthur, Franz had never considered him to be trust-worthy, but he had learned a long time ago, that ignoring the man only made him more persistent. Also, he had heard from other sources, that the man could be very formidable as an enemy. It was even rumored that he had taken up with a group that followed the teachings of that madman, Hitler.

Amanda's high-pitched laughter brought his attention back to them. *Lord, if she could only hear herself!* he thought as he watched her visibly preen at being the center of attention. Han's beady, little eyes would watch every gesture and move she made, as though transfixed. Seeing she had such a rapt audience, Amanda's wit and charm would flow like the wine they both consumed.

Jenny didn't enjoy the evenings, because she was forced to sit in the parlor until her bedtime. She tried to be as quiet as a mouse so they wouldn't notice her. She didn't like the man her mother was spending so much time with. Instinctively, she didn't trust him. He was always pulling on her curls and saying stupid things like, "How is our little violin player, today?"

Soon, she would sense that they had forgotten her presence and that's when she would quietly disappear. Sometimes she escaped to privacy of her room, but more often than not, to the garden.

Miss Cummings knew about Jenny's nocturnal wanderings and even knew where she went. Comforting Jenny was not easy. How do you explain to a child, Amanda's lack of maternal instincts? The woman was totally without understanding, and without a clue as to Jenny's needs.

Miss Cummings allowed a little smile to play around her lips as she patted her pocket where a telegram lay neatly folded. She started off down the path to the garden to find the "invisible" Jenny. Her smile grew broader as she thought about the telegram she had intercepted this morning.

"Jenny, child," she spoke into the dark shadows, "your father's coming to visit you!"

Chapter 13

A year! She could hardly believe it. When she first came here, she was convinced that she would never leave. The doctor was amazed at how much she had improved, and at her constant urging, had reluctantly agreed to let her go home. After all, the test results had been negative, showing the Tuberculosis to be in remission. He cautioned her that she must continue to rest to be fully recovered and to avoid a relapse. Early this morning, she had boarded the train in Dallas, and now it was chugging its way to the hill country. Ellen was ecstatic at the thought of seeing her children again. She had cried over their letters, knowing how much they missed her. Nora's letters had been as down-to-earth as the woman herself. She smiled as she thought about the "not so tough" ranch lady. Her eyes grew dreamy when her thoughts turned to Isaac. His letters had been very revealing, and they made her feel warm and tingly all the way to her toes! It had been so long since she had looked into his eyes, and the thought of seeing him again was both exciting and tantalizing. *Would the magic that had begun to weave its spell around their hearts still be there?* she wondered.

Ellen must have dozed. When she awoke, she noticed the porter had brought her an Austin newspaper to read. Idly, she turned the pages. One of the headlines caught and held her attention, causing her heart to beat faster. " Child Prodigy, Jenny McGowan, daughter of prominent publisher Jake McGowan of Austin, is in serious condition at a local hospital. After being in Europe for nearly a year, studying music, she was taken ill shortly after returning home. Currently, she remains under strict medical supervision where doctors are doing all they can to save the young child." The article swam before Ellen's eyes, and she knew that if she hadn't been sitting down, she would have fainted.

"I'm sorry, Jake, she's not responding to treatment," the doctor wasn't pulling any punches as he continued speaking, "There's nothing more we can do. It's in the hands of the Almighty."

He started to walk away, but Jake was quick for a big man. Using his large frame, he blocked the doctor's exit.

"You're telling me that my daughter may not make it, and that you and this entire hospital staff can't do anything about it!"

The doctor made a helpless gesture and tried to explain further, but Jake wasn't in the mood to listen.

"Bring in more doctors and I don't care what it cost! I want the best! Do I make myself clear?"

Jake's clenched jaw and fist made it abundantly clear. The doctor nervously tried again.

"Mr. McGowan, I don't think you understand." He had barely gotten the words out, when Jake grabbed him by the front of his coat. Thrusting his face close to the doctor's, he growled, "No, I think you are the one that doesn't understand. That's my daughter in there fighting for her life, and with my help and God's, she will have the best chance available to her! I want every effort put forth to find a doctor who has had success in treating pneumonia. I will beat this thing and God help the person who stands in my way!" Realizing that he still held the doctor by his coat front, Jake released his grip. Tiredly, he rubbed his eyes, while the doctor waited uncertainly. Then Jake spoke again as he observed the doctor slowly backing away.

"Look, isn't there any new medication for this type of infection?"

The doctor thought for a moment. "Well, I recently read about a new one on the market, but we don't have any here. It's called sulfa pyridine and it's supposed to provide a cure for some cases of pneumonia." He had barely gotten the words out when he found his coat front held once again in Jake's steel grip.

"You're telling me there is some medicine that will cure my daughter and you haven't made the effort to bring it here!" Jake's menacing face was inches from the doctor's. In vain, he tried to break free, but Jake only tightened the grip.

"Mr. McGowan," the doctor pleaded, "there's no positive proof that the medicine will have the desired effect on her."

"Just get the medicine!" Jake growled. He knew that he was behaving abominably, but he didn't care. Whatever it took for them to realize that he was serious about finding a cure for Jenny was worth whatever they might think about him.

He stood in the doorway of the room watching for some sign of life from his unconscious daughter. Slowly he walked over and pulled up a chair next to Jenny's bed. He picked up her small, lifeless hand, and bending his head he gently kissed each tiny fingertip. Drops of moisture fell on Jenny's hand. Puzzled, Jake reached up and touched his face. His cheeks were wet. Funny, it was the first time in his life that he ever remembered crying.

"Jenny," he groaned in agony, "Jenny, honey, please don't leave me."

Jenny's hand was wet from trailing it in the clear stream that flowed through a beautiful meadow with luscious green grass. She was laughing and skipping. The sun was so bright Jenny had to shield her eyes to look up. Far away she could hear music so melodious and enticing that her feet begin to carry her in the direction of the wonderful sound. Further and further she went looking for the source of the music. Suddenly, she found that she couldn't move. Something was keeping her firmly in one spot. She strained to break free and follow the sound of the divine music. Just as she thought she would make it, she heard a faint sound like a groan.

"Jenny, Jenny!"

Who was calling her? She frowned looking back along the path she had come. Somehow, the child sensed that the decision would be hers. Should she go back, or stay?

Amanda had paced back and forth so often one would think she was trying to wear a hole in the thick Persian carpet. She was impatiently waiting for Jake to return from the hospital.

This morning she had received a telegram from Franz Leonie. He was devastated at the news of Jenny's illness. A friend of his, a renowned physician, was coming to America for a symposium in Dallas, Texas. He agreed to make a side trip to see if he could help Jenny. Franz assured her that the doctor was famous for his remarkable accomplishments in the medical field.

Amanda hoped the telegram would put Jake in a better frame of mind. Heavens, the man acted like she was to blame for Jenny's illness. His mood had become black and ugly when she had refused to sit by Jenny's bed day after day. Even the doctors and nurses had the nerve to treat her with a certain amount of contempt, because of her absence.

That old hag, Miss Cummings, had dared to show her disapproval by deliberately avoiding her whenever possible. Amanda tossed her head and sniffed loudly. *Let them talk. I simply cannot sit and watch her die, and goodness knows, I have to remain realistic since Jake has gone off the deep end.* She continued to pace as she thought.

Why had everything gone so horribly wrong? It seemed Jake, Miss Cummings, and his awful mother portrayed her as the villain. Jenny was supposed to have helped her achieve her rightful place in Austin society, but the town snobs had rejected her, and embraced Jenny. Everything that she'd worked for was spoiled, because Jenny might die, and where would that leave her? Jake would throw her out without a backward glance. Amanda stopped pacing and shivered. Without her being aware of it, the room had grown quite dark and chilly as day faded into night.

Night sounds brought the croaking of frogs and the chirping of crickets through the open window in Ellen's room. She lay in the darkness half-listening to their music. Her mind was filled with the newspaper article she had read earlier today.

Publisher's daughter stable. Doctors say child is still unconscious, but otherwise there has been no further deterioration in her condition. A new drug, sulfa pyridine, is being sought as a possible remedy in the case.

Ellen sighed as she went over the article again in her mind. Suddenly, she came to a decision. The creak of her bedroom door claimed her attention as Lilly poked her head around the corner.

"Mommy, can I get into bed with you?" she shyly asked.

Ellen smiled and threw back the cover in silent invitation. Lilly giggled as she ran and jumped into bed next to her mother. They hugged, neither of them noticing that Jim had slipped into the room. He stood at the foot of the bed and pulled on the covers.

"What do you two think you're doing?" he laughed

"We're getting reacquainted." Ellen responded gaily, "and you may join us!"

"You know I'm thirteen years old now, Mother."

"Oh, yes," Ellen solemnly mocked.

"Too grown up to romp and play."

She threw a pillow at him promptly starting a free-for-all. Soon pillows and feathers were flying and the noisy threesome was having the time of their lives. Their horseplay was abruptly brought to an end by Ellen's sudden fit of coughing. She grabbed a handkerchief that was on the nightstand as more coughing spasms shook her body. Jim and Lilly were somber as they exchanged glances. Lilly quickly poured some water from the carafe on the nightstand and handed it to her mother. Her coughing subsided long enough for her to take a sip. She looked up into the worried faces of her children.

"Darlings!" she cried, "I'm okay, truly I am! See," she showed them the clean handkerchief. "Nothing here, no blood or anything. I just got too carried away laughing and playing."

She smiled at them reassuringly. They nodded, but the realization of Ellen's illness was sobering.

"We're really glad to have you home again, Mom," Jim stated, "but I think it's time for you to rest now. "Lilly," he commanded, "You better go back to your room." Obediently, she nodded her head, and gave Ellen a goodnight hug before getting up to leave. She had taken only a few steps when suddenly she came running back, and flinging her arms around her mother's neck, she sobbed, "Please don't leave us; please don't go away again!"

"There, baby, there," Ellen soothed as she rocked back and forth with Lilly.

Jim watched awkwardly not knowing what to do.

"You know I would never leave you unless I absolutely have to. Lilly," Ellen tipped her daughter's head back until they were making eye contact, "if I ever did have to go away, you and Jim have each other - plus, Nora and Isaac. So you see, I would not be leaving you alone. Okay?"

Lilly sniffed and buried her head on Ellen's neck once more.

"It's okay, Jim," Ellen said, looking up at him, "I think Lilly can sleep here tonight."

Jim hesitated a moment before bending down and kissing his mother's cheek. Softly, Ellen spoke,

"Goodnight, Son. I want you to know how very proud I am of you. You're growing into a fine young man." Jim smiled at the compliment and quietly left the room.

Soon, Lilly was settled and after her emotional outburst, seemed to draft into a deep slumber. Ellen relaxed and thought of Isaac. Their reunion had been very sweet. Both he and Nora treated her like precious china and she could hardly make a move without one of them fussing over her. She desperately wanted to confide in them, but she was afraid. Would they think of her as some terrible monster for giving up her child? What about Lilly and Jim? Wouldn't they hate her for lying to them and letting them think their little sister had died at birth? Moisture gathered in Ellen's eyes as she thought about Jenny, in the hospital, fighting for her life. The one salvation for her tortured conscience was in knowing that the McGowan's could afford the very best of care for her. "Oh, God!" Ellen prayed, "Forgive me and please, please, let my little girl live!" The decision she had made earlier was reinforced. Somehow, she would visit her in the hospital. Sadly, she knew that she would never have known anything about Jenny, had this tragic thing not happened. The article said that she played the violin, even studied in Europe! Trying to picture the little girl brought her peace, sending her into a dreamless slumber.

They assured him that Jenny was not getting any worse, but neither had she regained consciousness. It was morning, and once again, Jake had spent the night by his daughter's side.

"Nurse!" he bellowed, "I'm going to the cafe down the street and, if Jenny should wake up, I want someone to get me. Understood?"

The nurse looked at the unkempt, tired, man with pity showing in her kind eyes.

"You, bet, Mr. McGowan, I'll come get you myself."

"Thanks," he mumbled as he left the room.

The fresh air hit him, fully waking him up. He breathed deeply, thinking how good it was to be out of the hospital for a while. His constant vigil over Jenny was taking its toll, but he vowed that he would be there when she woke up. The cafe was alive with early morning raisers, but Jake chose a quiet spot over in a corner. A smiling, waitress brought him some coffee. After placing his order, he sat warming his hands on the steaming cup, and replayed in his mind the events leading up to his daughter's illness. He never should have allowed her to go to Europe without him. When, he was finally able to make the trip, what he found had enraged and appalled him. Jenny was a shadow of her former self, her unhappiness evident. Amanda had insisted that she was just homesick and that she would adjust given time. Against his better judgment, he had reluctantly agreed. However, on his second and last visit, he found the situation worse than before and Jenny's unhappiness was more pronounced. He called himself all kinds of a fool for not insisting that she return home sooner.

When he confronted Amanda, he was adamant about his decision. She had been furious with him and with Jenny. How the woman could call herself a mother was beyond him. Taking matters into his own hands, he had arranged for them to leave for America at once. His demands were met with one of Amanda's tirades, and when that didn't work, she played the martyr. Both ploys had been ignored, much to her chagrin.

Lucky for Franz Leonie, he had agreed with Jake. Secretly, he felt Amanda was a poor influence on the child, and her father could handle her much better. First-hand, he had observed the woman's inadequacies in the capacity of motherhood. Franz, had worried that Jenny's music had been affected by her unhappy state, but that had been laid to rest. The last night in his home, she had played the violin so superbly, he had almost wept with joy.

That fop, Hans Gunthur, had tried to interfere, much to his discredit. Quickly, Jake had put him in his place, informing him that he had absolutely no say in the matter. His dark, menacing look had been quelled by Jake's even darker one, and the man had practically ran from the room. Amanda's defense of her *suitor*, even after he had left with his tail tucked between his legs, had made Jake furious.

Her indifference toward Jenny had angered him further. Refusing to come to the hospital, she insisted it was because she was afraid and she couldn't bear to watch her suffer. If that was true, it was a poor excuse in Jake's book. His anger caused his face to darken and his thoughts were anything, but pleasant. Returning to his table with food, the smiling waitress was met with such a look of disapproval that she quickly served him and left.

Isaac pulled up to the curb and Ellen, hurriedly, got out of the Ford. They were in front of the hospital where she had insisted that he drop her off. The doctor at the sanitarium told her that she must have blood work done at least once a month to access the chemical reaction of the medication, and to make sure she was still immune. It was the perfect excuse to go to the hospital and no one questioned her request. In fact, Isaac had wanted to come with her, but she convinced him that it would be a waste of time. Instead, she insisted that he spend the time getting the required supplies, before they were due to head back. This pleased him, because with the extra time, he hoped to take Ellen to a nice restaurant. There was something important that he wanted to ask her. Promising to be back in an hour or so, he waved goodbye as he watched her climb the steps to the entrance of the hospital.

The strong disinfectant chemicals, designed to cover up the not so pleasant smells associated with hospitals, caused Ellen's sensitive nose to wrinkle. She waited impatiently for the switchboard operator to finish her call, before inquiring about the room number for Jenny McGowan. She was told to go to the children's ward on the third floor, and the little girl would be in a private room. Once she got there, she would have to inquire at the head nurse's desk about the room number. Smiling, and thanking the operator, politely, she hurried to the lift.

Ellen walked down the long corridor on the third floor, hoping to see a nameplate that would identify Jenny's room. Fear of too many questions, made her determined to avoid the head nurse. Her heart was pounding at the thought of seeing Jenny after all these years. Coming so early in the morning, she gambled on the hope that the McGowan's would not be there. It was risky, but a risk worth taking. Glancing up, she saw the name J. McGowan. The door stood slightly ajar. With hammering heart, she slowly pushed the door open, and quickly surveyed the room. The only one present was the slight figure lying perfectly still on a bed of white.

Dark curls framed the elfin face, and lashes the color of soot contrasted sharply against the white porcelain skin. Not daring to breath, Ellen stood beside the bed looking at her daughter. Fighting back tears and not taking her eyes off the slight figure, she sat down in the chair beside the bed. Desperately, she wanted to grab the little girl and run. Instead, she reached out and took the small hand in her own.

"Oh, Jenny," she whispered, "Where do I begin? I guess I should introduce myself. My name is Ellen, and I'm your mother." She bowed her head, and let the tears come.

Jenny had been searching for the source of the music, but the sound had grown fainter until she could hardly hear it. She was going back the way she had come, because someone had been calling her. The voice had seemed so far away, and just now she heard it again. Yet, she was puzzled, because the voice was one she didn't recognize. Her eyes searched the path ahead, and vaguely, as through a fog, she saw someone.

"Jenny," Ellen was saying, "you must live. There are people here who love you, and would be heart-broken if you left." Again the voice pleaded. "Please open your eyes! You mustn't go away. Please, Jenny!"

The impassioned voice would not let her rest, but kept pleading with her over and over.

Slowly, through the fog she came, and dimly she saw a woman. No, not a woman, it was an angel with golden hair. The angel was crying. Tentatively, the small hand moved, then lifted to comfort and touch the bowed head of the weeping angel.

Ellen froze as she felt someone touching her hair. *Who has come into the room?* she asked herself as panic rose up within her. Slowly, she raised her head, and at the sudden movement, the small hand dropped and lay still. Ellen eyes grew wide with astonishment as she realized that it was Jenny who had touched her. Excitement and joy filled her voice as she spoke to the little girl, again.

"Jenny, open your eyes, honey."

There was no response, but Ellen was not daunted. Earnestly, she spoke to her.

"I know you touched me. You're coming back. Jenny, I won't allow you to leave, again! Do you hear me?"

Voices could be heard in the hall, and Ellen knew she must go. The pain was almost physical, but the time had come to say goodbye. She knew beyond doubt that her daughter would live.

"Jenny," she whispered once more, "I love you! You're going to have a wonderful life. I'm proud that I was the one to give you life, but now I must let you go. Goodbye, darling, girl!"

Holding her fist tight against her mouth to hold back the sobs, Ellen rose and without looking back, she quickly left the room.

Head bowed as she fought to control her emotions, Ellen ran into a solid wall, or what felt like a wall. Tentatively, she raised her head and found herself staring into the eyes of Jake McGowan.

"What the devil?" he growled as his hands reached out to steady the slight figure that had run head first into his broad chest.

She was looking up at him as though *he were the devil* and had suddenly sprouted horns. His eyes narrowed as he realized she had come from his daughter's room. Ellen struggled in vain against the strong arms that held her.

"Nurse!" Jake yelled over his shoulder, "See if Jenny is okay!" The head nurse hurried around the struggling man and woman to see if any harm had come to her small charge. Heads would roll, starting with hers, if anything was wrong.

Panic set in as Ellen pitted her inferior strength against the giant that held her. Using her last ounce of strength and the heel of her shoe, she came down full force on Jake's toe. Surprise and pain made him let go of her long enough for her to take off down the corridor. His initial response was to go after her, but the excitement in the head nurse's voice as she called to him, made him forget all about pursuing the intruder. Rushing into Jenny's room, Jake was met by a sight that made his heart leap. She was awake and asking for him!

"Jenny!" he cried, as he ran to the bed and threw his arms around the small body,

"Honey, you're really okay! You've come back!" Jake knew he was babbling like a fool, but his precious daughter's life had just been handed back to him and he couldn't stop himself.

"Baby, Daddy, really missed you! Don't ever do that to me again, okay?"

The unfamiliar moisture was once again in Jake's eyes. Jenny's eyes were beginning to focus as her father's familiar face swam into view.

"Daddy," she asked weakly, "where is the angel with the golden hair?"

Humming a tune, Ellen busied herself fixing the evening meal. She was radiant and her new found peace added to the lovely picture she presented. In her heart, she knew it was because of her visit to Jenny in the hospital. That day by the child's bed, she had made her peace. Doubt over her decision no longer plagued her. Remembering the struggle with man in the corridor, and his fear that Jenny had been harmed, convinced her that her daughter was very much loved. Jenny was where she belonged, and she had a talent that only the McGowan money could nurture and develop. This was Jenny's chance to be somebody, and Ellen would not stand in her way. She had vowed to God that if He would allow her little girl to live, she would not interfere in her life or seek vengeance, because it would only bring sorrow. Ellen thought it would be a mortal sin to put another human being through what she had suffered. Amanda had deceived and robbed her, but now Jenny's happiness and needs must come first. Releasing Jenny a second time was the hardest thing that she had ever done, but it was the right thing, and it brought her peace. She was happy.

Isaac, the other reason for Ellen's newfound happiness, was thinking about his bride-to-be. It was good to see her well and happy. Gone was the sadness that had been so often in her eyes, along with the feeling that she was hiding something from him. Every since the day he had picked her up from the hospital, and she had dashed madly down the steps into the car, he had sensed the change in her. Alarm bells had set off a warning, when she had jumped into the car, out of breath and seemingly agitated about something. As he drove away from the hospital fear, that the tuberculosis was back, had been uppermost in his mind. When he questioned her, she assured him that everything was fine. Seeing the doubt in his face, she had turned playful and teased him until her earlier behavior was forgotten.

They had gone to a particularly nice restaurant and Ellen had looked so beautiful sitting across from him, with the candlelight playing over her lovely features, that all he could do was stare. There was so much that he wanted to tell her, but he felt tongue-tied and slow witted. What did he have to offer her anyway, he thought morosely. No land, no home or money to speak of.

STRADI'S VIOLIN

Sensing he needed some help with what ever was troubling him, she smiled at him and placed her small hand over his larger one. "You said that you had something important to ask me," she prompted. Looking into her eyes caused his carefully rehearsed speech to flee, and his only thoughts were of her.

"Darling," he cleared his throat and started again, "Ellen, I love you very much. Would you do me the honor of becoming my wife?" It came out in a rush and his voice was filled with self-recrimination as he tried to make amends. "Darling, I'm sorry! I didn't intend to blurt it out like that. I wanted it to be romantic, you know, the way a woman likes these moments to be."

"Isaac," she gently interrupted, "It's okay. You're a good man and the children adore you. You're strong and kind, and I feel very fortunate…"

"But," he interrupted hoarsely, the hurt evident in his voice, "You don't want to marry me, because you don't have any deep feelings for me." The surprise, or was it pity in her voice at his pronouncement, made him feel even worse.

"Isaac! Isaac!" Ellen's voice was pleading, but he couldn't bring himself to look at her. Gripping his hands, she spoke in her most commanding voice, "Isaac Rheinhart, you look at me, right now!"

Slowly, his eyes lifted to meet hers. The love he saw shinning in them, overwhelmed, and filled him with joy. He couldn't believe it, even when she spoke the words.

"I love you more than I ever thought possible, and becoming your wife would be a dream come true."

He was sure there were tears in his eyes as he smiled at her.

Nora, too, was thinking about the changes in Ellen. Mostly, she was thinking about the impending marriage to her foreman. They wanted to be married in June, at the ranch, with only herself and the children as witnesses to the simple ceremony. She smiled as she remembered the children's delight at the prospect of Isaac being a member of their family. It was easy to see by their respect and affection for each other, that it would not be a difficult adjustment. She recalled how a few nights ago, Isaac had confessed to Ellen and to her about not having any land in Montana. The guilt was eating him up and he felt he had to risk everything in order to start fresh with Ellen. After hearing his story, they had both derided him for not telling them sooner. They were sorry his dreams had been shattered, but secretly, each was not sorry that it hadn't worked out. Selfishly, Nora realized she didn't want to lose her family, because that's how she thought of them. Ellen was perfectly content living on the ranch and she didn't want to leave Nora.

The wedding present she had picked out for them would take a lot of effort on her part, in getting all the parties involved, to accept. Talking it over with her lawyer, all the arrangements had been finalized, and the papers were ready for signing. Making her bull-headed foreman accept the gift would be the major problem. She was giving each of them, including the children, a parcel of land from the ranch. They would all be partners and when she passed on, her share, along with the house, would go to Ellen and Isaac. It was all perfectly logical, as she had no family of her own, until Isaac, Ellen and the children had come into her empty life. Isaac would have to be reasonable. What else would she do with the ranch? No living relations meant that it would be auctioned off, and that was unthinkable.

Chapter 14

It was Thursday, May 6, 1937. Rose and Jake laughed as they watched Jenny anxiously search the sky with her father's binoculars.

It had been a couple of years since her brush with death from the dreaded pneumonia and she was once again the picture of health. The three of them had traveled from Dallas to New York City where they had spent the last few days shopping and attending the theater at night.

The maestro, Franz Leonie, was paying them a visit. His visits were too few and far between. He desperately wanted to see his little protégé and hear her play the violin. Being unconventional at times, he had decided that his mode of transportation to America would be via Germany's luxury airship, the Hindenburg.

Jenny's eyes had grown wide with wonder as Jake had described to her the magic ship that floated through the air. Her interest in it had been so great that he decided to take her to see the giant airship for herself, and to surprise Franz by being present at his arrival.

Amanda had not been in favor of the trip, stating that it was highly unnecessary and that she had better things to do. Jake and Jenny were not put off by her lack of enthusiasm, each, secretly, thinking they would have a better time without her anyway. Much to their delight, Rose had agreed to make the trip with them.

This afternoon they had traveled to the airfield at Lakehurst, New Jersey, to met the zeppelin. It was 5 P.M., and because of rain, it had been delayed. Almost an hour and a half later, the rain had stopped and the last rays of the setting sun occasionally broke through the thin cloud covering.

Quite a crowd had gathered in anticipation of the landing. Jake had his camera ready, and he spotted several other reporters setting up their cameras. He figured since he was here, it wouldn't hurt to take a few photos for the *Lone Star Chronicle*.

Dancing with excitement, her cheeks rosy, and eyes shining, she ran back to where her father and grandmother were standing. Jake lifted her on top of the car as the huge airship came into view. The whir of the giant engines could be heard above the din of the crowd. Everyone's face was turned upward in awe as the Hindenburg hovered barely two hundred feet above ground.

The reporters were scribbling in their notebooks while some were taking pictures, their flashbulbs popping in the fading light. The air was electric with excitement and Jenny stood spellbound then timidly began to wave as she noticed others around her were waving. She wondered if the Maestro could see her.

Uneasiness came over the crowd, as they noticed the great airship shutter as if something had stuck it severely, causing it inward distress. The crowd grew strangely quiet as they waited.

Franz Leonie had been looking out the observation deck windows, watching the mooring party as they scattered about the field doing their job. The engines were silent and the ship had stopped moving. Then he had heard a deep thumping noise that came from somewhere within, and the ship had shuttered, almost throwing him to the deck. Trying to figure out what had happened, he regained his footing and looked out the window once more.

The people on the ground had terror written on their faces, and many begin to scream. The mooring party dropped the ropes and began to run from the ship. All at once the sky seemed to light up, and the ship lurched viciously, throwing Franz backward. His head struck something hard, knocking him unconscious.

A frenzy of panic had broken out as people ran screaming from the horror in the sky. Jake had grabbed Jenny and his mother, and together they ran from the burning debris falling all around them.

After making sure they were well out of harm's way, Jake left a crying Jenny with her grandmother. Before either of them could protest, he was on his way back to the scene of the disaster.

The fire spread rapidly, and within half a minute the great airship was on the ground. Jake mingled with those trying to rescue people who had somehow managed to escape. Desperately, he searched for Franz Leonie, but the maestro could not be found.

Soot covered his face, and the smoke from the inferno filled his lungs. Coughing, he staggered to where he had left his camera, and sinking to his knees, he crawled to a nearby building. Feebly, Jake searched his coat pocket for his bottle of nitroglycerin. After slipping the pill under his tongue, he leaned his back against the wall and closed his eyes. In a few moments, he was breathing easier and the pain in his chest had all but subsided.

He sat hypnotized by the sight of the airship and as the flames lit up his reflection, his face looked like a statue carved out of bronze. The horror he had witnessed was replayed over and over in his mind. He watched as bodies were brought into the nearby hanger and laid on makeshift beds, knowing that soon he would have to see if the Maestro was among them.

Wearily, he buried his head in his arms. Someone was tapping him on the shoulder. Alarmed, he looked up into the fire-singed face of a man he barely recognized, Franz Leonie.

A few days later, the indomitable Franz was sitting up in his bed at the hospital, regaling visitors with the incredible events that had occurred on the Hindenburg. After falling backwards and striking his head on something, he came to in what had to be hell, with smoke and flames everywhere. He crawled along the floor, his hands and feet getting scorched by the heat. Pausing to look behind him, his heart almost stopped at the sight that met his eyes. A giant fireball was coming toward him! Quickly, he launched himself forward, and that's when his eyes fell on the closed hatch. Kicking it with all the strength he possessed, the hatch had opened, and he had dropped through, thinking it was surely the end. Fortunately, the airship hadn't been too far from the ground and he landed in the soft sand. Struggling to his feet, he got out of the way just as the Hindenburg plunged to earth. Shock set in and everything around him became a blur, causing him to wander aimlessly, until coming across Jake.

Everyone agreed that Franz Leonie was indeed a fortunate man. As it turned out there were many more just like him, only thirteen had not survived the disaster. Jake dispatched the pictures along with Franz's story to the *Lone Star Chronicle*.

Jenny sat wide-eyed through Franz Leonie's incredible story. She was very thankful that her beloved maestro had come to no harm. There was one thing troubling her, however. One thing he had not mentioned. Walking to his bedside, she sat down on the edge of the bed.

"Maestro," she questioned solemnly, "did you see her?"

Franz' heavy brows came together, as he searched her serious little face.

"Who, child?"

"The angel with the golden hair!"

Her eyes met his and he could read the sincerity in her expression. He was puzzled and his confusion clouded his features, as he looked to Jake for guidance.

"Jenny," her father said, "Mr. Leonie needs to rest now. Go with your grandmother, and I'll be along in a moment."

Obediently, she got up, but before leaving, she placed a goodbye kiss on Franz's check. Rose, too, stepped forward to say "goodbye."

"Mr. Leonie, I'm very happy to met you at last, but I'm sorry it had to be under such dire circumstances."

Eyes sparkling, he looked into her lovely face,

"Dear, lady, the pleasure is all mine, and I apologize that our first meeting couldn't have been more pleasant, but in the future, I hope to remedy that."

He took her hand as he spoke, and brushed his lips across the top of her knuckles. Quickly, she withdrew her hand and motioned for her granddaughter.

"Grandmother," Jenny's young voice carried clearly through the room as they were leaving, "why are you blushing?"

"Jake," Franz asked as soon as the door closed, "who is the 'golden haired angel' that Jenny spoke of?"

In response, Jake shook his head, "I don't know for sure, but when Jenny came out of the coma she talked about an angel. She insists that the angel made her come back, but that she was very sad about something."

"Well," Franz interrupted, "isn't that normal for a close to death experience?"

"Then why didn't you see the angel?" Jake shot back.

Franz smiled, "You've got me there. Maybe, only the truly innocent, like Jenny, can actually see and hear an angel." He shrugged his shoulders, "Who knows?"

"Well, there could be another explanation," Jake paced as he spoke.

Franz waved his hand in the air, "Like what?" He stopped pacing and stood at the foot of the Maestro's bed. "Like a real flesh and blood golden-haired woman!" He told Franz about the mysterious woman that he had struggled with right before Jenny's miraculous recovery.

Being the ever-practical Franz, he assured his friend that the poor woman had probably stumbled into the room by mistake, and that more than likely she had nothing to do with his daughter's recovery. It did seem to be the logical explanation, but it still bothered him.

Squaring his shoulders, he decided it was time to put the incident completely out of his mind. Now, about that little display of affection that Franz had shown his mother. Jake's eyes narrowed as they took in the amused expression on Franz's face when he brought up the subject.

"What was that all about?" he growled.

The sparkle was still in his eyes as he turned an innocent face to Jake, "Why, *Son*, what do you mean?" At Jake's outraged expression, he could contain himself no longer. He doubled over with laughter, causing Jake to forget his annoyance and join in.

Chapter 15

The wedding was lovely and very romantic to fourteen-year-old Jenny. Her grandmother was radiant, as she stood beside her new husband, greeting their guests. A beaming Franz was never happier as he watched his charming bride.

It had taken him over a year to get her to walk down the isle with him. Their feelings for each other had come as a surprise, neither of them expecting romance, in the winter of their years.

At first, Rose had been reluctant, worried about Jake's disapproval. Surprisingly, he had been very supportive of their relationship, even when it had turned serious. It was Amanda who haughtily proclaimed the whole thing a disaster. Franz had difficulty being civil towards the woman after she had shown her contempt for his lovely Rose. He avoided her whenever possible, much to her displeasure. However, he decided this might not be the wisest course of action. Amanda could be very vindictive whenever provoked and Jake or Jenny might be made to suffer the consequences. Compromise would be a small price to pay for everyone's peace of mind.

He felt a tug on his hand, and turned to a smiling, Jenny, who declared she would now call him Grandfather Franz.

"Dear child," he laughed, "nothing would delight me more! We are truly family now."

A short time later everyone gathered to say 'goodbye' to Franz and Rose as the couple made ready for their honeymoon trip to South

STRADI'S VIOLIN

America. Franz felt it his duty to show his wife as much of the world as possible, before the tyrant, Hitler, gobbled it up! For a moment, his countenance changed to one of great sorrow as he thought about his beloved Vienna. Hitler had annexed Austria into the German Empire. His home and lands had been confiscated for the *glory* of the Third Reich. Luckily, for him, it was during his courtship of Rose and he had stayed mostly in the United States, even removing most of his money and holdings from the Austrian banks and transferring them to America. The shock of Hitler's invasion had been a devastating blow. Shaking his head to clear his thoughts, he returned to the present.

Jenny hated the thought of not seeing either of them for a long time. She clung to her grandmother's hand as long as possible.

"You will be back in December, won't you? You know, for my winter concert?"

Seeing the uncertainty and sadness in her eyes, they both put their arms around her as Franz spoke.

"We wouldn't miss it for the world. My old friend, Professor Goltz, tells me that you are more than ready and it is his extreme pleasure to have you in his symphony!"

"Thank you, Mr. Leo—I mean, Grandfather Franz," she corrected. They both smiled and Rose hugged her close one last time.

"Jenny, I'll be back before you miss me!" she whispered.

Hoping for a breeze, she sat at the window in her room. Today would be another scorcher for sure. The Texas sun was burning up everything in sight.

She wondered how her grandmother and Grandfather Franz were doing and if it were this hot in South America. Her thoughts were interrupted by her mother's voice in the hallway as she spoke to Sarah. Fervently, she hoped her mother was not planning on taking her shopping. It seemed, she always had to be doing something or going somewhere. Why didn't she ever just talk to her? There were many things that Jenny wanted to talk about and questions that she needed to ask, but Amanda was never in the mood to talk or listen. Sighing, she slid off the window seat and crept into the hall. She hoped to find her father before her mother found her. She jumped as the bedroom door opened, then smiled in relief, when she saw it was her father.

"Well, what have we here? Are we hiding from someone?" he winked at her in a conspiring way. Jenny placed her hands behind her back, crossing her fingers.

"Dad, I've been giving some thought to the newspaper, and I think it is time I learned more about what you do," she stated in her most grown-up voice. "I believe I should come with you to the office today. What do you think?"

Jake's mouth twitched at the corners, as he pretended to give her request grave consideration. Finally, he spoke,

"Yes, I think that would be an excellent idea. Would you like to accompany me today?"

Uncrossing her fingers and flinging her arms around his neck, she smothered him in kisses as she squealed in delight.

"I'll take that as a definite 'yes'!" Jake laughed.

They left the house together, over Amanda's vehement protest. She insisted that a newspaper was not the place for a young lady to hang out. Anyway, why would she want to be around all that dirty ink and newspapers, when she could be out buying pretty clothes? Jenny was glad that her father was not moved by her mother's disapproval. It no longer concerned her, either. She had learned, by observation, that it wasn't just her that Amanda disapproved of - it was everything and everyone!

Muscles bulging as he lifted the last bundle of newspaper onto the moving conveyer belt, Jim Gibson, stopped to catch his breath. It was evident by the bronze skin, and hair bleached golden by the sun, that he spent a good deal of time outdoors. A young man of twenty, he possessed the handsome looks that could only be enhanced by maturity. The fact that he seemed unaware or simply not interested, in his good looks, made him even more appealing.

Jake McGowan had made good on the promise of long ago and hired him to work in his newspaper empire during the summer months. It didn't matter that he was starting at the bottom and the smell of ink and the black stains on his clothes didn't bother him either. In school, he discovered writing was his passion and he was good at it. One day, he'd be a reporter for the *Lone Star Chronicle*. He longed to work here full time, but Isaac needed his help on the ranch.

Two hours later, a bored Jenny sat watching her father while he talked on the phone to a business associate.

Isn't there anything interesting around here? she wondered.

Jake had finished his conversation and was racking his brain, hoping for an inspiration to cheer up his daughter. It was a mistake bringing her here without some planning. Anyway, he had done it simply because he knew that she wanted to get away from Amanda's constant manipulation.

Jake glanced at the door just as the Gibson boy walked by.

"Jim!" he yelled, startling Jenny, as he came around the desk.

"Yes, Sir?" Jim's handsome face appeared in the doorway.

"Welcome aboard, Son!" Jake was saying as they shook hands, "We're glad to have you here."

"Thank you, sir." Jim replied, wondering why his boss seemed so relieved. He noticed a young girl sitting in the corner, staring at him with her mouth hanging open. From far away, she heard her father's voice.

"Jenny, this is Jim, and I think he may be able to find something for you to do."

Which of the two were more stunned, it would be hard to say. Jim was silent for a moment, but his boss was looking at him expectantly.

"Er, yes, of course, Mr. McGowan."

He looked back at the girl. She was still staring at him and it reminded him of the way a dog stares at a bone. He shifted uncomfortably.

"Uh, Jenny, would you like to come with me?"

A tiny squeak, that sounded like a "yes" was all she could manage.

"Good, good!" Jake beamed at them as they left the office.

Red-faced with embarrassment, Jim hurried past the amused reporters with Jenny trailing behind.

Over the course of weeks, it became a common sight to see the boss's young daughter trailing behind the tall, handsome, young man that worked in the mailroom.

Jim had gotten over his initial embarrassment and even looked forward to his times with Jenny. On the days she didn't come, he found himself missing her lively chatter and millions of questions. Strangely enough, the friendship that had sprung up between them had not been a conscious effort on their part. In fact, Jim had done everything he could to discourage it, but Jenny was just as determined not to be ignored.

Mr. McGowan had been adamant on insisting that his daughter should learn the business from the ground up. Jim taught her how to read the scale that weighed the bundles and how to record it in the logbook. He, also, showed her how to bundle the papers, which caused the blacking from the ink to stain her clothes and hands. This infuriated Amanda, which led to more than one altercation with Jake. Finally, for the sake of peace, Jenny was allowed at the newspaper only two days a week.

The evenings, she spent at the symphony practicing for the Winter Concert. Jim was amazed and impressed when he learned that his young charge had become a member of the symphony at only eleven years of age!

Today, she was sitting on the dock in back of the *Lone Star Chronicle* eating an apple and watching Jim load bundles of newspaper onto a truck. She savored the sight of him, because their time together was fast coming to an end. School would be starting next week. How she hated the thought of not seeing him for a very long time. He was her best friend, her soul mate, and now they would have to be parted for, what would seem to her, an eternity. To say that she loved him would not have been far from the truth. All her adolescent longings and dreams were wrapped up in a fantasy and centered on Jim. If her father had known, he would have immediately ended the liaison and her mother would have moved heaven and earth to part them. This, she was sure would be the case and for that reason, she was very careful to avoid mentioning his name in front of her parents.

A young, but wise Jenny recalled her mother's frown of disapproval when she had mentioned his name frequently, after their first meeting. Sensing that the ax might be about to fall, she quickly adopted an air of superiority, dismissing his importance, and disclaiming him as a person of low class. This brought a frown from her father and a satisfied smile from her mother.

As Jim loaded the bundles of newspaper, his thoughts were on the young girl watching him. She had been awfully quiet today and kind of sad. He rubbed his head, thinking how uncanny it was, that they could almost read each other's thoughts. He was certain that she was feeling the same as he about their impending parting of the ways. They had grown so close, almost like best buddies, which was kind of strange, since she was just a kid. She knew everything there was to know about him and he about her. More than once, he had felt a sense of outrage at her woes, concerning her insensitive mother. It was very fortunate that she had a great dad like Jake McGowan.

Sometimes, he felt guilty talking about his family, especially about how wonderful and supportive they were. She liked for him to tell her stories about Lilly, sighing wistfully, about not having any siblings of her own. His stories regarding his mom, also, seemed to interest her. When he described Ellen, mentioning her golden hair, Jenny told him about seeing a golden haired angel when she was in the hospital.

The story he liked best was the one about the Hindenburg and the incredible escape of her Grandfather Franz from a fiery death. Smiling, he remembered how often he had insisted that she repeat the story.

Finishing his task of loading the newspapers, he observed Jenny as she took the last bite of her apple and tossed it away. Her long, dark, hair was tied back with a blue ribbon. Noticing how small she was, her frailty inspired in him a strong urge to protect. The thought of not seeing her again bothered him. It was unsettling to feel this close to someone he had only known for a short time.

Smiling and dark eyes dancing, she called out to him.

"Come here, and close your eyes. I have something for you."

Smiling in return, he obeyed, wondering what she was up to.

"Hold out your hands." she commanded.

Making sure his eyes were still closed, she reached into her pocket and pulled out an envelope. He felt something being laid in his hands, and opening his eyes, he looked down at the envelope.

"Well, open it!" she chided. There were five symphony tickets to the Winter Concert.

"Wow!" He looked at her, grinning from ear to ear.

"My family's gonna flip! We've never been to the symphony. Thanks!"

She was pleased that he liked her gift.

"You'll enjoy the concert and you'll get to hear me play my violin," she added, shyly.

Placing his hand on her shoulder, he spoke earnestly.

"It'll be great and I'm really looking forward to it, Jenny. I just wish the concert was next week instead of four months away!"

Her eyes sparkled up at him, happy that he would be anxious to see her again.

"Look, I'm sorry. I never expected this and I don't have a gift for you."

"It's okay," she quickly assured him, "and anyway, this is really to say 'thank you' for putting up with me all summer."

Looking at her, he was thinking how fast the summer had flown by and he had not been burdened at all by her presence.

"Jenny McGowan," he stuck his hand out for her to shake. "I'm glad we met!"

"Me, too!" she echoed and laughing together, they walked back into the building.

Chapter 16

Glasses full of eggnog clinked together as they toasted the Christmas season and each other.

The doors to the McGowan house had been flung open wide to invite friends, neighbors, and business associates to a party honoring their daughter's violin solo in the Winter Concert. Jenny had caused quite a sensation by being the youngest member ever to perform solo at a symphony gala. The annual Winter Concert was to be held next week and it was obvious by the enthusiasm at the party that everyone was looking forward to the event.

For Jenny, the most important people were there, her beloved grandmother and grandfather Franz. Keeping their word about returning, they had managed to surprise everyone by arriving early. It was like receiving an early Christmas gift. Missing them as she had, the only thing that kept her spirits up, was the wonderful summer she had shared with Jim. Privately, she told her grandmother about him, face shinning, as she related story after story. Rose smiled indulgently, acknowledging to herself, that her grown-up granddaughter was having her first real crush.

Amanda's smile turned sour as she observed Jenny and Rose with their heads together. Since they were not facing her, she couldn't tell what they were saying. Green with jealousy, she headed in their direction to break up the private discussion.

Jake had also been observing and seeing the determined look on his wife's face, he purposely intercepted her. A less than pleased glare at having been thwarted in her purpose was reward enough for him.

"My dear, you're looking exceptional tonight, even with that little green monster sitting on your shoulder!"

At her outraged expression, his knowing smirk did nothing to soften her disposition. She stomped off in the opposite direction and catching Franz's amused glance, he winked.

Strolling up to him, Franz spoke in the tone of a fellow conspirator, "Watch it, Son, I think you may have a tiger by the tail!"

Jake slapped him on the back, good-naturedly, as they both enjoyed a laugh at Amanda's expense. Their talk turned serious as they discussed world events. Mostly, they talked about America's policy of isolationism.

"I tell you, Jake," Franz remonstrated, his voice strong with his convictions, "the United States must get involved in the war in Europe!"

Jake tried to assure him that he was in complete agreement, but Franz was just warming up to his favorite subject. Some of the other men had joined them to listen to the impassioned Austrian as he spoke.

"When I lost my home to Hitler, I thought it was the end of the world, but, dear friends, I fear the worse is yet to come." Many were nodding their head in agreement, as he continued.

"A few months ago, France fell and, now, England must face Nazi tyranny alone. Surely, this will force your President Roosevelt to act."

"Sir," one of Jake's associates at the *Lone Star Chronicle* spoke up. "America has begun supplying England with billions of dollars worth of U.S. arms and supplies on credit. England will be able to continue the battle even if she runs out of money."

"Ah," Franz smiled, "then, perhaps, the United States has decided that isolationism is not the way."

This brought about a lively discussion on the role the U.S. should play. Most were against sending U.S. troops, insisting that it was not our war. Then Franz asked a question that caused serious doubts to some about remaining isolated.

"Do you truly believe that the tyrant, Hitler, will stop with the conquest of Europe?" The silence that followed was eloquent.

"I would, also, remind you that Imperial Japan has recently joined Germany and Italy to form the Axis Alliance. This unholy alliance will not stop with Europe and Asia, dear friends."

Heated debates broke out in the group of men after he had finished speaking. Sensing that he had probably said too much, he excused himself and left the room. More than anything, he needed to be alone for a few moments. Talk of the war always stirred him and reminded him of his loss. Frustration at being so helpless in the face of tyranny brought tears to his eyes. *If only I were a young man, I would go and fight the Germans!* he silently vowed.

At Jake's insistence, a worried Rose went in search of her husband. She found him in the study, sitting with bowed head, deep in thought. Her heart was stirred with pity as she watched him, knowing that he was thinking of Vienna. Going to him, she tenderly placed her hand on his shoulder. He reached up and patted her hand, reassuringly,

"My sweet, Rose, you are such a comfort to this old fool."

"Come, dear," she coaxed, "Let's join the others. Jenny is worried about you, and Jake, too."

Slowly, he stood and linking his arm with hers, they left the room together.

Why is she being so difficult about this? Jim wondered as he lay on the bed staring at the ceiling. His mother was usually enthusiastic about experiencing new things and going to different places, but his news about tickets to the Winter Concert had been met with fierce resistance. Even Isaac had been puzzled at her determination not to go. He sighed and turned over on his stomach. Perhaps with the rest of them excited about going, she would change her mind.

Ellen felt trapped. The family continued to badger her about going to the Winter Concert, especially Jim. They couldn't know that in her heart she wanted to go more than anything in the world, but she dared not. What if Jake McGowan, or, heaven forbid, Amanda should see her? They, most assuredly, would if Jenny were as fond of Jim as his stories indicated. Secretly, Ellen was pleased that Jim had met Jenny, but she never dreamed that their relationship would extend beyond work and that her daughter would invite the entire family to a concert! She sat on the edge of the bed that she had finished making, and, longingly, thought about seeing Jenny perform in the Winter Concert. It would be a dream come true, but unfortunately for her, it must remain a dream. Getting up, she walked to the dressing bureau, opened a drawer, and searched beneath her gowns and slips until her fingers touched the envelope. Carefully she pulled it out and taking it with her, she once again sat on the bed.

It was an official looking envelope with some fancy, Austin lawyer's name on it. Slowly, she took the document out and once more looked over the contents. Quite simply, it stated that Ellen had signed away all parental rights to her child, and that she had been legally awarded to the McGowan's. It also warned her to stay away from the child, and unless the adoptive parents wished it, her identity must never be revealed. Amanda's word had meant nothing even after promising Ellen that she could see Jenny anytime. It had all been a lie to get her to sign the papers. Long ago, she had realized this, and after being at the ranch for only a short time, the document had come in the mail, ending all of her plans to eventually reclaim her little girl.

Tears fell on the worn document, as she remembered that day, almost eight years ago, when she had stolen a few precious moments with her daughter. Then she recalled her encounter with Jake McGowan, knowing how close she had come to revealing her identity.

Only the fact that so much time had passed prevented her from destroying the only life that Jenny had ever known. She had vowed that she would never do anything to hurt her daughter, and she meant to keep the promise, even if it meant alienating her family, because of her refusal to attend the concert.

Unknowingly, to Ellen, Isaac slipped into the room and stood watching her, wondering what she was so intently reading that was making her cry.

"Ellen," he spoke her name softly.

With a cry of alarm, she stood and whirled to face him, knocking the document to the floor. Quickly, she retrieved it and stuffed it in the envelope, trying to shield the contents from her husband. When Ellen raised her eyes to Isaac, she noticed he was not looking at her with suspicion or condemnation. Instead, there was such of look of tenderness and concern that she had to turn away. A great feeling of unworthiness and helplessness overcame her. She felt Isaac's strong hand on her shoulder, turning her back to face him. Tiredly, she leaned into his strength and let the tears flow. Picking her up, he carried her to the bed and sat down, cradling her in his arms like a small child. Stoking her hair, he lapsed into his native German to speak words of comfort and love. Ellen smiled through her tears, knowing he always spoke German when he was deeply moved and wanted to express himself more completely.

Sensing that she was now in control of her emotions, he allowed her to slip from his arms and sit next to him on the bed. The envelope was still clutched in her hand.

"Ellen," he spoke in a voice deep with emotion held in check, "does the envelope have anything to do with the secret you have kept from me all these years?"

She looked into his face, realizing that this man loved her no matter what and the secret that she had guarded so carefully wouldn't make any difference. Making up her mind, she moved closer and grasped his hand.

"Isaac, I need to tell you something."

Even though it was December, the day was unseasonably warm. Isaac stopped to wipe the perspiration from his brow as he chopped wood.

Never, in a million years, had he expected to hear a story as strange and tragic as the one his wife had told him a couple of days ago. He continued to chop as he thought about her confession. She had been so fearful of loosing his love and respect, when, in truth, it had made him love her more. He was only sorry that she had carried the burden for so long by herself and he had chided her for not having more faith in him.

He thought about Lilly and Jim. They really should be told, but Ellen was adamant that they should not know. In fact, she had sworn him to silence and they would both carry the secret to their grave. He had promised her, but it hadn't been easy. To him, it was a potentially dangerous secret, especially since Jim was involved in Jenny's life, and it could all blow up in their face one day. When he expressed his doubts to Ellen, she had insisted that everything would work out for the best. Perhaps she was right, but he wished that he had some of her faith. Anyway, the immediate problem was the Winter Concert, because now it was clear why Ellen couldn't go. They had to think of an excuse that wouldn't arouse suspicion.

Sometimes, something tragic turns out to be a blessing, although, the people involved certainly didn't think of it that way. A day before the Winter Concert, Nora Thacker became seriously ill. Her temperature was dangerously high, so they bundled her up and took her to the hospital. Doctors and nurses hurried in and out of the room as the pioneer spirit struggled with the toughest battle of her life. The common cold, that she insisted it was a few days before, turned out to be double pneumonia. Her surrogate family worried and prayed as she slipped in and out of consciousness.

The cold front, accompanying the Winter Concert, put everyone in a holiday spirit. Jenny hummed a Christmas tune as she dressed for the performance. Tonight, she would not be required to wear the black uniform of the symphony. Since she would be performing solo much of the time, she was allowed to wear a formal of her choosing. Actually, her mother picked out what she would be wearing from Boswell's Department Store, but Jenny found no fault with the lovely dress. It was deep red velvet with white ermine trim around the neckline and the cuffs of the long sleeves. The princess styling hugged her young, slim, body. The dark, hair was long and softly curled to enhance and caress the lovely shape of her face.

Critically, she studied her reflection in the mirror, hoping that the dress made her look older and more sophisticated. Excitement lent a glow to her cheeks and the dark eyes sparkled. She pivoted, trying to see every angle, but disappointment clouded her view.

"Drat!" she exclaimed to the reflection staring back at her, "You look like a boy with a dress on!"

"Jenny!" she was interrupted by her father's bellow from downstairs, "We're going to be late!"

"Coming, Dad!" she called, as she stuck her tongue out at the reflection in the mirror and hurried out the door.

Jim gave a final adjustment to the bow tie, hoping that the hastily tailored suit that had belonged to Isaac fitted him properly. His family had insisted that he go to the concert, since Nora's condition was the same, assuring him that they would stay with her, and let him know if there were any changes. Excited as he was about Jenny's performance, he felt guilty about not being with Nora. She was like a grandmother to him and he hated seeing her suffer. Sadly, he thought about the woman that had taken them in and had been more than generous with her love and money. The day his Mom and Isaac had married, she had given them all a piece of the ranch. Isaac had raved and ranted, but in the end, he had seen things Nora's way. Jim smiled as he recalled a defeated Isaac, shaking his head in wonder, that he had finally met someone as bull-headed as he.

The loud blaring of a horn shattered his thoughts, and he ran out the door just as Isaac brought the car to a screeching halt. He was motioning Jim to get into the car as he spoke.

"Come, quickly! Nora has taken a turn for the worse. We must all be at the hospital."

Isaac's stilted words were filled with the pain of grief. Thoughts of the Winter Concert flew out of Jim's head, as they rushed back to the hospital.

Stalling for time, Jenny balked at being hurried up the steps of the symphony hall by her Father. She was searching among the people that were beginning to crowd the hall, hoping to catch a glimpse of someone very special. Even though it had been months since their last meeting, she knew that she would recognize him. Surely, he didn't forget. He had to be here!

Panic lent a hectic flush to her skin as her adolescent mind formed reasons why he might not come. Her immature thoughts were a confusion of self-doubt and insecurity. Taking a deep breath, she noticed her father looking at her strangely.

"Jenny, are you okay?" he asked, worriedly.

"Yes," she gulped, fighting back tears,

"I have to go now, Dad!" Before he could respond, she hurried into the rehearsal room.

A troubled Jake walked back to the crowded hall where his wife was busily trying to impress someone with the latest gossip.

He had never seen Jenny so nervous before. She had performed many times at various functions and it had never seemed to faze her. He thought of asking Amanda if she knew what might be troubling Jenny, but discarded the idea immediately, knowing that his wife would be of no help in that area. Looking around, he spotted the two people that could help, Franz and his mother.

Tears of sorrow ran down the grief-stricken faces as they watched the doctor pull the sheet over the face of their beloved Nora Thacker. Valiantly, she had fought, but lost the battle, and mercifully, she had slipped away, while still unconscious.

The concert was nearly over and the beautiful, talented daughter of Jake and Amanda McGowan had won the hearts of Austin. Jake had been terribly concerned when she took her place on center stage. Standing alone in the lovely red dress, she had somehow looked vulnerable and a little lost. The crowd had grown a bit restless when she hesitated, looking out over the audience, before she began. However, once she drew the bow across the strings, nothing else mattered, but the instrument that had captured her heart and soul.

With the symphony behind her, highlights from Handel's "The Messiah" were her crowning achievement. It brought the audience to their feet, many in tears, for a deafening ovation and tribute to an astoundingly, accomplished musician.

Head bent against the fierce north wind, Jim searched the pasture. He spotted what he was looking for over near the barbed wire fence. It was a large clump of "bear grass." The scientific name of the plant was unknown to Jim.

Every Christmas, for as long as they had lived with Nora, she would bring in a clump of the grass with the needle sharp blades, and using it as a centerpiece, she would cover the base with cloth and place pinecones and glass balls around it for a festive look. Then, much to the delight of Jim and Lilly, she would place gumdrops of different colors on the ends of the sharp grass. When no one was watching, they would snatch a gumdrop from one of the blades. Placing her hands on her hips, Nora would frown and declare that the mice were getting bigger every year to be able to eat so many gumdrops! This would send them into gales of laughter. Pretending to be put out by the candy's disappearance, she would replace them only to find them missing, again, in a day or two.

Determinedly, Jim dug up the clump of grass and placed it in the burlap sack. Slinging it over his shoulder, he headed back. Slowing his stride, as the sun came up over the horizon, he looked up at the ranch house. It was going to seem empty without the wiry, rancher that had ruled them with a velvet glove. He entered through the back door and noticed that no one was up, yet. Though it was Christmas, there was no festive atmosphere. Nora had been buried yesterday, and the creaks and moans caused by the wind, made the house appear to be in mourning for the absence of its mistress.

Carefully, he removed the "bear grass" and cleaned and cut the base to make it set nicely on the table. He searched the storage closet under the stairs, until he found the box marked "decorations." In the pantry, he found the large sack of gumdrops that Nora had purchased a couple of weeks ago. Busily working on the centerpiece, he didn't notice that Lilly had quietly joined him.

The sniffles caused by the tears that flowed down her cheeks, alerted Jim to his sister's presence. She and Nora had been very close and looking at the centerpiece had brought back memories. Putting his arm around her shoulders, he drew out a handkerchief and handed it to her.

"Here, wipe your nose," his voice was gruff with emotion, "and help me finish decorating. You can add the gum drops." Standing back, they surveyed their handy-work.

"Wow!" Lilly said, smiling at Jim, "It's beautiful!" Mischievously, and almost in unison, they each grabbed a gumdrop.

"Here's to you, Nora. Merry Christmas!"

Chapter 17

Gloomily, Jake sat in his office at the *Lone Star Chronicle*, drumming his fingers on his desk. He had a long talk with his mother about Jenny. Ever since the night of the Winter Concert, she had been moody and uncommunicative. Not knowing what to do, he had enlisted Rose's help. His mother's revelation of Jenny's adolescent crush on Jim had been a shock. He hadn't realized she was growing up so fast. His first inclination had been to go to Jenny and have a talk with her, but his mother had restrained him, begging him not to over react.

It wasn't that he objected to Jim because, in fact he had always been impressed by the young man. He was of good character and Jake instinctively trusted him. Anyway, he supposed that he had himself to blame after all he had thrown them together last summer. It was a delicate situation and he didn't have a clue as how to handle it, but one thing was certain. Jenny was too young to be thinking seriously about *any* boy. As for Jim, he wondered how his employee felt about his daughter. Because of the age difference, it was doubtful that he was even aware of Jenny's crush on him. Soon he would find out, because he had sent word requesting Jim to stop in and see him today.

Enthusiastically, Jim made his way to the *Lone Star Chronicle*. He wondered what was so important that his boss had requested that he come to the office. Hopefully, it concerned his future with the newspaper.

Entering the Chronicle, he faced the hub-hub of the noisy newsroom. Editors were rushing about frantically trying to meet deadlines, while reporters typed stories they hoped would receive top billing. The staccato rhythm of the typewriters was music to his ears and he yearned for the day when he, too, would be hard at work on a story. Wistfully, he watched them and looking up he discovered that his boss was standing in the doorway of his office watching *him*. He smiled, but noticed that Mr. McGowan did not smile in return. Instead, he motioned for him to come into his office. Feeling more than a little discomforted, Jim hurriedly went to join him.

For the next fifteen minutes, small talk and sidestepping seemed to be the substance of the conversation. Finally, Jake seemed to draw a deep breath, before plunging blindly into unknown territory.

"You're a fine looking, young man. I'm sure there must be some special girl that has caught your interest?"

The blunt change in conversation had Jim at a loss. He still had not figured out the reason for this meeting. Mr. McGowan was staring at him impatiently waiting for a response. Nervously, he cleared his throat, before attempting to speak,

"Well, sir, no, there is no one special. I mean I don't have a girlfriend or anything like that."

"Come, come, and don't be shy!" Jake interrupted, "I was young once, so I do know a thing or two. At your age, girls are all you do think about."

He smiled knowingly and winked. Jim was thoroughly confused. His boss was acting very strangely.

"Sir, I know you must have had a reason for asking me here and I hoped it would be about my future with the *Lone Star Chronicle*. It's been my dream since I was a kid shinning shoes down on the corner, and ever since you have allowed me to work here, I've thought about nothing else, but this."

The earnest way he spoke and the sincerity behind the words convinced Jake that he was hearing the truth. Glancing at his young employee's hopeful expression, he quickly came to a decision.

"What do you see yourself doing here in a few years?"

Jim stood and earnestly began to plead his case as though he were before some judge who could sentence him to life or death without a second thought. Passionately, he spoke of his desire to be a reporter and to write stories that would stir peoples' hearts and imaginations.

"Mr. McGowan, I know that if I'm given the chance, I'll make you and the newspaper proud of me! I'll write stories that will cause the *Lone Star Chronicle* to be the measuring stick for every newspaper in the country!"

The glow and excitement in Jim's face and eyes reminded Jake of himself at that age. He, too, had been full of dreams and ambitions.

"Whoa, Jim!" Jake held up his hands to halt the flow of words. "That's some ambition you've got there. I greatly admire enthusiasm and determination, but there's a little more to it if you truly wish to succeed."

"Just tell me what to do, I'll do anything!"

He could barely contain himself. He was on the threshold of his dream and Mr. McGowan had the power to make it all come true.

"Well, you're going to need more than a high school diploma and a fist-full of ambition. Although, that is a good start." He smiled as he said it to soften the blow. He could tell the bubble had burst, and Jim looked more than a little frustrated.

"Sit down, Son. I have a proposition for you." Feeling out of sorts and a little bit foolish, he did what his boss suggested.

"I know of a fine journalist school in New York. In fact, I went there myself."

Jake's voice droned on, but after he mentioned New York, Jim tuned him out as chaotic thoughts took over. *How could I possibly go to school in New York? I'd never be able to afford it.*

Noticing that Jim had turned quiet and thoughtful, Jake stopped speaking. Smiling to himself, he quietly divined the reason for his protégé's sudden lack of enthusiasm. Unfolding his arms, he came around the desk and stood in front of Jim.

"By the way, did I mention that the *Lone Star Chronicle* would, naturally, pay for your training?"

Jim's bent head snapped back and his look of disbelief mixed with hope, made Jake almost laugh out loud.

"What did you say?"

At that he did laugh and slapping the dazed young man on the back, he grabbed his hat and pulled him towards the door. "Come on,

I want to buy you lunch and we can talk some more about those ambitions of yours!"

Smiling so broadly that he felt his face would burst he followed his boss out the door.

Jenny was walking with her head down against the fierce north wind. Her cheeks and lips had been stung a rosy red and her hands felt frozen as they clutched her school-books. The large object she had run into had almost knocked the wind out of her.

He had been daydreaming about going to school in New York and had not even noticed the slight form that he had almost succeeded in knocking flat.

"I'm so sorry miss!" He said as he scrambled to pick up the books that had flown everywhere. From his crouched position, retrieving the books, he smiled and looked up.

"Jenny!" he exclaimed when he saw it was his young friend from last summer. The books were forgotten as he quickly stood and grasped her small hands in his large ones.

"It's wonderful to see you again!"

No welcoming smile lit her face as she withdrew her hands and quietly walked around him to gather up the pile of books. He laughed halfheartedly watching her small stiff back as she turned away from him.

"Don't you remember me, Jenny? I'm Jim, we worked together at the Chronicle."

Turning to face him, she haughtily replied, "Remember you, why should I remember you? Oh, yes, you're the boy I gave concert tickets to. I do hope that you and your family enjoyed the concert. Well, please excuse me, I must be going."

Something was not right. Jim sensed that he had hurt her deeply and she was hiding behind a wall of hostility. He silently cursed himself for not making the effort to let her know what had happened the night of the Winter Concert.

Head held high, she started to walk past him. His hand shot out to prevent her hasty departure.

"Wait, please, Jenny," he implored as she tried to struggle away from the hold he had on her upper arm. "Look, it is cold out here and this is not the place to talk, will you go with me to the cafe across the street? I'd like to buy you a cup of hot chocolate. Okay?" he smiled hopefully.

"Why should I go anywhere with you?" The disdain was evident in her tone and in the way she looked down her perfectly formed nose at him.

"How about, because we were once friends and friends give each other the courtesy of listening." The serious brown eyes and handsome face of Jim Gibson looking down at her melted away the last of her resistance. Allowing him to take her books, he escorted her across the street to the corner cafe.

After they were seated with two steaming cups of cocoa, an uneasy silence stretched between them. Jenny lightly traced the pattern on the tablecloth. She picked up her spoon then allowed it to clatter against the cup in sudden agitation.

Jim was busy thinking about how to explain the events of the past month that had seemed like years. Noticing that his companion was becoming restless, he decided that he'd better try.

"You know, Jenny, I actually put on a suit to wear to the Winter Concert. My whole family was very excited about going." *Everyone except my mother,* he thought, still not understanding her reluctance to go.

"So, what did you think of the concert. I don't remember seeing you there, of course, I was very busy," her eyes dropped to the tablecloth as she said this, knowing full well how desperately she had searched the faces in the audience.

"Jenny," he waited for her to look at him, "You must know how much I, my family," he quickly amended, "looked forward to being with you that night, but something tragic happened. One of our family members passed away."

Her eyes widened at his words,

"Oh, Jim, who? Not your mother!" she reached across the table grabbing his hand, her green eyes moist with tears. "I'm so sorry!"

"No, honey, it was not my mother. Actually, she wasn't even kin to us, but my sister and I had kind of adopted her as our grandmother. Her name was Nora and she owned the ranch where I grew up."

"How awful for you and your family, I wish I had known." Desperately, she wished that she were older so that she could express her feelings and say something comforting to him. Without words, however, he seemed to understand her compassion and her need to reestablish their special friendship. Soon, they were laughing and talking with the same familiar comradery of that special summer. After a while, Jenny noticed that Jim kept glancing at his watch.

"Am I keeping you from something?" she asked, secretly hoping he wouldn't have to hurry away.

"As a matter of fact, I'm meeting your father at his office very shortly," he replied.

"Oh, is it about what you and I will be doing at the Chronicle this summer?"

He could tell by her expression that it was a prospect she was eagerly anticipating. Hating to disappoint her he drew in a deep breath, knowing that he had to be the one to tell her or she would never forgive him. "Actually, I won't be here this summer."

"Wha...t?" she stammered, doubting that she had heard him correctly.

"I'm going to New York, Jenny." Watching the sparkle go out of her green eyes, he hated being responsible. "Please try to understand," he spoke earnestly, his eyes pleading. "My dream, for as long as I can remember, was to be a reporter for the *Lone Star Chronicle*. Your father has generously made a way for me to go to New York and study journalism. It's the opportunity of a life-time and I have to go!"

His impassioned words brought incredible pain to the young, impressionable, girl who adored him. Her eyes, moist with tears, stared at him, trying to make sense out of his words.

"Jenny, look, honey, you're young. Someday you'll meet some great guy and you'll forget all about me."

"No! Never! Please, don't leave, Jim!"

Not sure what to say after her outburst, he decided on another approach.

"Jenny, you know how much you love the violin. Well, that's how much I love journalism. You wouldn't want someone to ask you to give up what you love most, would you?"

Her passionate cry of, "I'd give it up—for *you*," surprised him further.

Not giving him a chance to say anything more, she quickly gathered up her books and fled from the cafe. Her hasty departure did not go unnoticed by the clientele who turned to stare at Jim, accusingly. Ignoring the whispers and stares, he continued to stay where he was for a few more moments. She was young; she didn't understand and she *would* get over her crush, and forget all about him. The nagging feeling that he didn't want her to forget him was bothersome. He shook his head to clear the thought. Focusing on the future, he hurriedly left for his appointment.

Jenny rushed into the house practically knocking Amanda down as she blindly ran upstairs to her room. The resounding slam of her door echoed throughout the house. She dropped the books and fell face down onto the bed, weeping as never before.

Amanda was startled, then annoyed at what she considered ill manners. Sternly, she called Jenny's name several times, but there was no response. Indignation and anger carried her to her daughter's bedroom. Without bothering to knock, she opened the door.

It was obvious that Jenny was crying, which further angered her. Crying showed weakness of character and was reserved for the emotional lower class. People with the proper breeding never cried and it was time her daughter learned how a refined, upper class citizen handled life's disappointments. Standing over the sobbing child, she roughly shook her arm.

"Jenny, stop that crying at once!"

She cried out in fright not having realized that her mother had come into the room. Sitting up, she turned her face trying to hide her puffy eyes and tear stained cheeks. Roughly, Amanda shook her arm once more, "Look at me when I speak to you!" she commanded.

"Please, Mother, I need to be alone right now." The hurt and pain in her eyes would have been evident to anyone with a sensitive nature, but Amanda possessed no such quality.

"Now, you listen to me, you spoiled little girl! Your father is a weakling and he has been far too lenient with you for your own good. The past few weeks, you've been moody and impossible to live with! I have decided that you must have proper training, therefore, you will attend a boarding school for young ladies in Houston." Here, she paused, waiting for some protest or outburst from her wayward daughter. At Jenny's silence, she continued the lecture, outlining each and every one of her daughter's shortcomings.

STRADI'S VIOLIN

Old Sarah Cummings was waiting for Amanda to finish upbraiding Jenny. She was going to have it out with her once and for all. No longer will I keep silent, she vowed. Her hands shook as she pushed thin strands of snow-white hair out of her wrinkle lined face. It's time Jake knows the truth too, she mumbled to herself.

A young, Mexican, housekeeper named Maria now took over Sarah's chores. When she was forced to retire a couple of years ago, due to poor health, Amanda had wanted to send her away, but Jake had insisted that she remain with them. The house was large enough and he saw no reason why she should have to leave the place that had been home to her for over fifty years.

Satisfied that things were now under her control, Amanda left a subdued Jenny. Smiling, she congratulated herself for handling what had become a problem for the past few weeks. She was positive that boarding school was what Jenny needed to mold her into a proper young lady and to get her away from Jake's influence. Closing the door to Jenny's bedroom, she had taken only a few steps when suddenly her former housekeeper confronted her.

"I know what's going on!" Sarah hissed. "All these years, I've kept silent, but no more, Miz High 'n Mighty!" The menacing features were thrust close to hers.

Amanda smiled cruelly into the age-lined face. "What does and old hag like you know and who do you think will listen to your senile ramblings?" Deliberately turning her back on the old woman, she continued to the top of the stairs.

"Wait!" Sarah screeched, running after her, "I'm not through with you!" she grabbed Amanda's arm as she spoke.

"Let me go, you old fool!" Amanda shouted as she shoved her away, causing her to totter precariously on the edge of the stairs and then to loose her balance, entirely. With a look of sheer terror and outstretched, hands toward Amanda, she tumbled backwards down the staircase. A piercing scream brought Jenny and the new housekeeper running. Jenny noticed her mother's attention was focused on something below. Hurrying to her side, she and Maria stared in horror at the pitiful heap at the bottom of the stairs.

"She lost her balance and there was nothing I could do!" Amanda was getting tired of repeating the words, first to a hysterical Jenny and Maria and then to the doctor and later to Jake.

Now, this weak-eyed, pompous, county coroner was forcing her to go over every detail at least twice. He was peering at her, owlishly, from behind his horn-rimmed glasses with lens as thick as a coke bottle.

"She was a sick, old woman and she simply lost her balance. Of course," she paused and looked accusingly at Jake, "if she had been sent away when she retired, this never would have happened!"

The coroner looked from Amanda to Jake noticing the strained atmosphere between them.

"Ah—um," he snapped the notebook closed and stood, "I think I have all that's necessary to complete the paperwork on this unfortunate accident. Thank you both for your cooperation."

He shook hands with Jake and briefly nodded to Amanda before making his exit. Amanda quickly took steps to follow him, but Jake blocked her path preventing her escape. She glared at him, her eyes narrowing to slits.

"Get out of my way!" The venom in her voice was unmistakable.

"What's the hurry? Everyone else is in an emotional upheaval over Sarah's *accident*, but you, dear wife, are calm and cool as always. Why, is that, I wonder? Did you happen to speak to her prior to the *accident*?" His cruel, mocking eyes watched her intently as he waited for a response.

She felt like attacking him physically, but knew that she would be the loser. Anyway, she wouldn't give him the satisfaction. Haughtily, she answered, and the loathing in her eyes was plain for him to see, "Sorry, to disappoint you, but I'm not some weak-minded, sniveling creature to fall weeping into your arms, because the hired-help fell down the stairs! She was a sick, old woman and now she's dead— end of story!"

Jake drew back at her deliberate cruelty and catching him off guard, she raced past him out of the room. He drew his chair in front of the fireplace, before sitting down. Amanda had left a chill inside him that even the fire couldn't warm. *Why was she such a cruel, unfeeling, woman?* He had asked himself the question many times. Poor Sarah didn't deserve to die this way. Perhaps, he had been wrong in keeping her here. She had been a part of his life for as long as he could remember and she was more like family than employee. His mother had been devastated at the news of her death, promising to get there as soon as possible. Jenny was inconsolable and refused to leave her room. Amanda acted as if the whole thing were a minor annoyance, to be forgotten as quickly as possible.

Leaning back in his chair, he massaged his aching temples. He shouldn't have goaded Amanda into a reaction, but he had to know if there were more to the story than she was telling. She had barely tolerated the housekeeper and he couldn't understand why. Sarah was honest, hardworking, didn't have a mean bone in her body. So why had Amanda not trusted her? He had known for a long time that this was the case, but the question that nagged him was, why? Did Sarah know something, a secret, maybe, that Amanda didn't trust her to keep? Jake groaned and closed his eyes. His thoughts had only made his headache worse.

The whole household was in turmoil, getting Jim ready for his big move to New York City. Isaac and Ellen had been stunned when Jim had first told them about his plans. Neither of them were truly happy about his leaving, especially Isaac. He had hoped that Jim would want to be a rancher and help him keep their ranch running smoothly and profitably. Listening to Jim as he enthused about his future in journalism, he remembered his own restlessness at that age. It was natural that the boy would want to explore the world. Maybe after he got it out of his system, he would come back here and settle down. In the meantime, Isaac had hired a drifter to help with the chores.

Ellen tried to maintain the right attitude as she helped Jim get ready, but she was having trouble letting go. This was her son, her little boy. Her eyes grew misty as she remembered what a little man he had always been. Now, he was truly a grown man and he certainly deserved to have this chance. Once again, she was indebted to Jake McGowan. She knew without his sponsorship, Jim would not be going to New York.

Lilly sulked in her room, eaten up envy and jealousy, as her brother prepared for a life vastly different from the one he'd always known. She could sense him becoming more and more withdrawn from them as he daydreamed about his new life. Staring at the pouting red mouth in her mirror, she thought of the excitement waiting around the corner for Jim.

How I wish it were me leaving this dreary, backwater, place! Just thinking about New York sent chills of delight running up and down her spine. She'd never been anywhere. There was a great, big, world out there waiting for her if she could only get out of here. She'd tried to tell Jim how she felt, but he hadn't really been listening to her. Instead, he'd tried, in vain, to get her to meet his boss's uppity daughter! What on earth would she have in common with a spoiled, little, rich girl. Heavens, they weren't even the same age, what would they talk about? From all she'd heard the kid was some sort of genius with the violin.

Dismissing the young girl from her mind, her eyes focused on the reflection in the mirror, noticing the drooping mouth. I've got to stop this, she thought, rising to her feet and once again looking into the mirror. She smiled and discovered a very pretty girl was smiling back at her.

Long, blonde hair, made lighter by the sun, and large blue eyes framed by naturally dark lashes, contrasted with the honey-gold of her skin. She pivoted slightly to better view her shapely body that was filling out in all the right places. *Not too bad*, she thought, *maybe I do have the ticket out of here after all!*

Jim wondered how he would get the entire luggage his mother had packed to New York. She had left nothing out, of that he was sure. Whenever he tried to protest that something wasn't needed, she just replaced it with something else! He was going to miss her. He was going to miss Isaac and Lilly, too. Leaving the security of his family and home had been a difficult decision, but the future was beckoning him so he pushed his feelings aside. After all, he wanted to avoid being homesick before he left!

There were plenty of other things to occupy his mind. The best thing of all was when Mr. McGowan had told him, that not only would he being going to school, but he would also be working at one of the world's busiest news rooms — The New York Tribune!

With the Spring Concert just around the corner, Jenny was busy with rehearsals. It was hard work, but she was glad, because it didn't leave much time for thinking. She hadn't been to the Juniper tree in over a month. The day of Sarah's funeral was the last time. Her father had come looking for her, because he knew it's where she went to think things through. That day they had a long and much needed talk. She had cried and he had held her. They had talked about Sarah and finally about Jim. It was hard at first, but her father had seemed to understand. Best of all, he didn't condemn or judge, but he listened. They had also discussed Amanda's plans for her to go to boarding school in Houston. She begged not to be sent away. Her father had promised to do what was best and she trusted him.

Jake was thinking about his talk with Jenny. He didn't want to send his daughter away, but he was concerned about her obsession with Jim. Her upbringing hadn't been exactly normal. For one thing, she had never had much interaction with children her own age. Having gained a certain amount of fame at a very young age, she had been in the spotlight, surrounded by adoring adults and music lovers. Sadly, he mused, she had never really been a child, and now it was time to grow up. Amanda wants to mold her into a replica of herself by sending her to a fancy girl's school in Houston. *By heaven!* he vowed, *I'll never let that happen!* Without consulting Amanda, he had talked to his mother and Franz. They had readily agreed with him. Jenny would live with them in Dallas and attend a private school. It was a prestigious academy, so perhaps, Amanda wouldn't protest too much. At any rate, it wouldn't matter if she did, because this time he was doing what was best for Jenny.

Chapter 18

It was the night before Jim's departure for New York. He was dressed in the new suit that his mom and Isaac had given him as a going away present. Lilly giggled while she looked him up and down. Mockingly she teased. "My! Big, brother, you *do* look spiffy!"

Jim smiled as he studied her appearance in return. "You don't look half bad yourself — for a kid sister!" She made a face at him, causing Ellen and Isaac to laugh at their antics. Ellen was filled with pride at the picture the two of them made.

Lilly was wearing her first party dress. It was a rose color with a draped neckline that hinted at her maturing bosom. The softness of the dress clung to her figure, swaying gently, when she moved. It was a romantic dress, and wearing it made her giddy with excitement. She was actually going out! So what if it was with her brother to some boring concert. She was going to the city and anything could happen!

Jim had gone ahead to bring the car around and was, impatiently, holding the car door open for her. Hurriedly, she kissed her mother and Isaac goodbye, before rushing out of the house.

A chair squeaked and came to rest on all four legs with a thud. Lilly turned at the sound. It was the new hired hand sitting on the front porch. His dark eyes glowed faintly in the fading light as he boldly stared at her. His leering smirk was almost frightening, but at the same time exciting. She smiled shyly and ducked her head before racing down the steps to the car. The man's eyes followed her, noticing how the dress clung to the ripe, young, body. Jim was frowning as he observed the man's stare.

Ellen and Isaac appeared on the porch, cautioning them to drive carefully and not to be out too late. Wistfully, Ellen watched the taillights of the car disappear down the road. How she wished she could hear Jenny play the violin! She comforted herself with the thought that Jim and Lilly would get to be there.

Despite the warmth of the evening, she suddenly shivered and turned to find herself staring into the eyes of the newcomer. Defensively, Ellen's hand flew to her throat.

"What are you doing here? You frightened me!"

Isaac had been absorbed in his own thoughts, and turned in surprise at his wife's outburst.

"Sorry, folks, I was just enjoyin' the evenin' air before turnin' in." Grinning at them, he tipped his hat and ambled off the porch, disappearing around the corner.

"Isaac, I don't like him, he frightens me!"

"Now, hon, we've had this discussion," he soothed, "I need help and he has the experience."

"Yes, I know," she sighed, "but what do you know about him?"

"What's there to know?" he countered, "As long as he does his job and knows his place, there shouldn't be a problem. But," he tweaked her small, up-turned nose as he spoke, "if it'll make you feel any better, I'll keep a close eye on him and from now on, I'll tell him the porch is off limits. Okay?" he stirred her into the house.

"Alone, at last!" He turned her in his arms and began to kiss her. Playful at first, then passionately as their mutual desire took over.

Melvin Yates smirked as he watched the lights go off in the big house.

"Guess I know what they're up to, since it's too early for even that yokel rancher to go to bed!" he sneered as he raised the whiskey bottle once more to his lips. Remembering Ellen's frightened look caused the sweat to pop out on his face. An almost uncontrollable blood lust overtook him. He fought it, knowing that soon he would not be able to. Once again, he pictured her frightened look and her hand going to her lovely, white, throat. Oh, yes, it was what turned him on. Seeing their terrified looks, hearing them beg for mercy. His eyes glazed over with lust as he remembered them—-one by one.

Jenny's dress was a stunning emerald green to match her eyes. The off-the-shoulder style with the large ruffle surrounding the neckline was perfect. The bodice of the dress hugged her like a second skin and the skirt was long and flowing. Her long, dark hair was sweep up on top of her head, leaving her slender neck bare. Tiny emerald earrings, a birthday present from her father, sparkled from delicate ear lobes. Tonight, she looked older than her fourteen years.

"Wow!" Jake said, as he walked into the room. She smiled at him. "Are you nervous, honey?"

"A little, but I'm excited, too. Dad," she reached up to adjust his bow tie as she spoke, "have you given our discussion anymore thought?"

He smiled and caught hold of her hands, drawing her with him to sit on the sofa. Anxiously, she waited for him to speak.

"I have good news for you, at least, I hope you'll consider it to be good news. How would you feel about living in Dallas with your grandma Rose and Franz?"

"Dad!" she cried, "Do you mean it?" At her obvious pleasure, he laughed.

"Yes, and I've, also, chosen a very fine private school for you to attend."

It pleased him to see her happy and smiling, again. She leaned over and kissed him on the cheek.

"You know, Dad, I'd rather stay with you," she told him somberly.

"Remember how you always trust me to do what is best for you?" She smiled and nodded.

"Well, kiddo, I think this is best for now and," he winked mischievously, "it'll keep you out of Houston!"

Lilly's cheeks were flushed with excitement as she and Jim walked into the lobby of the city auditorium. Men's heads turned as the blonde, beauty walked by. She caught their interested looks and blatant stares and it left her breathless and giddy with a heady sense of power that she had never before experienced.

Jim smiled to himself. He could feel his sister's confidence rise with each interested stare. She really was lovely, but he wanted her to be discerning, too. There were some men whose attention a girl could do without. One that came to mind was the man Isaac had hired. He made a mental note to warn her about him.

STRADI'S VIOLIN

Suddenly, Jim tensed as he caught sight of another stunning beauty. She was holding on to Jake McGowan's arm and on the other side, though not holding Jake's arm was an elegant, older woman. Briefly, Jim experienced a feeling of dejavu, as he looked at the woman that had to be Jenny's mother. Jake caught his interested stare and motioned him over. Before they could respond, the older woman disappeared in the direction of the powder room.

Jenny could feel the blood drain from her face as she watched the couple approach. He was the last person she expected to see and the fact that he was with a beautiful girl didn't help. A momentary feeling of panic made her wants to rush off somewhere and hide. Her father tightened his hold on her arm as though he sensed that she was about to take flight. Then, he was releasing her as he greeted the couple.

It was the first time she had ever seen him dressed up like this and he was devastatingly handsome. She took in his appearance at a glance and quickly looked away, feeling awkward and tongue-tied. As though through a dense fog, she heard her father's voice.

"Jim, glad to see you made it." They shook hands.

"Thank you for the tickets, sir. It's our pleasure to be here."

Her head snapped up in surprise at her father. He saw her accusing look and catching her hand, he drew her forward as he spoke.

"I couldn't let you go off to New York without hearing one of the most famous and talented violinist of our time, now could I?"

Jenny waited for the floor to open up and swallow her.

"It would have been a pity, indeed, sir, and my sister and I are eternally grateful to you." Jim countered, smiling.

It took a moment for the words to register. *Sister*, she thought, *did he say, sister?* Her interest piqued, she looked up once more as Jim formally introduced his sister Lilly. Her shyness was forgotten in her excitement as she spoke to the girl of whom she had heard so many stories.

"Lilly, I'm so happy to meet you. I feel that I know you already, because Jim has told me so much about you."

Lilly was staring at the young, girl who had suddenly come to life and was babbling about the stories Jim had told her. So, this was the concert violinist that Austin and the surrounding communities raved about. Why, she was hardly more than a child! However, Lilly noted, reluctantly, a lovely one. No wonder her brother was confused about her. Poor, Jim! She smiled and shook hands with Jenny, telling her how delighted she was to make her acquaintance. Next Jim's boss, Jake McGowan, captured her attention.

Wow! she thought, *for an older man, he is quite handsome.* Her thoughts must have been revealed in our eyes, because Jake smiled at her indulgently. While holding her gaze, he addressed Jim.

"I guess good-looks and charm must run in your family." He winked at Lilly.

"Thank you, sir, and might I say—"

"We don't have time for chit-chat," a waspish voice interrupted.

Their heads turned to take in the source of the voice, as she continued to speak.

"Jenny, you must go to the rehearsal room. I'm sure the Maestro is looking for you and, Jake, we must take our seats in the auditorium."

A faint sense of distaste washed over Jim and Lilly as they stared at the regal woman with the coronet of braids wound around her head, like a crown.

"Jim, Lilly, let me introduce you to my *charming*," he emphasized the word sarcastically, "wife, Amanda," he gripped her arm causing her eyes to sparkle dangerously.

"Amanda, this is Jim Gibson and his sister, Lilly."

"A pleasure, I'm sure!" she spoke in a stilted, bitter voice without bothering to so much as look in their direction.

Jenny was mortified by her mother's rude behavior and she couldn't bring herself to look at their guests.

"Excuse me," she spoke, her voice quivering slightly, "I must go to the rehearsal room." Apology written in her eyes, she forced herself to look at Jim and Lilly.

"Thank you both for coming, I hope you enjoy the concert."

Knowing that if she didn't leave now, she might disgrace herself by bursting into tears, she hurried away before either of them could respond.

Watching his daughter's retreating back, Jack's eyes hardened as looked into Amanda's mocking face. Masking his anger, he turned once more to the young couple who stood by, uncertainly.

"Jim, Lilly, I want to invite you both to our house after the concert," he sensed they were both on the verge of making excuses.

"I warn you, I won't take 'no' for an answer," he smiled warmly at them as he spoke.

"Jim, consider this as a kind of "going away party" since you're leaving for New York tomorrow. I've invited the entire Lone Star Chronicle staff, plus some other friends." He still seemed ready to refuse, so Jake turned his charm on Lilly.

"My, dear, if I were a younger man and not married," he looked wickedly in Amanda's direction, leaving the sentence unfinished. Then in mock regret, he spoke,

"Alas, I'll have to stand by, as the young men in my employment, vie for your attention and beg to be introduced."

Lilly couldn't stem the laughter that bubbled up at his playacting. She turned to Jim, her eyes pleading. He knew that she would never forgive him is he didn't allow her this opportunity and his boss had subtly reminded him that he was indebted to him, by his mention of New York. Reluctantly, he agreed to come.

"Good! I'll be looking for you so don't let me down"

"Whew!" Lilly fanned herself with the program as the couple walked away, "He's such a charming man. I wonder why he's married to that awful witch!"

Jim frowned at his sister, "I don't think my boss's wife should be a topic of discussion."

"Oh, don't be so stuffy! I just don't think she's a very nice person, that's all," slyly, Lilly cocked her head and looked at him, "Now, the daughter, she's another story, huh, Jim?"

"Don't go there, Lilly," he warned.

His expression and the seriousness of his tone convinced her to drop the subject. Timidly, she touched his arm.

"I'm sorry, Jim. Let's just have a good time, okay?" Relieved at her offered truce, he smiled and took her arm, "Shall we?"

Together they entered the auditorium and found their seats just as the lights begin to dim. The expertise of the musicians and the harmony of the finely tuned instruments, exploded into sounds that filled the listeners with awe and admiration.

Lilly, expecting to be bored, had found that she was spellbound by the music that filled the auditorium. Stealing a glance at Jim, she noticed that he, too, was caught up in the music.

Jake sat stiffly beside Amanda. Lord, the woman had a way of tying him up in knots. As the music worked its magic, his body slowly relaxed and he felt the tension begin to drain away.

Amanda's fist clenched and unclenched as she seethed with anger. Being deaf, ordinarily, wouldn't have stopped her from enjoying the concert. In the right frame of mind, she could feel the electricity and vibrations of the music. Tonight, she felt nothing, but a burning anger. Her mind was activated by the hatred she felt towards the man sitting next to her, but then, she hated most men, starting with her father.

The only man that had piqued her interest in years was the one she had met in Austria, Hans Gunthur. Jake hadn't allowed her to continue her friendship with him. When she had suggested inviting him to America for a visit, Jake had negated the idea in no uncertain terms. Even Franz Leonie had refused to be her ally, when she had suggested that he be the one to invite Hans. Jake always stood in the way of her getting what she wanted and she was tired of his contemptible ways.

Spitefully, he had asked that couple in the lobby, along with his cronies from the newspaper, to come to their home tonight, expecting her to play hostess.

The spotlight on center stage interrupted her thoughts and captured her attention, as Jenny walked onto the stage. Thunderous applause broke out and, smugly, Amanda looked around, watching the adulation of the audience.

Waiting for the conductor's cue, Jenny positioned the violin and at his nod, her bow was drawn into action across the strings. Her body, her mind, became one with the instrument as she brought to life a masterpiece of incredible beauty. Magic, pure and simple. The audience sat enthralled by the captivating, young mistress of the violin. Jim was mesmerized by every move she made, watching her long, delicate fingers as they caressed and commanded, bringing the instrument to life. Sophisticated, confident, this was a Jenny he had never seen before. This girl was alluring and compelling, and he fought the spell of her attraction with every fiber of his being. All during the conversation in the lobby, he had deliberately avoided either directly speaking or looking at her. Now, she was all he could see and it felt as though someone had punched him, hard, in the stomach.

STRADI'S VIOLIN

The final note sounded and the audience had come to their feet, in standing ovation. Before Jim realized it, Jenny was walking off the stage. He rose on unsteady legs feeling as though he had just lost a battle; against what, he wasn't sure.

The conductor was escorting Jenny back to center stage where a bouquet of roses was placed in her arms. Again, the audience showed their admiration as they applauded with renewed enthusiasm. She curtsied low and, holding the conductor's arm, was led away.

The concert was over, but everyone seemed reluctant to move. It was like being released from a spell as the audience slowly began to leave the auditorium.

"Jim!" Lilly was tugging on his arm, "Isn't she the most talented person you've ever seen?" Not waiting for him to answer, she prattled on, "I really thought this concert would be boring and you were only going out of curtsey to your boss and, of course, Jenny. And, well, I thought she would be just a spoiled, little, rich girl with no talent. Boy! Was I wrong! Perhaps, I *should* get to know her. Don't you think that she'll be famous, someday?" She was talking non-stop and without her being aware of it, they had reached the car and Jim was holding the door open. She jumped into the car eager to join the party that Jim's boss had invited them to.

As soon as they were underway, she resumed her incessant chatter. He wished that she would be quiet, so he could think. He didn't have the heart to rebuke her, though, because the excitement of the evening was making her talk more than usual.

Soon they were climbing as the road wound up a hill; then he was pulling to a stop in the circular driveway of the imposing mansion overlooking Austin. Lilly had stopped talking. She sat gazing up at the house. Smiling, he waited for her outburst of appreciation and a renewal of her chatter. Still turned toward the house, he noticed her shiver, slightly. Concerned, he reached out to touch her arm.

"What's wrong, Lilly?"

"I'm not sure," she turned a troubled face towards him, "for a moment when I looked up at the house, it was like I'd done it before. Do you know what I mean?" Instantly, he remembered how he'd felt when he first saw Mrs. McGowan.

"Yes, Kiddo, I do." Seeking to put an end to these weird feelings, he reached over and playfully rumpled her hair.

"Maybe, we should just leave if this house bothers you!" he teased.

"Oh, no, you don't, Jim Gibson!" she cried indignantly, "I'm attending this party with or without you!" She was out of the car and halfway up the steps, before he caught up with her.

The doors were flung open in welcome. Noisy conversation, laughter, clinking of glasses, and a smoke laden atmosphere, greeted the newcomers.

Lilly felt like a child that had just been turned loose in a candy store. The decor was stylish and elegant from the Persian rugs to the crystal chandeliers. She walked ahead in a daze and Jim started to go after her. Then he shrugged his shoulders. *Why not leave her alone and let her enjoy the evening*, he thought. Turning away, he went to join some friends from the Chronicle.

Lilly was so enthralled by her surroundings that she almost bumped into a server with a tray of drinks. She was offered a sparkling drink from the silver, serving tray. Eagerly, her hand went out to grasp the long-stemmed glass, but another hand reached it first. She looked up into the laughing eyes of Jake McGowan.

"Lilly, would you do me the honor of letting me get you a cup of punch?"

She looked at him knowingly, "Saving me from a fate worse than death, Mr. McGowan?"

"No, dear," he whispered conspiringly, "saving *me*, from a horse-whipping from that big, strong brother of yours!" Laughing and talking they made their way to the punch bowl and a table loaded with all sorts of delicacies. True to Jake's prediction, in a matter of moments admiring males seeking an introduction surrounded Lilly.

As Jim talked and bantered with friends, he allowed his gaze to wander over the room. He noticed that Mrs. McGowan was nowhere to be seen. Someone else was missing, too, someone he didn't want to think about.

Excusing himself from the group, he circulated through the crowd. He caught a glimpse of Lilly surrounded by eager, young men trying to win her attention. He shook his head. *You poor suckers*, he laughed to himself, *she'll have you eating out of her hand in no time*. As he continued his wanderings, an arm fell across his shoulders. Surprised, he looked around and found himself eye to eye with his mentor and boss.

"You certainly look gloomy for a young man on his way to New York tomorrow afternoon. Having second thoughts?"

"No, sir! I've waited for this all my life. It's finally going to happen and I owe it all to you."

"No, Son, it's due to your hard work, your ambition and your determination. I've always admired that about you, even when you were a skinny, little kid shinning my shoes."

"Thank you, sir, I'll try to make you proud."

Jake smiled, "You've already done that, Jim."

Their brief conversation ended as friends and colleagues intruded to offer their congratulations and engage them in other topics of discussion.

Soon a restless Jim moved on, seeking what, he wasn't sure. He found himself in a hall gazing up at the long stairway leading to the upper floors. As though, he had conjured up the object of his thoughts, she appeared at the top of the stairs. She was still wearing the green dress that left her creamy shoulders bare. About to descend the stairs, she caught a glimpse of him standing at the bottom, gazing up at her. Startled, she withdrew, ready to flee.

"Jenny! Wait," he pleaded, "Don't go, I need to talk to you."

She hesitated, praying that her mother would not wake up and come looking for her.

Amanda had refused to join the party, claiming that she had a dreadful headache. Jake had not been fooled by her ploy, but it didn't upset him either, since he knew it would be a relief not to have her disapproving stares and tantrums spoiling everyone's fun.

Jenny was allowed to join the party, even though her mother disapproved. However, Amanda had detained her, insisting that she stay with her and apply cool rags to her head. Then she had regaled her with tales of how the audience had responded to her performance. She had fairly gloated over the standing ovation that her daughter had received. Finally, she had fallen asleep, much to Jenny's relief.

Looking down at Jim, she saw that he was impatiently waiting for her. In fact, his foot was on the first rung of the stairs, as though he intended to come up. Making up her mind, she quickly descended the stairs. He was looking at her so strangely. Almost like he was seeing her for the very first time, she thought. He moved back as she reached the last step.

"Jenny, could we go some place private and talk, *please*?" he added at her uncertain look.

For a moment, she was tempted to refuse, remembering the last time they had talked, but the look in his eyes made it impossible not to give in.

"Well, yes, there is a place that we could go. It's my special, private place, but I'll take you there."

Relieved, he followed as she led him out the back entrance and through the garden. The night was warm and filled with the heady scent of flowers. A narrow, winding path ended on top of a cliff and silhouetted against the moonlit sky, was the tallest tree Jim had ever seen.

They reached a bench situated beneath the aromatic Juniper, where once seated, you were greeted by a panorama of stars. Looking down, one could see the twinkling lights of Austin far below.

"Wow! This is some private spot you have here, Jenny."

Smiling at his approval, it pleased her that he liked it.

"Yes, my father says it was his favorite spot when he was growing up and, also, his father's. In fact, his father built this bench, beneath the Juniper tree, especially for him."

"Juniper tree, huh?" Jim said, looking up at the scale like leaves overhead.

"Yes, it's probably over a hundred years old. Dad's great grandfather collected it as a sapling while on one of this many journeys. He loved the red cedar wood and wanted to see if it would grow here." Animatedly, she was telling how it had been nurtured by each generation and had flourished to a stunning size.

Jim stared at the purity of her profile as she spoke, thinking how young and vulnerable she looked. His intense stare made her nervous and shy. Her voice faltered and she grew quiet. *He was so handsome and she lo —*, but she must not think this way, because he was leaving tomorrow and he had made it clear that she was to forget about him. *Maybe, he's apprehensive about leaving and he just needs a friend to talk to*, she thought.

"Jenny," he spoke, jolting her out of her contemplation.

"I'm glad I was privileged to be at your performance tonight. You were, *are* sensational," he amended. His praise brought a glow to her cheeks.

"Thank you, Jim. And Lilly? Did she enjoy the concert?" He laughed,

"Did, she? That's all she talked about all the way over here."

There was an awkward silence as neither of them seemed to know what to say next. Suddenly, he spoke, causing her to jump.

"I'm leaving for New York tomorrow afternoon." His statement was met by silence. She was angry that he was reminding her again that he was going out of her life, perhaps, forever.

He stood, shoving his hands in his pocket. "Don't you have anything to say?" he spoke to her bowed head, but his words brought her head up, eyes sparkling with the force of her feelings.

"I thought I'd said too much already. A few weeks ago, I made a fool of myself. I really don't want to repeat the experience." Tears welled up in the lovely green eyes as she looked at him.

"Dear, Jenny," he resumed his seat, only closer this time, "Did I hurt you so very badly?" Shyly, her glance met his, with the love she felt for him plain to see, and it made him angry with himself for causing her even a moment's pain. He sighed. It was all so difficult, why couldn't it be simple?

Softly, she answered him, "Yes, you hurt me, but I'm okay, now. I mean... I understand that you're older and you don't have time to wait around for me to grow up." She stumbled over the words as she spoke, afraid of being misunderstood and embarrassing them both.

"Jenny," he interrupted, "you don't know how much I will miss you. You're a very special person and I don't want to lose you."

"Don't worry, Jim, I'll always be your friend," she assured him, sadly.

"No! I'm not talking about losing you as a friend," frustration made his voice harsher than he intended, "I'm not talking about friendship at all!"

Her heart was beating fast. What was he saying to her, she wondered, confused.

Groaning, he reached out and turned her face toward him. Cupping her face in his hands, he intently studied her perfect features, as though, committing them to memory. He could feel her heart beating wildly, but he knew that his was doing the same. The last thing he wanted to do was frighten her. He knew that if he allowed himself to kiss her, it would be impossible to control the intense passion this young girl had inspired in him. Keeping a firm grip on his emotions, he leaned forward and, gently, kissed her forehead. She was trembling and he could see the confusion in her eyes.

"Jenny, you are very precious to me," he stroked her flushed cheek as he spoke,

"Will you write to me while I'm away?" She nodded, not trusting her voice to work. Abruptly, he stood, pulling her to her feet, "I thought going away to New York and becoming a journalist was what I wanted. The *only* thing I wanted. I was wrong," he spoke heavily, as though it pained him to speak at all.

"Forgive me, Jenny, I have no right to ask this of you, but will you wait for me?"

Her heart skipped a beat as she realized what he was telling her. He wanted her to wait for him! Happiness lit her features, dazzling him with her beauty, as she gazed at him, awe-struck by the knowledge that she would have her dream, too.

"Oh, Jim," she whispered, "yes, I'll wait for you and I'll write to you every single day!"

The purity and unselfishness of her love made him want to cry. It would be torture being separated, but she was definitely worth the wait. Hand in hand, they strolled back to the house.

They were both quiet on the way home, each alone with thoughts of the evening. Lilly was in seventh heaven, because for her the party had been a new beginning. She already had a date next Saturday with one of the young men that she had met. *Oh, drat*! she thought, *I hope my mother and Isaac will be reasonable about this and allow me to go out with him.*

Her head turned toward Jim to ask his opinion of how they would react, but she noticed that he was deep in thought. In fact, it seemed that he was scarcely aware of his surroundings. Just before they left, she had noticed him in, what appeared to be, serious conversation with Jenny McGowan. She stole another look at him and noticed that he didn't look very happy. Her curiosity aroused, she decided to ask him about it.

He was reluctant to have his thoughts interrupted, but he could tell Lilly wanted to talk. It took him a moment to realize that she had asked him about his conversation with Jenny. His feelings were still so new to him that he wasn't sure he could put it into words.

"Well," Lilly was saying, "what were the two of you talking about? It looked *very* serious!" she teased.

He was in no mood for teasing, because this thing with Jenny had him all confused. His future was all mapped out, but now there were complications. He wondered if Lilly would understand. She was still waiting for him to say something.

"Lilly, something changed tonight," he explained, haltingly, "I have these feelings..."

"For Jenny!" she interrupted excitedly.

Glaring at her, he spoke harshly, "If you're not going to listen, then I can't talk to you!"

"Oh, all right, Mr. Grumpy, I'll shut up and let you talk! she flounced back in her seat, ready to sulk.

"I'm sorry, Lilly, this is difficult for me and to be perfectly honest, I don't think I'm ready to discuss it," he had softened his tone to take away the sting his words might cause, "Am I forgiven?"

Smiling, she nodded her head knowing that she could never stay mad at him for very long.

"Of course, and, Jim, I'm sorry for being such a brat. If you don't want to talk right now, I understand, but can I talk?" she added, the sparkle back in her eyes.

Jim laughed, "Can I stop you?"

The silhouette of the farmhouse against the big harvest moon was a welcome sight. The evening had been long and Lilly had talked his ear off. They pulled into the drive and he could see that his mother had left a light burning for them. Together they entered the house, intent on going off to bed. The excitement of the evening had finally taken its toll on both of them. Jim was in the process of closing his bedroom door, when he heard Lilly's mischievous, "sweet dreams, dear brother!"

Jim had thought that sleep would be impossible, but he hadn't counted on the stress of the last few hours that determined that his mind needed a rest from the turmoil. He was soon sleeping soundly and dreamlessly.

Jenny was blissfully happy and wide-awake. All her youthful dreams had culminated with Jim's desire for her to wait for him. She thought about how handsome and strong he was and what it would feel like to be held in his arms and kissed by him. Giggling and blushing at her thoughts, she allowed them to continue. *Kissing, what would kissing a boy be like?* she mused.

Jim had kissed her forehead, and she had been disappointed and at the same time elated. Turning on her stomach, she grabbed the pillow and pressed it to her body as though holding a lover in her arms. In her fantasy state, her eyes fell upon the clock that told her it was well past midnight. The bubble of reality burst in upon her dreams, sending her crashing back to earth. Tomorrow, it was already tomorrow! He would be leaving at 4:00 this afternoon and she had promised to meet him at the train station. Suddenly, she was overwhelmed with a strange sadness that made no sense, and, yet, she couldn't shake the feeling.

Chapter 19

Ellen had risen early, and was making a pot of coffee, her thoughts on her son's impending departure. She glanced up, surprised to see him standing in the doorway. His sleep-tousled hair gave him the appearance of a young child, and Ellen's motherly instinct wanted to take him in her arms and protect him from life's hurts. Placing another cup on the table, she poured the coffee, inviting him to join her.

"Thanks, Mom, that coffee smells great."

She watched as he sat quietly warming his hands on the steaming mug. He seemed preoccupied and uncommunicative.

Tentatively, she interrupted his thoughts, "Well, you two were certainly out late. How was the concert?" She waited anxiously for him to tell her all about Jenny's performance.

Finally, he looked up, "Mother, I need to talk to you about something." His tone was so serious that all thoughts about the concert flew out of her head.

"Son, is it about New York? I'm sure your Mr. McGowan will understand if you decide not to go."

"Mother, please!" he said impatiently, "It has nothing to do with New York. Well, perhaps, indirectly," he mumbled.

Ellen, frowned, her confusion mirrored in her face,

"I don't understand—you seem unhappy or unsure about something."

"My feelings are very confused at the moment. I thought I had everything all figured out, but..." here he paused as he tried to make sense of what he felt for Jenny.

Puzzled, Ellen was still looking at him and trying hard to understand why he seemed unsure of his future.

"There's a girl and I think I have feelings for her, maybe even love." There, he'd said it.

Silence met his comment and then she was smiling. "I think I understand your dilemma," she said knowingly, as she got up to pour more coffee into her mug, "You'll be in New York and she'll be here. I realize that a long distance relationship is not very satisfying, but if you truly care for each other, you'll wait," she stated confidently. It was obvious that he struggled with his desire to fulfill his ambition *and* his longing for this girl. "She must be someone special, Son, do I know her?" she asked, smiling.

"Well, no, that is, you've never actually met her, although I've talked about her. Mother, she's absolutely wonderful and talented and beautiful." The way his eyes lit up as he described her convinced Ellen that her son must have met someone truly wonderful.

"I wish she were older though. She's so young, but she really cares for me and she says that she'll wait. I just hope that Mr. McGowan will approve."

Ellen leaned against the counter facing him as she drank her coffee, wondering why Jake McGowan would need to approve. She was about to ask that question when Jim spoke again.

"Jenny is so sweet and innocent. I love her so much, but I don't want to frighten her."

She couldn't have made a sound, because she had stopped breathing, but Jim glanced up at her, the concern evident in his face. Everything happened in slow motion, the cup falling from her hands and crashing to the floor; Jim, calling her name, and racing to catch her as she pitched forward into the blackness, then nothing.

"You're up early!" Jake smiled at his rosy-cheeked daughter as she bounded into the kitchen. He was sitting at the table enjoying a cup of coffee and reading the newspaper. The kitchen was cozy and inviting unlike the formal dinning room that Amanda preferred. Jake was an early riser and often made his own breakfast before going to work.

"Hi, Dad," she responded, kissing him on the cheek, before sitting down opposite him. He studied her flushed face, noticing the brightness of her eyes and wondering what was different about her. She looked absolutely blissful. Her eyes met his then dropped to the brightly patterned tablecloth, fearing that he would see too much. He frowned, laying his newspaper aside.

"Okay, young lady, what are you up to?" The seriousness of his expression told her that it wasn't a question to be taken lightly.

"Dad, I'm just very happy, that's all. It was a wonderful evening and the concert was a huge success, don't you think?" She was talking way too fast.

"Oh to be sure," he responded, dryly, "However, I don't think the concert has anything to do with your present state of mind."

At his words, she felt a warm blush creep into her face and she sincerely hoped that he wouldn't pursue the matter. Her hopes were dashed by his next words.

"I noticed that you were talking to Jim last night just before he left."

Silence filled the room, as she frantically searched her mind for something clever to say. Before she could think of anything, Jake abruptly stood up.

"I've got to leave now, there are some pressing matters waiting for me at work."

She was both puzzled and relieved at his sudden need to go. He leaned over and kissed her gently on the cheek, searching her eyes for a moment, as though trying to read her thoughts.

Walking away was the hardest thing that he'd ever done. He wanted so badly to confront her about her conversation with Jim, because he was certain that things had changed between them. He sighed. They were both so young and Jim was leaving today. Perhaps it's for the best, he told himself as he left the house.

Jenny stood and looked out the window. I was going to be a lovely day, in spite of the fact that Jim was leaving. It would be difficult saying goodbye to him at the train station, but as long as he loved her, she could wait until he came back and then they would never be separated again. She grabbed an apple off the counter and headed out the back door. Dreamy eyed and happy, she climbed the path to the Juniper tree.

When she came to, she was in bed. A very worried Isaac was patting her hand, begging her to wake up. Jim and Lilly hovered nearby, equally distressed over their mother's condition.

Reality returned bringing back the memory of her conversation with Jim. In a shaking voice she asked Jim and Lilly to wait outside the door, while she talked to Isaac. They protested, insisting on taking her to the doctor, immediately. Knowing that this was something a doctor would not be able to fix, she turned pleading eyes to her husband, seeking his support. Isaac studied her expression and turning to the children, he asked if they would give them a few moments alone. As soon as the door closed, Ellen launched herself into Isaac's comforting arms.

"Oh, Isaac," she sobbed, you were right!" He held her, not understanding.

"Ellen, dear, tell me what has happened." She took a deep breath between the sobs.

"You were right when you said it might all blow up in our face one day!"

Once more, she subsided into heart wrenching sobs. He stroked her hair, hoping that by remaining calm, his distraught wife would settle down and tell him why she was in such a state. It seemed to be working, because she appeared to have regained a measure of control, as she looked at him with tear-stained face.

"At first, I thought it must be some cruel joke and that I didn't hear him correctly," her lips began to tremble as she continued, "but I did, Isaac, I did!"

Sensing that she was about to become hysterical again, he took her by the shoulders, shaking her slightly to make her look at him.

"Ellen, for God's sake, *please tell me* what you are talking about?"

"Jim!" she cried, "Is in love with Jenny!"

The silence following her declaration was eloquent. Isaac had turned pale.

"What did you say?"

"You heard me!" she cried bitterly, "Jim thinks he's in love with Jenny and as far as I know she feels the same. I've caused all this and, now, I'm going to lose my children — *all* of them!"

Isaac stared at her as he sat stunned and disbelieving at what he had just heard.

STRADI'S VIOLIN

The sound of her weeping returned as she lay back upon the bed, pressing her face into the pillow, seeking a route of escape from the disaster she had brought upon them.

"Ellen!" Isaac's voice pulled her back. "You've got to tell Jim, now!"

"No!" The pain and agony in her voice, caused him to flinch, but his eyes steadily sought hers, willing her to do what had to be done.

They continued to stare at each other and he could sense the battle going on, as she strived, to come to terms with the inevitable. Moments passed and the struggle seemed to end, signaling that something had been resolved. She looked pale and defeated, but when she spoke, her voice was calm and steady.

"Tell Jim and Lilly to come in." As Isaac went to open the door, Ellen braced herself. It was time to end the deception.

Solemnly, they stood waiting, their thoughts a jumble of questions, as they took in the revenges of distress evident in their mother's face. Their ever-youthful mother had aged before their eyes. Her face was puffy and swollen and the golden hair hung limp and lifeless.

Swinging her legs off the bed, she stood shakily to her feet. Isaac didn't try to stop her, sensing that she needed to be standing.

Jim, protested, but Ellen held up her hand, silencing him before he could continue. Her voice husky with emotion, she spoke,

"What I must say to you will not be easy for either of you," pausing, she looked at her son, "It will be especially hard on you, Jim."

Uncomfortable at the direction the conversation was taking, he started to interrupt, but she was speaking again.

"You both were so young when your father left. You may not remember how desperate, and poor we were but trust me; we were in great need. There was no one we could turn to, because there were no relatives to help us."

Exchanging glances, Jim and Lilly wondered where this conversation was leading.

"Do either of you remember that there was going to be a baby to care for?"

A slight frown wrinkled Jim's forehead as he nodded in response. Lilly had a faint recollection of being told that there would be a new baby brother or sister to play with, but something had happened and the baby had never been mentioned again. Why, now, she wondered, but before she could ask, her mother continued.

"The Depression was making things difficult for everyone, and I had just lost my job. I had no way of supporting myself or the two of you." Here she paused as though trying to collect her thoughts.

Impatiently, Jim shifted from one foot to another. This conversation made no sense to him. He couldn't see how it had anything to do with what had happened earlier.

"I'm not going to relate the entire story or the events leading up to it, because there is really no excuse for what I did," here her voice broke slightly, "But I do hope that each of you will be able to find it in your heart to forgive me, someday, and please try to remember how much I love you." She looked up, her eyes swimming in tears and pleading. They could stand it no longer as they both went to place a comforting arm around her.

"Mother," Jim's voice was rough with emotion, "what are you finding so difficult to tell us? You must know that we'll always love you and nothing you say or do will change that." He smiled briefly at Lilly, who was having difficulty keeping her emotions in check. She appeared on the verge of tears.

"You're going to have to stop this, you're upsetting Lilly and you know what a crybaby she is," he teased half-heartedly.

Ellen drew away, putting some distance between them. Soon, she knew they would not want to comfort her and they would probably despise her for destroying their lives.

Puzzled, they waited to hear what was on her mind. She chose her words carefully so there would be no misunderstanding about what had happened.

"I had a baby girl and I told you that she died at birth, but that was a lie. I gave her to a woman," she was looking directly at Jim as she spoke, "I gave her to a prominent family in Austin who could give her every advantage. Everything I couldn't. In return, I could start a new life with the two of you and we would never have to be poor or homeless again!" The tears were running down her cheeks as she pleaded, "Don't you see? It was for the best! Jim, it was for the best!" she sobbed, looking at him, begging him with her eyes to understand.

The frown that had appeared earlier on his brow increased with each word as his mind shuffled through the given information, seeking a common denominator. Flashbacks, forgotten memories were surfacing with each passing moment, piecing it together with horrendous results.

"What woman, who, Mother?" Lilly was asking with a breathless anticipation that grated on his raw nerves. Harshly, Jim interrupted, his eyes still on his mother,

"Shut-up, Lilly! What does it matter who she gave the baby to?"

Somehow, he had to keep his mother from saying it. His mind was telling him, but his heart rejected it with gut-wrenching intensity. He was pale and suddenly he felt like he might be sick.

Turning on his heel, he headed for the door. He had to get out of here. Isaac had been sitting quietly in the corner, witnessing the pain. He was on his feet and blocking his stepson's route of escape. Jim's tormented eyes looked into Isaac's sad, pity filled ones.

"Get out of my way!" he ground out, but the big man refused to budge. Anger boiled inside him. "Why are you doing this?" he yelled, as his fists clenched and unclenched, wanting badly to lash out and hit.

"Jim!" his mother's voice came from far away,

"Jenny is your sister!"

His world exploded and he was reeling with the after shocks.

"No...o!" Someone shrieked in agony.

His fists were striking a solid wall over and over as his heart along with his dreams lay shattered. He was unable to deny the truth he heard coming from his mother's confession. Isaac endured each blow until the storm inside of Jim subsided.

Chapter 20

Texas Ranger Sam Spaulding sat at his desk reading a report that had been sent from the Dallas office. It was a chilling report involving a series of murders believed committed by one man. From all accounts the man was a cold-blooded killer that preyed on innocent women. First raping his victims, then wrapping his hands around their throats, he choked the life out of them, leaving no witnesses.

Authorities could only guess at his whereabouts. The report suggested that all murders involving a female victim be carefully investigated to see if there were any similarities in the cases. It would be easy to tell, because this killer left a peculiar calling card. It seems that each of the victims, after being brutally choked to death, had a cheap string of pearls placed around their neck by the killer. He'd even been nicknamed, "the Pearl," by authorities. So far, homicide matches had been found in three states, New Mexico, Colorado, and Oklahoma. The identity of the person was unknown, however they did have a suspect. A woman had come forward insisting that the killer was her son, whom she hadn't seen in over fifteen years. She claimed he had tried to kill her once and he had frightened her so badly, that she had packed her things and left, abandoning him to the streets.

The Ranger finished reading and leaned back in his chair, closing his eyes. A man like that would be very cunning and difficult to catch. Fervently, he prayed that this one had not crossed the Texas border.

Melvin Yates stood looking at the ranch house, trying to determine why, at almost high noon, there was no sign of his boss, Isaac Rheinhart. Not that it mattered, because it would give him more time to recover from his bout of drinking last night. He snorted as he looked toward the house once more.

"Must have had quite a night with your little woman," he sneered, "Well enjoy yourself, you German bastard, because soon you won't be able to."

He thought about the news he'd been hearing, lately, about the tyrant, Hitler. Germans were getting less and less popular each day. He'd probably be doing the world a favor if he got rid of one of them.

Feeling his chin, he decided that a shave would definitely make him more presentable. It was important for him to keep up appearances. After all, he didn't want to offend anyone and give *Herr* Rheinhart a reason to fire him. There was a shaving strap and a straight edge razor in the tack room above a makeshift washbasin. Obviously, it had been useful long ago when cowboys got gussied up before a Saturday night on the town. Looking into a flyspecked mirror, he shaved his face, being careful not to cut himself. He had removed his shirt, revealing muscular arms and torso. The large hands were strong with power in them to crush whatever came within their grasp. His unruly, dark hair fell roguishly over one eye. They were the eyes of a man with secrets, dark secrets that would turn a person's blood cold.

His life had started out almost thirty years ago. Born out of wedlock to a woman who didn't want him and whose lifestyle was highly questionable to moral society. His mother and various "uncles" had either ignored or beaten him. He had never known a loving touch of any kind. Violence and anger were his only teachers. So, not surprisingly, somewhere between birth and adolescence, that spark of human decency or conscience had died. Human life was neither respected nor valued, especially where women were concerned. The only thing he could remember about his mother was the strand of pearls that she constantly wore. He was fifteen years old and she was berating him and cursing him, and all he could see was her delicate neck, draped by pearls. That was the first time the blackness had swirled in upon him…when it lifted, he was surprised to see pearls strewn all over the floor and his mother crying and cowering in a corner. She had screamed at him to get out and that was the last time that he ever saw her. Later, when he had come back, all her clothes and things were gone. He had shrugged his shoulders not really caring that he had been abandoned. From then on, he had drifted from place to place.

Hearing the loud bang of a door, he looked up and noticed that the young, sassy blonde with the delectable body had come outside. He remembered how she had looked last night when the dress had clung in all the right spots. Today, she appeared to be in distress over something. Quickly, he replaced his shirt, deciding this was his chance to get acquainted.

Lilly was unaware that she was being watched; her thoughts were on how her mother had lied to them all these years. Like Jim, her mind was still absorbing the shock of her mother's confession. Jenny McGowan was their little sister! It explained why that house had given her a case of the shivers. They had been there and their mother had given birth to Jenny, and then she had told them that their little sister had gone to heaven. She tried to imagine what Jim might be feeling, because for him it had been a betrayal of the worst kind. How awful to find out that the person you were falling in love with, turns out to be your sister! Oh, God, what a mess! The thought brought fresh tears to her eyes. She walked over to the porch swing and sat down, morosely lost in thought.

A large red rose, plucked from a near-by bush, was thrust under her nose. Startled, she looked up into the dark, dangerous eyes of the new hired hand. He winked at her.

"Pretty girl like you shouldn't have anything to cry about."

Embarrassed that he had seen her cry, she quickly looked away ignoring the rose he held out to her.

"Now, honey, there's no reason for you to feel bad. I just hate to see you so unhappy," he consoled, sympathetically.

Once more she looked up at him. He was giving her a dazzling smile full of boyish charm.

"Is there anything I can do?" As he asked the question, he seated himself on the swing next to her.

She had never been this close to him and it wasn't unpleasant. He was a handsome man and he seemed concerned for her, but she was vaguely disconcerted by his presence.

STRADI'S VIOLIN

"By-the-way, my name is Mel Yates, at your service!"

He looked at her expectantly and she realized that he was waiting for her to introduce herself. She knew that her mother and Isaac would not approve of her fraternizing with the hired hand. Following that thought was another one. So what if her mother didn't approve. How could she have any respect for someone that had betrayed her for years with lies and deceit?

Defiantly, she looked at him and still keeping eye contact, she slowly stood to her feet.

"It's a pleasure to know you, Mr. Yates. My name is Lilly."

The seductiveness of her smile and eyes were beginning to turn him on. His eyes caressed the white curve of her throat. The loud banging of the backdoor interrupted, causing them both to jump.

Melvin Yates took in the thundercloud he could see darkening the features of Jim Gibson, and stood to his feet, anticipating trouble. However, Jim wasn't even looking at him as he strode to his sister's side.

"Lilly, I just came to tell you "goodbye," I'm leaving now." Her eyes widened in surprise.

"But, Jim," she pleaded, "it's not time to go to the train station."

Knowing that he could not stay in this house one second more, his voice came out harsh and rather desperate, "Lilly, I have leave, now!" His statement brooked no argument. Silently, she placed her arm around his waist and together they walked around to the front of the house. His luggage was already stowed in the car. He turned to his sister once more, wishing he could say something to make her understand why he must leave. Instead, he hugged her.

"Lilly, promise me that you will take care of yourself and, remember, I love you," he squeezed her hand.

"Oh, Jim, do you have to go?" she cried.

Smoothing her long hair back from her face, he spoke softly, almost a whisper.

"Yes, more than ever, now."

"Jim, what about Jenny!" she blurted out without thinking.

Turning away, impatiently, he called to Isaac who was driving him to the station.

"I don't have time for this, Lilly. Just take care of yourself. I'll write to you when I get settled, okay?"

She could tell that it would be pointless to argue.

"Please be careful, Jim."

They embraced once more and he started to kiss her on the forehead, but unbidden, a picture flashed through his mind, causing him to wince in pain. Hurriedly, he transferred the kiss to her cheek before getting into the car.

Isaac gave his wife a comforting look as they both watched Jim say goodbye to Lilly. Ellen desperately wanted to hold her son and beg his forgiveness before he left, but she dared not make the first overture. He had made it plain that he wanted nothing more to do with her.

He glanced in his mother's direction once, but looked quickly away. Isaac was behind the wheel. He released the brake and then hesitated briefly.

"Are you sure you don't want to say goodbye to your mother?" he spoke gruffly, keeping his eyes straight ahead.

Jim laughed, cruelly, "What mother? I don't have a mother!"

Isaac's jaw clenched and unclenched. Controlling his temper, he decided to let it go. Jim was hurting pretty badly right now. He just hoped that once the pain was gone, he wouldn't allow stubborn pride to shut Ellen out forever.

As the car rolled forward, Lilly ran along side, waving goodbye. She waved until the car was out of sight. Slowly, she walked back to the house. Her mother was staring at where the car had disappeared down the road, with tears streaming down her face.

Lilly was moved with pity, but she was still angry. Sighing, she realized it would take time for them to heal, maybe a very long time. Ignoring her mother's pleading look, she walked past her into the house.

Melvin Yates had been watching and listening. He had figured out that some type of disagreement had caused a family rift. He smiled. It could work to his advantage. Soon, he would have the lovely, Lilly, right in the palm of his hand. He remembered the way she had looked at him before her brother had interrupted. Thinking about her brought the darkness swirling in upon him. He remembered her creamy skin. Her eyes, lips and the long, smooth neck. Sweat beaded his forehead and, vaguely, he felt the sting of pain. Slowly, the mist cleared. He looked down in surprise. The red rose had been crushed in his hand and drops of blood stained the petals where the sharp barbs had pierced his skin.

Jim watched as Isaac walked away leaving him at the train station. He knew that his stepfather was disappointed in him. The whole journey here, Isaac had tried to reason with him about Ellen, but he was not ready to listen. His life had been turned upside down by his mother's deception concerning Jenny. Dear, God, just thinking about her made him sick, because for his feelings to make the transition from sweetheart to sister was not, yet, possible. It would take time, but not right now.

He looked down at the ticket for New York City that was clenched in his hand. Making a decision, he walked determinedly to the ticket counter.

"Sir, excuse me, but I've changed my mind about going to New York."

The gray-haired stationmaster turned from the board where he was posting the train schedules. He stared at him over his spectacles.

"Well, young feller, where would you like to go?"

Jim looked at him in surprise. It hadn't occurred to him where he would go, but he knew that he could not carry out his dream to be a reporter, at least, not on Jake McGowan's and the *Lone Star Chronicle's* generosity.

He looked up to hear the man saying rather impatiently, "Son, I haven't got all day, what do you want to do?"

Jim licked his lips. He'd never been on his own, especially with no place to go and no plans. Quickly, making up his mind, he shoved the ticket through the window toward the man.

"Look, I've decided not to leave after all, could you please refund the money?"

He could tell by the old man's expression that he probably thought he was a lunatic. Taking the ticket, he paused,

"Are you sure this is what you want?"

Seeing Jim's determined look and the curt nod of his head, the stationmaster moved away to make the necessary adjustments to his books and soon he returned with the money.

Jim then asked him for an envelope and putting the refunded ticket money inside, he addressed it to Jake in care of the *Lone Star Chronicle*. After securing a promise from the stationmaster to have it delivered, he walked out of the train station, knowing that he was leaving all those he loved and his dreams behind. Outside, he paused, drawing in a deep breath. He had done the right thing by burning his bridges, and now was not the time for regrets. Knowing that he did not have a lot of money, he allowed his footsteps to carry him in the direction of the bus station. As he neared his destination, he noticed a boisterous group of young men. Their voices were loud and they sounded stirred up about something. One of them, a former classmate, called out to him.

"Hey, Jim! Are you joining the Army, too?"

"Yeah!" another one chimed in, "We're going to Europe to teach Hitler a thing or two!"

The others shouted their support at the prospect of humbling the tyrant.

In reality, joining the Army had been the farthest thing from his mind, but suddenly the idea appealed to him. After all, it was the perfect solution.

An olive drab army bus screeched to a halt beside the group and a man in uniform jumped down and begin barking orders. He looked them up and down as though they were the scum of the earth. Then he was in their face, baring his teeth and yelling obscenities.

"You baby-faced, Mama's boys, get your butts on that bus!"

Stumbling over each other in their haste to obey, they clamored aboard. He grinned to himself, swinging up behind them as the bus roared off down the street.

"Yes, sir, Uncle Sam's gonna love takin' care of you!"

Jenny was busy searching the crowd at the train station. It was almost 4:00 and the train was due to leave soon for New York. Standing on tiptoe, she peered over heads, searching in vain. He wasn't here! She was starting to have a bad feeling. Something must have happened to him, she reasoned, as her eyes darted back and forth seeking the familiar figure.

Grimly, Jake watched his daughter's desperation as she frantically looked for Jim. An envelope had been delivered to his office a short time earlier and he had been astounded to find enclosed, a refund for the ticket he had purchased for Jim. There was no explanation, nothing. Immediately, he had gone to the station in search of answers. The train master had confirmed that a young man, fitting Jim's description, had, indeed, been there and had asked for a refund. Other than that, he didn't have a clue as to Jim's whereabouts or plans. Jake had waited around, hoping that Jim would change his mind and return to the station. That's when he had spied Jenny and the reason for her being here was clear to him. He hated to see her hurt and it was obvious by the desperate look on her face that she was beginning to feel the pain. He walked up behind her and tapped her on the shoulder. She spun around, thinking that Jim had found her. A smile lit her features, but quickly fled as she met her father's disapproving stare.

"Daddy, wha —t are you doing here?" she stammered.

"I believe that should be my question to you!" Jake shot back, causing her to flinch.

At her downcast look, he deliberately gentled his tone, although, rage was boiling up inside him. *After all I've done for you, Jim, how could you do this?* he seethed to himself.

"Come, Jenny, its time to leave, now."

"But, Daddy," she started to protest, until the uncompromising look on his face halted her words.

He took her small, cold hand and placed it through his arm, leading her away from the train station. He could sense her reluctance as she kept glancing back over her shoulder, silently, willing Jim to appear.

Rose had finished watering her plants and stood watching the discontented young man as he skipped rocks across the pond. He was so handsome, well, she amended, not handsome in the conventional sense, but he had the rugged good looks that attracted the opposite sex like bees to honey.

It had been quite a surprise when he had shown up on their doorstep a week ago. All grown up, she hadn't known who he was until he introduced himself. She marveled at seeing him after all these years. He was the grandson of her beloved dead brother, Malcolm.

There had been some speculation between her and Leon as to why he should come here all the way from Boston. So far, he had not been very forthcoming as to why he had suddenly decided to visit his great-aunt in Dallas. Not that she was complaining, after all, he was family.

Garret Davenport lobed a rock and watched it skip along the water, to the other side. At the age of twenty-four, his tobacco brown hair was thick and wavy. He owed his trim body and healthy tan to the hours spent playing tennis and swimming. His features were nothing out of the ordinary, except that his lips were rather full, giving him a sensuous look that drove female acquaintances crazy.

Probably, his most arresting feature was his eyes. They were a smoky gray, turning almost silver, when he was happy or pleased, but they could quickly change to a flinty gray if something or someone upset him. Right now his thoughts weren't very pleasant and they persisted in hounding him, even as he tried to release them into the rocks, that he sent skipping across the water.

The only son of a wealthy lawyer, he had been expected to follow in his father's footsteps and enter the world of high finance and corporate law. Soon after graduating Harvard Law School, he had signed on as a junior partner in the law firm. Everything had gone well until he had involved himself in a scandal with the daughter of his father's partner. It was the age-old tale of a scorned lover and revenge. Wining and dinning the stunning Miss Sarah Infield had not been a problem. The problem had come later when he tried to break off the relationship. After his initial passion had cooled and he had gotten to know her better, he saw things about her that displeased him. Her selfish, spoiled ways begin to grate on his nerves. For both their sakes, he decided to end the affair.

Lovers never left Sarah Infield; she left them. Being dumped like a sack of garbage was something she could not endure. So to get even, she had lied, crying sexual compromise and ruin. Her plan had almost worked, but in the end, former acquaintances of the male gender, were secured to give testimony. The results had been unfavorable, but Miss Infield and her family continued to proclaim her innocence.

The scandal had wrecked havoc and a life-long partnership had been dissolved with much bitterness. Boston society was not quick to forgive, so to save his family further embarrassment, he had resigned his position and left.

Two places were never more different. Boston was sophisticated and somber. Dallas was backward and brash. It was his father's suggestion that he come to Texas and to his "aunt" Rose. At first, he had balked at the idea of going to a virtual stranger, but after meeting her, it felt right. She and her husband were kind and thoughtful. They welcomed without asking questions or prying.

Rose turned from her contemplative study of her great-nephew and hurried to answer the ringing telephone. On the other end, Jake waited impatiently for his mother or Franz to pick up the phone.

He had been astounded last night when Amanda had come to him and practically demanded that Jenny go to Rose at once. Normally, he would have baited her about her sudden change of attitude about their daughter living with his mother, but he, too, felt it was best for Jenny to go.

He needed to find out where Jim was without his daughter knowing. He had warned Jenny to put him out of her mind, but, in truth, he was worried. *Damn!* he chided himself, *I should have seen this coming.*

He was convinced that Jim's disappearance had something to do with Jenny. The boy would never have given up his dream unless he had come up against something that he felt incapable of handling. Jenny could be very persuasive when she put her mind to it and her infatuation with Jim had probably driven him away. He felt guilty for thinking this way, but it was the only explanation that made any sense.

"Mother...."

"Son!" she interrupted him gaily, "guess who has come here for a visit?" He didn't want to be rude, but he was in no mood for a guessing game.

"Mother, I'm calling about Jenny." Immediately, Rose picked up on the strain in his voice.

"Is she okay? Has something happened to her?"

"No, no, everything is fine, but could I bring her to Dallas earlier than planned?"

Rose sensed the urgency behind the request.

"Of course, you know that we would love to have her, but you sound so concerned. Are you sure everything is okay?"

Feeling on edge, he regretted the impatience in his voice, but he couldn't help it.

"Yes, Mother, I'll explain later. We'll be there sometime tomorrow." He rang off shortly, not giving her the opportunity to tell him about Garret.

Oh, well, she thought, *it'll be a nice surprise.*

Anyway, she was more concerned by his apparent sense of urgency. "Franz!" she called out to her husband, as she hurried away to tell him the news.

Jenny sat on the bench beneath the Juniper tree. Sadly, she remembered a couple of nights ago when Jim had come here with her. What could have gone wrong? Tears begin to flow once again. Her mother had been angry and exasperated over the amount of crying she had done last night. Only her father's intervention had curbed Amanda's relentless questions and condemnation. Finally, she had been allowed to escape to the privacy of her room, where she had lain awake, crying for hours.

On the way home from the train station, her father had told her about Jim returning the money for the train ticket and then disappearing. He said that Jim must have decided to pursue other interests and for her own good, she should just forget about him. She refused to listen, knowing in her heart, that Jim would not give up his dream without a good reason.

Then her father informed her that she would be leaving for Dallas as soon as he could arrange it with her grandmother. She cried and pleaded that she couldn't leave right now, but it had been obvious that her father wasn't listening.

She looked up at the bright blue sky, her dreams shattered, and demanded to know *why*. It just didn't make any sense. Even though she was young and inexperienced, she had known that Jim cared for her. He had been sincere when he had asked her to wait for him. Something terrible must have happened.

Restlessly, she stood to her feet and walked to the edge of the cliff and looked out at the vast expanse with the city of Austin sprawled far below.

"Where are you, Jim," she spoke aloud as though expecting an answer, but the only audible sound was the wind stirring through the Juniper tree.

Amanda sat in front of the mirror, trying to apply her make-up with shaking hands. Her nerves had been shattered since her confrontation last night with Jake. She had been trying to find out what had Jenny so upset, and she would have, too, if he hadn't interfered!

After sending Jenny off to bed, she and Jake had argued. Finally, he had relented and told her about Jim. She had been outraged that he had allowed their daughter to get involved with some boy that was obviously unsuitable! Heatedly, Jake had defended his protégé, insisting that he was both smart and ambitious. In turn, she had pointed out that if he were really such a paragon of intelligence, why hadn't he gone to New York? She questioned him further about the boy's background. Sarcastically, he reminded her that she had been introduced to him at Jenny's concert the other night, *and* to his sister. Racking her brain, she tried to remember, but she had been so upset with Jake that night, that she had barely glanced at the couple. At the time, it didn't seem important, but now she demanded to know his name.

"Jim Gibson!" Jake ground out through clenched teeth, "and he lives about 50 miles Southeast of here on the Thacker Ranch, with his mother, sister and step-father. Anymore questions!" Not giving her time to respond, he turned on his heel and left the room.

Jim Gibson, ...Gibson, she turned over the name in her mind as she slowly sank to the sofa.

No! It can't be! she cried, as memories from the past swooped in on her with terrifying clarity. The Thacker Ranch where she had sent Ellen Gibson and her two brats! Horrified, her hands flew to her mouth. She stood up in a rush as the full impact of it hit her.

Jenny and.... her brother! No, no, this can't be happening! she moaned, and putting her hands on either side of her head, she swayed back and forth like an animal in pain.

Refusing to take the blame for this fiasco, her bitterness and hatred found their target...Jake! *It's his fault, if he hadn't allowed Jenny to be around that boy, this would never have happened*! Her panic increased as she thought about what Jake had said about the money from the train ticket being returned. *Where was the Gibson boy and what if he had decided at the last moment that he couldn't leave Jenny?* Panic crept in as she thought of other possibilities such as Jenny finding out about her "real" family. And Jake, heaven help her, if he should find out the truth!

Even though, she had been against Jenny living with Rose and Franz, she quickly decided that getting her daughter out of town was of the utmost importance. Fear lent wings to her feet, as she had gone in search of Jake.

The trip to Dallas had been long and tedious. Jenny had been silent, refusing to be drawn into conversation. She was pale and Jake noticed that once or twice she had bitten down on her lips to stop their trembling. He felt frustrated and helpless. He was also very worried and wanted to question Jenny about what had transpired between her and Jim, because he was more convinced than ever that something had happened. Jim had seemingly vanished. Before leaving Austin, he had called the Thacker Ranch and Lilly had answered the phone. Her bubbling personality seemed to have gone flat and she had been nervous about something. In fact, he had sensed that she was reluctant to talk to him at all. Pretending that he had forgotten Jim's departure time for New York, Lilly quickly informed him that the train had left the day before, at 4:00 in the afternoon, and that Jim was on his way to New York.

Sensing, by the strain in her voice, that something was wrong, he had asked her if everything was okay. Hastily, she had assured him that *everything* was fine. Jake instinctively knew that Lilly was withholding something. He wondered if Jim had told his sister that he had decided not to go to New York and why. Determinedly, Jake vowed that once he got his daughter settled in Dallas, he was going to get to the bottom of this situation.

He felt relieved as he pulled up to his mother's house. He glanced at his daughter once more, but she had her eyes closed to avoid his unwelcome questions. Sighing, he knew that he must have handled the situation badly. Thank goodness his mother was around to help, because if anyone could get through to Jenny, it was Rose.

As soon as she caught sight of her grandmother and Franz coming down the path to greet them, she felt the prickle of returning tears. Her grandmother, if no one else, would understand and sympathize with her misery. She greeted Franz, but it was Rose she threw her arms around and clung to with fierce intensity. Rose smiled over her granddaughter's head at her bewildered husband. Reading the message in his wife's eyes, he discreetly moved away and went to help Jake with the luggage.

STRADI'S VIOLIN

He watched the family greetings from his upstairs bedroom window as he studied the distinguished looking, gray-haired man that was his father's cousin. He was large and powerfully built and it was easy to imagine him running a newspaper empire. Straining to see the dark-haired girl accompanying her grandmother into the house, he had his first glimpse of the famous Miss McGowan. Franz Leonie had sung her praises along with his aunt, until his curiosity was piqued. He had listened to them, half amused, thinking that surely they exaggerated the girl's ability with the violin. *For heaven's sake*, he thought, *from all appearances, she's hardly more than a child*! Allowing the curtain to fall back into place, he moved away from the window. He heard voices below as they entered the foyer. They would probably enjoy some private time together, he concluded, deciding not to intrude. There would be plenty of time to meet them later.

Picking up the newspaper, he resumed his perusal of world events. The United States was moving closer and closer to involvement in the war being fought in Europe. Already, American troops were being trained at break-neck speed and mobilized.

Laying the paper aside, he stood and paced, restlessly. Back in Boston, he had taken flying lessons and for several years, now, he held a valid pilot's license. His talents could be useful in the Army Air Corps. The only thing holding him back was the disapproval he knew would come from his father. The elder Davenport was firmly against U.S. involvement in the war. Normally, this would not have stopped him, but the recent upheaval he had caused pressed on his conscience and he was reluctant to disappoint his father again.

Rose accompanied her grand daughter upstairs to the bedroom that would be hers. She helped her put her things away and they talked, but Jenny had not confided in her about any of the things that were bothering her. Wisely, Rose did not push. Leaving her to freshen up before dinner, she went downstairs to find Franz and Jake.

As soon as she appeared, Jake confronted her about their "other" houseguest.

"Mother, Franz tells me that a long, lost relative arrived unannounced." His eyebrows rose in silent question, as he waited for her response.

"Actually, dear," she smiled while she patted his cheek as though explaining to a small child, "he's your second cousin." He looked at her sardonically as he spoke,

"Why the sudden interest in this side of the family?"

Rose could tell Jake was less than pleased by the "surprise" guest.

"Now, Jake, Garret's a good boy...you be kind to him!" she scolded.

Mockingly, Jake placed his hand over his heart, as though he had been misunderstood.

"Mother, have I ever been less than kind to one of your guest?" Wickedly, he winked at Franz, who was busy trying to hide his chuckles in a cough, causing Rose to turn on him.

"Don't you dare encourage him!" she warned indignantly.

"Yes, dear," he replied with false meekness, causing Rose to throw her hands up in despair over the two conspirators. She gave them one final, disapproving look before she hurried off to see about dinner preparations.

Jenny had finished her bath and was drying with a large fluffy white towel. Her dark hair had been secured on top of her head. Dark, damp tendrils hung down against creamy, flawless skin. Her thoughts, as usual, were on Jim. Pain showed clearly in the large green eyes. For the young girl just learning to explore her femininity and budding emotions, it was a tragic time. At least, she thought it so. She had no way of knowing that Jim had barely touched the surface of the woman that she would eventually be. For all her grown up ways, emotionally, she was still a child.

She wound the huge towel around her and left the steamy bathroom, her thoughts still filled with the tragedy of lost love. She bumped into something solid and almost lost her grip on the towel. Strong hands reached out to steady her. Looking up in alarm, she met the distinctly amused eyes of Garret Davenport. Frantically, she pulled away from him.

"Wha.*who*...?" her scattered wits were making her incoherent.

He bowed from the waist as he spoke, "The talented, lady McGowan, I presume."

Clinging to her towel as though it were a lifeline, she replied in her most haughty tone,

"*Who* are you and what are you doing in my grandmother's house!"

Her cheeks had turned a vivid red, whether from temper or embarrassment at her lack of clothing, Garret wasn't sure.

"I don't think that in your present state of... hmm..." he pretended to be at a loss for words, "undress, that we should introduce ourselves. Perhaps, you'd like to get put on some clothes first," he suggested, with amusement evident in his voice. She remained silent, but he could feel her rage.

"Come, little girl, don't look so tragic. That towel is quite fetching and, anyway, the woman's anatomy is not unfamiliar to me. Of course," he looked at her contemplatively, "you're not, yet, a woman, are you?"

Jenny's fury had mounted at his arrogance and at the way his strange, silvery eyes mocked her. Keeping the towel tightly in her grip and with head held high, she walked down the hallway to her bedroom. She felt his gaze following her as she walked past. At the door, she turned, her green eyes shooting sparks.

"I don't care *who* you are, my grandmother will have you thrown out when I tell her how rude you've been!" His laughter followed her into the bedroom and she slammed the door in her fury. Hateful man! She would never forgive him for his behavior. She hoped he would be gone when she went downstairs to dinner. Oh, no! Her hands flew to her hot cheeks. The fact the he was in the house and upstairs meant that he must be a guest! If that were the case, they would likely meet again.

"Oh, Lord," she moaned, "I'll just die of embarrassment!" Lying down on the bed, she squeezed her eyes tightly closed, trying to blot out his mocking face. Turning onto her stomach, she felt the tears slip past her closed eyes.

"Jim," she cried in desperation, "*where* are you?"

Garret was smiling as he made his way downstairs. His little cousin was quite a spitfire. Once again he smiled as he recalled her indignant outrage at his lack of manners. Well, he conceded to himself, he had baited her unmercifully. It would definitely be interesting to see how she would react when they met next.

He entered the parlor, treading softly, so as not to draw attention to himself and took in the tall, distinguished figure of Jake McGowan as he and Franz debated the handling of the war in Europe. He noted that the man's silver gray hair was as thick as his own and his body looked fit and trim. The legendary Jake McGowan, head of a newspaper empire, he acknowledged to himself. Silently, he studied the man that was Rose's son, and that Franz held in such high esteem.

The uncanny feeling that he was being watched caused Jake to pause in his conversation. Turning, he came face to face with the stranger that was scrutinizing him so closely. Returning the stare and allowing his eyes to do their own measuring up, he waited. A test of wills seemed to prevail between the two men.

Hesitantly, Franz interrupted their silent battle to begin the introductions. Each silently acknowledged the other as they shook hands.

Jake decided to break the ice.

"Well," he drawled, "So you are Uncle Malcolm's grandson." It was more a statement of fact than a question.

"Yes, I do have that distinguished privilege," Garret replied, sardonically.

Franz sought to break the tension as they continued to stare at each other like two combatants.

"Gentlemen," he interrupted, "Let's be seated and continue our discussion."

Jake chose a seat opposite the younger man. "Garret," Franz was saying, "We were discussing the impending war with Germany."

Franz was relieved to notice that the tension seemed to be dissipating, and he largely carried the conversation and the atmosphere was definitely more relaxed. Jake was smoking a cigar as he half listened, while watching Garret. He wanted to ask him point blank what he was doing here in Dallas instead of practicing law in Boston with his father.

Garret, too, was listening politely, while being aware of Jake's scrutiny. He could almost read the man's mind. He knew that Jake was wondering why he was here, living with *his* mother, with no apparent future plans.

Suddenly, Jake stubbed out the cigar and rose to his feet. "You know, Franz," he drawled, " I think that a *real* man would be thinking about joining the army and helping rid the world of the tyrant,

Hitler." His eyes spoke volumes as he looked pointedly in Garret's direction.

The implications were not lost on the younger man. He stood, his eyes glinting and sauntered over to Jake.

"Well, cousin, old man, take heart," he said, slapping him on the back, "They may run out of young blood and come looking for you!"

Jake sputtered at the man's insolence. No one had ever spoken to him like that, at least, not in his presence and still remained standing. His proud head came back and the fury in his eyes would have sent many a man scurrying for cover. Garret stood his ground, his eyes never wavering from Jake's face. What would have happened next, no one would ever know. Dinner was announced and a relieved Franz ushered them quickly into the dining room.

Lilly stared at the phone she was holding in annoyance. That was about the fifth time that a woman had called asking to speak to Jim. She told her before that Jim had left for New York, but the woman kept calling. What was even stranger, she had a Spanish accent. This time, Lilly had asked for her name, but the woman had hung up, quickly, without responding. Shrugging her shoulders and replacing the receiver, she decided to go outside for some fresh air.

The evening was warm and she could smell Nora's Rose garden. She smiled to herself, remembering how Nora had fussed over the giant blooms. Then her thoughts took a sobering turn as she wondered how Jim was coping with his pain. She was curious to know if Jake McGowan had gotten in touch with him. She hoped that Mr. McGowan wouldn't think too badly of her after their strained conversation yesterday, but after the revelation about Jenny, she had felt less than honest in talking to him. It was odd, but she felt guilty, like she had done something wrong. Sighing, she turned and as a shadow loomed in front of her, she let out a frightened cry.

"Oh, it's you!" she laughed, nervously, to make up for her sudden outburst.

Melvin Yates stood blocking her path. His eyes glittered in the evening shadows, giving him a sinister look that caused a chill to run down her spine. She shook off the feeling as his face came into the moonlight, giving him a softer appearance. He smiled at her and, gently, yet firmly, took her hand and placed it through his arm.

"Sweet girl, you don't have to be afraid of anything with me around to protect you," he drawled soothingly.

"You look so sad and I can't allow that. What can I do to cheer you up?" Answering his own question, he snapped his fingers, "I know! There's something real special that I want to show you. It's in the barn. Come on!"

He looked at her questioningly, as she appeared to be reluctant to go with him. She looked back at the house and Isaac's large figure was framed in the lighted doorway as he strained to see into the darkness.

"Lilly!" he called.

Quickly, Melvin drew back into the shadows so he couldn't be seen. She spoke in low tones, "I have to go in now." Without waiting for a response, she hurried to the welcoming light of the house.

Frustration made him almost frantic. He slammed his fist against the wall of the bunkhouse. Perspiration beaded his forehead, as he opened the satchel that held his belongings. He searched until he pulled out a long strand of cheap pearls, and staring at them he thought how beautiful that would look on Lilly. He pictured how they would look draped around her lovely, white throat. Carrying them to his bunk, he lay down and continued to run his fingers over their smooth texture. The action calmed his overwrought nerves. Tonight, he would have given them to her, if that German swine hadn't interfered! Swearing, he snapped the fragile string holding the pearls and watched as they flew helter-skelter over the bunkhouse floor.

Embarrassment gave Jenny's skin a feverish glow. She felt the heat sweep up her neck, as all eyes seemed to follow her to her place at the dinner table. Her father had risen and pulled out a chair for her to be seated. She was glad that she had left her long hair down, because it swung forward like a curtain, hiding her face from view.

"Garret," her grandmother was saying, "I want you to meet my lovely, talented granddaughter, Jenny."

The pride and love in Rose's voice left no doubt as to her feelings about the child. Garret rose and walked around the table and stood beside the blushing, young girl.

"Oh, and Jenny, darling, this is my brother Malcolm's grandson from Boston!"

Jenny's head remained bowed as though she were studying the pattern on the delicate china plate. It felt as though she were trapped in a nightmare and, from far away, she heard her grandmother's voice.

"I suppose you two could consider yourself cousins," her grandmother had happily declared. Barely lifting her head and still not meeting his eyes, she heard the rich tenor of his voice somewhere above her head.

"It is my distinct pleasure, Miss McGowan. I have heard so much about you that I feel we are acquainted already."

Jenny could hear the amusement in his voice. He paused as though waiting for a response, but when none was forthcoming he continued.

"Franz tells me that the two of you do a mean duet. I sincerely hope to have the pleasure of hearing you play after dinner."

She knew that her mumbled reply was less than gracious, but she had no intention of playing her beloved violin for this man! The small drama had not escaped the notice of Jake and Franz, who exchanged glances.

Garret winked at his great-aunt as he contemplated her puzzled demeanor over her granddaughter's strange behavior. He took his seat once again at the table, causing Jenny to sigh to herself in relief.

Sensing her granddaughter's discomfort, Rose began talking, hoping to divert everyone's attention away from her. It worked, because soon lively conversation filled the dining hall.

Slowly, Jenny lifted her head. Steeling her nerves she ventured a look in the direction of her grandmother's houseguest. She regretted it immediately; because the hateful man lifted his glass in a mocking salute and his strange eyes glinted at her wickedly.

Drat him! she thought to herself, *He's the interloper here and I will not be intimidated!* Firmly, she sat her glass down, then, swept her hair back from her face. Her expressive green eyes shot sparks of fire as she defiantly meet Garret's stare. This man would never make her cower or let down her defenses. She didn't like him and she would do everything in her power to let him know it.

Garret read the message in her eyes, but was not bothered by it. He smiled broadly and winked at her. Her look of distaste at his outrageous behavior and the dislike for him that showed clearly in her eyes, also, failed to impress him. Had he wanted to, he could have charmed her as he had countless others, but he wasn't sufficiently interested. For all her implied sophistication, she was too young and too inexperienced for his taste. Oh, she was very pretty and no doubt, one day would be quite a beauty, but before she would become an interesting woman to him or any man, she had a lot of growing up to do. He doubted if Jake McGowan would want that to happen too soon. From what he could tell, she was just another spoiled, little rich girl. Her daddy probably took care of every problem that came her way. Heaven help her if she ever had to think or act for herself.

Feeling bored and suddenly out-of-sorts, he turned his attention back to the conversation around the table. Determinedly, he put Jenny McGowan entirely out of his thoughts.

Amanda was beside herself with worry. All her attempts to find Jim had failed. Her housekeeper, Maria, had called the Thacker Ranch numerous times for her, with no results.

She thought of arranging a meeting with Ellen and demanding to know what was going on, but she was afraid of Jake finding out. After all there may be nothing to worry about, she reasoned with herself. Now that Jenny out of Austin, maybe the problem would resolve itself.

After dinner everyone retired to the parlor and soon Franz had coerced Garret into a game of chess. Sensing that this was his final opportunity to talk with Jenny, Jake approached his daughter with some trepidation, hoping for a sign that she had forgiven him. Her sullen expression was not encouraging.

"Er, Jenny, could I have a word with you in the study, *please*," he added for good measure.

She nodded her head slightly, but clung to her grandmother's hand, insisting that Rose come with them. This was not the way he wanted it, but under the circumstances, he had no choice. Rose diplomatically tried to make an excuse not to come, but Jenny would have none of it.

After they were comfortably seated in the study, Jake decided that attack might be the quicker way to find out what had happened.

"Jenny, I know your grandmother is not up to speed on recent events, but I must come directly to the point. I'm going to ask you point-blank and I hope you will answer me truthfully," he paused, momentarily, and seeing the stubborn set of her jaw, he knew this would be an uphill battle, "Jenny, at the party, I saw you and Jim in deep conversation and I also know that he disappeared from the party for a time. Were you with him?" Her eyes flicked toward him briefly, but his question was met with silence.

Rose felt uncomfortable, eavesdropping on a private conversation, but obviously this was something gravely important or Jake and Jenny would not be at such odds.

"For God's sake, Jenny!" Jake exploded, "I'm on your side. I'm just trying to make sense out of what has happened." Her eyes filled with tears as she looked at him.

"You blame me for Jim's disappearance!" anguish filled her voice.

"That's absurd!" Jake bellowed.

Rose stood up. "That's enough, Jake. Can't you see that you're frightening the child? I don't understand all that has happened, but I'm sure Jenny didn't have anything to do with the young man's disappearance."

"Mother, I think you should let me handle this," Jake interrupted.

Facing Jake, she stood her ground. "Well, I do understand this - nothing is ever resolved by screaming and yelling. I'm sure if you will come over here and sit by your daughter and *try* talking to her calmly, everything will make sense."

Defeated, Jake did as his mother suggested. Jenny still wasn't looking at him.

"Sweetheart, I love you and I know that I've handled this pretty badly. I only want what's best for you and I can't stand to see you unhappy. Jenny, please look at me!" Slowly, she did as he asked. In silence, he searched her eyes seeing the pain and confusion.

"My darling girl," he held his arms wide, "can you ever forgive me?" With a loud sob, Jenny threw herself into her father's arms. "Oh, Daddy," she cried. I love you, too. I'm so worried about Jim." Her tears fell faster as she agonized over something she didn't understand.

"Daddy, what did I do wrong?" she sobbed brokenly. Jake was stroking her hair as he tried to calm her, "Honey, listen to me, you didn't do anything wrong! Please, stop crying. You will make yourself ill." Over his daughter's head, his eyes met his mother's. "Thank you, Mom," he mouthed.

Rose smiled. She had known that once they came to an understanding, Jenny would let down her defenses and she would be willing to talk to Jake.

After regaining a measure of control, she told Jake everything, including the conversation under the Juniper tree. He listened intently and from what she told him, he still had trouble putting the pieces together. It was more puzzling than ever. Jim had wanted to go to New York. He also cared for Jenny, enough to wait for her to grow up. Maybe, Jim had gotten cold feet and was worried that he would disapprove of his intentions toward his daughter. No, he rejected that notion immediately. So why had Jim decided not to go to New York and where was he now? Jake's thoughts ran rampant as he considered different possibilities. So what or who had changed his mind? Maybe something had happened at home. Yes, he decided that had to be it. His thoughts were interrupted as Jenny tugged at his arm.

"Daddy, where is Jim?" Her eyes filled with tears once more.

"Jenny, I promise you, when I get back to Austin, I'll do everything in my power to find out." She hugged him in relief. "Thank you, Daddy, that's all I wanted."

Rose had been listening as intently as Jake, and she, too, was concerned about the young man's whereabouts. However, she felt that Jenny had been drained enough from this emotional upheaval.

"Come, child, it is time you were in bed. I'll fix you a nice cup of warm cocoa to make you sleep."

Garret watched from his upstairs bedroom window as Jake said "goodbye" to his daughter. As he watched, he brooded over the events of last evening. Jake, Aunt Rose and Jenny had disappeared for quite a while. When Jake had returned to the parlor, he seemed to be in a better frame of mind. Garret confessed to himself that he had played chess very poorly, causing Franz to cluck at him reprovingly when he made a wrong move for the second time. His concentration was lost, once again, when Aunt Rose and Jake had remained aloof, talking in quite, somber tones. Franz had given up in disgust, after winning three games in a row.

Garret slowly pulled the curtain aside so he could see more clearly. It appeared that Jenny was pleading with her father about something. Jake reached out and patted her shoulder reassuringly. She stood on tiptoe and kissed his cheek. His face somber, he ducked into the car and then waved to her as he put the car in motion. She stood for a long time watching the car disappear down the road. Garret wondered what that was all about and if it had anything to do with him. He supposed not, because if he were no longer welcome here, he was certain that Jake would have taken great pleasure in asking him to leave.

Chapter 21

He bolted upright as the first notes of the bugle sounded reveille. It never failed to startle him and, groaning, he fell backwards on his bunk.

"You'd better move your butt, Gibson, the Sarge will tear you apart if you're still there when he comes in."

His Army buddy, Ed Wallace, determinedly shook the bunk bed as he stood over him grinning from ear to ear. Jim opened one eye and peered up at him, thinking how much he looked like Alfalfa of the Little Rascals.

It was funny how the army threw people together who would have otherwise not met. Most were from vastly different backgrounds and had they passed on the street probably would not have acknowledged each other.

The Sarge had drilled it into them that everybody in your platoon was your buddy and it was your duty to look out for each other. Soon they would face the enemy, shoulder to shoulder, and then it wouldn't matter a hill of beans who you were or where you came from.

Ed Wallace was a backwoods, boy from Tennessee. His colorful rendition of life in the Tennessee hills had drawn Jim to him or perhaps the writer in him had been drawn. At any rate Ed was often the subject of the material that he wrote about in his journal.

He had decided that keeping a journal would occupy his mind and satisfy the writer in him. It would help him to keep his thoughts clear and on the task at hand. He would not, *could not*, think about the past or why he was here instead of New York.

Hearing the thud of approaching footsteps, he quickly assumed the position beside his bunk. The door burst open and Sergeant Flannery strode inside. Planting his feet wide, with hands on hips, he quickly surveyed the quarters. Then with voice booming, he roared.

"Okay, you sweet, little Mama's boys, get your gear together! We're goin' for a stroll!"

Instantly, they knew what that meant - full field gear and weapons. They were training for war. A war that seemed far away and unreal to them and some, naively, thought it would be over before they finished basic training.

Ellen placed a handful of spring flowers from the garden on Nora's grave. Kneeling, she stared at the headstone, almost as though she were willing the woman to appear.

"Oh, Nora," she spoke softly, "I've made such a mess of things! I wish you were here to advise me and tell me that everything will be okay."

Wistfully, she shook her head at her fanciful thoughts. She didn't have to hear Nora speak to know exactly what she would say and do. She might berate her for her duplicity, but then she would say that there was no use crying over spilled milk and to get on with her life. But most of all, she would tell her to be honest and to stop making excuses. That would mean confronting Jenny and the McGowans. Jenny would probably despise her just as Jim and Lilly did, but at least there wouldn't be anymore hiding from the truth. Perhaps, in time, they would even forgive her. Tears of self-pity filled her eyes as the pain over her relationship with her children weighed heavily upon her.

Suddenly, a bee, that had discovered the flowers, buzzed around her and then sharply stung her on the hand. She leapt up grabbing her injured hand and quickly pulled the stinger out. Then she began to laugh uncontrollably, sinking to her knees once more.

"Nora, you certainly know how to get my attention. I've been moping around and feeling pretty sorry for myself. I guess it's time I started acting like a mother and a wife. I made a terrible mistake, but it is time to move forward and to take back my family. Smiling, she kissed her fingertips and touched them to Nora's headstone.

"Thanks, dear friend."

Jake sat behind his desk at the *Lone Star Chronicle*, contemplating his next move. He stared at the rain beating against the window while lost in thought. It was evident that he should get in touch with the Gibson family and let them know their son was missing. He wondered how they would take it and if they would blame him for Jim's disappearance.

The shrill ringing of the telephone interrupted his thoughts. Quickly, he grabbed the receiver and barked. "Jake McGowan, here!" There was total silence and then a voice that he immediately recognized was speaking, "Mr. McGowan, this is Jim."

"I know who the hell it is!" The expletive shot out of his mouth before he could stop it. "Where are you and why did you bail out on me," he started to say Jenny, but changed his mind, "and the Chronicle?" The anger and disappointment in his voice made Jim flinch, and he knew that this would not be a pleasant conversation.

"Sir, please, let me explain." His request was met with silence and then, reluctantly, and because his curiosity demanded it, Jake allowed him to speak.

"First of all, I'm in San Antonio, at Fort Sam Houston." He paused, waiting for his former boss to say something, but the only sound coming from the phone was Jake's labored breathing.

"I've joined the army," he continued, "and soon I'll be shipped overseas." He waited once more for some response, but none was forthcoming.

"I felt it my duty to join up, you know, with Hitler causing such a stir in Europe and the Japanese starting to make some noise." He laughed halfheartedly, hoping Jake would finally say something.

When he spoke, he caught Jim off-guard, causing him to almost drop the phone. "When were you going to let me in on your little secret? I assume your parents knew about your plans!"

The bitterness and sarcasm in his voice were like blows to Jim's body.

He sighed, "I know you are disappointed...."

"Disappointed doesn't even begin to cover it!" Jake growled in response, "When were you going to tell my daughter that you have changed your mind?"

Jim's hand trembled as he held the receiver. "Sir, you don't understand," he pleaded.

"You're damn right, I don't understand!" Jake thundered into the phone, "Is it your habit to take a young, impressionable girl out in the moonlight and fill her head with all sorts of nonsense, then disappear out of her life?"

"Mr. McGowan, please, it wasn't that way. I really meant what I said to her, but then I found out there are some extenuating circumstances in my life that has changed my future now and forever where Jenny and the *Lone Star Chronicle* is concerned." His voice was gruff and pleading, almost as though he was fighting to keep from breaking down altogether.

"Please believe me, sir, I never meant to hurt her and I'd do anything I could to change things, but our future together is impossible. Other than that, there is nothing else I can tell you." The defeat in his voice was unmistakable.

Jake turned a deaf ear to the sound. "What do you mean, there's nothing else you can tell me? You owe me more than just a flimsy excuse about some obscure circumstances in your life!"

"I can't tell you any more than that," Jim interrupted, "Believe me, I would like to, but it's not up to me."

To Jake is sounded like a brush off and he wasn't buying it. "Then I want you to understand this…stay away from Jenny and stay away from me. I don't want to see or hear from you ever, again. Is that clear?"

Jim tightened his grip on the phone as though he were afraid to let go. "Sir, please tell Jenny…." Click. The line went dead and he knew that Jake McGowan had hung up on him and that all ties between him, the McGowan's, and Jenny had been severed forever. He told himself that it was for the best, but he was glad that it was raining, because when the rivulets of water ran down his face, it mingled with the tears, hiding them.

Ellen was humming a tune as she dressed. She was going into Austin to see Jake McGowan at *the Lone Star Chronicle*. It was time to set the record straight and she wanted to get it over with, before she lost her courage. Carefully, she applied her make-up. She studied her features wondering if she still resembled the woman that had run into Jake McGowan all those years ago. No, she thought, he would not recognize her.

In truth, her features had matured, leaving her even more lovely. The passing years and added affluence had lent an air of sophistication, which she previously lacked. Her blonde hair was styled in the forties fashion favored by Hollywood. As she applied the finishing touches to her hair, she was very pleased with the results.

Standing up she impishly declared, "Betty Grable, eat your heart out!" The blue organdy dress matched her eyes. Looking in the mirror, she shook her head at the short hemline of the dress. She still wasn't used to showing so much leg, but with the shortage of materials and the United States sending everything they could to aid in the war effort, it was inevitable. With one last admiring look in the mirror, she left the room. On her way downstairs, she heard the shrill ringing of the phone in the kitchen. By the time she reached it, Lilly had already answered.

"Jim, is it really you? How is life in the big city?" Lilly prattled on without giving him a chance to answer.

Ellen watched with aching heart, hoping that he would want to speak to her. She really didn't think there was much chance of that happening and when Lilly handed the receiver to her, she almost dropped it from her trembling fingers. Lilly smiled at her, encouraging her to speak into the phone.

"Jim," she spoke his name hesitantly almost afraid to breathe for fear the connection would be broken.

"Mother!" Ellen's heart leapt at that word. She thought he would never call her that again.

"Mother, I'm calling from the army base at Ft. Sam Houston in San Antonio." He paused to give the news time to sink in.

"Son, why?" She knew the answer, but still had to ask.

"Under the circumstances," he interrupted, "I thought it best not to go to New York. I joined the army and I will be going overseas in a short time."

"Oh, no! " Ellen moaned. Just when she thought her heart couldn't break anymore, this! She took a deep breath, determined not to cry.

"Look," Jim was saying, his voice wavering as though he were having difficulty, too, "I get a few days furlough at the end of my training. I'll come home, if that's what you and Dad want."

"Son, I know I speak for Isaac when I say this, we love you and you will always be welcome here."

"Thank you," he stammered, "I just thought after all that's happened…"

"None of it your fault!" she stated passionately, "Jim, if you want, we can talk about it when you are here." There was a moment of silence that seemed to last forever.

"Mom, tell Lilly to be good and say hello to Dad for me and I'll see you guys soon. I'll let you know when as soon as I know for sure."

He rang off before she had a chance to comment. It was evident that Jim was not ready to talk about the past, but Ellen was confident that his calling her "Mom" and asking to come home was the first sign that things would soon work out between them. She sat there still holding the receiver, going over the conversation again in her mind as Lilly tried, impatiently, to find out what Jim had said. Ellen looked at her blankly for a moment; then, running out the door, she insisted that she must talk to Isaac.

Lilly hurried to catch up with her mother as Ellen ran, calling Isaac's name. Instinctively, she knew that it had something to do with the conversation with Jim and she wondered what was said that caused her mother to look both happy and sad at the same time. Still, the fact that Jim had bothered to call and had asked to speak to their mother must mean that things were going to return to normal.

Ellen found him down at the corral, where he was busy heating the branding iron. It was time to brand the new calves.

"Isaac!" she called as she continued rushing toward him, her face flushed. He looked up, startled at first; then, he smiled at the charming picture she made. Her hair was wind blown, making havoc of her carefully styled coiffure, and the blue dress was flying higher with each stride, leaving a lot of leg to admire. Finally, she arrived in front of him, out of breath. He grasped her by the shoulders to steady her. At that moment, a disgruntled Lilly came rushing up behind her mother.

Isaac backed away holding up his hands, "Whoa, what's going on here? Two pretty ladies all out of breath and wanting my attention!" He playfully winked at them both. Then his expression sobered as he noticed they were not joining in his lighthearted banter.

"What's wrong?" he now demanded, looking from one to the other.

"Oh, Isaac!" Ellen cried, "We just received a phone call from Jim."

"What! Is Jim okay?" Isaac had grabbed her shoulders once more. She leaned into him and rested her head on his shoulder. He looked over her head at Lilly, his eyes demanding an explanation, but Lilly could only shrug her shoulders and shake her head, indicating that she knew nothing.

"All right, Ellen," he withdrew, holding her at arm's length and looking into eyes that were just barely holding back the tears, "What's this all about?"

She sniffed as she continued looking at him. "Jim," she stammered, "is coming home for a visit soon."

Relief washed over Isaac. "That's wonderful, hon!" he enthused, beaming down at her. Then a frown lit his features as he realized that Jim hadn't been gone long enough to be coming home from New York, unless, he had decided that it wasn't for him after all.

"Isaac," she gently touched his arm bringing his attention back to her, "Jim, has joined the army at Ft. Sam Houston in San Antonio!"

The words came out in a rush, but she knew it was the only way she could get them out. Isaac and Lilly were clearly stunned, disbelief clouding their features.

Amanda was certain that time was running out. Soon Jake would know the entire story about Jenny. If the Gibson boy had confided in Ellen at all and she was sure that he probably had, then he knew by now that Jenny was his sister. The only satisfaction it brought her was in knowing that Ellen wouldn't be blameless in their mutual deception. After all she had signed the adoption papers and agreed to tell her other two children that their little sister had died. *Yes*, she thought smugly, *Ellen would certainly have to shoulder her share of the blame*. Amanda smiled to herself, if she told the story just right, Ellen would carry most of the blame. Jenny needed to hear the story from her. Yes, she must be the first to tell Jenny just what kind of mother she was spared from knowing!

Amanda quickly packed a bag, not in the least worried that she was leaving practically everything she owned. When she reached her destination, she would buy new things. First, she was going to Dallas to see Jenny and tell her the whole sordid story regarding her real mother's betrayal. Then they would take the train to New York and from there an ocean liner to England.

She grasped the latest letter from Hans Gunthur. Once more she scanned the contents of the letter. Hans was urging her to come to Austria and be a part of the new world order. His admiration for Hitler was mesmerizing. This was her chance to join him and thousands before it was too late. Hitler would rule the world and only a precious few of the inner circle would escape the holocaust to follow. Already, Hans had been given a post of authority within Hitler's regime. If she would join him, they would prosper together with Hitler's blessing. All she had to do was get to England. Friends of the new regime would get her into Austria. That old fool Franz Leonie should have returned to Austria. In all probability, his home and land would have been restored to him. Amanda sneered. The fool actually thought Hitler was a tyrant. Hitler was trying to make the world a better place to live. Why did people oppose the man and his cause so much? She dragged the large bag and her train case out of her room onto the landing. Maria was on her way up the stairs and almost ran into her struggling with the bags.

"What is this, Senora? Maria asked, clearly puzzled by her mistresses packed bags. Amanda did not wish to be detained, but she needed the housekeeper's help.

"Maria, go and call," she was fishing the slip of paper out of her handbag as she spoke, "this man and this is his number. Tell him I need his services immediately and if he hurries there will be a bonus!"

"Who is this man, Senora and where are you going?" The woman's curiosity had been piqued.

"Just do as I say, Maria! When you have finished, come back up here and we will talk." Maria shrugged and walked away. She had given up long ago trying to understand the ways of her employer. The woman was loco.

Amanda watched as Maria dialed the number. Her mind was racing ahead. She had run into an acquaintance last week, a Mrs. Frye, who complained bitterly of her housekeeper's retirement and how hard it would be to replace her. She would give Maria her pay with a nice bonus if she promised not to return here and send her to see Mrs. Frye with a letter of introduction and glowing praise. That should take care of things nicely. How she would have loved to see Jake's face when he came home and found no one here! Hopefully that wouldn't happen too soon. Since she wasn't taking a whole lot with her, it might be some time before he realized that she had left Austin. He would think that she had gone out on some errand and taken the housekeeper with her, which would not seem unusual.

It was several moments before Amanda realized that Maria had finished the phone call and was telling her that the driver would arrive at the appointed time. The woman's eyes widened at the amount of money her employer was insisting that she take.

"Do you understand, Maria?" her eyes bored into the housekeeper, "you must never return to this house or tell anyone that I am leaving?"

Solemnly, the girl nodded. Amanda breathed a sigh of relief. She was confident that Maria wouldn't be a problem because, for one thing, she was not very articulate in the English language. She hastily wrote a letter of introduction and gave it to Maria. "Take this to Mrs. Frye and she will employ you, but you must never tell her anything else. I told her in the letter that we will be away from Austin for some time and that it seemed unfair to keep you when I know how badly she needs someone. Hurry! You must leave as soon as your things are packed."

Chapter 22

Jenny and Franz were enjoying a stunning repertoire, she playing the violin and he the piano. They often practiced this way, giving them both the satisfaction of competition and total involvement in the piece they were playing.

Rose often stopped to listen as she worked in her garden. Today was no exception. She smiled to herself as she listened to the outpouring of their souls. The heavenly sound of the music they made was like nothing she had ever experienced.

Sighing, she thought about Garret. He was never around to hear them play. She suspected that her granddaughter was to blame for that. She was sure that Jenny had learned Garret's habits well and manipulated her own activities to coincide with his absences. It was funny how those two avoided each other. If they did come in contact, the air was charged with electricity and they were distantly polite to each other. Rose wasn't sure why, so she decided it must be the age difference. Garret was sophisticated and worldly, and her granddaughter was naive and *headstrong*.

Hearing the sound of footfalls on the path, she glanced up in time to see Garret rounding the corner of the garden. The music filtering through the open windows wafted toward him, stopping him in his tracks. He looked puzzled for a moment, as though, not sure where it was coming from. Frowning, he moved forward, seemingly unaware of Rose's presence. He stopped at the French doors, the entrance to the music room, and gazed open-mouthed at the pair, who were oblivious to everything and everyone, but their music.

Garret would not have believed it if he had not heard with his own ears and seen with his eyes. Jenny McGowan was a master musician. He had laughed to himself when they bragged about her ability, thinking them to be prejudiced and single minded where she was concerned. Smugly, he believed that they had overstated her talent with the violin and that she was probably mediocre at best.

The fact that she played in the Austin Symphony had not impressed him either, since he believed Austin to be just another hick town. Also, he admitted to himself, he had not wanted to believe that she was any good, because she had steadfastly refused to play in his presence, which had angered him. Now, there was no denying the girl's ability.

Slowly, he turned toward Rose. "I had no idea," he stammered. His features appeared stricken as he raised his eyes to her face. "I didn't really believe that she could possibly be as good as you said! How long has she been playing?"

Rose smiled as she reached up to pat his cheek. "Don't take it so hard, Garret. You're not the first non-believer. There were others—until they heard her play! As to how long she's been playing, well, I believe since the age of six. That was when my Franz first heard her play. He believes she is destined for greatness; few have ever possessed such talent. The violin that she plays was once his, but when he heard her play, he said that it belonged with her, so he made it a gift. It is not an ordinary violin. If you were to examine it closely, you would see a Maltese cross and the initials A.S. enclosed within a double circle." Rose looked at Garret, but she doubted that he had heard what she was saying, his attention was fixed on Jenny. Then he spoke and she knew that he had been listening after all.

"What does the markings mean?" he asked, without taking his eyes off of the young girl who was so enraptured in her music.

Rose laughed softly, "My dear, it means that it was made by the most famous violin maker of all time," she paused briefly to make sure he heard, "Antonio Stradivari!"

The shock on Garret's face was almost funny.

"My, God!" he exclaimed, "Does she know?"

"Oh, yes," Rose assured him, "she knows. Jenny and the violin are one. I think it would break her heart to be separated from it. It is as though Stradivari had fashioned that particular instrument especially for her."

Garret excused himself and quietly made his way to his room upstairs. He lay down on the bed thinking about all he had heard. He still couldn't believe it. This young, inexperienced girl had the most incredible gift inside her! She hadn't looked the same when she played her music. Somehow, the music had transformed her. She was the most beautiful person he had ever seen.

He rolled over as he thought about the picture she made. One thing was certain; she was definitely going to be a woman that men would want to possess. Strong emotions were aroused by the music she played and as she matured those emotions would erupt into passion. He sat up suddenly, trying to shake off the mesmerizing power of his strange thoughts.

The sound of a car crunching on the gravel below brought him to his feet. Slowly, he walked over to the window and looked out. The driver was opening the door for an eloquently clad woman. She was tall with a regal like bearing. The sun glistened on the rich color of the hair that was wound around her head in braids. After helping her out of the car, the driver resumed his place in the car to await further instructions. The woman looked at the house almost as though she dreaded approaching it, but with quick determination she walked toward the front door.

Since Rose had not mentioned expecting company, curiosity bade Garret to go and find out the identity of the uninvited guest. He reached the front door just as Amanda had allowed the knocker to fall once. Startled by the sudden opening of the door, she fell forward and Garret caught hold of her just in time to save her dignity. Face flushed, she was ready to upbraid whoever had opened the door so abruptly. The shock of coming face to face with a complete stranger left her speechless.

Garret could sense the tirade that would soon be forthcoming by the way she now drew herself up as though preparing for battle.

"My apologies, Madam. Please come into the drawing room and have a glass of sherry." He was smiling into her eyes and holding her hand as he led her into the room. Amanda's mind was a flurry. Who was this man? She was certain that she had never seen him before and as far as she knew Rose and Franz had not employed a butler.

"Forget the glass of sherry! I demand that you take me to my daughter at once!"

Her words were like a blast of Arctic wind. Her eyes shot sparks of fire at him as she waited for him to do as she had commanded.

"Well," he drawled, "you're obviously a woman who knows her mind." By the look on her face, he could see that his sarcasm would get him nowhere fast, so he tried another tactic.

"Look, lets start over. My name is Garret Davenport and I'm a relative visiting from Boston." He waited, expecting her to reciprocate by telling him her name. Amanda never did the expected. Haughtily, she walked out of the room without a backward glance.

Just as she reached the hallway, Jenny and her grandmother stepped through the French doors from the music room. "Mother!"

"Amanda!" they cried in unison.

"What a charming greeting," Amanda sneered.

Rose was taken aback for a moment. It was rare indeed for Amanda to be in her home and she couldn't imagine what had brought her here. Perhaps something had happened to Jake! Her hand trembled slightly as she held it to her chest. "Is there anything wrong, is Jake okay?"

Rose held her breath as she waited for Amanda to answer.

"Your concern is touching and, yes, everything is okay. Why shouldn't it be?" She dismissed Rose's concerns with a wave of her hand. "I was bored in Austin and I'm simply here to do some shopping. I want to replenish Jenny's wardrobe." Her eyes now bored into Jenny's. "Go upstairs and get dressed, we are going out!" she commanded.

"But, Mother," Jenny, stammered, "You know how I hate shop...."

"That will be enough! You will change your clothes and come with me right now. Also," now she turned toward Rose, "don't expect her back for dinner. We will dine out and then perhaps go to the theatre."

Rose felt completely helpless. After all what Amanda was asking was not anything out of the ordinary. It was the fact that Jenny didn't want to go that troubled her.

STRADI'S VIOLIN

"Amanda," Rose was saying, "Aren't you tired from that long trip? Why not rest tonight and then you two could go out on the town tomorrow." She should have known better than to try to reason with her daughter-in-law.

"I don't recall asking for your opinion. I will not tolerate your interference in my plans." After her stinging retort, she turned to Jenny once more. "I believe you should be getting dressed." Her demeanor and tone brooked no argument.

Garret had followed Amanda into the hallway and her conversation, if it could be called that, with Jenny and Rose was clearly overheard. He still could not believe his ears. The woman was an absolute tyrant. How did someone like Jenny wind up with a mother like that? Maybe cousin Jake had a good reason for that chip on his shoulder. He watched as Jenny slowly made her way up the stairs. He and Amanda both made eye contact at the same time. Hers frosty, his like shards of ice as they bored into hers.

"What are you staring at?" she demanded.

Disdainfully, he walked toward her, "A very rude, selfish woman is my guess."

His manner and words made no secret that he disliked her intensely. His imposing stance blocking her way made her slightly nervous.

The arrogance! she fumed to herself. She drew herself up for battle, just as Franz made an appearance.

"Amanda, what are you doing here?" he asked without preamble.

"Nice to see you too, Franz," she sneered. Belatedly, he realized his manners bordered on rudeness.

"Please forgive me, dear," he spoke as he took her hand, "How nice to see you and what may I ask brings you to our humble home." His eyes twinkled at Garret as he spoke and right away Garret knew that this was a game that Franz played to keep this woman off balance.

"That's better," she said sulkily as she withdrew her hand from his, "After all you are the only one on this side of the family with any real manners. You may come into the drawing room and get me a sherry. Perhaps then, I'll tell you why I'm here."

Her attempt at being coy almost made Garret sick. He turned on his heel and headed toward the stairs.

Amanda's voice rang out for his benefit, "Your guest or whoever he happens to be is very rude!"

Garret would not give her the satisfaction of looking back. He took the stairs two at a time. He started toward his room, but something made him go the other direction. He found himself in front of Jenny's door. He started to knock, but stopped. The sound of her muffled crying had reached his ears. For several moments he stood there listening, wondering what to do. Hesitantly, he raised his arm and softly tapped on the door.

At the sound, Jenny quickly dried her eyes and tried to look as though she was trying to decide what to wear. "Come in," she said tentatively. Slowly, Garret opened the door, knowing that she would not be expecting him.

Her reaction was immediate. "Get out!" she yelled, pointing at the door. She made a disturbing picture with her temper flaring, a wisp of hair over one eye and the strap of her slip riding down on one shoulder. However, it was the curve of her young breast that was keeping Garret rooted to the spot.

Angry with him for not moving, she grabbed the pillows off the bed and threw them in his direction. He dodged them easily and laughed, until he saw her reaching for something a little more substantial. The vase on the table was quickly raised, but never left her hands.

Garret, with lightening speed, had grabbed her from behind and wrestled the vase out of her grasp. She was spitting mad, like a little cat. She turned on him with claws ready, but once again he was too quick for her. His arms wrapped around her vise-like and they both fell backwards onto the bed. Quickly, he turned and pinned her beneath him with her arms above her head. She twisted and turned and tried to release herself from his grasp, but finally she lay still as she realized the futility of what she was doing. Her breath was coming out in little gasps and her face was flushed. The hair she had earlier pinned on top of her head had come loose.

Garret gazed at the enigma before him. She was like a kaleidoscope that changes patterns and shapes. One moment, she was a precocious child, next a superb musician, then a shrieking shrew, and now, a captivating siren. His head was spinning with the different faucets of her personality. He wished that he had not wasted all this time in getting to know her, that he had stormed her defenses until he discovered her true identity. Ultimately, he knew, she was worth it after all.

Her eyes searched his and she wondered why she had ever thought his gray eyes were ice. Now, they reminded her of smoke – and fire. His sensuous upper lip was slightly curved in what appeared to be a smile. Then he spoke, awaking her senses and releasing the lethargy that had momentarily overtaken her.

"I heard you play the violin," he rasped as though it was difficult for him to speak of it, yet, wanting her to know.

In silence, her eyes continued to search his, waiting for...she wasn't sure what.

He released her hands and reached up to cup her face. She tugged on his hand to pull it away, but he resisted. Then slowly, he lowered his head and she felt the searing touch of his lips as they claimed hers. His mouth plundered the sweetness of her lips again and again. Passionately, without holding back his assault continued as though determined to provoke a response. At first, her lips were cold, unyielding, from the shock of her first kiss, but then they seemed to ignite and burn with a fire of their own. A growing passion within both excited and frightened her, and her arms betrayed her as they reached up, and wrapped themselves around his neck. Garret raised his head, and stared into her eyes. It was as though time stood still as they continued to look at each other. Neither of them heard the door open, but the loud gasp that followed was like being splashed with a pail of cold water. Garret's head snapped back and he encountered Amanda's rage filled eyes. Jenny turned her head, and as Garret reluctantly released her, she sit up trying to shield her state of undress. She knew that her mother would not let this incident go without extracting every ounce of dignity from her and making her pay for her indiscretion.

His worse nightmare had come true. Texas Ranger, Sam Spaulding could no longer deny the facts. He stared at the box containing several strands of cheap pearls and visibly shuttered.

It started a few weeks ago, with the discovery of the first victim. Her parents had been disbelieving and then horrified by their only daughter's disappearance and untimely death. A farmer had discovered the body along side the road just outside of Austin. She had been sexually molested and then strangled. Her battered body was nude except for a cheap strand of pearls around her neck.

The ranger's fist struck the table in frustration and anger. Three more young girls had been found over the past few months. "The Pearl" was definitely here. But *where*, specifically, was the question that nagged him. He had talked with Jake McGowan at the *Lone Star Chronicle*. Getting the word out was the best thing that could be done for now. Jake had agreed with him and the Chronicle was running several articles in an effort to alert people, especially women, to the danger.

Where are you? You murderer! Sam seethed to himself.

The car chugged over the ruts in the road, sending the driver bouncing, his head hitting the roof. Melvin Yates cursed at the old jalopy that he was forced to drive. Still, it got him around and away from the farm, which is what he needed. *Yes, sir, a man needs a little diversion from time to time.* He smiled to himself, thinking about the young girls that had submitted to his charms. His smile turned to a snarl as he thought about Lilly. She was always avoiding him and the anger, that was ever present in him, was beginning to build. *Who does she think she is anyway?* He eyes glazed over with passion as he thought of the ways that he would make her submit. *Before I leave here, she will be mine*! he vowed to himself.

Amanda was furious with her daughter, but controlled the emotions that threatened to overflow. She had other things on her mind. A plan had been formulated with her friend, Hans Gunther, and she would not jeopardize it. She had told Jenny that her behavior would not be tolerated. She also indicated that she would apprise Jake of what had occurred. This brought more tears from Jenny and a contemptuous snort from Garret. She turned on Garret to lash out at him, but he held up his hand for her to stop.

"Madam, don't even try it!" Turning on his heel, he had slammed out of the room.

She had also set Rose and Franz straight in the matter of their guest, upbraiding Rose for allowing a rake such as Garret into the house. Franz had quickly leaped to his wife's defense, stating that Garret was not only a guest, but also a relative. More words had followed. Amanda did not waste any time taking Jenny out of their house, along with all of her belongings. Rose was very distraught and begged and cried for Amanda to reconsider. Haughtily, Amanda reminded her that Jenny had been allowed to visit, because of the trust that Jake placed in them. She doubted that their allowing a cad and a rake to seduce his daughter would please Jake. Those were her final words as she left with a tearful and reluctant Jenny.

Despite Amanda's prodding and pushing, she managed to turn back for a final look at the house. As she glanced upward, to the second floor, she saw the curtain move. It was Garret and he was staring down at her, his expression unreadable. Her grandmother stood just inside the front door with a handkerchief pressed to her eyes. Franz stood beside her, his expression sad. His eyes glinted strangely, as though he was struggling to keep from crying. Rose looked so small and forlorn that Jenny's heart felt as if it were breaking into a thousand pieces. A strange feeling came over her, causing her to shiver. As she continued to stare at them, it was like she was seeing them all for the last time. Tears blinded her eyes as she stumbled to the waiting car. Immediately, the car was set in motion, and before she knew it, the house with those she loved so dearly, was left far behind.

Garret watched as the car drove out of sight. He cursed himself for not exercising more control. After all Jenny was still very young. Then he remembered her response to his kisses and he knew that she had stirred him more than any woman he had ever known. He didn't care a wit about Amanda McGowan, or Jake for that matter. What they thought about him wasn't important either, but he did want the respect of Jenny McGowan very badly. He knew that so far he hadn't done anything to make her particularly fond of him, especially with this latest fiasco. He was sure that Amanda would defame him at every available opportunity and Jenny was young. She would dutifully listen and do whatever Amanda wanted. However, their paths would cross again, he vowed, because he had unfinished business with Jenny McGowan.

Morosely, Jake sat at his desk staring into space. The cup of coffee his secretary had brought him was forgotten and was now cold and unappealing. He was thinking about the phone call from Jim. Well, the mystery was solved and he guessed that by now Jim's parents must know their son's whereabouts. He still didn't understand, and Jim hadn't wanted to explain saying that it wasn't up to him. None of this made any sense and the only thing left for him to do was pay a visit to the Thacker Ranch. Somehow, he knew that he would find the answer to all his questions there. Having made the decision, he abruptly stood up grabbed his hat off the desk and headed out the door. His secretary stared after him wondering why her boss had left without telling her where he was going.

Ellen was humming as she sat at the kitchen table, making plans. She was jotting down a list of Jim's favorite foods. Hope had boosted her spirit, because he had called and wanted to come home. Jim's future was not what he had planned, and now he belonged to Uncle Sam. It didn't help knowing that she was to blame for the chaos. *Will he truly be able to forgive me?* she wondered, sighing as she stared into space. *What about Jake McGowan*, she thought. Probably, they should contact him and let him know that Jim did not go to New York. She suspected that he was already aware that things had not worked out. He would certainly have some questions and she supposed it was only fair that he be told the truth. She had planned to go to the *Lone Star Chronicle* and talk to him today, but then Jim had called. Silently, she scolded herself for using Jim as an excuse to prolong the inevitable. Would Jim expect her to talk to Jake McGowan? She sensed that it was exactly what Jim wanted her to do. Why had she put it off, again? *Coward*! A voice whispered to her. Yes, she was afraid of the confrontation, and the condemnation from which the formidable Jake McGowan would not allow her to escape.

The gray roadster pulled up to the front of the Thacker Ranch. From inside the house, Ellen could hear the purr of an engine. Jake turned the key and abruptly the sound ceased. Ellen got to her feet and walked to the front door to see who had come to visit them. She didn't recognize the car, but the imposing figure that got out was one that she remembered. Jake McGowan! She trembled and suddenly felt faint. This would not do, she must not let him know how unnerving this visit would be. Straightening her shoulders, head held high, she went to open the door.

For a moment, Jake just stared at the house. He wondered what the occupants would be like. He hadn't decided how he was going to handle the situation. He just sensed that it was time to meet the rest of Jim's family. Maybe, they would be able to explain to him why Jim had abandoned his dreams. As Jake's foot rested on the first step leading up to the porch, the front door opened. A woman stood silhouetted in the doorframe, her features hidden by shadows.

"Hello, I'm Jake McGowan from the *Lone Star Chronicle*," he stated as he continued to climb the steps. Still she said nothing, and as Jake looked up, he smiled, "Lilly, I'm sorry. I didn't recognize you, at first."

"I'm not Lilly, she's my daughter," came the softly spoken reply. She opened the door inviting him to come inside. Jake realized his mistake as he drew even with the woman. As his eyes adjusted to the light, he saw that she was an older version of Lilly and extremely attractive.

Leading him into the parlor, she indicated for him to be seated. She settled across from him and braced herself for some sign of recognition. None was forthcoming, but he did appear to be studying her. She decided that she would have to be the one to break the silence.

"I'm Ellen Rheinhart," her eyes met his as she held out her hand in greeting. Jake's large one engulfed hers.

"It's a pleasure to meet you, but I must warn you that my business here is not entirely pleasant." Taking a deep breath, he continued, "Mrs. Rheinhart," his voice was gruff, "I need some answers from you regarding your son, Jim."

Warily, she nodded her head as she waited for him to continue.

Jenny was waiting for the lecture that she was sure would be forthcoming. Instead, Amanda seemed preoccupied, almost like she had forgotten Jenny's presence. She sighed and leaned back against the seat and watched as the buildings and houses flew by. With heart-wrenching clarity she replayed the scene in her bedroom with Garret. Why had he come into her room? And why had he kissed her? He didn't even like her and she certainly was not fond of him. Uncomfortably she remembered the kisses they had shared, but she was sure that it didn't mean anything to him. Garret was the type of man who had just wanted to teach her a lesson, and make her pay for all the times she had ignored him. He had spoiled her stay with her grandmother and grandfather. She would never forgive him!

"I will come straight to the point. I received a phone call from your son and he told me that he has joined the army," he watched Ellen as he spoke, trying to gage her reaction to his words. "He said that he could not go to New York as planned, but he refused to tell my why, and that is my question to you, Mrs. Rheinhart, why?"

Silence followed his question. What could she say to this man? She could make up a story, but what would that solve? Too many lies had been told in the past and now, she knew that Jim depended on her to tell the truth. Clasping and unclasping her fingers, she struggled with how to tell Jake McGowan her deepest, darkest secret.

"Mother, where are we going?" Jenny sat upright, alarmed at the unfamiliar sights.

"We're going to the train station." Amanda stated matter-of-factly.

Jenny's eyes widened as she stared at her mother. "Wha...why?" she stammered.

Amanda snorted in disgust, "Stop acting as though you're being abducted. I've decided it is time to pay my sister a visit. Since she has never met you, I want you to accompany me."

"But, Mother, what about Dad, does he know? There was something important that he was going to find out for me. Please, Mother I need to go home first." Her eyes had filled with tears as she pleaded.

Amanda's eyes narrowed as she studied her daughter's distraught condition. "The fact that I am going to take you to my sister's won't matter to him and I know all about the *important matter*," she stated sarcastically, "It's that boy from the newspaper, the one that you met last summer. Isn't he the reason you want to go home?"

"Mother, please you don't understand. Jim disappeared and Dad promised to find him. He was supposed to go to New York, but we don't believe that he did."

Amanda wasn't really listening to Jenny, because she decided at that moment that it would be to her advantage to tell her the truth. Well, the truth as she, Amanda McGowan saw things.

"That boy is your brother," she stated it simply without raising her voice.

Jenny was sure that she had misunderstood her mother. She knew that she had said something of monumental importance, but her mind had not comprehended it. Moving her mouth, she failed to form a response.

"I said that boy, Jim Gibson, is your brother!" She repeated it so there would be no mistaking her this time. Smugly, she waited for the words to soak in.

Jenny's features became pinched; her breathing was rapid and shallow. Struggling to keep from fainting, she tried to speak once more. "Wh...why are you saying this to me. How could such a thing possibly be true! Mother, why are you lying?" Jenny put both hands over her eyes, because Amanda features were unrelenting, adding credence to her words. She sobbed brokenly and wondered why her world was coming apart.

"Jenny!" Amanda's commanding voice made her look up. "It is time that you were told the truth. For years, I have wanted to tell you, but Jake forbade me to speak of it. It was your grandmother and he that kept this terrible secret from you!" She was watching to see if her words were having the desired effect. The tortured look in Jenny's eyes, gave the answer. Satisfied, she continued. "Your mother was a woman of the streets - you know what that means, don't you? She looked for her comfort where she could and took what was offered by men to ensure her way of life." Amanda sneered as she said this, hoping to destroy any sympathy that Jenny might start to feel towards the woman who gave birth to her.

"Anyway, she got herself in trouble - pregnant. It wasn't enough that she had two other illegitimate children, but now there was to be a third. The economic depression took its toll on her lively hood, plus the fact that she was with child and becoming larger every day. Soon, she was in dire trouble - and that's when she came to me."

Once again, she looked at Jenny, who appeared to be in shock. "I know this is a terrible thing for you to hear, but once you know the story, you will come to appreciate how much I have sacrificed for you. Do you want me to continue?" Mutely, Jenny nodded her head.

"Well, she came to the house one day, dragging her poor underfed children in tow. She was about to give birth and had no money or means of support. I felt dreadfully sorry for the children - they looked so helpless and lost. I brought them into the house to feed them and that's when the woman went into labor. There's no need for me to go into all the details, but that is when you were born. Afterwards, the woman told me that she could not possibly raise another child. She knew that I had no children, and she took advantage of my weakness in confiding to her that I desperately wanted a child. So, she offered to sell you to me."

A startled cry came from Jenny's lips, "she...she sold me?"

Amanda was impatient with the interruption. She had formulated the events in her mind and wanted to conclude the story quickly. "Just let me finish and then you can ask questions. Where was I? Oh, well, no, I would not agree to that kind of blackmail. I told the woman that I would adopt you and raise you as my own. In return, she and her two children could start a brand new life, with my help. I sent them to the Thacker Ranch outside of Austin. Apparently, I didn't send them far enough away," she stated dryly. She sat thinking about how much better it would have been if she had sent them out of the state or better, yet, out of the country!

Jenny was tugging at her mother to regain her attention. "Mother, have you told me everything?"

Her eyes studied Jenny's tear streaked face, seeing the effect that her half-truths were having on her. *Good*, she thought, *soon I will not have any more trouble with her. She will be completely obedient and dependent on me.* "Unfortunately," this time she spoke aloud, "that is not the end of the story. I wish it were, truly, I do."

Jake was pacing back and forth, but he stopped in front of her, staring at her as though he were trying to see inside her head. "You gave away your own flesh and blood!" His voice was hard and bitter and he looked at her with such loathing that it felt like a knife was being twisted inside her. "What kind of woman are you?" The disgust was evident in his voice.

"My wife is loving and caring and a *wonderful* mother, that's what kind of woman she is," thundered the deep gravely voice of Isaac Rheinhart. They both turned in surprise, not having heard him come in.

Ellen was relieved at the interruption. After telling her story, Jake had raved and ranted like a madman, hardly allowing her a word in her own defense. She had told him practically everything, except about Amanda's duplicity. If he were an astute man, then he could figure out the details himself. She had also left out the part about the visit to the hospital. Heaven knew he was upset enough without her bringing that up!

Jake walked over to the tall, blond giant, sizing him up. He was obviously a man of integrity with an honest face. His hands were callused, his skin dark from long hours of labor in the sun. Right now, Jake didn't care about that. He was angry and felt somehow betrayed.

"Your wife is such a paragon of motherhood that she gave away a small, helpless, baby and her son has run away from her and joined the army!" he sneered into the face close to his own.

A giant fist drew back and connected with his jaw, leaving Jake reeling and stumbling backwards.

"No! Isaac!"

He heard a woman scream, just before he hit the floor and everything went black.

Amanda fussed with her gloves, pulling them off as she spoke,

"I truly regret having to tell you this, but Jake, the man you have known only as your father, is not who he appears to be. There is a dark side to him that only I have been witness to and also a victim to, like you." Here, she paused, to make sure that she had Jenny's full attention. The now silent, ashen-faced girl was definitely listening. Satisfied, she continued,

"Jake is ruthless, cruel and used to getting his own way. He is a womanizer and a drunkard. Oh, I know you've never seen him that way, but he is adept at keeping these things secret. Furthermore," she continued, "he never wanted children even though he knew how desperately I wanted a child."

A low, moan escaped Jenny's lips, as though, she were trying to speak. Amanda ignored her, wanting to drive her point home, before she was expected to answer any questions. "When I told him about the woman who gave birth to you and that she did not want you, he was very unsympathetic. In fact, he said that you should be sent to an orphanage, but I wouldn't hear of it. I begged and pleaded with him to let me keep you. At first, he refused to even consider it, but finally I appealed to his ego, by telling him that it would make him more respectable and that people would admire him for this Christian act of charity. Reluctantly, he agreed. It is true that for a time, he took to fatherhood better than I had hoped. However, I am the one that took care of you and saw to all of your needs. Furthermore, it is I who always had your best interest at heart."

After all the moments of silence, Jenny found her voice, "I don't believe you! Daddy loves me and he would do anything for me!" she cried passionately.

Amanda sneered, "That is what he would have you and the rest of the world believe!"

Trembling, Jenny interrupted, "Wha—at did he say about me?" her voice wavered and broke as she asked the question.

Amanda's eyes searched her daughter's, seeing the fear and doubt that clouded her reasoning. She knew that it was only a matter of time before she would be obedient and submissive, giving her no more cause for worry. It would be as it was supposed to be from the start, Jenny would belong to her completely—no Jake, or Rose, or Franz, or anyone else to interfere.

"Well, since you asked, I will tell you this one thing," she paused for effect, "He would often say to me that he could see the flaws in your character and that he suspected that you were becoming more and more like your real mother. He despaired of your ever becoming a decent woman."

So caught up in her story, it was a few moments before she realized the impact of her words. When she stopped to look at Jenny, she could see the spark had gone out of her eyes. She looked vulnerable and lost. *Good!* Amanda thought, *Now, she will do as I say without any trouble.* Satisfied, she sat back and closed her eyes to get some rest, leaving a wide-eyed, frightened, young girl to stare hopelessly at the shattered fragments of her life.

Chapter 23

Jake watched the sun come up as he sat beneath the Juniper Tree. Tentatively, he reached up and touched the bruised area on his jaw, wincing at the pain. A few hours ago or was it an eternity ago, he had been to see Ellen Rheinhart. What she had told him had stunned him to say the least and then his anger had taken over and he had berated her without mercy. In the middle of his tirade, Isaac Rheinhart had come in and put a stop to his hurtful words. For that, Jake was grateful. He had been totally out of line, but he couldn't seem to stop himself.

Deep down he had known that Amanda had not told him the entire truth, but after his first look at Jenny, it simply had not mattered. She had given new meaning to his life and she was the reason he was still alive. Amanda had not kept any of her promises to him and he had not cared. Jenny was the center of his universe.

He thought about Ellen Rheinhart and how difficult this must have been for her. She was a delicate woman and very attractive. He couldn't help but wonder how different things might have been if he had met her all those years ago. It was strange how when he first saw her, he thought it was Lilly, because there was something so familiar about her. Later, it had dawned on him, but he didn't tell her. She was the "golden haired angel" that Jenny talked about, and the woman who had rushed headlong into him that day in the hospital. He believed that Isaac Rheinhart had spoken the truth when he said that she was a loving, caring woman. No woman could inspire that kind of loyalty in a man unless it was true.

Slowly, Jake extracted himself from the bench. He felt stiff, and old. Yes, he felt very old this morning. Sighing, he picked up his discarded jacket and started down the hill toward the house. He was trying to decide if he should talk to Jenny first or confront his wife, who he knew would lie vehemently about everything. Amanda was in for a shock, because he was sending her away. He didn't care where, just as long as she was out of his and Jenny's life. The thought of getting rid of the poison that had ruined much of his life, gave him a livelier step. Walking faster, he glanced up at the house. It was strangely quiet...too quiet. A foreboding overtook him and he ran the rest of the way. His chest was hurting before he reached the door and he fumbled in his jacket for his bottle of pills. Shaking, his fingers finally removed the cap and he gulped down several of the pills. He collapsed in a chair and waited for the medicine to take effect. It felt as though a giant hand was gripping his chest and his breath was being slowly squeezed out. *Panic, don't panic* he told himself.

"Jenny!" he called her name weakly. He knew that she wasn't there, but it somehow brought him comfort to speak her name. The ringing of the phone startled him and he hoped the housekeeper would answer it, but the ringing continued sounding loud and demanding in the too silent house. Clutching his chest, he forced himself out of the chair and staggered to the loudly ringing phone in the hallway. He grabbed the phone and fell heavily against the wall and slid down all the way to the floor. The pain was becoming steadily worse and he barely managed to get the receiver to his mouth. He could feel himself starting to black out and he fought to remain conscious. Hearing his mother's voice gave him the determination he needed to speak.

Rose could hear labored breathing on the other end of the line, but nothing else.

"Jake, Jake! Is that you, Son? Answer me, please!" her voice shook as she cried out, "Oh, God, Jake are you ill! Is it your heart?" Miraculously, she heard his voice. Gripping the phone so tightly that it seemed her fingers were embedded, she listened.

"Mother," he spoke faintly, "Please help me – I think I'm going to pass out..."

The rasping of his labored breathing told her how serious the situation was and she knew that he must be alone. She had called to advise him of the situation regarding Amanda - how she had demanded that Jenny go with her. Obviously, Amanda had not just taken Jenny shopping, or they would have been back in Austin by now. Fear gripped her as she realized the precarious situation that her son was in.

"Jake! I am going to hang up and call the Austin authorities and then I will call you back. Jake, do you hear me!" Barely, she discerned his whispered "yes..." and knew that would have to satisfy her.

As Rose waited for the authorities to call her back regarding Jake's condition, she frantically threw clothes into a suitcase. She had to get to Austin. Jake needed her now more than ever.

Garret had come down the stairs, with his own suitcase in tow, finding a distraught Rose almost hysterical with fear. He and Franz had managed to calm her long enough to find out what was going on. Garret had quickly taken the situation in hand and insisted on driving them to Austin. At first, Franz had refused, but Rose had come to Garret's defense and insisted that he should drive them.

Guilt had weighed heavily on him and the opportunity to do something to partially redeem himself was God-sent. He started at the sudden shrill ringing of the phone. Before it could ring again, Rose had grabbed it. He and Franz hurried to her side and waited impatiently until she got off the phone. Her face was ashen and her hands trembled. For the first time Garret was aware of how frail she was as he gently led her to a nearby chair. Franz was leaning over her with a glass of water. At his urging, she sipped the water and took a calming breath.

"He's alive!" she gasped, "And they have him at Austin General Hospital. Apart from that, that's all the authorities know. Please," she gripped Garret's arm with surprising strength, "take me to him!"

A frown furrowed his brow as Isaac drove the few miles to Mills Feed Store. He was thinking about the encounter with Jake McGowan the night before. Ellen and Lilly had berated him for hitting the man, but as far as Isaac was concerned, he had gotten off lightly. Still, he grudgingly admitted, he shouldn't have let his temper get the best of him. He supposed he might have felt the same if he had been in Jake's shoes. Ellen's past had certainly stirred things up for a lot of people.

Pulling into the parking space in front of the feed store, he cut the engine and got out. Mills Feed Store had a number of goods stacked outside on the long veranda and Isaac casually glanced around to see if there was anything he could use. The front entrance was stacked with newspapers, and he picked one up to see if there was anything new on the war in Europe. Quickly, he scanned the paper and then he saw it. The letters seemed to stand out and burn themselves into his brain.

Newspaper Tycoon Jake McGowan Hospitalized in Serious Condition.

The owner of the feed store walked out onto the porch, "Ah, Isaac, what can I do for you today?" he offered good-naturedly.

The sound of his voice startled Isaac from his trance-like state. He looked up uncomprehendingly. "I'm fine!" he stammered as he tossed a coin for the newspaper to the man who was concerned by the unnatural parlor of Isaac's skin.

"Say, why don't you come in a sit for a spell?" he offered with a worried frown.

Isaac shook his head without speaking and ran to the truck, yanking open the door and jumping inside. He started the motor and gunned the truck into reverse. Gravel and dirt flew in every direction as he drove off in a cloud of dust with the storeowner looking on in alarm.

He was driving wildly and he knew that he must get control of the situation. Pulling off the road, he stopped the truck. Slowly, he picked up the newspaper and read the article. It didn't say very much just that Jake was in serious condition. There were no other details. He laid his head on the steering wheel. "God," he groaned, "what am I going to do?" His thoughts ran riot as he considered the possibilities, none of them very comforting. *What if he dies? I didn't think that I hit him that hard. The law is probably looking for me right now.* Then came a more sobering thought. *I have to get home to Ellen before she finds out.* He slung the paper aside as he started the motor once more. He hated thinking about what might happen to his family if he were arrested. Still, he reasoned, he must consider the facts. Before he turned himself in, he needed to tie up some loose ends. He drove as fast as he dared, feeling that he was in a race against time.

As soon as he reached the farm, he would get rid of Melvin Yates. In the last few weeks the man was becoming more hostile and sullen.

Ellen should not be left to deal with him. His thoughts led him to take a detour. He drove past fields of cotton and corn to the shanties where the Mexican farm laborers and their families lived.

He had met Juan Alvarez several days ago and was very impressed with him. In Mexico Juan had worked mostly on ranches, so the work would not be unfamiliar to him. He had not been in this country very long, but he had taught himself English. Others had also told him that the man was honest and a hard worker. Not understanding it, yet aware that he and Juan had somehow been simpatico in spirit, he knew that this was the right thing to do.

Isaac barely allowed the truck to come to a complete stop before he swung his large frame out of the cab. He had already made up his mind, he would ask Juan and his family to come and live at the ranch and work for him or for Ellen, he amended to himself.

He strode to the front door of the shanty. The screen was torn and a cotton sheet served as a covering to keep the flies out. "Juan!" he called out as he banged on the doorframe.

A small Mexican woman greeted him, but her English was very limited. She understood that the giant American was looking for her husband. She pointed to the cotton fields behind the shanty. Hurriedly, Isaac made his way to the fields and the woman watched with a puzzled frown on her face. She wondered why he was so anxious to see her husband.

Juan was on his knees pulling the cotton out of the hull on the lower part of the plant. It was backbreaking work and he thought that perhaps he had made a mistake leaving Mexico. He was barely making enough money to feed his family and his two children worked in the fields with him. He glanced up and could barely make out the figure of his son far up the field on a different row. His son, Jaime, was only fourteen, but already he slaved in the field when he should have been in school. At least, that had been the plan. Juan shook his head sadly and sighed. Turning, he looked a short distance down the row of cotton that he was working, and there his daughter, Margarita, labored, her lovely face hidden by the large straw hat that she was wearing. He knew her mouth would be fixed in a pout and her eyes would be sullen and hostile. She hated the hard labor they were forced to do just to get by. Margarita was sixteen and he knew that before long, she would find a way to leave this life that she despised. Juan sighed again. His dreams for himself and his family were not working out. At that moment he heard a shout, and looked up, shading his eyes from the sun. Someone was shouting his name and striding towards him. It was Isaac Rheinhart! The giant blonde man had always treated him with respect and he liked that. So many of the gringos treated the Mexicans with contempt and ridiculed their language and way of life, but Senor Rheinhart had never done that.

Isaac was out of breath by time he reached the man that he had come to see.

"Senor Rheinhart, what may I do for you?" he questioned as they shook hands.

Isaac decided to be brief and to the point so he wasted no time in explaining what he wanted from Juan and his family.

Margarita was watching them, knowing that her eyes were hid by the large brim of her hat. She wondered contemptuously, what the gringo wanted with her father. Probably wanted to hire him to do more work and pay him little. All gringos treated the Mexicans like slaves. She noticed that her father was smiling, something that he rarely did now, and nodding eagerly. They shook hands once more and Isaac strode off with her father watching and still smiling. He turned towards her then and motioned for her to come; then he called across the field to his son, Jaime. No more cotton fields! They were going to live on a ranch and he would do the work that he loved so much. They would have a nice place to live. Perhaps his children would go to school after all! Smiling from ear to ear, he crossed himself and looked up into the bright sunlight sky.

"Gracias, El Senor, gracias!" he cried.

Rose kept a steady vigil beside the hospital bed. No amount of urging by her husband or Garret could persuade her to give up her post. She was going to be there when her son awoke. The doctors said it was a stroke, probably brought on by his heart condition. Garret and Franz had gone to the house to see if they could find any clues as to the whereabouts of Jenny and Amanda. Rose stretched and got up, her body stiff from sitting in one position so long. She looked at her son. He looked so peaceful. She touched his hand. It was cold, so cold and she rubbed it with her own hands trying to instill warmth. "God, please," she begged, "let him live!"

Garret had gone over the house with a fine toothcomb, searching for something, anything that would tell them where Amanda had gone. He knew they weren't still in Dallas, because he had located the driver that Amanda had hired. He was reluctant to talk at first, but after Garret had explained some very unpleasant consequences to him for his part in all this, he decided it might be to his advantage to cooperate. He said that Amanda had paid him to drive them to the train station in Dallas and they had boarded a train for the east coast. Then he had returned to Austin and that, he swore, was all he knew.

From what Garret could tell, it looked as though Amanda had not planned on coming back. He searched all the closets and drawers. That's when he found the letters. Frowning, he read the letters that Hans Gunthur had written to Amanda. They sent a chill down his spine. Surely, the woman would not be crazy enough to attempt to leave the country with Jenny. He carefully stuffed the letters inside his coat. It would not be a good idea for anyone to know about this, until he could find out more. Franz said they had a housekeeper, and apparently, she too, had disappeared. He wondered if Jake had found out that his wife had taken their daughter and fled. Perhaps that had brought on the stroke. Garret's lips curled in an unfamiliar snarl. His anger toward Amanda, like a physical presence. He wondered if Jenny was frightened or if she was in any danger. "Damn the woman!" he slammed his fist against the doorframe in frustration, "If anything happens to that girl, she'll pay, I swear it!"

Needing fresh air, he strode outside and up the path to the Juniper Tree. By the time he reached the top of the cliff, his anger had abated somewhat, allowing him to think clearly again. He knew that he must use his wits to figure out what had become of Jenny. He took in his surroundings. It was so serene and peaceful up here with the city of Austin sprawling far below. Sitting on the bench, his thoughts turned again to Jenny. He'd overheard a conversation between Aunt Rose and Franz. It seemed Jenny had been pinning for someone. He was desperate to know with whom she imagined herself in love. Distastefully, he pushed the thought away. She was far to young to be in love with anyone. Restless, he got up and walked back toward the house, hoping that Jake would wake up soon, because he had a lot of unanswered questions that were burning him up inside.

Melvin Yates had watched Isaac drive off earlier that day and had decided it was time to make his move. He could feel the law closing in on him and knew that is was just a matter of time before the Texas Rangers came here looking for him. His latest victim lay in a shallow grave about a mile from the ranch. If the body were discovered, they would be crawling all over this area. He had always been smart enough to know when it was time to move on, but he had a couple of things to take care of first. Meticulously, he oiled and cleaned the shotgun and then loaded it. He shoved his belongings into his duffel bag. The last thing he took out of the drawer was a single strand of pearls. Smiling, he put them into his pocket and grabbed the shotgun off the bed. He walked out the door and headed straight for the main house.

Ellen was standing on a stool in the large pantry looking for the tomatoes she had canned last season. Just as she was about to reach for a jar, she heard the backdoor open and close.

"Isaac, is that you? Where on earth have you been? I've been so worried about you," she paused waiting to hear his voice, but all she heard was the creak of a board as someone approached the pantry.

"Lilly, is that you?" her voice sounded uncertain and a little nervous. Suddenly the door to the pantry swung wide and Melvin Yates stood in the doorway. Ellen almost lost her footing and would have fallen, but he caught her roughly and pulled her down. She glared at him and demanded to know what he was doing in the house. Smugly, knowingly, he brought the shotgun up. Ellen stared in horror then closed her eyes, waiting for the blast that would end her life.

A few miles to the north, Texas Ranger Sam Spaulding was talking to a local rancher. They were talking about cars - old cars. The suspect that he was after was seen driving an old jalopy.

"You know, Ranger Spaulding, I do recollect seeing an old car like the one you described. I believe my neighbor has one like it."

The ranger tried not to sound impatient, but time, he felt sure, was running out. "Which neighbor, Mr. Davis? How far does he live from here?"

"Well," he scratched his head for a moment, "I do recall seeing that hired hand, that works for Isaac Rheinhart, driving around here in an old car. The Thacker Ranch is about five or six miles down the road."

STRADI'S VIOLIN

Sam knew it may or may not be the man he was looking for, but he wasn't taking any chances. Barely, taking time to say goodbye, he jumped in his car and sped off toward Thacker Ranch.

"You just be quiet and do what I tell you and everything will be fine." Melvin had grabbed Ellen's hair and forced her face up to his. His breath was foul and smelled of stale beer. Ellen almost gagged, before he let her go. "Now, where is that pretty little daughter of yours, huh?"

She was silent and once again he grabbed her hair and forced her close to him. "Woman," he growled, "I asked you a question and you'd better answer and answer quick!"

Her heart was thudding so hard against her chest that she was sure he could hear it. Melvin thought about killing her right then, but he wanted to keep her alive until Isaac returned. Just then he heard a sound. It was Lilly coming down the stairs.

"Mother, where are you? I thought I heard you talking to someone."

Before Ellen could cry out a warning, Melvin shoved the shotgun against her stomach.

"Don't make a sound," he whispered cruelly, "or I'll kill the girl." Reaching into his pocket, he took out a filthy rag and stuffed it into Ellen's mouth. He noticed some rope, used for stringing clothesline, hanging on a nail above his head. He grabbed it and quickly tied her hands behind her back. Then grabbing her feet, he roughly tied them together. The look of pure terror on her face made him almost laugh out loud. He loved to see the fear in their eyes. Shoving her down on the pantry floor, he repeated his warning, that if she didn't cooperate, he'd kill the girl. Carefully, he stepped out into the hall.

Lilly had just turned the corner at the foot of the stairs and walked right into the barrel of the shotgun. She jumped back in surprise that was quickly replaced with fear as she stared at the weapon pointed menacingly at her. She glanced up into the sneering face of Melvin Yates.

"Well, little gal, I was just coming to look for you." He reached out a hand to caress her hair, but she jerked away.

"Where is my mother?" her voice shook as she spoke. He laughed cruelly.

"She's fine for now, but that could all change - unless you decide to cooperate," he added snidely.

"Where is she?" she cried, her eyes wide with fright. Panic and fear lent wings to her feet as she ran past him oblivious to the shotgun he held. She ran into the kitchen and noticed the open door to the pantry.

"Mother!" she cried as she ran to where Ellen was lying on the floor. Frantically, she grabbed the rag out of her mother's mouth and sobbing, she clawed at the ropes that bound her hands and feet.

As soon as Ellen could catch her breath, she screamed at Lilly to run, "Get out of the house! Run!" her frantic cries fell on deaf ears, because Lilly had no intention of leaving her mother. Tears of desperation were running down her face as she tried to untie the knots.

"Oh, God, no!" Ellen cried as Melvin grabbed Lilly's hair and yanked her to her feet.

He dragged her across the room and when he reached the kitchen table, he laid the shotgun down and sat down in a chair. He wrapped both arms around Lilly, trapping her arms at her side.

She twisted and turned and kicked with all her might. Laughing, he watched her vain struggles. It amused him when they struggled so hard. He always wondered why they spent their last few moments on earth fighting. *I would be so much better if they would just relax and let it happen.*

Isaac was driving fast, but he needed to see Ellen and tell her how sorry he was that he had messed things up so badly. The truck swerved as he turned the corner to the ranch on two wheels. It rocked and, for a moment, he thought it might turn over. He had kicked up so much dirt that he could barely make out the drive leading up to the ranch house. The brakes squealed as he brought the truck to a stop by the barn. He jumped out and made a beeline to the back door of the house.

Ellen had heard the squeal of the tires and looked at Melvin to see if he had heard as well. The man was oblivious to his surroundings; a look of pure lust and evil dominated his face. His hands were caressing the now whimpering Lilly as he touched her where no man had ever dared.

Isaac was calling Ellen's name as he came into the house and stopped short as he took in the scene before him. Lilly was sobbing and Melvin Yates was holding and stroking her. A cheap strand of pearls lay twined around her neck, where her torn blouse was open exposing nearly all of one breast.

Some moments in life seem to come in slow motion. Ellen watched helplessly and screamed a warning, but it was as though she was trapped in a nightmare and no one could see or hear her.

Isaac was yelling at Melvin to let go of Lilly and Melvin had jumped to his feet and grabbed the shotgun. As Isaac dived at him, the roar of the gun blotted out everything. Then came a moment of stunned silence, as all eyes took in the horrific scene.

A man stood silhouetted in the doorway.

"Drop the rifle!" the voice commanded.

Melvin Yates brought the shotgun up to fire again, but he was not fast enough. The ranger's 45 fired and the bullet hit him in the middle of his forehead. He fell heavily to the floor and didn't move.

Lilly had dropped to the floor and was cradling Isaac's head in her lap. The ranger checked to make sure Melvin Yates was dead. He walked over to where Lilly sat weeping over Isaac and looked down. Keeping his face devoid of expression he turned to help Ellen. She was frantically trying to get to her husband. He pulled the knots free and the rope fell from her hands and feet. She crawled over to where Isaac lay, and sobbing, she called his name over and over.

Ranger Sam Spaulding hated this part of his job. The part where the innocent paid for what the criminally insane did. At least, Melvin Yates wouldn't be able to hurt anyone else. He had seen to that when he shot him between the eyes. Now, his only regret was that he had not gotten here in time to save the man who lay mortally wounded on the kitchen floor.

Isaac was looking up at Ellen, wondering what had happened. The sound of the shotgun had been deafening, but now he felt nothing. He just felt sorry that he would not be able to comfort Ellen or take care of her. He could feel the life's blood leaving his body and knew that he was growing weaker, but he had to speak.

"Ellen!" her name was faintly spoken, and she bent over him to catch what he was saying.

"Sorry...didn't mean to hurt..." the words were so difficult to get past his lips. Ellen was crying and pleading with him not to speak. Once again, he made the effort,

"Must.... speak! Jake... McGowan?" The question in his voice puzzled her. What was he trying to say? Blood bubbled up through his lips and his breathing was tortured. Struggling, he tried again.

"Love... you...God, forgive...me!" the last was spoken fervently as a prayer.

Then he stopped struggling and peace settled over his features as his eyes became fixed and the breath left his body in one long, shuttering, sigh.

"No, Isaac!" Ellen screamed, throwing her arms around his body and weeping brokenly.

The Ranger stood, silently watching, as the two women grieved over the man who would never again be able to speak to them or bring them comfort. A shotgun blast at close range could cut a man in two and Isaac Rheinhart had been shot in the middle. Sam Spaulding was surprised he had lasted long enough to speak.

Chapter 24

A moan escaped his lips and he opened his eyes. At first he couldn't see clearly, then the room came into focus. He looked slowly around. His eyes came to rest on a slight figure whose head was bent as though in prayer.

"Mother," he said weakly.

Rose's head snapped up and she was leaning over him, frantically calling for the nurse. She didn't have to wait long. The nurse, followed by the doctor came running. They quickly urged Rose out of the room to begin the examination. The doctor prodded and poked until an irritated Jake began to complain.

"Well," the doctor said, "everything is as we expected," he was smiling at Jake as he spoke. Jake was not amused.

"What the hell does that mean?" he growled.

"It means that you are very lucky."

Jake snorted and said something unpleasant under his breath. The doctor was undaunted by Jake's attitude as he continued, "You had a stroke and that's why your left leg has no feeling in it. You are partially paralyzed." Jake tried to sit up, but the doctor restrained him.

"You mean that I won't be able to walk?" he choked out.

"Mr. McGowan!" the doctor was looking at him sternly, "You have had a stroke and, yes, there will be some difficulties. However, given time, you may be able to walk short distances. You will have to use a cane."

Jake had turned his face away.

"You are very fortunate," the doctor waited for a response, but didn't really expect one.

Jake was thinking, not about himself or what the doctor had said, but about Jenny. How was he going to look for her? He knew the night he had the stroke that Amanda must have gone away and taken Jenny. He turned and faced the doctor, "Would you please ask my mother to come in here?" The doctor nodded and walked out. He knew that with a man like Jake McGowan, it would take some time for him to adjust to his condition.

Jake waited impatiently for his mother to appear. He knew that she was being delayed by her desire to find out from the doctor about his condition. Right now his condition was not important. He needed someone to find Jenny and quickly. He was worried about the lies that Amanda would tell her.

When his mother finally did arrive, she was not alone. Franz was with her and someone that he never expected to see again. Rose rushed over to the bed and embraced him. After he had reassured her that he was going to be okay, he looked up and his gaze locked on Garret.

"What in blazes are you doing here?" The scowl on his face was meant to intimidate, but Garret stood with feet firmly planted and glared back at him. Then for Rose and Franz's benefit, he visibly relaxed, and smiled, "Hello to you, too, cousin!"

Jake was not amused and continued to glare at the man. "I asked you a question and I expect an answer!"

"Now, Jake," Franz broke in, "Garret is the one who got us here so quickly."

As Jake's displeasure turned to Franz, Rose spoke up, "I insisted that he bring us! Do you hear me, Jake? I insisted!" Rose was struggling for composure. Everything that had happened was beginning to take its toll on her.

"For God's sake, Franz," Jake bellowed, "take her home so she can rest!" Amid protest from Rose, she was ushered out the door by Franz and taken home.

STRADI'S VIOLIN

Garret made no move to leave. Jake's eyebrow rose inquiringly as he looked at him.

"In case you're wondering why I stayed," he stood looking somberly down at him with his hands in his pocket, "I just want you to know that it's not your charming personality that's keeping me here."

Impatiently, Jake pointed to the chair, "Sit down! I don't like you towering over me!"

Garret turned the chair around and straddled it, resting his chin on the back of the chair his face almost even with Jake's. "Is this better?" he asked blandly.

"If I weren't in this bed!" Jake sputtered darkly.

Garret put up his hand, halting the flow of words, "I stayed because I want to talk to you about Jenny."

He had Jake's full attention. "What do you know about Jenny?" he demanded, his eyes watchful.

Garret decided that to evade the question would only make things worse.

"I know that she is on a train to the east coast," the words were softly spoken. His eyes never wavered from Jake's. He read the question in them and before Jake had a chance to voice it, he answered, "I found out from the chauffeur that your wife hired in Austin."

"Damn, Amanda!" Jake broke in, "I should have guessed she'd do something like this!"

"What do you mean?" Garret asked, "Has she done this before?"

Gloomily, Jake stared at Garret trying to decide how much he should tell him. The younger man correctly interpreted his indecision and standing up abruptly, he stated matter-of-factly,

"You either trust me or you don't. I know that we got off on the wrong foot, but I think I can help." He waited for Jake to say something, but if his expression was anything to go by, then he probably didn't stand a change in hell of gaining his confidence. He was on the verge of leaving, when Jake came to a decision. He had fought with his misgivings, but in the end, common sense won. He needed Garret's youth, vitality and his ability to get around. Jake grimaced as he tried to move his left leg. Yes, he admitted to himself, he needed Garret. "Sit down!" he growled, as he looked up at the man moving towards the door.

"Look, I'm not staying unless you're willing to trust me," Garret's expression brooked no argument.

Jake sighed, "Please, sit down." His quietly spoken words and look of defeat made Garret uneasy. Casually, he walked over and once more straddled the chair. He stared into Jake's face. "I like it better when you growl."

Sardonically, Jake stared back, "I'm willing to tell you the whole messy story and not leave anything out, but" he paused here making sure he would not be misunderstood, "I want the same thing from you."

Garret smiled knowingly, "Quid pro quo! Is that the way it works, cousin? You tell me your story in exchange for mine? Well, I guess that could be considered fair. Okay, it's a deal!"

Shaking his head, Jake frowned at the younger man, "Boy, you do try my patience!"

Garret was still smiling as he got up and turned the chair around. He sat back down and leaned back, folding his arms across his chest. Then the smile vanished and with somber expression, he spoke, "I'd like to hear that story now."

Jenny had not slept in the last twenty-four hours. Even though she was young and somewhat naïve, she knew that somehow Amanda's story did not add up. For one thing, her father had never mistreated her. His love for her had been the strong point in keeping things on an even keel even when Amanda's volatile nature threatened to disrupt their lives. Always, he had supported her and she had never sensed that he was displeased with her character. She couldn't believe all the things that Amanda had told her about him. They couldn't be true, they just couldn't. Her head hurt from trying to make sense of everything. Jim was her brother, and Lilly, her sister! Then there was the matter of Ellen. Why, had her Mother not wanted her? Fresh tears rolled down from eyes still red from weeping much of the night.

Jim was on his way home. Sergeant Flannery had called him aside and told him that he would be going on leave earlier than scheduled, because there was some sort of emergency at home. The Sarge's usual mode of address when he spoke to a recruit was either an insult or an order, but he had been very serious, his voice grave as he talked to Jim.

He had wanted to ask questions, but Sergeant Flannery had not given him the chance. He frowned as he looked out the window of the train. What could be wrong?

Garret paced the floor. He was staying in Jenny's room. As he walked by the dresser, he picked up a brush. It had a long strand of dark hair caught in the bristles. He stared at the strands, as though by sheer will, he could conjure up their owner. Abruptly, he dropped the brush and resumed his pacing. His mind was going over everything that Jake had told him about Jenny's life. How could her mother have given her up?

The things that Jake had told him about Amanda did not surprise him. She was a harsh woman used to getting her own way and she was not a fit mother for Jenny. Why Jake had allowed her to stay in his and Jenny's life was beyond him.

Jake had been pretty sure that Amanda had figured out that her lies regarding Jenny's real mother were about to be exposed.

She had run and he doubted if she planned on coming back. Well, he was going after her and he would bring Jenny back home, forcefully, if necessary. Jake had also told him about Jim and how Jenny had fallen in love with him. Knowing Amanda she had probably taken great delight in informing her that Jim was her brother! The emotional impact could be devastating to a young girl.

His suitcase was packed and stood at the foot of the bed. The honking of a horn broke in upon his thoughts. He peered through the window and saw the taxi parked on the circular drive below. His expression was grim as he grabbed his bags and headed downstairs to the waiting taxi.

The steady sound of the train rolling down the tracks had lulled Jim to sleep. The sun came up over the horizon bathing everything in its golden glow and the warm rays penetrated Jim's sleep laden eyes. He was fully awake when the train pulled into Little Junction.

Almost before the train came to a full stop, Jim had grabbed his duffel bag and was anxiously waiting for the porter to put the steps down allowing him to leave. Longingly, several girls eyed the handsome soldier in uniform as he ran past them to the station platform.

Spotting Lilly, he almost shouted her name, but something about the way she looked, stopped him. Her eyes were infinitely sad, her features withdrawn. He had a gut wrenching feeling that whatever the news, it was bad. Slowly, he came towards her, noticing that she was not alone, but not knowing the Mexican man that stoically stood beside her. Just as he had almost reached her, a man stopped him. It was Arlis Mackey, who lived on a neighboring farm.

"Jim Gibson, is it really you? I know your Ma will be glad you've come home," he was patting him on the back as he spoke, his features somber, "Your Pa was a good man. Too bad that crazy...."

"Senor!" the sternly spoken word stopped him from completing the sentence. The Mexican man that Jim had noticed earlier was looking at Arlis Mackey as though he might strike him if he didn't shut up. Which would have been comical, because he was well over six feet tall and the Mexican was probably only a little over five feet.

Arlis looked guilty and shuffled his feet awkwardly, "Sorry, Son. My mouth sometimes runs away with itself. Be seein' ya' soon." He ducked his head, and quickly walked away. Judging by the few words that his neighbor had managed to say before being interrupted, Jim knew that it was far worse than he could have imagined. Lilly ran up and grabbed Jim around the neck, holding on to him as though she would never let go. As he stroked her hair, while she continued to cling to his neck and cry, he looked over her head at the compassion filled eyes of the Mexican. Abruptly, the man reached for Jim's duffel bag and slinging it over his shoulder, he walked towards the waiting car. Motioning with his hand, he indicated that he wanted Jim to follow.

Once, he had settled Jim and Lilly in the back seat where they could talk, he climbed in the front seat and put the car in motion, heading to the ranch. He thought about what he and his family had come upon. Was it just a short twenty-four hours ago?

They had wasted no time in packing up and going to the ranch. Senor Rheinhart had told him to come as soon as possible. When they arrived, everything was in chaos. Reporters, lawmen, people curious to see what was going on, were swarming all over the place. Isaac Rheinhart had been brutally murdered, by a crazy killer, known as "The Pearl."

He had instructed his family to wait outside while he sought to speak with the wife of his deceased benefactor. He had found Ellen in a state of shock along with her daughter and seeing the need for some action, he immediately took charge. He felt that Senor Rheinhart would have wanted him to protect his family from the questions and stares of curious onlookers and reporters. Calling his family inside to help, they had taken Ellen and Lilly upstairs and firmly, yet politely, refused to let them be further interrogated by lawmen or reporters.

Even though Ellen had no idea who they were, or why they were there, she was grateful for their presence.

Juan's thoughts were interrupted by an anguished cry from the back seat. He didn't turn around, but grimly keep his eyes focused on the road ahead. There was no doubt that the soldier had been informed of his father's death. He didn't wish to intrude upon his grief.

Jim was wracked by remorse and pain far worse than he could ever have imagined. He and his stepfather had not parted on the best of terms. His stubborn refusal to forgive his Mother had put up a barrier between them and now Jim bitterly regretted it. Lilly held him and they both wept openly, each trying to make sense of the tragedy that had robbed them of a father for the second time in their life.

Ellen sat in the darkened front room, waiting for the arrival of her son. She was oblivious to the storm that was approaching and the clouds that had caused the premature darkness. Her hands were sedately folded in her lap, her eyes staring straight ahead at nothing. Her soul had shriveled up inside her, hiding from the pain and grief that the last twenty-four hours had brought. A strange calmness had taken over, allowing her to view things rationally and without emotion. She had refused to go to the train station, demanding that Lilly go in her place. Juan had volunteered to go with her.

Juan and his family had broken in on their lives in the midst of the terrible ordeal. They had taken over without being asked and she had not minded, especially, when Juan had told her about Isaac's visit and invitation. If Isaac had trusted Juan, then that was enough for her.

She had given them the entire upstairs, except Lilly's room, for living quarters. They had refused at first, insisting that the bunk house should be their home, but Ellen could not bear to see them in the place where Isaac's killer had lived. Humbly, they had accepted her offer to live in the ranch house. All the arrangements for Isaac's wake and funeral had been made and Juan had scarcely left her side through it all. She would have been totally lost without him.

The sky was gray and overcast. Pete Driskoll, the Editor-In-Chief, for the *Lone Star Chronicle* was debating on whether or not he'd need an umbrella. He was anxious to visit his boss in the hospital. He wanted Jake to know that everything was okay and they had a top story that definitely would sell newspapers. It was too bad about that farmer, though. He shook his head, sadly contemplating the fate of the latest victim of the killer. At least, Ranger Sam Spaulding had made sure that there would be no more deaths due to the man they had dubbed "The Pearl." Shooting that scum had made him a hero to a lot of folks.

Jake was sitting up in bed. He was extremely annoyed with the doctors and nurses. Home is where he wanted to be, but they insisted that he wasn't ready. He cursed the weakness in his limbs that made him helpless as a baby. Thoughts of Jenny and what she must be going through plagued him without mercy. He hoped to God that Garret would be able to find her.

At his request, the Mexican had dropped him off in front; then, driven around to the back, taking Lilly with him. She had not minded, because she knew that he needed a few moments alone, before coming inside.

Jim stared at the front of the ranch house, knowing that it would never look the same to him. Why had this happened, he wondered, as the wind from the coming storm kicked up a sudden gust, causing him to turn his face away from the stinging, sand. Isaac was a decent God-fearing man. Violence had never been a part of his nature. Why, then, had he suffered such a violet death? It didn't seem fair. It was a nightmare of a homecoming, he thought, as he climbed the steps to the porch. He looked around as though expecting to hear Isaac's booming voice calling out in welcome.

Chapter 25

"You ungrateful child! After everything I've done for you, you are refusing to do this one little thing for me?"

Amanda was furious, but Jenny would not budge. She clung to her beloved violin. How could her Mother ask her to sell it? She had lost everything dear to her, but the violin, and she would not part with it.

"How do you expect us to get to Europe without money?" Amanda demanded to know.

Jenny shrugged her shoulders, because she didn't know and really didn't care. She had no desire to return to Austria and that awful man that her Mother liked so much. Anyway, she thought they were going to visit her Mother's sister in Virginia, but Amanda had changed her mind and decided to go directly to New York.

Amanda was still glaring at her daughter fully expecting her to give in. They were standing in front of an establishment that bought antiquities and she knew the violin would bring a nice sum of money. The tickets for their trip to Europe were more costly than she expected. Also, there was the matter of hiring someone to take them into occupied Austria. She had raved and ranted trying to get her way, but that had not moved her willful daughter. Heavens! She was supposed to be grateful to her for telling her the truth about Jake and Ellen. Her eyes glared as she looked at her once more. Maybe she was more like Ellen than she imagined. She remembered how stubborn that one had been! Slyly, Amanda decided to change her tactics.

"Look, Jenny, why don't we just go inside and ask the proprietor to take a look at the violin? Just to see how much money it's worth. Wouldn't that be nice to know?"

Jenny shook her head, "I don't care how much it's worth, I won't sell it!" She was clutching the case to her bosom and defiantly glaring back at Amanda.

There was only one thing left to do. Amanda brought her hand up and struck her hard across the cheek. The momentary surprise, coupled with outrage, caused Jenny to drop the case.

Immediately, Amanda grabbed the violin in triumph. Jenny's hand was pressed to her cheek where a large red welt was forming. She stared at her mother in stunned disbelief, and the large green eyes filled with tears, which spilled down her cheeks. Something in her expression told Amanda that she had gone too far. With one last, accusing, look in her mother's direction, Jenny turned and ran down the street. The sound of Amanda's voice demanding her to stop, spurred her to run even faster. She disappeared from sight, never once having looked back.

Jenny ran as one possessed, without thought or reason. How many blocks, she had no idea. Her headlong flight took her into the path of an on-coming car. The driver frantically put on his brakes and tried to swerve, but the scream and the thud as the car struck the small target, was unmistakable.

A crowd had gathered to view the unconscious, young girl, when an elegantly clad woman, wearing a fur boa, stepped from the vehicle.

"Pierre," she spoke in a foreign accent, "what can you tell; is she badly hurt?"

The chauffeur was bending over Jenny, intent on seeing if there were any broken bones. The woman spoke again, in her thick French accent,

"Well, what do you think?"

He looked up, "Madam, perhaps we should take her to the hospital. There doesn't appear to be any serious injuries, but she is still unconscious."

"Wee, I think that is best, also. Please put her in the car and do be careful!" Quickly, he complied and motioning the crowd aside, he drove slowly toward the hospital.

Suzanne Rendot looked down at the still form of the young girl, whose head was cradled in her lap. It was unfortunate that they had hit her, but perhaps it would turn out to be a blessing! Her hand reached out and caressed the dark hair away from the perfect features.

"Mon dieu!" she exclaimed, gently touching the large red welt on her cheek, "Who did this to you little one?"

As she continued to stare at the mark, the long dark lashes fluttered open and she found herself staring into a pair of frightened, green eyes. Jenny struggled away from the arms that held her and pressed herself against the door of the car.

"What am I doing here? Who are you?"

Amanda was frantic. The ship to England was leaving this afternoon and she still hadn't found Jenny. Pacing back and forth, she thought about what to do. She had believed that her daughter would come to her senses and probably be at the hotel when she arrived. After all, she was an intelligent girl and wouldn't have any trouble getting to the hotel on her own.

Going ahead with her plans, she had taken the violin into the antique shop. The proprietor had turned up his nose when she showed him the violin. After closer inspection of the instrument, he had discovered what she had known he would. It had the unmistakable markings of the master and maker of the violin, Stradivari. He had tried to mask his excitement, but Amanda recognized his delight at the thought of possessing such a rare instrument. After lengthy bickering over the price, they had finally settled on a sum that pleased them both.

He was startled, when he opened the front door, by the dark spectra that rose up from seemingly nowhere. Quickly, he reached out and switched on the light.

"Mother!" he choked out as he recognized Ellen.

She straightened, her arms hanging limply by her side. He rushed over and his arms enveloped her, holding her close as though he were trying to absorb her pain. Feeling her stiffness, he slowly released her and stepped back. There had been no return of the embrace and no emotion of any kind was evident in her face. Breaking the uncomfortable silence, she spoke.

"Thank you for coming. I think you should go into the parlor, now, and see your father."

The voice was that of his mother and yet, it wasn't. She had spoken impartially as though speaking to a stranger. Hesitantly, he followed her as she walked ahead of him. Turning, she stopped outside the door to the parlor, and spoke to him once more, "You make yourself at home. I have to go and see about supper now."

"Mother!" the agony and grief in his voice was unmistakable. Pleadingly, he looked at her, but her features remained stoic and calm. "I have to attend to something, now. You stay here and talk to your father." Quickly, she turned away and was gone.

"Coward!" she berated herself as she sat on the bed in her room. How she had longed to return his embrace! But, she told herself; she dared not. If she allowed any emotion, she would go to pieces and that would never do. She had to be strong. Isaac and Nora were counting on her. Suddenly, she smiled, "Isaac, doesn't he look handsome in his uniform?"

Candles were lit in every available corner of the parlor. Their light cast an eerie glow over the casket positioned in the middle of the room. Slowly, he walked over and looked down. There was a sheer cloth spread over the open casket and he could clearly see the man that he had called "Dad" for most of his life. Isaac looked peaceful, as though he were simply napping. As he stood looking at him, he allowed his emotions to run their gambit, letting loose the memories of a lifetime. He remembered the first time he saw Isaac. He was just a kid and the big man had taken him riding in the old Ford.

"Oh, Dad!" he whispered, " I wish I could talk to you and tell you how I feel." The touch of a hand on his shoulder startled him. It was Lilly and he put his arm around her, drawing her close, while they shared their sorrow.

After a few moments, he turned her to face him, "Lilly, I have to know! What happened? How?" The pain and anguish in his face was almost more than Lilly could stand. She continued to stare at him without answering. He shook her slightly, "Please tell me – did he hurt you?" She pulled away and whimpered like an injured animal, with her head bowed, and chin almost touching her chest. "Lilly, for God's sake tell me what happened!" He reached for her, but she pulled away again, only this time she raised her torment filled eyes to his face, "Jim, he was so horrible! He was going to kill us! If Isaac hadn't arrived when he did..." here her voice faltered, and Jim could see that she was reliving the nightmare. He tried to comfort her, but she shook her head, and backed away, then turned and ran out of the room. He let her go, because he was fighting his own guilt over the matter of Melvin Yates. The night of the Spring Concert he had seen the way the hired hand had looked at his sister, and he had intended to warn her. However, with everything that happened it had slipped his mind. Now, it was too late. He should have been a better Brother, a better Son. Again, he stood looking down at the man who had raised him as his own. "Dad," he cried brokenly, "I'm so sorry!"

Jake had turned a deathly shade of gray, causing his Editor-in Chief to rush out of the room in search of a doctor. They came on the run expecting to find him unconscious, but he had rallied from the shock, and was in the process of getting out of bed.

Pete Driskoll had not known of his bosses' relationship with the Rheinhart's when he filled him in on The Chronicle's top story. Hearing about the brutal death of Isaac Rheinhart at the hands of Melvin Yates was nearly Jake's undoing.

"What happened to the woman and the girl?" the choked out words were barely discernable. An alarmed Editor-In-Chief had rushed to the side of his bed, "My God, man! I'll go and get the doctor!"

"No!" Jake cried, as he watched the frightened man edge towards the door. Jake's hand shook as he pointed at him. "Tell me!" he rasped, "Tell me what happened –the woman and the girl! Tell me, damn you!"

"Mr. McGowan, please be calm! Mrs. Rheinhart and her daughter are fine."

While Jake struggled with whether or not to believe him, the distraught man took it as an opportunity to make his escape.

As it was, the doctors were unable to calm Jake or stop him from leaving the hospital. They threatened and pleaded, but to no avail. Finally, washing their hands of him, they released him from the hospital. Unfortunately, he was unable to walk because his left leg was still unresponsive. He commandeered a hospital wheelchair and instructed his Editor-In-Chief to take him home immediately.

Their final words of warning were still ringing in the ears of Pete Driskoll. Sternly, they had admonished his boss about the hazards of leaving. If he were to suffer another stroke, it could very well be his last. He was sweating and wringing his hands, wondering how Jake's family would feel, knowing that it was his fault, that Jake had ignored the doctor's warnings and left the hospital.

The woman with the strange accent had managed to calm the frightened, young girl by the time they reached the hospital. A doctor thoroughly examined her, finding nothing broken.

However, there was a problem. It seemed that she had lost her memory. Over and over they had tried to find out her name, but the girl was unable to remember anything, not even why she had run in front of the car.

The French woman took the doctor aside, "I would like to help. What do you think is wrong with her?"

The doctor was not sure how to answer the question. "Well," he hesitated, "she is fine physically, but mentally there appears to be what we call Amnesia," he waited for his words to sink in before continuing, "The blow to her head when she was hit by the car could be responsible."

"Doctor, how long will she be this way? She touched his arm and looked at him imploringly as though willing him to tell her what she wanted to know.

"Madam, I truly wish I could answer your questions, but we just do not know enough about this type of injury. She could go to sleep and wake up in a few hours remembering everything, or it could take weeks, even years, or," he paused ominously, "she may never remember."

Suzanne Rendot thought quickly as she took in the doctor's words. She came to a decision. "Doctor, I wish to be responsible for the girl and take her with me."

"Wait!" the doctor held up his hand, to try and halt the events that were happening too fast, "We must call the police or the social services in this matter. After all the girl's family must be around here somewhere."

The woman smiled at him as though she were dealing with a less than bright child. "Do you really believe that a decent family would let a young girl wander the streets of New York? You and I both know how many homeless children there are around here. Also, you must have noticed the mark on her face?"

"Yes," he answered gruffly, "I did wonder about that. I don't believe it had anything to do with the car hitting her." He was frowning darkly as he thought about what type of person had administered that blow on an innocent child.

Suzanne Rendot knew that it was time to use all of her persuasive powers.

"Surely, you must see that she is in need of someone to care for her," she looked at him expectantly, willing him to agree with her.

"But, Madame, her clothes do not look like those of an orphan, and I really do not have the time to argue with you in this matter," he spoke emphatically, hoping to put an end to their conversation, but he underestimated the will of the woman to whom he was speaking.

"Then, doctor, I suggest you take care of your patients and leave the welfare of the girl to me." Not giving him time to reconsider, she called to her chauffeur to take Jenny to the car. Meanwhile, she was busily digging in her purse. She withdrew what appeared to be a substantial amount of money. Practically waving it beneath his nose, it did wonders for mellowing the doctor. He reasoned within himself that the woman was probably right about the girl being homeless. Also, the child looked as though she needed someone to be kind to her. He decided not to interfere, except to give some instructions regarding her care.

"Make sure she is warm and comfortable. In a few days, I should probably see her again."

"You have been very kind," she spoke as she adjusted the fur boa to keep out the cold night air, "but I doubt we will be in this vicinity."

At his look of alarm and doubt in allowing the woman to leave without knowing where they were going, she quickly reassured him, "Doctor, I simply mean that, well, you can see that I am wealthy and I shall employ my private physician to look after her," as she spoke, she was pressing the large sum of money in his hand, "That should cover your charges with a little left over, hmm, doctor?" without waiting for a reply, she swept out of the hospital.

Staring down at the money in his hand, the physician felt the unmistakable stirrings of guilt for allowing his integrity to be compromised.

Several hours had passed, and hope faded quickly with no sign of Jenny. Amanda grew more anxious with each passing moment. Finally, when she could delay no longer, she had come to the dock. Then the gangplank had been lowered asking the few passengers to come aboard. Reluctantly, Amanda boarded the ship. She stood at the rail of the ship, looking at the crowd milling around the docks, but the one she looked for was not among them. Hope gave way to despair and she fought back tears, vowing not to cry.

It had been raining for several hours, but that had not stopped friends and neighbors from paying their last respects. So much food had been brought in that Juan's wife was having difficulty finding room for all of it. The kitchen had been scrubbed clean and there was no sign of the violence that had occurred, but Ellen and Lilly could not bring themselves to enter that particular room.

He stood at the door looking at the sky as lightening flashed and the elements seemed to be in turmoil along with his emotions. He was utterly weary from the strain of the long day. Welcoming people, accepting their condolences, making polite conversation had taken its toll.

His mother had scarcely made an appearance, refusing to leave her room for more than a few moments. Lilly had tried coaxing her out, but she had flatly refused. Finally, Lilly had given up and she, too, eventually disappeared. Sighing deeply, he could sense the weariness in him demanding that he rest. The humid air felt almost suffocating and he removed his shirt. His muscular body gleamed like polished bronze. Taking off his shoes to make as little noise as possible, he climbed the stairs.

Quietly, Jim opened the door to his bedroom. Lightening flashing across the sky caused the room to light up momentarily. He couldn't be sure, but it looked like someone was sleeping in his bed. Frowning, his hand found the light switch.

The bright light caused Margarita to bolt upright in bed, the covers falling from her scantily clad body. Boldly, she faced the intruder, sparks flying from her brown eyes. Her long, dark hair with its streaks of reddish gold was helter-skelter and she fought with it to keep it out of her eyes.

Jim knew that she was Juan's daughter, but he had only seen her from a distance and had never spoken to her. Still, the sound of her feminine voice with its thick, Mexican accent surprised him.

"Well, what are you staring at, Gringo, and what are you doing in my room?" she decided that attack was her best defense. It bothered her to see him standing only a short distance away, his muscular chest and arms bare. In fact, she had noticed him from the moment he had come home. Everything in her rebelled at the way she had felt when she saw him step out of the car. Handsome and blonde in his soldier's uniform, she had scolded herself for staring at him from the upstairs window. Determination and pride had kept her away from contact with him and now here he was in her room!

His voice was deep with a tinge of weariness. "Pardon me, but this is my room. Why are you in my bed?" He was looking at her suspiciously as though she had planned the whole thing. It made her Latin blood boil. He watched her face as her emotions ran high and it was obvious that she was no shrinking violet, but a girl who spoke her mind. Jim tried again,

"Look, senorita, you are very fetching sitting in my bed, but I am dog tired and I would appreciate it if you would just leave. Comprende?" he had sauntered nearer the bed as he spoke. The tone of his voice was condescending and slightly insulting. The day had been long and trying. Now, he just wanted to rest. She probably thought she was doing him a favor in trying to entice him. The sheer garment covering her body didn't exactly hide her assets from him. The curve of her breast was very inviting.

In San Antonio, he had heard tales of the lovely senoritas who offered comfort to the lonely soldier. For a few drinks, they would do almost anything, including spending the night in a stranger's arms. He had never been tempted to find his pleasure that way. Being old fashioned, he wanted more than a romp in bed. He wanted the respect and love that included marriage and a family.

That she was very tempting there was no denying. If he weren't so tired and emotionally drained, maybe just this once he wouldn't object to her brand of comfort. Something, about the way he was looking at her, must have alerted her to his thoughts.

"You Gringo pig!" she shrieked while grabbing an apple off the nightstand. Now, she was completely exposed standing in the middle of the bed. Her anger was such that she could barely speak, "You think I am here for you? All you gringos think the Mexican girls are for your pleasure! You think we are poor peasants who will fall at your feet! Well, Senior Gringo, comprende this!" Brazenly, she drew back her arm and released the apple.

The apple whizzed past, narrowly missing his head and smacked hard against the opposite wall. Now, he was angry. Perhaps, he had misunderstood, but she had no right to throw that apple at him. After all, she was the interloper standing in the middle of his bed shrieking at him.

Purposely, he strode to the side of the bed and reached up and dragged her down. Kicking and screaming, she tried to get free, but his strong arms held her fast. He sat down on the bed and dragged her across his lap face down. Her attractive posterior was an inviting target and he wasn't going to pass up the opportunity. Squirming and shrieking obscenities at him in her native tongue, she fought, but his superior strength held her firmly. He had administered one stinging blow to that soft part of her anatomy and was about to deliver a second, when the door to the bedroom swung open. Juan, his wife, Ellen and Lilly were staring open-mouthed at the couple on the bed.

Ellen was the first one to break the silence, "Jim, what are you doing? Let go of Margarita!"

The shock of seeing his daughter on the lap of senior Jim had momentarily robbed Juan of his speech. Now, he approached the couple still on the bed, "Why are you spanking my daughter?" his question was reasonable, but it all seemed so silly to Jim, and he wondered the same thing as he looked into the accusing eyes of the girl lying across his lap. Slowly, almost reluctantly he released her.

All the fight seemed to have left her. She stood up crossing her arms over her breast. Her head was slightly bowed, and her hair provided a curtain that hid her face. Before Jim could apologize, she ran to her mother, who promptly covered her with part of her robe and together they left the room.

A gathering of family and friends were there, as Isaac was being laid to rest next to Nora in the family cemetery on the ranch. Even though the rain had stopped, the sky was overcast and the October wind held a definite chill. Ellen, dressed in black, stood next to Jim who was wearing his dress uniform. He reached for her hand and drew it inside his for warmth. She smiled at him, silently thanking him. Even through the black veil of her hat, he could see that her eyes were infinitely sad.

The pastor was speaking, reminding them of what they had lost. Reading from the Bible, he remonstrated over Isaac's qualities, comparing him with men of like faith.

Jim looked over at Lilly wishing that he could comfort her, but was relieved to see that her grief had found release in the tears flowing down her cheeks. Stealing a look at his mother, he wished that she could cry. She was staring straight ahead, seemingly oblivious to her surroundings.

Jake was watching from a short distance away. Desperately, he wanted to be next to Ellen and tell her how sorry he was for everything, but the wheelchair prevented him. Rose and Franz stood behind him. Jake had told them the whole story and they had asked if they could come here with him. They wanted to meet the woman who had given birth to their beloved Jenny.

The SS Franklin was a freighter that carried a few passengers. She was carrying supplies to England and the handful of people that were brave enough or foolish enough to want to get to Europe.

Amanda's room lacked the luxuries found on an ocean liner, but she hadn't noticed. She lay on the small bed in the fetal position. A moan escaped her lips; things had not turned out the way she had planned. She knew that the ship had left the port and now she was on her way to a new life, but she felt no comfort in that knowledge. Somewhere in New York City, Jenny would be alone and frightened. What on earth had possessed her to run away? Suddenly, Amanda sat upright. She should not be on this ship; she should be in New York looking for Jenny. Running to the door, she yanked it open and began yelling for the captain. Someone told a passing crewman to do something about the madwoman that was making too much noise. She slapped the crewman's hand away when he tried to restrain her, "I demand to see the captain, now!" she screamed at her tormentor.

"Lady," he made the word sound like an insult, "the only thing you're going to see is the inside of your room! I will be glad to call some of my friends and believe me," he said menacingly, "you will go with us!"

Glancing around, she noticed that people were staring at her. "What are you looking at?" she demanded. Her clothes were in wild disarray and wisps of hair had come loose from the perfect coronet of braids. Frantically, her eyes darted from one to another. With clenched fist, she screamed at them, "What are you accusing me of? Tell me! Tell me!" her demands were met with uneasy silence. Only their eyes accused and some held pity. Turning, she ran wildly back to the cramped room and flung herself across the bed, weeping brokenly.

The service had ended and people were slowly leaving. Some lingered to speak to the grieving widow. Impatiently, Jim watched and nodded politely when spoken to. As his eyes wandered over the crowd, he noticed a man in a wheelchair. He was some distance away and there were two other people with him. Something about the man seemed familiar and excusing himself, he made his way towards him. He could hardly believe his eyes. It was Jake McGowan.

Jake watched him approach and wished that he could get up out of the wheelchair instead of helplessly waiting for Jim to acknowledge him. His eyes traveled upward to meet those of the young man standing in front of him. Jake vainly searched for the familiar, good-natured boy who wanted to be a writer for the *Lone Star Chronicle*. What he saw was a soldier in uniform, his eyes betraying none of his emotions. In fact, his eyes were slightly distrusting and definitely harder than Jake remembered. The silence was uncomfortable and Jake decided to break it.

"Jim, I'm so sorry about..." before he could complete the sentence, he was curtly interrupted.

"Where is Jenny? I would like to see her," the sharp tone of his question and demand left no room for formalities. Jake resisted the urge to let his temper take over, trying to place himself in Jim's shoes. "Look, I didn't know that Jenny was your sister before, but now I know the entire story," gruffly, he extended his hand as he spoke, "I came down hard on you and I'm sorry."

Jim's eyes flickered for a moment in surprise at Jake's admission. Then hardened again, as he spoke, "I still would like to talk to Jenny."

"So would I!" Jake mumbled, but before Jim could ask him what he meant, Ellen and Lilly had joined them.

"My God!" Ellen seemed to come out of her frozen state as she stared in horror at Jake and the wheelchair. Beneath the veil of her hat, she had paled considerably. "What happened to you? Did Isaac...?" her voice trailed off. Surely, this couldn't be the result of the punch he took from Isaac.

Quickly, Jake tried to reassure her, "Ellen, Mrs. Rheinhart," he quickly amended. This has nothing to do with your husband. I have a heart condition that caused a minor stroke. I'm fine and with a little help, I'll soon be walking," he smiled as he spoke, hoping to soothe her and not add to her sorrow.

Slowly, then faster, tears began to fall. Everyone seemed out of focus as the facade crumbled and all of the emotions that she had carefully locked inside seemed to surface at the same time.

Jim immediately stepped in, not allowing for further conversation. Ellen was weeping uncontrollably as he steered her away. Lilly looked at Jake briefly, and shook her head, silently warning him not to interfere.

Jake looked up at his mother and Franz, grateful that they had remained silent throughout the encounter. "Lets get out of here!" he spoke abruptly, not wanting to engage in conversation. His mind was churning with all the things he'd wanted to say. How he longed to make her understand that none of this was her fault or Isaac's. It just wasn't the right time. He looked down, cursing the wheelchair and the legs that wouldn't obey him.

Garret was impatient. He had followed Amanda's trail to New York and still he had not found Jenny. In desperation, he hired a private eye to help him find her.

They found the hotel where Amanda and Jenny had stayed, but there were conflicting views on where they had gone. People at the hotel remembered Amanda, but they had little recollection of Jenny. The desk clerk told them Amanda had asked directions to a shop that dealt in antiquities. It seemed that one person remembered seeing Jenny leave with Amanda, but another one said "no, that wasn't possible, because she didn't return with her." They were also confused about where Amanda had gone when she checked out of the hotel. One said that she had mentioned traveling to Europe, but he wasn't sure if she had found a freighter carrying passengers. For good measure, he also threw in his opinion about it not being a very good time to travel on the high seas with Hitler's U-Boats roaming around.

Discouraged by the reports, but refusing to give up, Garret had decided to see if he could find the antique shop that Amanda had inquired about. The private investigator thought that it wouldn't hurt to go down to the docks and see if he could find out if there were any ships going to Europe that would be carrying passengers. They parted ways agreeing to meet back at the hotel at a later time.

Garret found the street where the shop was located. He stood outside, wondering why Amanda would go to an antique shop. The sign read *antiques bought and sold here*. Frowning, he entered the shop. A bell tinkled above the door announcing his arrival. At that moment, a rather large man emerged from the back room. His eyes measured Garret's clothes and recognized the expensive cut of his suit. Greedily, he rubbed his large hands together.

"Welcome to my humble shop." He bowed his head slightly in Garret's direction. The proprietor's manner held a smugness that irritated Garret and made him want to tweak the man's beefy nose. Controlling the impulse, he turned what he hoped was a charming smile on the man. "Good afternoon." With the pleasantries aside, he came directly to the point.

"I need to know if a woman and a young girl paid you a visit yesterday. The woman would be in her late forties, very tall and her hair would be braided in a coronet around her head."

"Sir!" the man had raised his hand solicitously to interrupt the flow of words, "You cannot, surely, expect me to remember the many people that have been in and out of my shop."

"No!" Garret's eyes were flinty and his voice had taken a harder tone, "I don't expect you to remember everyone that came into your shop, just this one woman."

Garret's manner and tone of voice had caused the man to stiffen and his demeanor was uncompromising. He looked down his beefy nose that had turned an unbecoming red, "I think it would be best if you left my shop!"

Garret frowned and moved toward the man, causing him to take a step back. His eyes darted back and forth seeking a quick exit. Calmly, Garret reached into his coat.

"Please!" the man screamed, "Don't hurt me!" He flung his hands up trying to ward off the physical harm that he knew was surely coming.

Garret smiled, his eyes hard, and pulled his wallet out of his coat. He extracted some rather large bills and held them out to the stunned proprietor. "Would this improve your memory?" Sardonically, he watched as the man pulled a large handkerchief out of his pocket and mopped his perspiring forehead.

"This is most unconventional. Normally, I do not take bribes, but you have upset me and I feel that I am due compensation." His large hand shook as he reached for the money in Garret's hand. The money was pulled away out of the man's reach.

"Just a moment, I want to see if your memory has improved first!" Garret stated emphatically, "Did the woman and girl come into your shop?"

The disgruntled proprietor sighed deeply, before answering, "Yes, the woman you described was here, but there was no young lady with her. She was alone and we did some business and she left. End of story!" His eyes were on the money just out of his grasp. He reached out, but Garret refused to let go, "Not so fast, friend. This is a large sum of money and if you want it, you're going to have to do better than that!" Garret's eyes held his momentarily, causing the disgruntled proprietor to stiffen and glare at him in stubborn defiance. Garret knew that the man would not cooperate unless he made it worth the effort. "Look, I'll double the amount of money."

"Humph!" the man sneered, "I have yet to have any of your money. Why should I trust you?"

"Okay," Garret conceded, "point taken. Here is the money, but if you want more, I will need some answers."

Greedily, the man counted the money and his eyes widened, and he appeared to smack his lips in anticipation of the rest. Impatiently, Garret watched him, "Well, what did the woman have to sell?"

"What makes you think that she sold me anything?" he countered, smugly, "There are lots of lovely things that…Oh!

He was rudely interrupted by an angry Garret, who had grabbed the front of his coat. Their faces were inches apart. "What did the woman sell? I won't ask you again, but I will throttle you to within an inch of your miserable life if you don't tell me!"

The menacing look on Garret's face convinced him that it was time to stop playing games. However, he made a last ditch effort to regain some measure of dignity. "If I tell you, will you give me the rest of the money and leave my shop?" Garret released his hold on the man's coat and stepped back.

"Let's have it and you had better tell me the truth. I will make you no promises, because you could be an accomplice to a kidnapping."

The man paled considerably and would have offered a protest, but Garret continued, relishing the hold he now had over the unfortunate proprietor, "If you are wise enough to cooperate, then perhaps the police will not have to be involved."

The man was sweating profusely. He stumbled over to the counter and reached behind it, pulling out the violin case.

Now, it was Garret's turn to pale. Purposely, he strode over to the man and grabbed the violin case out of his hands. Opening it, he searched the violin for the markings that would identify the maker. Yes, there was the Maltese cross and the initials A.S. enclosed within a double circle! He looked up at the man standing quietly beside him, his eyes blazing,

"You do realize that this was not the property of the woman who sold it to you? It belongs to a young, girl and I doubt that she would ever part with it willingly."

Knowing that it would be futile to argue, he nodded his head in agreement, "Yes, now please take it and get out of my shop!" The man was clearly at the end of his endurance. Solemnly, Garret tipped his hat, "a pleasure doing business with you," and turning on his heel, he left with the beloved violin tucked beneath his arm.

The private investigator was waiting for him at the hotel. His expression told Garret that the news would not be good. Asking questions and talking to the right people, he found out that Amanda had bought two tickets on the SS Franklin bound for Europe. Garret sat down holding his head in his hands. His voice was muffled when he spoke, "God, what am I going to tell Jake? This could kill him."

The investigator laid his hand on the younger man's shoulder, "I think perhaps the FBI should investigate now. The authorities could be waiting for them when they arrive in England and the girl could be brought back to her father. It's the sensible thing to do. Shall I call the FBI for you?"

Garret looked at the man as though he had taken leave of his senses. "No!" the expletive came out harsher than he intended. At the man's startled look, Garret stood up, "Look, I want to thank you for all your help," he was taking money out of his wallet as he spoke, "this is a family matter and until her father says otherwise, we will handle it."

"But," the man stammered, "it is out of your hands now."

"Jake McGowan is very well known and he has many connections. Trust me, friend, he will know what to do."

The man shrugged his shoulders and walked away with a generous amount of money. Garret stared after him, knowing that the investigator did not understand his refusal to bring in the FBI. He was confident that Jake would know exactly how to handle the situation without allowing it to be turned into a public scandal.

His thoughts turned to Jenny. He hoped that she was not too frightened by Amanda's insane plan. He wondered how Amanda had talked her into it. His expression hardened. The woman deserved everything she was going to get, but Jenny was innocent. He prayed that Jake would be able to bring her home where she belonged.

Turning back to the hotel desk, he booked a room for the night. As soon as he was inside his room, he picked up the telephone, "Operator, I need to place a call to Austin, Texas." He poured himself a drink, knowing that he would need fortification before talking to Jake.

Chapter 26

Jim paced the floor. He was thinking about all that had happened after Isaac's funeral. He needed to talk to Jake McGowan, but most of all he wanted to see Jenny. His mother had told him the whole story of how Jake had come to the house asking questions. She told him how shocked Jake had been when she told him the truth. It was what happened after that he had trouble getting her to talk about. Finally, at his insistence she had told him that Isaac had hit Jake, knocking him down. He approved of what Isaac had done; He would have done the same thing for what Jake had said about his mother. Then, he laughed sardonically at his own thoughts. Hadn't he felt the same way as Jake when she had told him the truth?

At least, he was grateful to Jake for one thing. Seeing him in a wheelchair had been the catalyst that Ellen needed to release her grief. She had cried for hours after they had taken her home.

"Jim." his name was barely audible, but he heard her. Whirling around, he looked at her in surprise. "Mother, what are you doing up? You should be resting."

She was wearing an elegant black dress. Her hair was down except for the sides that were pulled up in the fashionable forties style. She was clutching her purse at her side.

"Are you going somewhere?" Some sixth sense told him what she had in mind.

"Yes, and I was hoping that you would come with me." Her eyes avoided his as though she was afraid of what he might see. Taking a deep breath she spoke, "I'm going to see Jake McGowan and Jenny. Will you come with me?" This time she did look at him, her eyes pleading.

Jake spent a restless night. He had talked to Garret and he was horrified at what Amanda had done. He had trouble believing that she would go that far. Garret convinced him that it was true and he told him about her selling the violin. He was very grateful to Garret for getting it back, but he wished with all his heart that it had been Jenny instead. Now she was on her way to England, but Amanda would have a surprise waiting for her when she got there. Thankful for the many connections he had all over the world, he had made a few phone calls. When they arrived, Jenny would be taken from Amanda and returned to him. Amanda would be given the option of staying there and continuing with her plans or returning to the United States and facing charges of kidnapping with treason thrown in for good measure. Smiling, he felt sure that Amanda would choose to remain in Europe.

Rose thought she'd never seen a woman more lovely than Ellen Rheinhart. The black dress was a perfect foil for her blonde hair and fair skin. Only her eyes hinted at the tragic events that had befallen her. Graciously, she shook hands with the elder Mrs. McGowan, showing a smile that was tinged with sadness.

Jim stood tall and handsome by her side. He, too, was polite, but distant. Rose could tell by his determined demeanor that he would not be put off and she sincerely hoped there would not be any trouble. She led the way into the parlor where Jake was waiting for them, then discreetly left the room.

Jake's first reaction at the sight of Ellen was the same as his mother's. She was a stunning woman. He wished that he could get up to greet her. Looking into her eyes, he could tell that the sight of him in the wheelchair troubled her. He watched as Jim solicitously seated his mother in the chair across from him, and then, seated himself a short distance away.

A few awkward attempts at conversation were made, until Jim impatient for answers came straight to the point, "We need to speak to Jenny, where is she?"

The abruptness of the question caught Jake off guard. He faltered for a moment, then, quickly regained his composure. Looking straight at Ellen, he spoke softly, "I'm sorry to have to tell you this, but Amanda has taken Jenny to Europe."

"What!" the word exploded from Jim, "You are kidding, right? At Jake's silence, Jim stood up. Anger held in check emanated from his body. "What are you trying to pull? Are you hiding her from us?" His fist clenched at his side. His eyes, boring into Jake, demanded an answer.

"Sit down!" Jake's voice and the expression in his eyes, brooked no argument, "You're upsetting your mother."

Ellen had turned pale at the news of Jenny's whereabouts. She had no doubt in her mind that Amanda would do this to keep her from being reunited with her daughter.

"Please, Jim, sit down," she begged. Turning to Jake she pleaded for him to tell them what had happened. Reluctantly, Jim took his seat and waited to hear what else Jake had to say.

He told them all that Garret had found out in New York and what was being done to get her back. They had listened intently and asked questions. Jim had wanted to know who Garret was and why he was looking for Jenny. Patiently, Jake explained that he was a relative and that he had sent him to look for her in his place.

Finally, not being able to sit still any longer and wanting to go somewhere to think, Jim had excused himself. He headed out the back door and straight for the Juniper Tree

"Jake," Ellen's eyes filled with tears as she spoke, "is this," she gestured to the wheelchair, "the result of the altercation between you and my husband?"

Jake was shaking his head, "No, Ellen, this is something I've been battling for years. It has nothing to do with Isaac." He looked into her eyes as he spoke and felt himself drowning. Abruptly, he looked away to break the effect.

Ellen wasn't sure. She watched him for a moment, trying to decide if he was being truthful or trying to spare her more grief. Noticing how abruptly he looked away filled her with despair.

Yes, she thought, *he's trying to spare my feelings*. Nothing he could say would erase the guilt, because she knew that Isaac had felt it, too. Before he died, he had wanted Jake's forgiveness and hers too. *My, darling, Isaac, I'm the one to blame for keeping quiet all these years,* Ellen thought, as tears of remorse welled up and threatened to spill down her face. Thinking of the danger that Jenny might be in, brought her further grief. *Oh, Jenny, how will you ever forgive me?*

The size of the Juniper Tree still impressed him. He stood staring up at it for some time. Slowly, he wondered over to the edge of the cliff. Austin lay sprawled before him, but in broad daylight it just looked dingy and dirty. He remembered the starlit night when he had been here with Jenny. It had glowed and twinkled with a thousand lights. It seemed like a lifetime ago.

He turned away and walked over to the bench where he had sat with Jenny. Sitting down, he relaxed and imagined her here with him. They would have a lot to talk about and their conversation would definitely be different than before. Life seemed so unfair. After he had finally come to terms with the fact that she was his sister, he couldn't be with her, because Amanda McGowan had stolen her from them a second time.

Angrily, he stood and paced. By the time Jenny was returned home, he would be off somewhere fighting a war. Maybe, he would never have the chance to know his baby sister. Lost in thought, he forgot time and was surprised to notice that the sun was beginning to go down. He looked at his watch and realized that he had been gone for several hours.

When he came into the house, Jake was waiting for him in the kitchen.

"Jim, your Mother was tired and I had my chauffer take her home, and," he paused as though unsure of himself, "I wanted a chance to talk to you."

Jim folded his arms and looked down his nose at the man in the wheelchair.

"I was under the impression that you never wanted to speak to me again. Isn't that right, Mr. McGowan?"

Jake laughed as he wheeled the chair over to the icebox and opened it. He took out a carton of milk. "You're not very forgiving, are you? By the way, would you get a couple of glasses out of the cupboard?"

Giving Jake a dark look, he did as he was asked. "Now, sit down and taste some of the best apple pie in the county. My mother made it!" He winked at Jim and waited for him to be seated. His expression sobered and as he looked at the young man across the table, memories came flooding back. "You know, Jim, Jenny and I used to eat our breakfast together. Right here. It was the best part of my day," his voice choked up and he had to clear his throat.

Jim looked away. He hated seeing the pain and sadness in Jake McGowan's eyes and he hated seeing him in a wheelchair. Most of all, he hated that Amanda had taken Jenny away.

He looked back at Jake. This was the man he had admired for so long and who had given him his job at the *Lone Star Chronicle*. He was also the man who had given him his dream that had been shattered by events beyond their control. Jake McGowan was a victim of circumstances just as he had been. So, why was he holding a grudge? Staring at the man sitting across from him, he felt an overwhelming urge to go back in time. Since that wasn't possible, maybe they could do the next best thing. Feeling a little foolish, but knowing that it was something that he had to do, he stuck out his hand, "shall we start over? Hello, Mr. McGowan, my name is Jim Gibson."

They were both smiling as they enthusiastically shook hands. For Jake, as his eyes beamed at the young man across from him, it was like having a heavy weight removed from his shoulders.

The day was bright and crisp, but the weary traveler that disembarked from the train was feeling pretty low. He hailed a taxi to take him to the mansion on the hill that overlooked Austin. Garret knew that they would all have to be patient, before they would see Jenny again. He sighed and hoped that Jake would be able to bear the long wait for the ship to reach England.

Seriously, he didn't think that he should be here when she returned. He doubted that she would anxious to see him again after their last encounter. The guilt was eating him up, and he felt that somehow he was to partly to blame for all her recent trouble.

Before he was aware, the taxi had pulled into the circular drive. After paying the driver, he wearily carried his bags up the steps and into the house. He sat the bags down in the hallway and walked into the parlor. He could have announced his presence, but he felt like having a few moments alone.

Rose walked into the room, surprising Garret as he stared out the window at nothing; His thoughts were dark and troubled. They looked at each other across the room and each tried vainly to think of something to say. Garret broke the silence, "I guess you think I'm a monster," he turned his face way from her as he spoke and his voice sounded bitter and filled with regret.

Rose closed the distance between them and gently touched his face, causing him to look at her. "I don't think you are a monster. Perhaps, you had a lapse in good judgment, though," she gently admonished. Her eyes were filled with understanding as they observed the misery and pain etched in his features. They both understood without saying it, what she referred to.

"I swear to you, Aunt Rose, I never would have harmed her, but you are right. I used poor judgment. I should never have touched her, much less kissed her. She is just a child, for God's sake!"

His disgust with himself was plain to see. It was obvious that his conscience had dealt harshly with him, and Rose could not help but forgive him for his indiscretion. Again, she touched him lightly to turn his attention back to her.

"Why did you do it, Garret?" her softly spoken words were barely above a whisper, and the man listening from the hallway, strained to catch her words. Jake's lips were tight with anger, but something had kept him from interrupting his mother and Garret's conversation. He, too, wanted to hear the answer to that question.

Garret's eyes held hers a moment before he spoke,

"You remember I had just heard her play the violin?" she nodded her head as he continued speaking, "The music was magic. It transformed her." His eyes sought hers, once more, trying to make her understand. "I felt something I had never felt before and I guess for a moment, I saw her as the woman that she will eventually become. I know it doesn't make much sense, but I wanted to hold on to that image."

He remembered the way she had looked. The passion for her music making her appear older and more mature that her years. It had awakened something deep inside him. With an effort, he brought his thoughts back to the present. Sardonically, his sensuous mouth curled,

"I know that doesn't excuse my behavior and I know it's my fault that Amanda took her away."

Rose held up her hand to stop his self-recriminations, "No, Garret, it is not your fault. True, Amanda was looking for an excuse to do what she did. I know, now, that she had planned all along to run away with Jenny. Her past was finally catching up to her and she was afraid of Jake's retribution for all the pain she has caused. Franz told me all about her flirtation and continuing correspondence with Hans Gunthur. She and that man planned this whole thing!" the latter was spoken with a harshness seldom used by Rose, "That woman has taken my granddaughter to Europe, and God knows what danger! Oh, Garret, I don't know if I can bear it!" Her face crumpled and covering her eyes, she burst into tears.

The sound of her weeping almost drove Jake over the edge. His white-knuckled fingers gripped the wheelchair.

Garret's arms went around her as he led her to a chair by the window. He produced a clean white handkerchief and handed it to her.

"You must not allow yourself to be upset by all this. Jake has everything under control. He must have told you why I went to New York?"

Rose looked up, "Yes, he did, but it was too late, wasn't it? They are already on their way to Europe!" Fresh tears rolled down her age-lined cheeks.

"Aunt Rose," he knelt beside the chair, taking her hands into his own. They were ice cold and he began to massage them as he spoke, "Your son knows people who can help and once they reach England, the authorities will take over. Before you know it, Jenny will be back here safe and sound, and," he paused here as anger crept into his voice, "Amanda will be out of the picture for good!"

The room had grown quiet, and both Rose and Garret sensed his presence at the same time. His wheelchair was framed in the doorway, but his features were shadowed.

"Mother," he moved the chair forward into the room as he spoke, "I wonder if you would mind leaving us alone for a few moments? I need to speak to Garret," he paused, "about his trip to New York."

His tone was strained and Rose sensed that he was not as in control as he was trying to appear. She worried about him. This whole thing was a terrible strain on him emotionally and physically.

"Jake, can't this wait? Poor Garret is tired. He just got here and you need to rest as well."

"Mother!" his voice sounded harsh even to him, "I'm not a child! I will decide when I need to rest!" The scowl on his face and his tone of voice caused Rose to flinch as though in pain. Jake felt instant regret, but she was already leaving the room. He would apologize later.

Garret was frowning and his countenance mirrored Jake's as they looked at each other.

"You snake!" Jake snarled as he moved the chair closer to the younger man, "I trusted you and you push your damnable attentions on my innocent daughter!"

The fire in his eyes made Garret wonder for a moment if Jake might come out of the wheelchair and physically attack him. Calmly, though inside he was a mass of nerves, he poured a drink from the decanter setting on the table. Before pouring the fiery contents down his throat in one swallow, he eyed Jake, "Would you like one?"

Jake noticed that the younger man's hand shook as he set the glass down on the table. He spoke as he poured himself another shot of whiskey, "I gather you were listening to our conversation?"

"Yes, and my mother is right about one thing. You didn't cause Amanda to take Jenny away. In that respect, you are blameless," he spoke the words grudgingly, "but," and this time the words came out harsh, the anger evident, "You should not have touched her!"

Garret slammed the glass down on the table, spilling the contents.

"Don't you think I know? I've regretted it ever since it happened! Believe me, I would not have harmed a hair on her head!"

"So you say!" Jake snarled not willing to let him off the hook.

"Give me the benefit of the doubt!" Garret returned.

"I'll tell you what I'll give you." Jake pulled himself up straighter, his eyes glittering. "I'll give you twenty-four hours to get out! I appreciate what you did in New York even though I suspect it was more from a guilty conscience than anything else. Under the circumstances, it would be best for everyone if you left. I don't want you here when Jenny returns. Do I make myself clear?"

The two eyed each other like warring combatants.

"Yes, cousin Jake, I get the message and I don't need twenty-four hours to think about it!"

He grabbed his coat and hat and walked to the door where he paused. Deliberately, he turned and looked at Jake. "I'm leaving this time, because, like you, I feel it would be for the best, but," he stressed the word, "someday, I'm coming back whether you like it or not!"

Jake heard the rattling slam of the front door and slumped in his chair. The anger drained out of him, leaving him weak. Deep inside, he grappled with remorse and guilt much like Garret, but for a different reason. He had lived in a fool's paradise too many years. Amanda was his nemesis for allowing his heart to rule his head.

Chapter 27

Jim was digging a new hole for the fence post. The sweat poured off his face and bare chest as he worked. Margarita stood watching from a short distance away. She had overheard him tell her father where he was going this morning. After he left, she had saddled the mare and ridden off in the same direction. It didn't take her long to spot him. His bronze muscles rippled as he worked.

Stopping to catch his breath, he wiped the sweat from his brow and stood leaning against the shovel. Some sixth sense caused a prickling sensation along his spine. Dropping the shovel, he shaded his eyes from the blazing sun and searched the terrain. He smiled even as he visibly relaxed.

"You can come out, now. I promise not to give you the spanking you deserve!"

Feeling foolish, she stepped from behind the mesquite tree and stood looking at him, uncertain as to whether she should stay or run away.

"Is there water in that canteen?" He was pointing at the canteen she was holding at her side. Impishly, she held it up, "Si, Senor Gibson, it is water and if you are nice to me, perhaps I will give you a drink."

She came closer. Her eyes were teasing. Appreciatively, he watched the gentle sway of her hips in the jeans that appeared to be molded to her body. One side of her peasant blouse had fallen down, leaving her creamy shoulder bare. Her hair tumbled down her back, the sun picking out the reddish streaks and setting them ablaze. The dark eyes watched him as closely as he was watching her. For a gringo, he was a fine looking man, she thought.

Holding out the canteen, she stood several feet away. Keeping his eyes locked with hers, he stretched out his arm and reached for the canteen. Instead of taking it as she expected, he grabbed her arm and pulled her off balance. She fell against him, gasping at the contact of his hard, lean body. The muscled arms came around her, drawing her completely against him. She tilted her head back, looking up at him through half closed eyes. Her lips were slightly parted and inviting.

"What do you think you are doing, gringo?" her voice sounded breathless as though she had been running. He could feel her heart hammering against his chest. Smiling, he reached out and stroked her head, going all the way down the length of her hair to the small of her back. Surprised, she looked at him, and he could tell that she had expected something entirely different.

"It's the way we calm the fillies," he smiled, his eyes dancing mischievously, "You know, the ones that get all excited whenever the stallion comes near!"

Pushing against him with all her might, she swung out of his arms, "You...!" the rest of the epithet was spoken in Spanish. Jim laughed, understanding a few of the curses she aimed at him. "I should have known better than to be nice to you!" she sputtered indignantly. Angrily, she strode away to where she had tethered the mare.

"Margarita!" the sound of her name on his lips stopped her.

He sauntered over to her. If she expected an apology, she was soon disappointed. Lazily, his eyes appraised her as he handed her the canteen.

"You dropped this. By-the-way, if I hadn't let you go, you'd still be in my arms."

Anger blazed in her eyes and she swung up into the saddle, intent on getting away from him. Easily, he caught the reins, stopping her, "One more thing, Senorita, I don't need you to be nice to me. Comprende?" he spoke softly, his eyes holding hers. Grabbing the reins from him, she gave the little mare a kick in the side that sent her galloping off. The sound of his laughter echoed in her ears long after he was out of sight.

Returning to his work, he thought about their brief encounter. He didn't know why he had deliberately baited her, but he had enjoyed her fiery response. The shooting sparks in her brown eyes and the agitated rise and fall of her breast, as she reacted to his outrageous remark, had ignited something within him. He had badly wanted to kiss her and he could tell she had wanted the same thing, but sometimes you had to be cruel to be kind.

Stopping to rest, his thoughts continued. Truthfully, he would like to get to know her a whole lot better, but there wasn't time. Just a little over three weeks left of his emergency furlough, and he would be rejoining his company. The war didn't show any signs of ending, and soon, and they would be shipping out - destination unknown. Yes, he thought, it would be wise to forget all about the lovely senorita. Anyway, he reasoned, there were other things to think about. He and Jake had come to an agreement. Any stories that he wrote regarding the war and a soldier's life were going to be published in the *Lone Star Chronicle*. That is, Jim sighed with resignation, the ones that got past the censors.

Juan watched his daughter leave the stables and storm into the house. Thoughtfully, he looked in the direction from where she had come galloping in on the little mare. He knew that Senor Gibson had gone off in the same direction only this morning. Sighing, he shook his head. No good would come from this. Senor Gibson was now the head of the household and someday he would be married, but not to the daughter of a poor Mexican. He loved his daughter and did not want to see her hurt.

Just as the sun was setting in the west, Jim drove up. He was tired and dirty from his long day repairing the fences. Unloading the pickup, he carried his equipment into the barn. Juan greeted him and offered to help, hoping for an opportunity to talk to him about Margarita.

The atmosphere was strained and awkward where usually they worked amicably, talking and laughing. Jim wondered about the change. He noticed the Mexican kept darting glances at him, his expression troubled and somber. Finally, Jim decided to break the tension by asking, "Is there something troubling you, Senor?"

Juan took off his hat holding it in front of him and looked down at his feet, trying to find the right words. Conveying his thoughts into the English language was sometimes difficult.

"Senor Gibson, you and your madre have been very kind to me and my family. I do not wish to offend, because I am grateful for the opportunities we have been given here," he paused wondering what to say next.

"But?" Jim was looking at him expectantly, one eyebrow risen in question.

"Well, Senior, I will get to the point. It is about my daughter, Margarita." The last came out in a rush, as though he was glad to get it out in the open. "She is very head strong, as you may have noticed, not without faults." Holding his head high, he looked straight at Jim. "I love her very much and do not want her to be hurt. One day, when you are a father, you will understand."

Jim was not a fool and he understood very clearly what Juan was trying to say. The undercurrents that passed between him and Margarita had not gone unnoticed. He was subtly warning him not to hurt his daughter. Jim smiled and rested his hand on Juan's shoulder,

"Do not worry, Senor Juan, I would not intentionally hurt your daughter. As you know, I am a soldier and I will be leaving soon."

"Si, Senior, I know this, but it only takes a moment to break a heart." His expression was one of deep concern and Jim could not ignore it.

"Look, I'm not going to tell you that I don't find her attractive, because I do. If I were not leaving so soon, I would like to get to know her better." His words did nothing to allay the man's fears.

"Senior Jim, I know that most gringos think of the Mexican as ignorant and poor," Jim started to protest, but Juan continued speaking, "It is true that we come from a poor country with only two classes of people; the very wealthy and the very poor. My family falls into the latter category; we are self-taught with little or no education. I brought my family here, because I wanted them to have a chance at a better life. However, Senior, we know our place and it is not proper for you and my daughter to be together."

A long time later, as Jim lay in bed, he thought about what Juan had told him. He didn't believe in class barriers or race barriers for that matter. Isaac had taught him that all men were created equal and it didn't matter where he came from only what he was like, inside.

STRADI'S VIOLIN

Eyes fluttered closed and as he drifted off to sleep, his last thoughts were about brown eyes and long, wild hair with streaks of fire.

Rose smiled as she watched Ellen and Jake. They were talking animatedly and laughing about a story Jake had told her about Jenny. Choking back her emotions, she tried not to think about her granddaughter. She was so worried and she knew that Jake was, too. Ellen's visits helped to keep things on an even keel. Ellen refused to think anything other than positive. She was so sure that soon Jenny would be returned to them. It seemed she could not hear enough about Jenny's life. Jake had shared pictures with her and had even given her one of Jenny posing with the symphony. Rose looked back at the laughing couple. *It should have been you*, she thought to herself. Ellen would have been perfect for Jake. The phone interrupted her thoughts and she hurried off to answer it.

Ellen was smiling and Jake was drowning, again. He looked forward to her visits. She made him feel like a little boy in a candy store staring at all kinds of delicious treats and not knowing which one to pick. Every facet of her personality was a treat to him and it was hard for him to decide which one he liked best. He never tired of listening to her, but she didn't talk much about herself. One thing was apparent to him; she would never have abandoned Jenny without good reason. He had been wrong to ever think that she could. Ellen wouldn't let him apologize. In fact, she refused to talk about the events of Jenny's birth and Amanda's part in it. One day, he would make her tell him the whole story.

Rose was talking to Garret. He rang to let her know that everything was okay. She was aware that he and Jake had had a disagreement, causing him to leave without saying goodbye.

Rose wished with all her heart that the two of them would get along. Garret and Jake were very much alike. Both were stubborn and proud. Garret told her that his father was displeased with him, because he had joined the air corps. As soon as he finished training, he was going to England to fly with the Royal Air Corps in raids against Germany. Rose begged him to be careful and to keep in touch.

Jim left the *Lone Star Chronicle* feeling very pleased with himself. He had written several stories about Army life. His journal had proved invaluable in retelling the stories. The editor was as impressed as Jake with the material and they had enthusiastically set to work getting them in print. The stories would sell newspapers to the public anxious to hear about the life of a soldier. Humming to himself, he walked a little further down the street. Then a flash of light caught his eye. Sunlight was trapped in the fiery tresses and he blinked to make sure he wasn't dreaming.

Margarita was standing in front of the Belleview Theater, looking up at the billboard. His feet should have propelled him away from the temptation. Instead, he found himself standing next to her. His voice startled her, "What are you doing here?" he was smiling as he spoke, his eyes traveling leisurely over her as though he were memorizing everything about her.

Drawing herself up, she clenched her fist. How dare he speak to her after their last encounter! She wanted to turn her back on him and walk away, but somehow she sensed it was what he expected her to do. Well, she wouldn't give him the satisfaction! Tossing back her wayward hair, she turned to look at him, "My father came into town for some supplies and I came with him. Is that all right with you, Senior?"

The saccharine sweetness of her smile did not hide the smoldering fire in her eyes. Jim was not deceived and his richly masculine laughter told her so. "I saw you looking at the billboard. Do you like Westerns, Senorita?"

"I wouldn't know. I've never been to a theater or seen a movie," she told him sullenly.

He was silent and she wished that she hadn't told him. He probably thought she was very ignorant and stupid. Turning, so he wouldn't see the sudden tears that sprang to her eyes, she started to walk away. A masculine hand shot out and gripped her arm, halting her.

"Margarita, would you like to see the movie with me?" She turned to look at him to see if he were teasing her again. His expression was sincere. "Please!" he whispered close to her ear, causing her body to tingle with unexpected pleasure. Forgetting why she was mad at him, she allowed him to propel her to the theater entrance. He bought two tickets from the girl at the ticket window and they went inside.

The lobby was impressive and Margarita was drawn to the freshly popped corn. Jim smiled as he watched her. She was like a small child, discovering a whole new world. The moment was shattered by a rowdy, threesome, who deliberately blocked their path. Harold Lassiter was smugly looking them up and down. "Well, well, Jim Gibson. I hear you're an army boy now."

He and his friends snickered, and Margarita moved closer to Jim as though seeking protection. Her action didn't go unnoticed by the pock marked leader. He leered and moved closer.

Jim remembered Harold Lassiter from his school days and his memories of him were anything, but fond. Harold was the school bully who had a reputation for violence and mayhem. It was rumored he'd spent time in the county jail. Deliberately, Jim moved in front of Margarita, blocking her from Lassiter's view. His eyes were steely as he made eye contact with the interloper. "We're going in to see the movie. I suggest that you be on your way," his tone brooked no argument.

The shifty eyes of Harold Lassiter looked back at him. "Now is that any way to treat an old school chum? Anyway, I have no objection to you seeing a movie. Hell, where you're goin' you probably won't get to see another movie for a long time," he looked at his buddies and winked, "that is if you come back at all!" They snickered as though it were a huge joke.

Taking Margarita's arm, Jim moved forward, but once again, his path was blocked.

"As I said, I have no objection to you seeing the movie, but the spic," he turned and pointed at Margarita, "is not welcome in our theater."

Anger swept through Jim and he grabbed the front of Harold's shirt. "Lassiter, I will give you and your hooligan friends two seconds to get out of here!" he snarled.

Harold backed up, pulling out of Jim's grasp, and held up his hands. "Hold on, soldier boy, I don't want to fight with you, but you need to understand how things are around here. We don't allow her kind into our theaters. The Mexicans and the Negroes know their place even if you ain't too smart!" seeing the look of disgust and menacing look that Jim was directing at him, he quickly added, "look at her, she knows that she don't belong here."

Margarita had turned pale and she was visibly shaking. She turned to Jim, her eyes pleading with him to take her home. There were several onlookers watching to see what would happen next.

"Personally, I don't know why you're getting so upset over a little, Mexican, wh—."

The sentence was never completed. Jim's fist connected with the pock marked nose, breaking it. Then all hell broke loose with Harold Lassiter yelling and screaming at his friends to help him, while his nose bled profusely. Lassiter's buddy grabbed Jim from behind and held him while the other one punched him in the stomach and face. Before the owner and several of his employees could break up the fight, Margarita had jumped on the back of the man beating Jim and began plummeting the back of his head. The police arrived and the melee was over as soon as it had begun. Lassiter and his buddies were hauled off to jail amid loud curses and protest.

Mr. Duncan, the proprietor of the theater, invited Jim and Margarita into his office to escape curious onlookers.

James Duncan entered the office carrying an ice pack, which he offered to Jim.

"Son, I'm sure sorry this happened. Are you going to be okay?"

Jim nodded and winced as he applied the ice pack to bruised area around his eye. His lower lip was split and bleeding slightly.

The heavy-set, balding, proprietor looked apologetically at Margarita before he spoke,

"Try to understand the way things are around here. I don't make the rules, but you can't just waltz in here and not expect some repercussions."

"Wait a minute!" Jim interrupted, "are you condoning Lassiter's attitude towards Mexicans and Negroes?"

The man looked ashamed and his eyes didn't quite meet Jim's. "As I said, I don't make the rules," he muttered.

Jim staggered to his feet, and Margarita quickly lent him her support to steady him. He looked straight at the man watching them. "No, you don't make the rules, you just follow them! No matter whom they hurt, isn't that right, Mr. Duncan?" the disgust in his voice was unmistakable. Jim looked down at the young woman whose arms were around him. Her head was bent slightly, hiding her expression. "Come on, Margarita, let's get out of here," he said softly. She looked up at him then, relief evident in her face.

James Duncan kept his eyes on the floor as they left. He felt badly, but there was nothing he could do. It was known fact. Mexicans and Negroes didn't come to the white man's theater. It just wasn't proper.

The British steamer, SS Franklin, was at the tail end of a convoy of ships headed for Europe. Mainly they carried supplies, but they also carried a few passengers. Radio silence was maintained, because any signal could alert enemy ships of their whereabouts. They communicated whenever necessary by light signals using Morse code.

Captain Horace Adams stood on the bridge. It was a clear day and the sea was only slightly choppy. Scanning the horizon and watching for foreign ships or spotting the sinister periscope of a German U-Boat, was everyone's duty and the captain was doing just that.

His mind wondered to the strange woman in cabin seven. It was reported that she hadn't been seen in several days. He had checked the passenger lists and it showed that the woman was traveling with her daughter, but no one had seen the daughter. Also, when he had questioned the crewman in charge of passengers, the man's memory was vague. He said the woman had given him two tickets when she came aboard. Passengers were eager to get settled and there were several people clamoring to get aboard, so he couldn't remember if he'd actually seen the daughter or not. Sharply reprimanding the crewman for not being more alert, he had dismissed him.

Frowning, the captain turned away. He would have to confront the woman now and find out what was going on. It was ludicrous for anyone to be going to Europe at this time and to take a child on such a journey was unthinkable. He assumed the woman must have a good reason to attempt traversing the seas with German U-Boats around. Sincerely, he hoped that the ship's line had explained the dangers involved. He scowled as he thought about those dangers. If it were up to him, they would not take any passengers. Looking around, he scanned the sea once more. If a German U-Boat were to spot them, they would be sitting ducks.

Taking his first mate and the crewman with him, they went below. As they stood in front of cabin seven, the Captain rapped sharply on the door. They waited expectantly, but there was no sound. Rapping louder on the door, he called out, "Madame, this is Captain Adams and I need to speak to you!" Leaning against the door, he listened for any sound. He thought he detected a moan. With both fists, he pounded on the door, demanding that she open it at once.

"Ah, Captain, excuse me," the red-faced crewman spoke.

His patience worn thin, he turned his attention to the younger man.

"Well, what is it, man, speak up!" His bushy brows were knit together in a dark scowl and his expression told the crewman that whatever he had to say had better be good.

"Begging the Captain's pardon, but our records show that Mrs. McGowan is, um., handicapped. She is deaf, but," he quickly added, "she reads lips very well and her speech is impeccable."

"What!" the captain bellowed, "Why didn't you tell me this before?" Not waiting for an answer, he turned to his First Mate, "Mr. Kenniston, I want you to get some men down here to remove this door!"

"What about the daughter," the hapless crewman asked.

The Captain poked his finger into the man's chest as he ground out the words, "If the daughter were in there, she would have answered the door by now, unless she's deaf, too!"

He was breathing hard with his face inches from the other man's, daring him to make a comment. Turning back to his First Mate, he scowled, "Didn't I give you an order, Mr. Kenniston?"

"Aye, right away, Captain!" The First Mate hurried out of the cabin before incurring anymore of the Captain's wrath.

Getting the door open didn't take long. Captain Adams entered first. The room was dark and the air was musty and smelled sour as though someone had been violently ill. Quickly the light was switched on.

Amanda groaned and turned over shielding her eyes from the light. He strode over to the bed and looked down at the woman. The once proud coronet of hair had come loose, and was tangled, covering most of her face. Her gown was soiled and wreaked of unpleasant odors.

"Please," she whimpered, "the light...my head. It hurts so badly!"

Knowing that she would not be able to talk to him in this state, the Captain quickly issued orders for the ship's medic to come at once.

An hour later, he spoke with the medic, who reported that Mrs. McGowan suffered from Migraine headaches. However, he asserted,

STRADI'S VIOLIN

it appears that there is something seriously amiss. Her behavior was far from normal. He further warned the Captain to proceed cautiously in dealing with her.

Margarita and Juan helped Jim to his room. By now he was feeling badly. Every bone in his body ached and he just wanted to lie down. Swearing them both to secrecy, he asked that they not tell his mother. Ellen would worry and he could see no reason to upset her. Juan agreed with him, but he was visibly upset by their unfortunate encounter in town. He helped to make him as comfortable as possible, shaking his head and frowning, as Jim winced at every movement. Margarita insisted on applying a cold wet rag to his forehead. Finally, after much protest, they had left him alone.

Before she could escape into her room, her father had insisted upon hearing the whole story. Afterwards, he had reprimanded her sharply for being so foolish. He knew that his lecture was harsh, but for her sake, she must learn her place. Finally, he finished, and watched her hurry off to her room. Without telling her, he had come to a decision regarding her future. It would break her mother's heart, but he was sending their daughter back to Mexico. A marriage would be arranged.

In her room, Margarita paced back and forth. She was worried about Jim. She couldn't get it out of her head that she was to blame for the incident. Her Papa was right, and from now on, she would stay in her place. Hadn't he warned her that she was not to get involved with Senor Jim? Defiantly, she plopped down on the bed. It seemed that Mexicans in this land were of little value other than as field hands or gauchos. Falling backwards on the bed, she stared at the ceiling. Jim was off limits to her. She should have known better, she scolded herself. From the first time she had laid eyes on him, he had filled her thoughts, and she had known it was futile.

Rolling off the bed, she stood. Not anymore, she vowed. Sighing, she looked into the mirror above the dresser. The mane of dark hair with its fiery streaks was like a cloud around the small, determined face. Silent tears ran down her cheeks. She would rather die than to put him in harm's way again, she thought, as she brushed away the tears.

Amanda rocked back and forth in the middle of the bed. Her hair had been combed into some semblance of order and her nightgown had been discarded and a clean one took its place. However, it was evident that something was terribly amiss.

Captain Adams stood at the foot of her bed and watched her as she clasped her hands around her legs and rocked back and forth, muttering. He had tried to question her, but she had avoided all of his questions or simply ignored him. His patience was wearing thin.

"Woman! Mrs. McGowan!" he amended, "Where is your daughter?"

She continued rocking. He strode around the bed and grabbed both her arms. He shook her as his face appeared close to her own. "Madame," he ground out, "where is your daughter? Read my lips and answer me!" Frustration was evident in his command as he shook her once more. Her skin was the color of parchment as her frightened eyes looked into his face. Violently, she pulled away from him, and resumed rocking back and forth. This time her eyes, recklessly wild, watched him. Suddenly, she pointed at him and began to scream,

"Jake, you fool! Get out of here! I've beaten you. You'll never find her! Never! She belongs to me and she hates you. Do you understand, hates you!" with that, she began to laugh gleefully.

The captain turned away in disgust, but her laughter echoed in his ears long after he had left the cabin.

Jim groaned in his sleep and restlessly kicked off the covers. Margarita stood watching him, her heart aching. She had been awakened from a deep sleep, and immediately, she had slipped on her robe and made her way to his room. His forehead felt warm to her touch. Taking a washcloth, she dipped it in the bowl of water beside his bed and wrung out its contents. Carefully, she sat down on the bed and applied the smoothing cloth to his brow. She pressed it gently over the dark bruise covering the left side of his face and then his split upper lip. He groaned again and slowly opened his eyes. Margarita quickly got up intent on leaving the room.

"Don't...go," he begged, his voice low and raspy, "I need you." He reached out and tugged on her arm pulling her down on the bed once more.

"I just wanted to make sure that you're okay," she stammered. Her head was bowed and her long hair hid her face from him.

He stroked her arm, but still she wouldn't look at him. Frowning, he reached up and pushed back her hair, but she tugged away from him and stood beside the bed.

"Margarita, please sit down."

Her head told her to leave the room, but her heart was not listening. Heaping condemnation on her wayward heart, she did as he asked. Still, she did not speak, but sat as she did before, with head bowed.

Wincing, at the soreness in his body, Jim sat up, pushing the pillows against the headboard for support. Quickly, she reached out to help him. "You must lie down," she warned gently.

"Then, you must not fight me," he countered. He took hold of her arms and drew her down beside him. Helplessly, she looked at him.

"That's better. Now, I can see your eyes when they shoot sparks of fire at me!" Struggling, she tried to gain her freedom, but he held her fast. Once, he groaned as her elbow made contact with a sore spot on his abdomen. Afraid that she would injure him further, she stopped struggling. "Please, I must go to my room. It is very late and you need to rest." It was a token resistance and they both knew it.

He tried to smile, but his swollen, split lip refused to cooperate. He pushed her wayward hair back from her face. Cupping her face with his hands, he continued to stare at her.

"What are you looking at, Gringo?"

"I'm looking at you, Senorita," he countered. "Do you know how beautiful you are?"

Sullenly, she watched him not trusting herself or him. Did he think that she was his for the taking?

Sighing, he released her and lay back down. Not looking at her, he spoke,

"I won't hurt you. I'm too weak to do anything more than just hold you, if that's what's worrying you. Maybe, you should go back to your room, now."

He sounded resigned and a bit lonely, and that touched her more than his words. Pulling off her robe, she turned out the bedside lamp and lay back down. Then turning on her side and facing him, she put her arms around him, drawing closer. Jim stiffened for a moment, and then relaxed. The heat of their bodies radiated between them. Neither of them spoke. Miraculously, they slept.

Captain Adams rubbed his forehead, as he watched the lights flash their signal to the other ships. He needed to break radio silence, but the others would have to agree. Mrs. McGowan needed medical attention that he could not provide and someone needed to be aware that the daughter was missing. No one had seen the girl, but two tickets had been purchased, so she had to have come aboard. Mrs. McGowan's behavior was not normal, giving room for him to ponder the unthinkable. Certainly, her present state pointed to a mind-altering calamity. It was obvious that she hated her husband and perhaps getting rid of the child was her revenge. Possibly, she had somehow disposed of her daughter and thrown her overboard. The results of such an action could have preyed upon the woman's mind, and turned her into a raving maniac. It was all speculation on his part and he hoped that he was wrong.

The sun was peeping through the windows as the household began to stir. The sights and sounds were all normal to those who went about their business. The two entwined in each other's arms were oblivious to the stirrings. Her head rested on his chest and his arms held her fast.

In the hallway, Juan spoke in lowered tones to Ellen. He explained the events of the previous day, not to alarm her, but in preparation for what she would see when she looked at her son's bruised face. Ellen was appalled by what had happened. Jim was usually an early riser, and the fact that he was not up worried her.

Vaguely, Jim was aware of a warm body pressed against his own. He opened his eyes and took in the sleeping beauty whose arm and leg was thrown across him in abandonment. He studied the creamy, purity of her face and the incredibly long eye lashes. Taking a deep breath, he took in her intoxicating fragrance. Idly, he picked up a long, sun-kissed lock of hair and twisted it around his finger. Gently, he tugged.

Slowly, she opened her eyes, "What are you doing, Senior Gringo?"

"Good morning, sleepy-head," he smiled into her eyes.

She stared back at the handsome man who had so captivated her heart. He looked much better this morning. She reached up and touched the split lip, satisfied that the swelling had almost gone. He watched as her eyes and fingers continued their fascination with his lips.

Ducking his head, he pulled her hand away, and captured her lips in a searing kiss. Breathless, she struggled, but the effects of the kiss were draining away her resistance.

Lifting, his head, he looked into her dazed eyes. What he felt was totally unexpected. Even though he knew that he was attracted to her, he never dreamed that kissing her would be so captivating to his senses. Again, he took her lips, and their touch was like a flame. So engrossed in each other, neither of them heard the soft knock on the door.

Knocking gently, but not hearing a response, she opened the door. Ellen's gasp brought a worried Juan to her side. Neither of them spoke, as they stared at the couple oblivious to the world around them.

Perhaps, it was the sudden feeling of being observed or maybe, it was Ellen's tiny gasp that broke through the barriers of their passionate embrace. They broke apart and gazed into each other's eyes, sharing the moment. Something, indefinable, kept them mesmerized. The fact that they were not alone had not fully registered.

Estella, Margarita's mother, had watched Senora McGowan and her husband enter Jim's room. Wondering what was going on, she made her way down the hall. She looked past the heads of the two in the doorway and her eyes grew wide at the sight of the couple still entwined.

Margarita hastily pulled away from Jim, and was tugging at her gown. It had ridden up and showed a lot more than she would have wished. Jim was reluctant to let go of her, but she was determined to get away. Defiantly, he looked at the three people who seemed to have lost their ability to speak.

Margarita stood beside the bed, groping for her housecoat. She was all thumbs and the housecoat appeared to have developed a life all its own. Vainly, she searched for the sleeves, but the elusive housecoat slipped from her shaking hands and fell to the floor. Four pairs of eyes were riveted on her.

Tears of frustration threatened her eyes. Angrily, she tossed the wayward housecoat aside, and stomped her foot. Her wayward hair had fallen over one eye and sitting down on the side of the bed, she began to weep.

At the sight of her daughter's shame, Estella began to wail and speak in her native tongue. She cried and waved her arms hysterically while Juan tried in vain to calm her.

Not sure what to do, Ellen looked at Jim for guidance. His face was bruised and his lip still slightly swollen. He got off the bed, his chest was bare, but he was still wearing his jeans from the day before. He motioned Ellen to his side. Hurriedly, she came to him and gently touched his bruised face. "Mother, please get them out of here. I need to speak to Margarita." She searched his eyes, wondering what he was up to.

"Jim," she hesitated, uncertainly.

"Mother, it will be okay. We didn't do anything wrong. Let me handle this." His determined look made her give in.

However, Jim hadn't reckoned on Estella's determination to right the imagined wrong to her daughter. In vain, Ellen tried to escort the couple from the room, but Estella was having none of it. Running around Ellen, she went straight for Jim. Spitting out a Spanish word that summed up all her feelings, she yelled at the gringo who had disgraced her daughter. Her small fists beat against his chest as she berated him in her native language. Jim, allowed her to vent her anger, then he gently captured her hands in his own.

"Mrs. Alvarez, you don't have to worry. Margarita is a good girl. Nothing happened between us last night," he spoke matter-of-factly, his eyes never wavering from hers. Looking at her husband, she waited for him to interpret the words into Spanish.

Juan was shaking his head as he came and stood beside his daughter. Estella, still eyeing Jim suspiciously, backed away and went to stand beside her husband. He looked at Jim, accusingly. "I told you, Senor Jim, this would not work. You and my daughter are different people. Our culture, our language, is not the same as yours. Surely, you must see that I am right." Not waiting for an answer, he turned his attention to his daughter.

"Margarita," his voice was stern, "didn't I tell you to stay away from Senor Jim?"

Sighing deeply, he looked at his daughter's averted face. Quickly, he made a decision that would affect all of them. "It was a mistake for us to come here, and now we must leave. I think it is time to go back to Mexico."

His announcement caused all eyes to focus on him. Margarita's head snapped back as she stared in disbelief at her father. Ellen was about to protest, but Jim gently restrained her, and went to stand in front of Juan. "Senor, I know that you are upset, but why would you want to leave? It is I who will be leaving soon, so your problem will be solved. My mother needs you, and I am asking you to stay for her sake. Isaac would have wanted you to stay," he added for good measure and seeing the uncertainty on the man's face, he pressed the issue. "Week after next, I must leave and rejoin my unit. They have already shipped out – only God knows where," he stated flatly, his expression grim at the thought of leaving.

Juan spoke briefly to his wife in their native tongue, and then turned back to Jim.

"Senor, I hear what you are telling me, but you do not understand. We must go back to Mexico, because it is time for Margarita to be married. As her parents, it is our duty to provide a good husband for her," he held up his hand as he sensed that Jim was about to interrupt, "I blame myself for what has happened, and I will do my duty as a father. Margarita understands this, Senor."

Jim's eyes caught and held Margarita's. He saw abject misery in their depths. This was not what she wanted. He looked at Ellen, silently asking forgiveness for what he was about to do.

"Senor, what if your daughter was compromised? Would she still be taken to Mexico to find a husband?

Startled, Juan stared into Jim's eyes as though trying to read his thoughts. "What are you saying to me? I do not understand," his voice was gruff, and his fist clenched and unclenched. It was plain to see that he was finding it difficult to remain calm.

Once again, Jim sought Margarita's reaction. Her eyes had widened, and were filled with questions as she looked back at him. Jim's mind was made up as he turned back to Juan. "Senor, I should have told you the truth. I am very sorry. I assure you that I am a man of honor, and I intend to do the right thing."

A tiny gasp left Margarita's lips. Ellen couldn't believe what she had just heard. The stunned look on her face must have alerted Estella that things had, indeed, been as she suspected. Weeping, she threw her arms around her daughter.

Juan was still staring at Jim as though he had taken leave of his senses. He opened his mouth to speak, but nothing came out. Jim decided to finish what he had started, "Senor Alvarez, Senora Alvarez," he addressed them formally and waited until he was sure that he had their full attention, "Would you allow me the honor of marrying your lovely daughter?"

Hands clasped behind his back, Captain Adams paced back and forth in his cabin. Deep furrows were etched in his brow as he tried to think about what to do with Amanda McGowan. The other ships had not offered a solution, other than the obvious one, which was to keep her confined. He had concluded that she was deeply disturbed, but he was not sure if she was capable of doing harm. The question of the daughter was still bothering him, but it was possible that she had never come aboard the ship. He was forced to maintain radio silence, and he would have to wait until they reached England, before he could find out the whole story.

The one thing that he had decided was that Amanda was to be kept in her cabin under lock and key. Her meals would be brought to her, and she would be watched. If the woman were a menace, then he would take the necessary steps to see that she was properly restrained. He stopped pacing long enough to pick up his cap, and place it on his head. It was time for the evening meal, and he would be taking it with Mrs. McGowan. He walked out the door wondering which one of them had truly taken leave of their senses.

"Jake," Ellen passionately declared, "he's not thinking clearly about this. I know that he did not compromise that girl!"

She had gone directly to Jake after the fiasco that had taken place this morning in Jim's room. He listened patiently, then, methodically knocked down each of her objections. If he read between the lines correctly, Jim was not doing this out of a sense of duty or for any other reason, other than the obvious one. He wanted to marry the girl.

"You don't understand," she spoke as she paced back and forth, "he's doing this to keep her father from taking them back to Mexico."

This time as she walked by him, he caught her hand, and gently tugged her down onto the chair across from him. "Don't you think that you should let Jim make this decision? After all, he will be going into combat soon, and he has a right to some happiness before he leaves. I don't believe that Jim would be doing this unless he had strong feelings, perhaps, even love for this girl," he spoke to her quietly, but with authority. She was not looking at him, and for some reason that irritated him. "Ellen, look at me!" he commanded.

Her eyes fluttered up to meet his, wondering why he sounded impatient.

"I think that you need to look into your heart, and ask yourself why this marriage is objectionable to you," before, she could protest, he continued, "Is it really because you think that Jim has a misplaced sense of duty, or, perhaps, it's because he would be marrying a Mexican?"

"What a foul thing to say!" she had risen to her feet, and was glaring down at him. She pointed at him, her hand trembling. "If you could think that about me, then you don't know me at all!" Tears filled the hurt, blue eyes, and spilled down her cheeks. Grabbing her coat, she turned and ran out of the room with Jake calling her name. The slamming of the front door brought a curse from Jake's lips.

Angrily, he looked down at his legs. Physical therapy was helping, but he was an impatient man. The next time Ellen ran away from him, he wanted to be able to go after her.

She had misunderstood him, because he had suggested the need to explore her feelings. He wasn't accusing her of anything, but he knew that she was worried about what had happened in town. Perhaps, she was right to have reservations. Maybe, Jim was getting in over his head.

Ellen was becoming much too important to him. Her laughter, her big, blue eyes that told him more than she probably wanted him to know, all contributed to his impatience. Reading her eyes was becoming his favorite pastime, and that disturbed him. Berating himself for his impatience, he remembered the hurt look in those eyes.

Chapter 28

The day dawned clear and cold, but the wind was calm. The parlor had been decorated with candles and flowers. A piano had been brought to the Thacker Ranch from Jake's house, and Franz Leonie was going to provide the music. Jake had generously offered his house to them for the occasion, but Jim had insisted it be at the ranch.

Margarita should have been in her room preparing for the most important day of her life. Instead, she had slipped away and gone riding. Her thoughts were troubled as she reigned in the horse and dismounted. She walked to the edge of the cliff and looked out over the valley below.

Jim's announcement that he wanted to marry her had thrown her into ecstasy and despair. Yes, she acknowledged to herself that she loved him, but were they right for each other? All the odds were against a mixed marriage. She didn't want to go through another disturbing scene like the one at the theater. Would Jim have to fight with hooligans every time they went out in public? The most troubling question of all was why did Jim want to marry her? To save her honor, but they both knew there was no need. She shook her head as though to clear her mind. Knowing that she should have protested, and demanded to know his reasons for wanting to go through with this marriage, didn't help her disposition. Her boot kicked at a rock, sending it cascading down the cliff.

The man watching her, smiled as he saw her spurt of temper taken out on the hapless rock. Her back to him, she stood with hands on her hips looking out over the valley. His eyes appreciated the feminine silhouette that was definitely provocative in the tight jeans and form-fitting jacket. "Senorita, does jumping from a cliff seem preferable to marrying a gringo?"

Her startled exclamation, made his smile broaden as he walked toward her. She was facing him with her back to the cliff. Defenseless, she stood her ground, while nervously pushing her wayward hair out of her eyes as she defiantly waited for him.

Moving close to her, his stance was dominant and male, as he looked deeply into her eyes.

"So, many questions, but no answers, little one?"

He was being gentle, but Margarita wanted none of it. She wanted answers!

"I have thought about it, and I do not wish to marry you." Her tone of voice and the sparks in her eyes told him that she was ready for a fight. Lazily, he picked up a strand of her hair.

"Ah, but senorita, I very much want to marry you." Smiling, he tugged on the strand, disconcerting her, so that he could pull her into his arms. She tried to resist, but he was much stronger and determined. Twisting her arms behind her back, he brought her in contact with his body. The heat of their bodies fused them together in one searing moment. She gasped at the passion that held her as captive as his arms. He, too, was struggling with the moment, his breathing labored. Deciding that it was not the time to frighten her, he spoke, lightly, "I think I am the one who has been compromised. Is this the way you get all your men?"

How could he make light of the way she felt? Quickly, she hid the hurt in her eyes. The heel of her boot came down hard on his instep, causing him to groan in pain. Taking advantage of her freedom, she ran to her horse. She had barely made it, when she was grabbed from behind. His arms around her waist, he lifted her up. Their legs tangled and they both fell to the ground. She struggled to crawl away, but his arms captured her and pinned her beneath him. Lifting himself slightly, so she wouldn't be hurt, he held her arms above her head in a vise-like grip. Twisting and turning, she wore herself out, while he watched and waited. The grim look on his face told her that he was angry. Defeated, she lay limp. Satisfied that she was through struggling, he pushed the hair out of her eyes. Warily, she looked at him, and waited.

"The next time you act like a spoiled brat, I'm going to throw you over my knee and administer a sound spanking to your delectable backside! Is that clear?" his tone brooked no argument. Her hackles rose, but controlling her temper, she smiled up at him provocatively. Still looking stern, he smiled to himself. She was a spitfire and would probably give him hell, but he loved her. Reluctantly, he released her and got up. He extended his hand and pulled her up, also. Shakily, she dusted the dead grass and leaves off her jeans.

"Senorita, we have a date at 2:00 this afternoon. I suggest you get back to the ranch, and make sure that you're ready. If you're thinking of not being there, I will come looking for you and I can promise you that the little tiff that just happened was my gentler side! Comprende?"

He turned away going to his own mount.

Wiping her perspiring hands down the side of her jeans, she decided to ask him the question that haunted her. "Senor, why are you marrying me?" she blurted it out quickly, before she could loose her nerve.

Sliding his foot in the stirrup, he swung into the saddle. He studied her as she waited in anticipation of his answer. Instinctively, he knew what she wanted to hear, but he was still unsure of her. How did she really feel about him? He knew that she hadn't wanted to go back to Mexico. Would she be grateful that he had saved her from an arranged marriage? His expression was distasteful. He did not want this girl's gratitude. What he wanted was her love and respect.

Margarita had her answer. She had seen the look of distaste that passed over his face. It was obvious that he didn't love her. He was just being kind. What had she expected from him, confessions of undying love? Frustration made her feel like screaming and weeping.

"Margarita," he had dismounted and was walking toward her. She averted her head so that he wouldn't see the tears that threatened to spill over. He wanted to reassure her, but he didn't know how. They barely knew each other and they would need more than the few days left to get acquainted. "First of all, since we going to be married in a few hours, I would like for you to call me "Jim." Look, I know that this is hard on you. I guess we don't know each other very well, but I do want to marry you. I'm sorry that I will have to leave you so soon after we're married, but I promise you that if...when, I do come back, I'll do everything in my power to be a good husband."

Miserably, she looked at the ground. Gently, he raised her chin so that she was looking at him. "I know this is not what you wanted to hear, but I don't have all the answers. We'll have to find our way together. Is that okay with you?" Mutely, she nodded her head.

He waited for her to mount, and they rode back together. Neither of them spoke, each with their own hopes and doubts for the step they were about to take.

The maestro was playing the piano for the growing number of people who had crowded into the parlor as they waited for the bride and groom. Franz Leonie was thinking of a dark-haired little girl with green eyes as he played. Tears stung his eyes. Would they ever see Jenny, again? If she were here, she would be playing the violin and he would be accompanying her. Why did Amanda take her away, especially to Europe? Of course, he knew the answer to that. Hans Gunthur had persuaded Amanda to come to him.

Rose sat nearby watching her husband play, and she, too, was thinking of her granddaughter. Sadly, she wondered what would happen to Jenny. Jake was so sure that they would have her back once the ship reached England. The authorities would be waiting for Amanda, and she would be given an ultimatum. Rose shuttered and felt faint. For some reason, she was dreadfully afraid that she would never see Jenny again.

Jake stood in the shadowed corner of the room. He leaned heavily on the cane. For some time, he had been walking, but this was the first time in public. The music that Franz was playing had been a particular favorite of Jenny's. It brought back memories of her laughing, and playing the violin. "God," he prayed, "please let my little girl be all right." He had been thinking about her all day, and the music had brought her closer than ever. Sadly, he wondered how long it would be before they would be together, again.

The woman who entered the room distracted him from his unhappy thoughts. Her blonde hair shimmered in the light streaming through the window. She was wearing a pale blue suit that hugged every curve. "Ellen," he breathed her name like a silent prayer.

Jim appeared, next, wearing his army dress uniform. He looked handsome, but a little uncomfortable in the starched confines of his attire.

Jake came toward him, smiling at the astounded look on Jim's face as he watched him walk with the aid of the cane. When he reached his side, Jim laid his arm across Jake's shoulder.

"Sir, this is wonderful! I can't believe it!" Smiling broadly, Jake responded,

"Well, now, you can't have your best man in a wheelchair!"

Ellen's eyes were shinning. At first, for her handsome son, but, now, Jake McGowan held her attention. He was walking! The dove gray suit emphasized the gray streaks that covered most of his hair, and gave him such a distinguished aura. The fact that he was a handsome man had not escaped her, but, never, had she felt the effects of his attraction as much as this moment. As though sensing her stare, he slowly turned, and looked directly at her. Then she did something that she had not done in years. She blushed. Wildly confused, she looked away, bringing a smile to Jake's mouth.

The first strains of the Wedding March caused all eyes to focus on the staircase. The vision that appeared at the top of the stairs brought a murmur from the crowd below. Proudly, Juan escorted his daughter down the stairs, and deposited her next to Jim.

She had never been lovelier. The fragile dress was antique lace, and had belonged to her grandmother. Tiny pearl buttons went from neckline down to her tiny waist. The ivory hue of the aged lace brought out the dusky rose complexion of the girl wearing it. The matching lace manila covered her dark, fiery, tresses.

Juan patted his wife's hand as she openly cried. She had begged her husband to take them back to Mexico, but he had refused. He looked at his wife, and for a moment, wondered if this was all a big mistake. However, knowing that his daughter was marrying an honorable man, and would be well cared for, eased his conscience.

Jim's eyes glowed as they took in the lovely vision that would soon be his wife. For a moment, he felt the pain of their impending separation.

STRADI'S VIOLIN

Lilly stood next to Margarita. She, too, looked lovely. The magenta suit was a perfect foil for her blonde hair. The only thing that detracted from her beauty was the sadness in her eyes.

The tragic events of Isaac's death had taken their toll. Jim wondered if the vivacious sister, that he once knew, would ever reappear.

Jenny, his little sister, should be here, too. It would be a long time before he saw her again. He remembered the wonderful summer they had spent together, and how they used to tell each other everything. Longingly, he wished that he could talk to her right now.

The minister was speaking to him. Mentally, he shook off the melancholy feelings. Nothing was going to spoil this day.

The crew of the SS Franklin was having trouble seeing their esteemed Captain escorting the "crazy" woman around the deck. The few passengers thought it was the captain, who had gone off his rocker. Captain Adams neither knew, nor cared what others thought. By offering his friendship, he had finally coaxed Amanda McGowan into leaving the cabin.

At first, for her safety, and others, he had her confined to quarters. Gradually, as he spent time with her, her sanity appeared to have reasserted itself. She began to trust him, and seemed to look forward to their time together as much as he did. Fearing that being cooped up for so long might be harmful to her, he made it a point to escort her around the deck for at least an hour every day.

Amanda had begun to open up, and talk a great deal, but one thing troubled him very much. No matter how subtly he tried, the subject of Amanda's daughter, was met with hostility. She would demand to be taken back to the cabin, and would refuse to talk to him. He could only conclude that Amanda and her daughter must have quarreled. He wondered at her ability to arbor such bitterness, and suspected that her husband must have something to do with it. It was a long voyage, and he was a patient man. Sooner or later, she would confide in him.

Margarita sat at the dressing table combing her hair. She tried to look like a happy bride, but her reflection mocked her. She threw down the brush, and got up to finish dressing. Jim, and the others would be waiting for her to come down. They were catching the late train to San Antonio for a brief honeymoon. She didn't remember much about the wedding. The vows were a blur, along with the guests, who gushed and awed over the bride and groom, keeping any reservations they might have had about the bride to themselves. Her nerves had been raw, and she barely looked at Jim. Anyway, he was probably ashamed of the way she looked. Her mother had insisted that she wear the antique gown because she had worn it at her own wedding, and her mother before her. Distastefully, she tossed it aside. Lovingly, she caressed the cream colored skirt with the bolero jacket. Jim had given it to her for a wedding present. It was her first store bought outfit. His mother had given her nylons and frilly underwear, along with a gown and robe for her honeymoon. She had never worn such things before.

As soon as she set foot on the stairs, there were cheers, and good-natured laughter. Jim was subjected to unmerciful teasing from some of the employees of the *Lone Star Chronicle*. Despite the ribald comments, he waited for her at the bottom of the stairs. His eyes watched in appreciation at the way the cream suit clung to her body. The short skirt did little to hide her shapely, long, legs. Someone whistled, and he frowned, but still did not take his eyes off her. When she was standing next to him, he offered her his arm. Together they walked through the crowded room, amid cheers from well-wishers, and people with last minute advice.

Her father waited for them at the car. He was driving them to the train station. Despite his attempts to hide the car, the bunch from the *Lone Star Chronicle* had managed to tie tin cans to the bumper, and write with white shoe polish "just married" all over the back window. Shrugging his shoulders, good naturedly, he smiled. These Gringos were as crazy as the Mexicans.

If the newlyweds thought they were alone at last, they couldn't have been more wrong. Guests climbed into cars, and followed them to the train station, honking their horns. Jake offered to take Ellen to the train station in his car. She thanked him politely, and was about to refuse when she realized how childish that would be. He wasn't fooled by her lack of enthusiasm, but he hoped the ride to the station would give him the opportunity to apologize.

Ellen had other ideas. She talked non-stop, asking questions about his physical therapy, and how wonderful it was that he was walking; how long had he been walking; why had he not told anyone?

Restraining his impulses was not easy. He clamped his teeth together so tightly, that he was sure that he would have lockjaw. On she prattled, until he thought he would go mad if she didn't allow him to say what was on his mind. Abruptly, he pulled the roadster to the side of the highway, allowing the other cars to pass. He turned the ignition switch off. Ellen was suddenly quiet, wondering why they had stopped.

Turning to face her, he reached over, and pulled her into his arms. His mouth found hers before she could protest. It was not a gentle kiss. His lips were firm, and demanding. The softness of her lips, and her yielding response went to his head faster than his most expensive wine. The kiss ended when neither of them could breathe, and he felt drugged, but immensely satisfied. It had proven what he had sought to know, that she was not indifferent to him.

Ellen forgot that she was supposed to be angry with him. Then she was angry for forgetting. The kiss had thrown her into a state of confusion. It was totally unexpected and unforgivable. He had no right to make her feel this way! She pushed against him with all her strength, breaking their physical contact. He allowed her to, only because, he knew that she was angry.

"I thought we were friends!" she sputtered through clenched teeth.

After the kiss they had just exchanged, he was amazed at her attitude. He looked at her uncompromising profile. The rapid rise and fall of her breast told him just how agitated she was over what had happened between them. "We're a lot more than friends, so get used to it, Ellen."

His self-assured reply did not set well with her. "Listen to me, Mr. "know-it-all," Jake McGowan! I refuse to be railroaded into something I'm not ready to accept."

He folded his arms across his chest, and glared at her. "Are you going to sit there and tell me that you didn't want me to kiss you?" not waiting for an answer, he supplied his own, "You enjoyed it as much as I did, and if you weren't so stubborn, you'd admit it!"

It was the proverbial straw for Ellen. She wrenched the car door open, and jumped outside, then slammed the door with all the force she could muster. Jake opened the car door with equal force, his face a mask of anger, "Ellen, you get back in this car, now!"

Not speaking, she turned her back on him, and began walking down the side of the highway. The high-heels she wore didn't make the prospect of a long walk very inviting, but it was preferable to spending another moment in his company. Stunned at her behavior, Jake sat in the car for a few moments, watching her. Once she cooled off, he reasoned, she would see how foolish she was being. He waited. She stumbled a few times, but never once looked back. Jake sighed. He had underestimated her, but he wasn't giving up.

The couple boarding the train turned and waved one last time before disappearing from view. They were barely seated when the train began to pull out of the station. Horns still blared, and people waved, trying to catch a last glimpse of the departing bride and groom. Jim waved as he watched their friends and relatives disappear from sight.

He settled back as the train picked up speed heading toward San Antonio. He glanced at his bride, and she looked anything, but radiant. She looked tense, and very unhappy. "Sweetheart, put your head back and close your eyes. You look beat. Perhaps, a little sleep is what you need." He spoke tenderly, wanting to ease her tension.

Sarcastically, she brushed aside his tender concern, "What is wrong, Senor? Are you afraid your bride will not be able to perform for you, tonight? Afraid that you will be cheated out of your husbandly rights?" The hurt look in his eyes caused her to falter for a moment, and wonder if she had gone too far.

Quickly, he masked the hurt, and adopted an air of teasing amusement that was sure to rile her, "Perhaps, I was a little worried," he drawled, "I do want my lovely senorita to be in top form tonight!"

"Oh!" she sputtered indignantly, "For your information, now that I am married, I am not a "senorita," I am a "senora"!" her eyes sparkled with temper.

He laughed, and then drawled close to her ear, "Not, yet, my lovely, senorita, not until we've been very intimate! Then you will be my "senora," my woman!"

His words caused her to blush profusely. Turning away from him, she closed her eyes determined not to speak to him. A tear slipped past, and rolled down her cheek. He was cruel to tease her. She wanted to be more than his woman. She wanted to be his "querida esposa," his beloved wife in every sense of the word.

Jim relented. He could tell that his teasing had upset her, but her remarks, implicating that he only wanted one thing from her, had hurt him. He seriously doubted that the short time they would have together would be enough time to convince her otherwise. Maybe, he shouldn't have married her, he thought. It wasn't fair to leave her so soon, before they would have a chance to know each other. Closing his eyes, his thoughts turned to the war. He would be going overseas soon. By God's grace, maybe, the war would be over before he got there.

Realizing that everyone had already driven past them, in their frenzy to get to the train station, Ellen decided that she had no option other than riding with Jake. He was driving slowly, keeping pace with her. Suddenly, she stopped and walked to the car. Jake reached over, and opened the door for her. Without a word, she got into car, and they resumed their ride to the train station. Jake was wise enough not to make any comment. They rode in uncomfortable silence.

Ellen was dismayed; they had missed seeing Jim and Margarita off. Relieved, she saw that Juan and Estella were still there. She hurried over to them, and asked Juan to take her back to the ranch. Looking puzzled, he raised his eyes to look past her at the man waiting beside the roadster. Senor McGowan looked formidable and angry. Juan wanted to ask questions, but the look on the Senora's face advised him to use caution.

Jake was angry. Now, on top of everything else, she was blaming him for their tardiness. He watched as the car pulled away from the train station with Ellen inside.

Margarita had temporarily put aside her unhappiness as the taxi drove them downtown. Never had she seen such a place. To her surprise and delight, Mexicans were everywhere. There were bustling mercados on nearly every corner. Reminding her of some of the cities in Mexico, San Antonio was a mixture of "old world" charm, and American hustle and bustle. Soldiers roamed the streets, some with lovely senoritas in tow, while others searched aimlessly for one last fling, before being shipped overseas.

The taxi pulled into the circular drive of the Hotel La Mansion. Jim smiled as he helped her out of the taxi. Her eyes sparkled in awe as she took in her surroundings. The large white stucco hotel was majestic, and she had never seen anything like it.

They entered the tiled courtyard, where large stone urns with blooms of bright red flowers provided a garden atmosphere. Couples sat at tables intimately hidden among the ferns and a profusion of colorful flowers. Next to a sparkling fountain, a Mariachi band was playing.

A bellhop took them up a winding staircase to a room at the end of the hall. He opened the door with a flourish, and waited for them to enter. The dark oak furniture was impressive. There was a large tiled bathroom. French doors opened to reveal a private patio.

Seeing the look on Margarita's face made Jim glad that he had accepted Jake's wedding gift. At first, he had been reluctant, but Jake had insisted on paying for their stay at the La Mansion. The luxurious hotel was one of Jake's favorites when he was in San Antonio.

The bellhop left, and suddenly there was just the two of them. Uncertainly, they looked at each other. Then they started to speak at the same time. Jim laughed to ease the tension.

"I think the first thing we should do is have something to eat. Would you like to go downstairs, or have something brought to the room?"

Margarita was a bundle of nerves, and eating was the furthest thing from her mind. Staying in the room wasn't a good idea either, so she hastily agreed to go downstairs. After freshening up, they left the room. A bellhop eagerly showed them the way to the dining room.

The German U-Boat was tracking the convoy. Moving beneath the waves like a shadowy menace, creeping nearer and nearer its target.

Amanda was having a nightmare. She had tossed aside the covers, revealing a gown soaked in perspiration. Her hair had come loose, and clung wetly to her body. Fear caused her to moan in desperation. Childishly, she wished that the ship would continuously traverse the seas, and never make land. Premonition, and her fear of what Jake would do to her when she reached England, made dread her constant companion. Leaving Jenny alone in New York had been her ultimate folly. Jake would not have cared that she left him, but because she had taken Jenny, he would hunt her to the ends of the earth. She laughed out loud at her thoughts. Maybe she was being ridiculous. Jenny was probably with Jake right now. Once again, she moaned in fear. Something was telling her that when she reached England, they would expect Jenny to be with her. Darkness claimed the troubled mind that could not accept reality, and she began to thrash and moan, "O God! What have I done?" she wailed over and over.

The sounds and wails coming from her cabin did not go unnoticed. A seaman rushed to the captain's quarters to inform him that the "crazy" woman was at it again.

The U-Boat maneuvered to get into firing position. The Germans loaded the torpedo into the tube, and waited for the signal to release their deadly cargo.

Hurriedly, Captain Adams pulled on his uniform. It was the early hours of the morning when he had been awakened. He hoped that he would be able to calm Amanda down without having to wake the medic. He hated resorting to drugs to calm her. Grabbing his cap, he hurried to Amanda's cabin. Unlocking the door, he entered to find her on the bed writhing from side to side. Quickly, he pulled her up, and wrapped his arms around her, gently rocking back and forth. Her wails subsided, and he brushed the damp hair away from her face. "My dear, you must tell me what troubles you! I cannot help you if you shut me out. Do you understand?" the gruffness in his voice belied his emotions. Desperately, he searched her eyes for some sign of recognition. The eyes staring back at him were wild with fear. Suddenly, she crumbled and her head fell against his shoulder. "O Horace!" she cried. He had allowed her to call him by his familiar name, but only when they were alone. Stroking her hair, he spoke softly, "My dear Amanda, what ails you so; you must tell me!"

Dinner was not as perfect as Jim had hoped. His bride barely touched her food. Their conversation was strained, and by the time the last course was served, there was silence between them.

Once inside their room, Margarita was ill at ease. She moved around aimlessly wondering what to do next. Jim was searching in his suitcase. "Here it is!" he stated triumphantly.

He had pulled something out of the suitcase that resembled her wedding gown. She did a double take. It was her wedding gown! She grabbed the garment out of his hands.

"Why did you bring this? To make fun of me?" Tears were stinging her eyes, as she defiantly waited for his answer.

Hands on hips, he stared at her. "I brought it, because the girl in it was a vision of loveliness. I wanted her to wear it for me, and I wanted to undo the pearl buttons, and remove the dress from her body. Then I wanted to make her a part of me," the sincerity coupled with the hurt in his voice was evident, "You seem to think that everything I do is designed in some way to hurt you. I guess for you to trust me is too much to ask." Grabbing his jacket off the bed, he strode out of the room, slamming the door behind him.

Legs shaking, Margarita sat down on the bed, still holding the wedding gown, she buried her face in the lace and wept.

"Fire One!" the U-Boat captain ordered. The whooshing noise that the torpedo made as it left the tube would have struck fear in the heart of every person aboard the SS Franklin, if they had been able to hear it.

First Mate Kenniston was near the rail looking seaward. He suddenly stiffened as he looked down. His eyes grew wide with fear as saw the wake of the deadly torpedo coming toward the ship. Vainly, he tried to shout a warning, but before he could form the words there was a horrific explosion.

The other ships in the convoy were well ahead of the SS Franklin. The U-Boat was pursuing and preparing to fire her other torpedoes at the remaining ships.

A sailor from another ship heard the roar of the explosion, and saw the flash of light. Panic ensued as he rushed to spread word of the destroyed freighter. Lifeboats were quickly swung out in anticipation of the coming destruction.

Wearing her wedding dress, she stood in the center of the room, her heart pounding, as she heard the rattle of the key in the lock. Hesitantly, Jim opened the door. The soft lighting in the room illuminated the young, girl who looked poised for flight. She was wearing the controversial wedding dress, which surprised him. He walked to the chair next to the bed, and took off his jacket. Next his removed the offending tie, and breathed a sigh of relief, as he undid the top two buttons of his shirt.

Margarita stood still, watching his every movement. Walking toward her, he gazed into her eyes, their hypnotic effect held her spellbound. He stopped in front of her. Slowly, he reached out and caressed her face. Then his fingers trailed across her cheek, and down to her lips, tracing their outline. Her breathing seemed suspended for a moment, and he felt her tremble.

"You are very beautiful," his voice was low and husky, "Why are you afraid of your husband, mi esposa?"

She tilted her head back, and looked at him. The genuine concern in his eyes convinced her that he was serious.

"Jim, I am sorry that I do not know the right words, or know what to do, but I have never..." the rosy hue in her cheeks deepened, "I have never been with a man. You are my husband, but you are a stranger."

Smiling at her, he drawled, "Well, since we did get married this afternoon, and our honeymoon will be relatively short, I think we should stop wasting time, and get better acquainted."

She missed the amused gleam that had entered his eyes. Unbuttoning his shirt the rest of the way, he pulled it off and tossed it on the chair. Her eyes were mesmerized at the sight of his muscular torso. The bronzed skin gleamed in the softly lit room.

"Come, Senorita," he taunted. "You've seen me this way before. In fact, the first time, you threw an apple at me, remember?"

This time she did not miss the amusement that danced in his eyes.

"You're making fun of me," she scolded, "do all gringos treat their wives so badly?" Her full, pouting lips were an invitation to be kissed.

He reached out and took her hand. It was cold. He drew it to his chest, and pressed the fingers flat over his heart. "There, do you feel the beating of my heart?" no longer was he teasing, but somber, "My heart is probably beating as fast as yours. Our fears and anxieties are the same. This is my first time, too."

Stunned, she looked at him in disbelief. This tall, handsome man that she married was telling her something profound. "But..." she stammered, "you have never...?"

Gently, he smiled at her confusion, "No, my lovely bride, I have never! I've been out with lots of pretty girls, and enjoyed their company, but kissing is a far as it went." He lifted her hand, and pressed his warm lips to her wrist. An electric current shot through her body, surprising her. "When you know me better, you will realize that I'm old fashioned in a lot of ways. I don't believe in the double standard."

Margarita quietly studied this enigma, who was her husband, with newfound respect.

"Margarita," he whispered, "We can learn this together, do you trust me?"

Her eyes sought his. They were filled with desire, and something more. Something indefinable that brought peace to her heart. "Si, yes, I trust you!"

He smiled; it was the answer he'd hoped for.

Mayhem, and destruction was everywhere. Smoke and flames billowed from the gaping hole in the SS Franklin. Here and there a splash was heard as those who survived the explosion jumped into the cold Atlantic waters. What was left of the ship would soon disappear beneath the waves, leaving only debris. More explosions were heard as the other ships in the convoy met a similar fate.

As the sun came up over the horizon, it cast an eerie glow on the water where the convoy of ships bringing supplies to England, were last seen. Now, there were no ships, only a few lifeboats carrying a handful of survivors, and the waves dispersing the debris. A captain's hat floated by, then was picked up by a wave, and carried further out to sea.

Beneath the waves, a woman floated. It appeared that the flow of the current was aiding her performance of the Macabre. Long, auburn tresses swirled around the lifeless body of Amanda McGowan, providing a burial shroud for her final resting place in the depths of the ocean.

The day dawned gray and cold. Brisk winter air had filtered down from the North causing the South Texas city of San Antonio to finally succumb to winter.

The entwined couple was oblivious to the change in weather, or to the time of day. It was past the noon hour, and still they slept. It had been a night of discovery and magic. They had moved slowly in their desire to know each other, savoring every moment.

It had begun with the wedding dress. One by one Jim had undone the tiny pearl buttons. Each bit of skin that was revealed, he had kissed. To Margarita, every place his lips touched burned. By the time he had undone the last button, they were both breathing with difficulty.

Then he had kissed her lips, and she had begun her exploration of his body. Timidly at first, touching his chest, and then growing bolder as their kisses deepened, and became more passionate. Pushing the dress off her shoulders, he watched as it slid to the floor. The lacey bra barely covered her small, firm breast. Lace panties, a garter belt, and nylon stockings covered her lower body. His eyes burned with passion as they roamed over her partially clad form.

Holding his gaze, she had sat down on the bed, and unhooked her stockings from the garter belt. Then she started to remove them, but Jim stopped her. His hand burned where it touched her thigh, and he slowly slid the stocking down one leg. The pulse in her neck was beating rapidly. He pressed his lips to it, as he slid the other stocking off. They continued to kiss and caress as he removed her lacey bra. The sight and feel of her bare breasts against him drove him over the edge. Lowering his body fully on hers, he savagely found her lips, and the flames of their mutual passion raged out of control. Their lovemaking had lasted through much of the night.

A radio played softly beside the bed. A popping noise, then static, and crackling sounds interrupted the harmonious melody and disturbed the slumbering couple. Vaguely, Jim heard the announcement that was coming through. Heart pounding, he bolted upright, coming fully awake as he heard the voice of the President, and the words "Pearl Harbor has been attacked!"

History would forever call it a day of infamy. The date was December 7, 1941.

The End – Stradi's Violin, Book I